# AUTHOR'S NOTE

*(& Content Warnings)*

This story is my heart and soul. I'm offering it up to you, my reader, here in these pages.

Before embarking on this journey with me, you should know that the main characters face grief, depression, anxiety and self-doubt that we have, most likely, all faced at one point or another.

There is a lot of humor written in between the tough moments and I hope it will bring a smile to your face, despite what the characters are going through.

I've always said that trauma forges the best humor.

However, if these topics are highly triggering for you, I recommend reading one of my others.

I began writing this novel in May 2022 after I'd found out my dad was battling cancer. I'd always thought my own story would end differently than Ara's, but I ended up having more in common with her than I ever imagined.

My hope is that Ara's story will make you, my reader, feel seen and maybe just a little less alone.

# LAST *Letters* TO ARA

# LAST *Letters* TO ARA

THE LAST SERIES

KAYMIE WUERFEL

First published in September 2023 by Kaymie Wuerfel

*Cover design by coversbyjules.crd.co*
*Editing and formatting by Allusion Publishing*
*www.allusionpublishing.com*

ISBN (paperback): 978-0-6457951-0-3
ISBN (ebook): 978-0-6457951-1-0

www.kaymiewuerfel.com
Instagram: @kayywuerf
TikTok: @kayywuerf

# PLAYLIST

*How Do I Say Goodbye - Dean Lewis*
*The Funeral - Band of Horses*
*Unsteady - X Ambassadors*
*Heal - Tom Odell*
*Young & Sad - Noah Cyrus*
*Enchanted (Taylor's Version)- Taylor Swift*
*Photograph - Ed Sheeran*
*Here With Me - d4vd*
*All of the Stars - Ed Sheeran*
*All For You - Dean Lewis*
*Wings – Birdy*
*Try – AkaFO*
*Marjorie – Taylor Swift*

To my dad.

1 December 1961 - 1 December 2022

May we meet again.

JANUARY
Dear Ara

# CHAPTER ONE

## Present - Ara

Do you believe in soul mates?

Not the cheesy kind of soul mates you see in the movies. The kind that magically don't hate the way the other person chews or doesn't get annoyed when they leave their socks on the floor. I'm talking about that soul-deep connection you find with any other soul.

It could be your best friend. Your grandparent. Your brother. A cousin. You understand each other on such a basic level that you never need to explain yourself. They are your person, without a doubt. For me, that person was my dad.

*Was.*

As of a week ago, in fact.

Today is his funeral. Well, technically the pamphlets says that it's a "celebration of life well-lived" but I can assure you that there will be no celebrating on my part. They should call it "a day of dumping truckloads of salt into a gaping wound that will never heal." That would be a more apt description.

It was something that had never occurred to me, that one day Dad would die, and I would have to attend his funeral. I know that's stupid. I mean, everyone dies. I just never considered *him* dying. Especially of cancer, after having kept it a secret from everyone until the very day it took him.

You might be wondering how a daughter doesn't know that her own dad has cancer. Well, I can tell you. He was clever, and he didn't want me to know that his life would soon come to an end. I've thought about it every day for the last seven days, trying to figure out how I didn't see through his explanations.

When you don't know something is wrong, things are easy to write off when given an answer for everything. His coughing was due to the "mold" they'd found in his office, nothing too serious, of course, but he would be taking some time off work while it's fixed. He was tired because he discovered he had an allergy to such "mold." He would be going to the hospital for standard checkups after being in long-term contact with "mold."

Fucking *mold*. I'm *such* an idiot.

At first, I was in shock. Dad had never even had a cold for as long as I'd been alive. He had even gotten up and walked away from a motorcycle accident without a scratch on him. He was supposed to be invincible.

Until he wasn't.

After the denial came the anger.

How could he keep something so serious from me? How could he deny me the opportunity to say *goodbye*?

But the anger lasted only as long as it took me to imagine him trying to form those words. Having to tell his daughter, his best friend, that he is going to die. That he is being ripped away, far too soon, and there is nothing that either of us can do about it. Even if he'd tried to tell me, I know he never would have been able to get the words out. And I never would have been able to hear them.

Even if he *had* told me, it wouldn't be any less painful. He would still be gone, and I would have had to see the only person I've ever depended on go through the kind of misery nobody deserves. It would have changed me forever. By keeping it from me, he's preserved my memory of him, and I know that's what he wanted. It's what he thought would be best for me.

I can't be too mad at him, anyway. It's hard to be mad at someone who's gone.

The funeral people, an official term according to me, asked if I'd like to get up and say a few words about him, surely expecting me to say yes. Most people would get up there after their loved ones die, to go on some sappy tangent about how much they loved them and cry their eyes out for the world to see. When you really love someone though, they know it through your actions. You don't have to make a dramatic speech in front of a crowd to prove it.

So here I sit, quietly reliving our best memories, surrounded by people who didn't really know Dad at all, while some random priest who is part of a religion we don't belong to, preaches about how this was someone's *plan* to take my dad, which somehow makes it okay.

Well, ladies and gentlemen, it's better than watching me pour snot all over the podium.

See, Dad and I kept our cards close. We didn't shout our love from the rooftops or share our sense of humor with any random person who passed us by. We saved it for those who truly mattered. Each other. The extended family, people from work, and an old buddy from high school who hasn't made an effort to see Dad in twenty years, didn't know him the way I did.

To be honest, I didn't even realize so many people *had* known him, until I saw how many people showed up to his service. These people only knew him as a friendly, yet reserved man, who was raising his daughter by himself. They saw him as a hard worker and successful, someone they could probably depend on in a pinch. As if that's all he had to offer to the world.

They don't know how much the world will suffer, how much *I* will suffer, without his dry, but hilarious sense of humor. His great, booming laugh that he saved for special occasions. The way a few of his words could right any wrong. The safety of his arms when everything seemed to be going awry. The thoughtful actions that he saved just for me.

The preaching finally comes to an end, followed by music, which I suppose is meant to sound uplifting, even though it fucking sucks. A slideshow of photos comes on, and I'm not prepared for the wave of grief that hits me, as photos of me and Dad come onto the screen. These people must have FBI-level connections to get access to these because I wouldn't have handed them over in a million goddamn years.

Most of them are those overpriced photos they take when you visit a theme park (we live in Florida after all) or go on an excursion, but a few are from the first few weeks after I was born when my mother was still alive to capture those moments. They've even managed to get a few from the recent years where strangers volunteered to help us capture a moment.

With every photo that makes it onto the screen, I'm reminded again and again that these are the last of it. These are the last of our memories and we'll never get the chance to make new ones. Dad is *really* gone. The universe decided to take away the only person I could ever count on, and I don't even get to tell him that I love him or thank him for being my dad.

The last photo comes on the screen, and I realize that it's also the last photo we took together, six months ago on my twenty-second birthday. Six *damn* months went by, and I didn't think to capture a single moment we shared. I'd thought we had all the time in the world.

Just then the music ends and people are...*clapping*?

I hate them all.

More than I already did.

• • •

We are ushered into the next room where finger food and drinks await. Someone ought to make these things look less like a cheap party and more like someone will be missed. This whole "positive outlook" thing is a crock of shit.

I spy an empty corner and decide to make my way over, hopefully before anyone notices me. I've just about made it when a man I've never seen in my life approaches. "You must be Sarah. My name is Phil, I knew your father."

I cringe at the use of my actual name and give him a nod, intending to pass him by.

"He was a good man, your father." He chuckles, *actually* chuckles. "He saved my ass from the IRS a time or two. Got me a good gig pretty recently, as well."

"How cool," I say, intending for the conversation to come to a fast halt. He can take his IRS stories to someone who cares.

"Yeah, our offices have been in the same building for years. I was lucky to know him."

"Nice," I say and this time I make a point of giving him my shoulder and heading in the opposite direction. Another corner will have to do.

I've made it all of five feet before the next onslaught. This time, it's the receptionist from Dad's office. "Hey there, sweetie, how are you holding up?"

*How does she think I'm holding up?*

"Fine, thanks." I look around for somewhere that isn't filled with people, and I come up optionless. Before I can make a run for it, everyone standing in this dreadful room notices me all at once. It's like a scene from a horror movie as they all start to slowly walk toward me and I can't get my legs to move.

I endure person after person, sharing endless streams of cliché words they probably stole from a Hallmark card on their way over. As if a stranger saying

"I'm sorry for your loss" does anything to fill the vast, gaping hole in my chest that was ripped open with a single phone call.

If Dad were here, he would find a way to calm my racing heart, resolve my inability to take such a level of emotion and human interaction. He would come up with something funny, using humor to ease what I'm going through, and we would probably strike a bet on how many times we'd hear "He was a good man" and "You have my condolences." The loser would buy the other a chocolate frosty from Wendy's and call it a day.

Except here I am, alone. Utterly fucking alone. Just like I will be for the rest of my life.

I don't wait for whoever is speaking to me to finish their sentence as I finally get my legs to work, leaving the haunted house behind me.

Less than an hour later, I arrive at the only place I'd want to be right now, trying to think after the unthinkable and finding relief in the chaos of the busiest terminal at Tampa International Airport, the way I always do when I need to take my mind off something. Thankfully, my favorite seat is empty, allowing me to be alone without making it excruciatingly clear that I am exactly that. There is something peaceful about watching people going on about their lives as if a tragedy didn't just happen in your own.

I've never felt this level of soul-wrenching emotion, not even when I received the news of his death. Having no idea he was battling cancer, I assumed they had the wrong number. Of course, they never expected that their patient's daughter would be in the dark about his terminal diagnosis, treating it like just another afternoon call.

Deep down, I had known something had been off for months. Not just because of the coughing and the mold, the time off work and doctors' visits, but because Dad hadn't seemed quite himself. We had this unspoken rule where if the other person didn't want to talk about it yet, we gave them time. So I let it be, convincing myself that if it were something serious, he would tell me.

In my bones, I knew that Dad would never have abandoned me just before the holidays for some accounting convention in New York, nor would he have stayed for the expensive fifties and over holiday retreat he'd received as a gift. Though I didn't believe his story for a minute, I'd hoped he was on a secret getaway with a woman whom he wasn't ready to share with me yet.

*If only.*

If only he had just been nervous to introduce me to a woman. If only he was out, living his life after missing my mother for the last twenty years. If only he would be back in town at the end of this month. If only he wasn't taken away from me and sent to the unknown place one goes after death.

Part of me wonders where that place exists. Is he sitting in Heaven with the perfect ratio of chocolate brownie and vanilla ice cream? Is he hovering around somewhere, watching over me? Does he have a one-way looking glass into my life whenever he wants?

What if I'm having hot, sweaty sex when he decides to pop in for a peek? For the first time since he died, I crack a smile at the thought of how mortified he would be at discovering such a thing. My smile falters as a deep clearing of the throat draws me from my thoughts, back to the present.

I blink, clearing my mind a little, and look over to where the sound came from. Someone is a few chairs down, staring expectantly. A guy, to be more specific. He looks like James Dean and Adriana Lima had a love child with his dark, glossy waves, styled to perfection. I can't help but notice that he has the kind of bone structure celebrities pay big money for. High cheekbones. Strong chin. Perfectly sized nose. Chiseled jawline. His full lips start to lift into a grin on one side...is that a *dimple*?

I decide immediately that I don't like him. Nobody *that* good looking is worth knowing. He's probably Captain of the Tinder squad, out here looking for a stray flight attendant thinking he's in for an exciting weekend. I barely withhold my sound of disgust.

"I guess you didn't hear me," he says politely.

At least he doesn't *also* have an accent.

Tinder Boy's eyes are a piercing green, clearly questioning whether I'm mentally sound. Maybe if I ignore him for long enough, he'll think I'm not and he'll leave me alone.

"I asked what you were smiling about." Tinder Boy is good, he's got the nice guy act down pat. I don't even feel like showering yet.

I still don't answer him, though. This time it's because I realize I probably *am* mentally unsound. I mean, I was smiling to myself about my dead dad catching me during hot sex. The fact that one would have to actually be *having* sex to get caught is neither here nor there.

"Are you waiting for someone to get off their plane?" He doesn't give up easily, this one.

"No."

"Then why are you sitting in the airport?"

"Are YOU waiting for someone to get off their plane?" Maybe he's also in the airport thinking about a dead parent catching him doing the deed.

Not likely. That territory of unhinged thoughts is strictly population: me.

He chuckles. "Actually, I'm not," as if that's explanation enough.

Tinder Boy's expression is hard to read. His eyes seem genuine, tinged with something close to surprise, maybe even a little curious. When paired with his slightly raised brows and uneven smile, he looks...dazed. A little taken aback, even.

"Okay." End of conversation.

"So then what are you doing waiting on this side of security, if you're not waiting for someone?"

"Minding my own business." I look pointedly in his direction.

His answering smirk does things to me. *Weird* things.

I decide I *really* don't like him.

"Are you from around here?"

"No, I just did a cross-country road trip to a random airport, because why not?" My voice drips with sarcasm.

He laughs again.

"I'm Theo," he says as he holds out his hand. I can't even remember the last time someone my age offered a handshake. It's like an archaic method of interaction to my generation and it has me thinking. What if he's one of those guys who doesn't wash their hands?

"Don't worry, I wash my hands regularly." He jokes, leaving his hand extended a moment longer.

I *definitely* don't like that he managed to string my thoughts together.

Theo finally drops his hand, still grinning and not looking the least bit put-off by my refusal to shake his hand. It makes me uneasy. What could this guy want so bad not to be discouraged already?

"What's your name?"

*Aaaand that's my last straw.*

"I'm leaving," I say as I abruptly stand up.

"Why are you leaving? We just started talking."

"You were the one doing the talking."

"Come on, at least tell me your name before you go." That dimple makes another appearance, and it quickly becomes what I hate most about him, along with his eyes and his hair and his jaw and his...everything.

"My name is Gertrude Agnes Cocksuck," I say with a straight face.

Theo lets out a terrified snort, but sobers himself quickly. "You're joking."

"Guess you'll never know," I say with a shrug and make my way toward the elevator.

As if my parents would be *that* cruel. They were only cruel enough to name me "Sarah" along with every other American household welcoming a daughter in the late nineties. Paired with the last name "Scott" they may as well have named me Jane Doe. Actually, that would have been more original.

After meeting about seventeen other Sarahs before the third grade, I finally decided to go by "Ara." It's one of those names that everyone will pronounce differently, but whatever way they end up saying it is still better than Sarah.

But Theo will never know that.

I allow myself one more look before the elevator doors come together. Theo is still standing by the chairs, hands in his pockets, the look on his face sending chills over my entire body. For a split second I consider jutting my hand out to stop the elevator doors from closing. I imagine what it could be like, acting on a whim and seeing where this went.

Then I remember what trusting someone inevitably leads to. I remember that the only person in the world that I *could* rely on is dead and I just spent the day at his funeral. *That's* what I should be thinking about, not a random stranger from the airport, even if he does look like he fell out of a *GQ* spread.

I decide right then to forget all about Theo.

I'll never see him again anyway in the randomness of running into someone at an international airport.

It will be easy.

Since my usual spot seems to be occupado, I guess I'll be forced to be miserable in the comfort of my own home. The elevator doors close and I don't let him cross my mind again as I get home, open a bottle of wine, and push play on the next *Gossip Girl* episode.

# CHAPTER TWO

## Five Years Ago - Ara

"Come on, Ara. I promise it won't be that bad."

"The only reason you can say that with such confidence is because you're not a girl in high school."

"And I could never be more grateful for *that*," Dad mumbles under his breath, just loud enough for me to hear. I try to hide my grin and fail. "Too late. I saw that."

"Ughhhh, come on, Dad!! I'm not even going to prom, why do I need to try on one of those silly dresses?" The truth is they're not silly at all, but if I admit that, this whole "not going to prom" thing gets a lot more depressing.

"I thought we were still *considering* going to prom. We should be prepared."

"You say 'we' as if we're in this together, but it'll just be *me* sitting in a corner all night. You of all people should understand why I have no interest in going." I never use a whiny voice, but desperate times call for desperate measures. Engaging full whiny mode. "As if I want *another* excuse to see the kids from school. They'll eat me alive for not having a date."

"Then I think you should at least have the experience of dress shopping," I groan, ready to fight him on that, too, but then, "Your mother would have wanted it."

Every word I was prepared to slew comes to a screeching halt. Dad never brings up my mother. He just loaded the big guns on me.

"I don't want you missing out on these experiences just because I'm your dad and it's something girls usually do with their mothers." His voice is quiet, sad. Dad never gets sad. "I want to make sure you have *every* experience in life. I want you to enjoy being young."

"Dad, I've never felt like I was missing out on a single thing." I reach over to the driver's side and touch his arm. "I'm just...not like the other kids. It's not your fault I'm *different*."

"Being different makes you *special*, Ara. Someday, you'll find the people who will appreciate that," he tells me again for the thousandth time. "I won't let you miss out on things just because you haven't made friends yet."

"But *you're* my best friend, Dad. I don't need anybody else."

"Well then, as my best friend, please do this for me."

"You're really serious about this, aren't you?" Dad never pushes me to do anything that I don't want to do, so this must mean a lot to him. With what recently went down with Cameron, he's been extra worried about me.

"I'm really serious," he says.

"Fine, but I'm only trying on the most hideous ones I can find."

"No deal. You have to try on *at least* one that you like."

"What if I don't like any of them?"

"Then we will drive to other stores until we find one that you do."

As much as I love Dad and want to make him happy, I can't contain my groan. It's not that I don't want to spend my day looking at the dresses. I would be utterly fascinated to explore the materials and stitching which are used. I just don't want to try any of them on. With my luck, one of the Barbie bitches from my school will be there just in time to snap an embarrassing photo of me to put on Twitter or Instagram.

"Fine. One dress that I like, but nothing more."

"Fine."

"If we see anyone I know, we have to leave."

"Agreed."

Joke's on him, I'll never find anything I like.

A moment later I realize that the joke's on me. These dresses are beautiful.

Everywhere I turn, there is gorgeous dress after gorgeous dress. I can't help but wish that someday I would be able to create something as beautiful as these gowns.

One in particular catches my eye. It reminds me of something that a Disney villain would wear, rather than one of the princesses. The tulle is a sparkly black, rather than pink or blue, with a sweetheart neckline and layered tulle starting from the waist, flowing all the way down. I hate to admit it, but I immediately love it. "That one."

Dad wisely keeps his mouth shut as I ask the lady to put it in a fitting room for me.

A deal is a deal. One dress and I can go home.

I step inside the spacious changing room and unceremoniously kick off my Converse, followed by my t-shirt and jeans. I leave on my bra, because I need as much help as I can get in the boob department. I refuse to look at the price tag because based on the luxurious design of this store, I won't want to know.

I've only just stepped into the dress as the sales lady pops her head in to see if I need help with the zipper. Does no one teach these people how to knock!?

I can't stay irritated for long because...this dress? *Wow.*

Dad won't let me leave until he's seen what I've chosen to try on, so I pick up the layered skirts and head out. My dislike for the lady increases after she insists I stand on the gigantic pink podium in front of a great big mirror.

The look on Dad's face melts my annoyance. This man, of little emotion and little words, is on the brink of tears. My heart softens and I give him a genuine smile.

"Do you want that one?"

I shake my head. "Dad, it is way too expensive, and I still don't want to go to prom."

"Because of the other girls?"

I nod. Though if I did go, this would undoubtedly be the dress I'd wear.

"You look so beautiful, Ara."

"Thanks, Dad."

Maybe dress shopping isn't so bad after all.

• • •

"Can I pick the movie tonight?" I ask, as Dad flicks on the TV. "It's the least you could do after torturing me."

"Don't be dramatic, it was just a bit of shopping." Eye roll. "And why? You don't like the movies I've been picking?"

"I can only take so many Star Treks in a row..."

"And you think *you* can pick better?

"I'm not saying that they will be better for you, but since you've been punishing me with your movie choices, I get to choose at least one."

Dad groans. He knows it's only fair. "In that case, I'm going to make some popcorn so I have something to distract me from whatever vampire garbage you're surely about to choose."

This makes me laugh. Dad always makes his own popcorn from scratch, and it shits all over what you get at the movies.

I open Netflix and scroll straight to the Romance section. I'm not ashamed of loving a good chick flick. I know Dad secretly enjoys them, too.

After flicking through the ones I've already seen way too many times, I find the perfect one for tonight. *P.S. I Love You.*

"Dad! Can you bring some tissues back with you?" I call to him in the kitchen.

I hear him grumble something about needing strength, and I can't help but smile. He's going to get emotional, and he knows it.

A few minutes later, he walks back into the living room with popcorn and tissues and some chocolate that he must have had stashed somewhere, and I think about how lucky I am to have him as my dad.

# CHAPTER THREE

## *Present - Ara*

I wake up to incessant knocking, shooting upright way too fast I nearly give myself a brain aneurysm. I'm still on the couch, surrounded by empty wine bottles and dirty cereal bowls. If I don't do dishes soon, I'll be eating with measuring spoons.

*Classy, Ara.*

Glancing up to the TV, I find my reflection looking back at me through the "Are You Still Watching" screen. I have, no doubt, seen better days. The knocking continues, reminding me of why I'm awake right now.

Grumbling about knocking etiquette, I stand to wrap myself in a blanket but realize there is no need. I'm still wearing my clothes from the funeral yesterday. Even worse? I slept with my bra on.

The knocking still doesn't stop.

"One second, please!!" I yell, not the least bit friendly. I mean, for fuck's sake, who knocks like that this early? Except, a look at the clock tells me that it's 12:30 pm on a Monday, aka not early at all.

"I can't leave until you take this!" The delivery man yells from the other side of the door.

*Ugh.* I hope this isn't some strange attempt from Dad's lawyer to get ahold of me. It's only been a week and he already expects me to come by his office. I throw the door open just before he starts another round of knocks.

"Can I help you?" I don't mask my irritation. The delivery man is so out of breath that he's barely leaving oxygen for the rest of us. Though, I shouldn't judge. The stairs take it out of me every time.

"I'm just here to deliver this letter," he says, trying to catch his breath, as he holds out a letter wrapped in a pretty, gray envelope. It's old-fashioned, not anything official from a lawyer, but I'm still not interested.

I'm about to close the door on him when I spot the handwriting on the envelope. For a moment, I am utterly frozen. All I can do is stand here, weighing the options.

More than likely, the loss of Dad and my inability to connect with anyone else has officially driven me bat-shit crazy? Although, it could also be a dream. I discreetly reach down and pinch my leg.

*Nope. Not a dream.*

Insanity then.

Or could the wine still be clouding my judgment? Probably not, seeing as though I've never even had enough to get drunk, just a glass to soften my thoughts and make me sleepy. Nobody needs to know that I start the moment I wake up, and timing it out so a bottle gets that delicious haze lasting throughout the entire day.

"Are you okay there, darling?" Even the delivery man knows that I've lost it.

I rip the envelope out of his hand and close the door. As an afterthought, I yell "Thanks!" through the door. I'm not usually this curt with people, but I'm worried that I am on the verge of a mental collapse, and I don't want any witnesses.

Walking the short distance between my door and the living room of my small apartment, I sit down on the shabby chic couch I got for free on Facebook Marketplace, and stare at the envelope.

It is unmistakably Dad's handwriting. Which isn't possible.

I grab my keys, phone, wallet, shoes, and purposefully avoid the mirror in my entryway as I rush from my apartment.

Not sure where I was headed at first, I guess it isn't a surprise when I find myself at the checkout of the Publix liquor store. With a bag holding my footlong chicken sub and donuts in one hand, I awkwardly use the other to pull out my ID for the cashier.

Not that he particularly needs to see it. I've been here almost every day since I received the call about my dad. At first, I thought it would be too embarrassing to purchase seven bottles of wine all at once. Turns out, coming back every day is *so* much worse.

He nods.

I pay.

I run back to my car.

I don't know why I was in such a hurry to get back to my apartment. I've done nothing but sit here, staring at the letter until I register that it's gotten dark enough that I can't read his handwriting anymore.

I switch on the lamp next to my couch and stare at it some more.

I take a deep breath.

I know I need to do this at some point.

It's probably just something about the will.

I open the envelope.

*Dear Ara,*

Tears start spilling the moment I begin reading, blurring my vision. It's as if I can hear his voice with every word I read. Wiping my tears away, my vision clears enough that I can try again.

*Dear Ara,*

*I can see it now. You're probably turning into a permanent fixture in that living room of yours, while binging some god-awful teenage angst show and eating too much cereal.*

*I know you're probably sad about the fact that I'm no longer there to sit on that damn couch that I wish you'd let me replace, asking silly questions while I pretend to forget the names of those vampire boys you like. If this letter has been delivered when I intended, then I gave you a week, but now it's time to go back out into life, even if you think it won't be the same without your old man.*

*When you were born, I knew I made a best friend that day. When we lost your mother just a few weeks later, I didn't think that I could give you everything you needed on my own. I thought for sure losing her and realizing that would make it the worst day of my life.*

*Well, I was wrong.*

*The worst day of my life was undeniably when I found out that I would be leaving you too soon. Neither of us would be ready and there wasn't a damn thing my stubbornness or the medical field could do about it. You're probably angry with me, thinking that I should have told you when I found out, but I hope you can forgive me. I wanted the last of our time together not to be sad, but to be exactly as fun as it has been to be your dad. Please don't worry about not getting to say everything you wanted to.*

*Our bond has never had to rely on words before, and it doesn't now. I know how we feel about each other, and you didn't need to say it out loud for me to know. Our affinity transcends the laws of the physical world, and I will take your love with me wherever I go.*

*That aside, I knew I couldn't leave this Earth without feeling like I've done something to make it any easier for you. So, I got to thinking.*

*Remember that movie you made me watch a few years back? The one with that good looking Irish guy who writes letters to his wife? I pretended to hate it, but you caught me crying in the kitchen and I blamed the allergies I've never had? You know the one.*

*Well, the guy in that movie had the right idea. This is the only way I can help you get through this without physically being there. Writing these letters has become the only way I can still be there for my little girl, even when I'm gone.*

*This is letter number one.*

*I'm going to send you a letter every single month for the next twelve months. I've also stored up a few for the other big moments in your life that I will miss. Don't worry, you'll get them at the right times, I've made sure of it. I just couldn't give them to you ahead of time and risk you peeking when you get sad.*

*Each month, I'm going to give you a task and each month, no matter how difficult, you have to complete the task. It is the only thing I ask of you. It is the only way that you can help me move on to wherever I'm headed to next without an overwhelming sense of guilt.*

*My task this month is an easy one, but don't go thinking I'll be letting you off the hook for the rest of the months, too. But we need to start small. Here is your task for this month:*

Get out of your apartment.

Go on a walk and look at the world.

Go to our favorite breakfast place and order the usual.

Remember to appreciate what it's like to live.

*I guess that's technically four tasks, but come on, they're small. I know they'll feel monumental after this loss, but you've got to do it. You've got to get back out into that world and start making memories again. If there is one thing I've learned these past few months, it's that life is too short.*

*I know that you already know this, but I should have told you more often.*

*I love you.*

*I'm proud of you.*

*I can't wait to see where this life takes you.*

*Love,*

*Dad*

Pretty sure I'm not still crying only because I have physically run out. For a man of few words while he was alive, he really just had to go and use every word that hit me like a gut punch in death.

My feelings instantly become pandemonium beneath my skin. It's an uproar made of my sadness and my anger, an anarchy of rage for the universe which took him away too soon, and the despondency that comes with knowing I'll never again find comfort in resting my head on his shoulder.

Despite everything, Dad has found a way to help me get through this. He found a way to reach me, to be here when I need him the most, regardless of the cruel universe ripping him away.

Underneath the anguish, the lawless free-for-all of what I'm feeling is overwhelming gratitude that even in death, he would never abandon me. Knowing that I won't be going through this alone, that he will be able to guide me through his letters gives me a sense of security and a little, glowing kernel of something else.

Something which looks a lot like hope.

# CHAPTER FOUR

## *Present - Ara*

*Get out of your apartment.*

Standing on the sidewalk just outside of my apartment, I take a moment to appreciate the nice weather that never lasts for more than a handful of months. Florida's year is pretty much divided into two parts: hell and survivable. Hell takes place between May and September thanks to the heat, humidity, torrential rain, potential hurricanes, and mosquitoes. October through April are usually pretty decent, wonderful even, especially if you're one of the snowbirds who comes from up north.

A fresh breeze brushes through my hair, taking my waves in every direction. I pull my cardigan tighter around myself, wishing I wore a jacket instead. It rarely gets below sixty degrees, but this morning appears to be one of the flukes. Feeling cold is a bit of a novelty in Florida and warrants bundling up in the heavy clothing that only gets worn a couple of times a year.

*Go on a walk and look at the world.*

Not sure why I wasn't allowed to look at the world while sitting on my ass, but okay. Cardio has never been my friend. Nor has any other form of exercise, for that matter. Sadly, I was born without the ingredients that make one enjoy waking up early, working out, and liking salads. Instead, I was blessed with the love for lazy Sundays and pretty much anything one could buy at a food truck.

I head toward the little park at the center of Hyde Park Village, just down the road from where I live. It's a beautiful place with a lot of charm. Everything in Florida is pretty beachy and starts to seem generic after you live here long enough, but this park is a little slice of heaven with its giant oak trees, surrounding greenery, and antique wrought-iron benches.

I've always loved New York from afar, and this scenery reminds me of the bits of it that I've seen in pictures and movies. If I close my eyes and think hard enough, I can even pretend that I was brave enough to take a risk, that I'm in New York right now chasing after my dream that seems like a distant blip on the horizon now. The cold breeze and sounds of ruffling leaves make it almost convincing, until I open my eyes and remember I'm the girl who works in a café, living in fear of the dark, lurking shadow of my life called change.

After one loop around the park, I figure that I've done enough walking to check that off the list and decide to take a seat on one of the beautiful benches. Gorgeous to look at, terrible on the ass.

I don't know how long I sit there, watching people go by. Some hurry past and some look like they've got all the time in the world. I can't help but wonder where they might be headed.

A woman goes by in her designer Pilates outfit that probably costs more than my car, likely a resident from the more expensive area down by the water.

A man walks by with flowers. It's a colorful display with no roses, so they aren't intended for a lover, so it must be someone's birthday. Maybe his mother. I continue to watch him until he stops at one of the carts to buy a balloon which reads 'Happy Birthday'.

*Nailed it.*

This is the only form of human interaction I enjoy, the kind that happens from far away and doesn't include any real interchange. Afterall, the best way to avoid being maimed by a tiger is to stay out of its habitat and far enough away from its claws.

I'm stalling. These first two tasks were surprisingly doable, nice even. It felt good to have an excuse to shower and get out of the house to breathe some fresh air.

But the next task?

*Go to our favorite breakfast place and order the usual.*

I have to walk into a place, filled with memories of Dad, and not break down? Technically, I could just walk in, order the usual and get out of there before it's even ready. He didn't specify that I had to sit down and eat at our table.

But I know what he intended, and my cowardly way out would eat away at me if I chose that route.

Dad wants me to learn how to still love something we did together, even if I do it alone now. The thing is, I don't want to love it without him. I want to keep everything we did together wrapped up in a tiny box and preserve it forever.

Be that as it may, there is only thing I would hate more than learning to love something without Dad, and that is to let him down. His only request is that I complete his tasks every month. Dad never once let me down, so I won't let him down either.

The thought alone forces me to my feet.

• • •

The familiar bell jingles as I let myself inside where I'm greeted by the heavenly smell of coffee, bacon, and pancakes, three of my favorite things. Food being my love language, the prospect of stuffing my face with food for the soul *slightly* lifts my spirits.

Emphasis on slightly.

We started coming here when I was little, and it wasn't long before it became our favorite spot. The Diner is one of those old, retro-looking places that you hope never changes for as long as you live. It's got the black-and-white-checked floors with red-leather booths and swivel barstools. The walls are filled with black-and-white photos, giving you the feeling that you've traveled through time.

My stomach lets out an embarrassingly loud gurgle, and thankfully no one is at the counter to think I'm harboring an alien creature under my shirt. The "Please Wait To Be Seated" doesn't apply once I see that my usual booth is open. Even though I don't need to look at the menu, I grab one as I go by so I can look busy.

Susan notices me as she walks by with about fifteen plates in her hand. I will never understand how she manages to do that without wearing the food. I give her the best smile I can manage, which is pathetic, after she mouths "Be right there."

The Diner was opened by her grandfather and was passed down to her before he passed away from old age. Susan once told us that she had grown up in these booths and couldn't stand the idea of it being sold off to a developer with no heart. As a kid, I thought she might have a crush on my dad, but over the years I learned that she is married and treats all of her regulars with such care.

"I can't help but notice that you have no regard for the rules of society." The newly familiar voice sends every nerve in my body on high alert.

This can't be happening. I knew who it was as the first word left his mouth, but I confirm the knowledge with a look to the booth across from me, finding the guy I met at the airport sitting only a matter of feet away. Theo is *here*.

"*Huh*?" I don't let myself dwell on why I recognized his voice or why I bothered to remember his name. I don't even consider the unlikelihood of running into the same stranger two days in a row because I'm too busy imagining how to wipe that smug look right off his face.

"You walked right past that 'Please Wait To Be Seated' sign without even looking over your shoulder." His smug look slowly transforms into a grin. "What a menace."

He's...*teasing* me.

"Are you stalking me?"

He laughs a little and shakes his head. "How could I stalk someone if I don't know their name?"

"Sounds like a question you should ask a serial killer." I'm not giving this guy anything on me.

He laughs again. "Know how I could find one?"

Susan chooses that exact, wonderfully helpful moment to approach my table and greet me by name. "Good morning, Ara! Just you today?"

*Shit.* I look around Susan to see Theo sporting a triumphant grin. It's... infuriating. Now he knows my name.

"Officially stalking!" I mouth at him before turning back to Susan to let her know I'll have the usual.

Before I can get the words out, it hits me that I didn't react when Susan asked if I would be by myself. The delayed realization clangs through me, almost as if it's the first time I'm getting the magnitude of it.

*Just me today.* By myself. Sitting alone. Eating alone. The way I'll do everything from now on, accompanied only by my shadow and an empty seat serving as a reminder of what was taken from me.

"Everything okay?" Susan asks with a concerned look.

"I'm fine." I go for a happy face and end up landing somewhere near 'circus exhibit' instead. "Just me today and I'll have my usual."

Susan hesitates like she wants to stay and make sure I'm okay, but thinks better of it and heads back toward the kitchen.

"I like your name. Is it short for something?" Theo's voice is less teasing now, taking on a more somber tone as if he perceived the shift in my demeanor. At least he's observant.

"Yeah, it's short for Sarah." I hear the slide of jeans on leather and look up to see Theo sitting in front of me.

"Mind if I join you?"

"Do I have a choice?" I look down, noticing he's holding a mug of black coffee. I can't help but crinkle my nose. Who drinks black coffee unless they want to torture themself?

Theo lifts his brows. "Do you have an issue with my preference in coffee?"

I open my mouth to say something snarky, but I'm interrupted by, "One coffee with extra, extra cream," Susan says, *sooo* conveniently. "Food will be out soon."

Theo bites his lip and looks down at his coffee, trying very hard not to say whatever witty bullshit he's thinking. After he manages to suppress the urge, he slowly lets his bottom lip go and runs over the spot with his... oh my God, why am I looking at his mouth?

"Do YOU have a problem with MY coffee preference?" I fire his own question back at him, sounding defensive in my own question.

"Can you really call it a 'coffee preference' if it's mostly milk?"

"Does this normally work with your Tinder dates? Stalking with a side of immature badgering?"

"You tell me," he says with a wink.

This time, I'm happy to see Susan approaching the table, right up until she opens her mouth. "Mickey Mouse pancakes with chocolate chips and fresh strawberries."

I want to evaporate. *I know what I ordered, Susan.*

"Please," Theo motions to my plate, "continue with your lecture on maturity as you eat your Mickey Mouse pancakes."

I want to strangle him. "Why are you here?"

"You looked like you could use some company."

"No. Why are you *here?* At *this* diner."

For someone who is normally so quick with his answers, this one takes him a little too long, setting off the warning bells in the back of my mind. "I heard they have great waffles."

Anyone with half a brain cell would realize he's not being forthcoming and would immediately abandon ship, but the inescapable look in his eyes has me retracting my claws. I'm intrigued. Regardless of what he says, something tells me that Theo is here because I am here, and part of me gets a little thrill at the thought, even if it's just a certain lady-bit (in dire need of attention) interfering with my instincts and I'll be dead by the weekend.

"What's your name again?" I say over a bite of pancakes.

Theo gives me a look saying, *I-know-that-you-know-my-name-but-I'll-play-along.* "Theo."

"Theo." I try it out on my tongue. Interesting one would come all the way here for the waffles, yet not order any. "You're not eating."

"I already ate, you can ask Susan if you don't believe me." He winks. "I'm an early bird."

"Of course, you are." Gross.

"I write best early in the morning, before the rest of the world is awake."

"What do you write?" I try to conceal my genuine curiosity, but it doesn't work.

"Whatever comes to mind that day." Theo knows he's got me on the hook and isn't going easy. If he's going for the tall, dark, and mysterious thing, it's fucking working. "What do you do, Ara?"

"I work in a café." I hate this part. Where I inevitably have to tell someone that I do nothing of consequence, that I'm not in college, hardly pursuing a dream or on any kind of path. Glancing up to catch the judgment pass over Theo's face, surprise ends up passing over mine instead when I see nothing of the sort.

"Which café?" he asks with such authentic curiosity that I almost forget that I shouldn't tell him, self-preservation and all that. I don't like how unfiltered I seem to feel around him. A bit longer at this table and I might as well give him my birthdate and Social Security number while I'm at it.

"As if I'm going to tell a stranger where I work, especially when that stranger is already stalking me."

"I won't need to resort to stalking for long," Theo says with such unassuming conviction, it's got my stomach doing flips while I try to convince myself that it sounded douchey, not disarmingly attractive.

I clear my throat. "Someone seems wildly confident in themself."

"Someone else seems wildly dedicated to fighting everything I say."

*Touché.*

Our eyes meet and I forget why I've been fighting at all. Somewhere distant, my logical side is shouting, accompanied by that darker part ready to sink its teeth into me, but I'm already lost. Stolen away by the green of fairytale forests in far-off worlds, flecked with golden magic and a soul within that is full of kindness and depth, shadowed by the kind of things one can't gather from just one look. They're the kind of eyes which have seen both the beauty and ugliness that this world has to offer.

The urge to uncover what lies behind those shadows will soon become overwhelming. I rarely find anyone interesting enough that the desire to get to know them could become equal in measure to my fear of doing so. There is just something about him that's...captivated me. Which is just unhinged, considering I'm in the middle of an existential crisis, having lost the person I love most and realizing I have no idea where my life is headed.

If I stay here any longer, I'm going to start asking questions about his past and he will surely want to learn about mine. That would require opening up, delving into my past while I struggle to face my present. I can't risk putting myself in such a vulnerable position or making said crisis any worse.

Susan clears her throat and we both jump. She's got the check and I need to make my next move. Though every bone in my body is begging me to stay, a single thought in the direction of broken trust drives me from the booth.

"You've got this one, right?" I give him a little wink. "Make sure you leave Susan a good tip since I'm a regular." With that, I leave Theo and his bewildered expression behind.

As I walk out of the diner my heart begins a violent, uneven assault on my ribcage. I can't tell if it's my body screaming at me to go back to him, or because of the sick pleasure generated by Theo's stunned face at my sudden departure.

Letting out an evil little giggle, I make my way down the sidewalk, back toward the park, and I can't help but think of Dad's fourth task for today:

*Remember to appreciate what it's like to live.*

I pretend like that appreciation that I'm feeling right now has nothing to do with Theo.

# CHAPTER FIVE

## *Five Years Ago - Ara*

W*eird.* Dad is home early. Normally, I'm home from school and already finished with homework by the time he can get out of the office. I insert my key into the front door, giving it the special jiggle that makes it turn, and let myself inside. I don't make it past the threshold before my backpack and books clatter to the old, hardwood floors.

My dad has always been a simple, practical man, just like our home. Even the rooms which have been renovated keep the same, old-fashioned vibe that makes you feel right at home. Except for right now, as silver reflective streamers flow down from the ceiling, a new one taped only inches away from the last, creating a sea of shininess.

I slowly clear a path to walk, feeling like I'm making my way through the jungle in an alternate universe, and finally spot my dad standing in the kitchen, next to a giant bowl of punch. "Did someone break in?"

Dad's face slackens. "What do you mean?"

"Who did all of this?"

"I did."

Though it seems like the obvious answer, I can't make it click in my head. "You decorated the house?"

"Yes."

"Why? And why are you in a suit?"

"It's a special occasion."

"No, it's not."

"Yes, it is. It's prom night."

No way. "I'm not going, no matter what crap you try to guilt trip me with."

"You don't have to."

"Well, they'll arrest you for being creepy if you try to go by yourself."

Dad rolls his eyes, and I can't help but see our similarities when he does that. "We aren't *going* to prom. We are *having* one." He gestures to the obnoxious decorations. "Here."

A prom I don't have to leave the house for and brave the torment of shitty teenagers for hours on end? "But I don't have anything to wear."

Dad smiles. "Go check your closet."

I can't resist. Dropping the façade of unaffected, I take off in a sprint to my room, through my door, and throw open the closet. The beautiful, black, Disney villain dress that stole my heart hangs perfectly in the center.

I pop my head out of my room to see my dad standing in the hallway, a safe distance away. He's not blind, so I know he can see the tears well in my eyes as I look up to the ceiling to blink them away.

Dad knows how much this means to me, it's why he went through all of this effort. I don't have to blubber all over him for it, it'll just be embarrassing for both of us.

"It's the dust," I say with a sniffle, motioning to my eyes.

"Yeah, I noticed it when I was in there earlier." He clears his throat. "It got me too."

I smile because we both know there is no dust.

"Do we have to dance?" I ask.

"Hopefully not."

"Good. I'll be dressed in five."

FEBRUARY
Dear Ara

# CHAPTER SIX

## *Present - Ara*

It's been five weeks since Dad died. It's been four weeks since I received his first letter. Part of me still worries the first was a fluke and I'll never receive the next, but Dad always keeps his word. The letter saved that day, and being able to look forward to another one is what helps me get through the hard moments.

Sometimes I wake up convinced it was all a bad dream, only to put myself through the loss again when I realize it wasn't a bad dream at all. Sometimes I open my thread of texts with Dad ready to send a joke, just to remember he will never receive it. Sometimes I embrace the pain, calling his phone over and over just to hear his voice on the other end when I reach his voicemail. I don't know what I'll do when one day, my call no longer gets answered.

Every day I feel the loss of him over and over in different ways. If I was going through life based on my emotions, I would most definitely be spending most days in bed. The only thing which is getting me out of it is work and the wrath I'll face if I don't show up.

My unusual work hours are something I've always sort of appreciated, never having to wake up early for work, now more than ever. Working from 5 PM to 1 AM at the café allows me to be home during the delivery window, regardless of what day the letters arrive, so I'll never miss one.

The schedule is probably the only thing about my job that I mildly tolerate. In fact, I try not to think about my situation too much. There's nothing to be proud of being almost twenty-three, working nights at a café, heading to destination nowhere.

Most parents would be disappointed in their child becoming a business degree dropout such as myself, but not Dad. He understood that I didn't want to spend four years of my life preparing for something that I didn't love. He always encouraged me to pursue something that brought me joy, because if you love what you do and you do a good job, it will inevitably lead to success. The only issue with that is, when you love something, failing becomes even scarier. So I decided to play it safe, get a temporary job until I figured out something that I can do which I don't hate.

With his support, I didn't realize that dropping out of college and working at a café would become something to be embarrassed about. I first noticed it when I told my 'friends' that I would be dropping out. None of them could understand where I was coming from, and they kept talking about how disappointed their families would be if they made that choice.

It got worse when a distant family member would ask how my classes were going and I'd have to inform them that I dropped out. They always assumed it was because I got some incredible opportunity, such as an apprenticeship on Wall Street or something. Do these people live in the same world as me? We live in *Florida*. The biggest opportunity here is getting on a front page in some local yokel newspaper for riding an alligator naked.

Plus, that amazing stuff doesn't happen in real life. In real life, you drop out of college to start working at a café, and when you tell people, they get that shitty condescending look on their face because they think you're a failure. Since when does someone's career choice decide that anyway?

For example, Dad loved solving problems, finding things which didn't add up, and numbers, in general. So, he became an accountant. It wouldn't be most people's dream job, and everyone assumed he was boring because of it. But he wasn't.

I'm not sure at what point in my life I started to feel like I was running out of time, but I did. One day I woke up and found myself looking at my life through their eyes and felt disappointed, too. Dad's advice about achieving success is sound, but my dilemma is that I don't love anything career-worthy. Nobody is offering fifty dollars an hour to binge watch Netflix.

Finding the café gig was a total accident. I had just got back from dropping out of college, ending a bad relationship, and an even worse friendship, thinking maybe I could figure out what to do with my life by watching others.

I ended up coming to the same airport terminal, every night, just watching strangers go by. One night on my way out, I stumbled across the "Help Wanted" sign at the café just before security.

I went inside and got the job right away. Even though I had no skill set, sucked with people, and had no work experience, they were desperate. It's not easy finding people whose lives allow them to work the night schedule for crap pay.

The job sucks. My manager is named Karen, which is fitting. In fact, I think they invented that term *because* of her. She is stingy about any time off (even when your dad dies) and never misses an opportunity to let you know what you're doing wrong. Giving a single word of encouragement would probably make her drop dead.

Why don't I quit if I'm so miserable?

It's the question that I ask myself every day as I get ready for work, the answer remaining the same, never noble or admirable in any way. It comes down to the fact that I have nothing better to do.

Stepping in front of my long mirror, I take a moment to assess myself. You can't really tell by looking at me that I lost the person closest to me last month. My reflection is pretty much the same as it's always been.

Long dark hair, naturally tan skin with even tanner freckles. My eyebrows, which are just a bit too thick, frame my weirdly colored eyes. Some old lady in Walmart stopped me to say that my eyes were the color of chocolate sapphires once, her favorite stone, but I just think they're bizarre.

Sadly, my frame hasn't changed either. You'd think that I'd have lost some weight after barely eating for weeks on end, but no, I'm still stuck with a shape that's just slightly too soft. Not in that curvy bombshell way either, no. I'm permanently stuck in the middle of both ends of the beauty spectrum. I'm not thin enough to be on the skinny side. I'm rocking a B-cup, at best, and nobody is turning to watch me walk away, meaning I don't qualify as curvy either.

It's never really bothered me, not being most guys' cup of tea. I don't think I would do well with that kind of attention anyway. It just bothers me that I'm stuck at average in almost every area of life. You'd think I could at least fail at life *while* being hot.

All the girls swoon over my long hair and say that they would kill for my thick eyebrows if they were "properly shaped." I can guarantee they don't want everything else that comes with it, aka body hair. Not sure why thick hair is only acceptable in *certain* places, but God forbid I have some hair on my arms and lower back. The reality is you can't get one without the other, and I sure as hell can't be bothered trying to get rid of it.

I throw my hair up into a bun that is decidedly more messy than cute, following it up with some concealer under my eyes in an attempt to cover up those bags. A dust of powder across the rest of my face, and a swipe of mascara for each eye to finish it off. That's as much of an effort as I can manage.

Looking at myself in the mirror, despite my best efforts, my reflection is a pretty exact representation of the rest of my life: mediocre and a bit sad.

The clock on the wall reminds me that it's time to leave for work. I move to the great big windows, the feature which made me instantly fall in love with this place. My apartment is what HGTV would call shabby-chic, or what I like to call shitty-cute. Everything is a bit old and worn, but the neutral tones make it look like it's on purpose.

I shut the blinds, blocking out the golden sunlight which filters in all day, keeping it bright while reminding me there is an entire world out there. Plus, it makes my fake plants look even more realistic since it's an environment where real plants would thrive, if someone ever remembered to water them.

My phone buzzes with another alert, this time it's a message from Dad's attorney, informing me that he needs to meet with me urgently. No, thanks.

Grabbing my keys, I take another look at my place.

At the very least, I'm fortunate to have this little slice of heaven beside Hyde Park.

• • •

No matter how many times I drive to the airport just for work, I never get over the feeling of excitement, as if I'm about to head off on an adventure. My brain can never convince my heart that I'm not getting on a plane to New York, finally taking off to pursue my dream. It beats and beats and beats until I walk up to the café and see Karen looking at her watch. I already know that when she lifts her gaze to mine, it will carry nothing but undiluted disdain.

Karen is one of those people who is just plain unhappy and there is nothing the rest of us can do about it. I used to show up early, but all I would get was an irritated reminder that I was an over-achieving nuisance who won't be paid extra for arriving before my shift. Now, I show up for my shift every day on the dot, which is accompanied by a grimace and some growling from her for cutting it so close.

"Good evening, Karen," I say as I make my way past her. I receive no answer which is fine by me. Less is more where she is concerned.

Walking past the kitchen, the guys wave in tandem, and I give them a nod in greeting. Dan and Joel are good guys, friendly even, but like everyone else, I've kept them at arm's length. Secretly, I think they're great. They've worked here longer than I have, and I know they've covered my ass with Karen more times than I can count.

On my first day, I had made a massive mess in the back of the kitchen. I got ahead of myself and tried to carry multiple plates and ended up dumping them all over the floor, wasting the meal, and breaking several plates. The customers were angry about the delay, so Karen came back to find out who was to blame, and before I could say anything, Joel, the cook, stepped up and claimed full responsibility. I've never forgotten that.

I'll also never forget the time where Dan, the dishwasher, came out to help me bus tables. There had been a particularly rowdy group who stayed well past closing after seeing someone off, despite my increasingly unfriendly reminders. The place was a mess after they finally left, and I knew I'd be there long after everyone else went home. Dan came out and stayed to help me until everything was spotless.

If I were to have any friends, it would be them. They always joke around together in the kitchen when Karen isn't paying attention and I've always *wanted* to join in. But that darker part of me repeatedly ensures that I don't, reminding me what happens when I start to care about people.

Our break room is situated behind the kitchen, painted a cheerful yellow, and has a nice little table with chairs. I stuff my purse into my cubby and hastily snatch my apron. No need to poke the grizzly by taking too long.

It's a Sunday evening, meaning it will be pretty slow tonight. Low on tips and high on my patience. Karen likes to use these evenings to order me to do meaningless tasks. Before she gets the opportunity to badger me about anything, I make a beeline toward a table nobody has bothered to clean up.

A feeling passes over me, similar to when you can hear footsteps and know exactly who they belong to. This presence is one that I would recognize anywhere. I ignore it, hoping this awareness is being conjured by my imagination and will leave me untouched. Deep, heaving breaths reach me a moment later, and I can no longer deny it.

Any normal person would expect to turn around, finding an old man who has trouble getting around or a young boy racing invisible monsters. They would even expect to see fucking Usain Bolt standing there with his gold medals, because even *that* would make more sense than who I know stands behind me right now. *Theo.*

*What. The. Hell.*

"Do you know how many places there are in Tampa Bay that can be classified as cafés?" he asks, finally regaining some of his breath as he reaches over and grabs a glass of water from the table. I open my mouth to warn him that it's probably not very sanitary, but he's already chugging it. "Think in the *hundreds.*"

I haven't seen Theo in almost exactly one month, which I've spent trying and failing to forget about his existence. He's plagued my thoughts and crawled under my skin, refusing to leave. Nobody has affected me this way, abducting my thoughts and disarming me with his smile. When Theo is around, everything else falls away, and it scares the living hell out of me.

The last time we met has played in my head over and over. Sometimes I even imagine how it could have played out differently had I stayed in the diner that morning. In a parallel universe where I have the power to overcome my anxiety, we could have talked until closing time, learning everything there is to know about each other.

"I made it to *quite* a few of them before I realized something obvious." His babbling brings me back to the present, where I always choose to run. "I met you in the airport."

He laughs incredulously, taking a deliberate step in my direction. "I met you in the *airport!!!*"

Am I processing this correctly? "You're telling me... that you spent the last *month* driving around Tampa Bay...to find *me*?"

Theo nods shamelessly, no qualms in sharing this insanity.

"Now I definitely have to quit." It doesn't come out nearly as grumbly as I intended it. In fact, it almost sounds like that's a hint of a smile in my voice? *Am I holding back a smile?*

A conquering grin spreads across Theo's mouth as his unstyled curls cascade over his brow, a hint of perspiration leaving a dewy glow across his smooth, light gold skin. It does nothing to taint the clean smell emanating my senses, a mixture of fresh forest greenery that I can't quite place with a hint of cinnamon, his chest still rising and falling with effortful breaths.

Stalking back to the kitchen before my jaw can fully disconnect from the rest of my face, I close the door behind me, resting with my back against it, sending Dan and Joel to a jarring halt. Water drips to the floor as Dan suspends a half-washed plate while a burger hovers over the grill, carefully balanced on Joel's spatula, mid flip. They're looking at me like I've been inhabited by an extraterrestrial.

"*What*?" I ask. They look at each other as if to confirm they're not seeing things.

"Well," Joel begins, keeping his happy yet worn face sober. "It's just..." He trails off and glances through the windows of the kitchen doors toward Theo.

Dan tries next, "What he means to say is..."

"Never mind." If they're about to say anything about Theo showing up, I don't want to hear it.

Joel continues anyway. "What I wanted to say was that strapping young fool is looking at you like he's just stumbled across a glass of water in the middle of the desert."

"He is NOT looking at me like that." This is both the longest conversation I've ever had with them, and completely mortifying.

Dan lets out a low whistle, drying off his hands before running one over his cropped, silvering hair. "Must be someone special if he's got you this wound up."

*Someone, please, drop a nuke on me.*

Grabbing the freshly laundered napkins, I flee the kitchen, ready to try my luck with Theo rather than experience another moment of whatever *that* was. Except, Theo isn't standing where I left him, sending a sinking sensation into my stomach. I guess he finally took the hint. The hint which wasn't a hint at all, but a plea.

A plea for what? I'm not sure. All I know is that when he's around, things seem a little less bleak. Maybe it's because I'm so busy fighting him every step of the way, I can't focus on what I've already lost, and the time I'm losing every day, another cog in the wheel.

Regardless, there has to be an explanation for *why* he keeps showing up unannounced and *how* he keeps finding me. Our generation doesn't have to exert any effort beyond a swipe of the finger to land their conquests. What could possibly drive Theo to show up at this café, breathing the way I do after climbing a flight of stairs?

My thoughts wander as I fold the napkins. Would I open myself up to Theo if given the choice? The better question would be *could I*? Most of the time, I feel like those decisions are out of my control in a way. As if after I'd experienced a certain amount of hurt, *something* decided I no longer deserved the power to make my own decisions and took over, determined to keep everyone out. There is this deep sense that it's never been *me* who wants to shut people out.

There is no doubt that I am physically attracted to Theo, but it doesn't end there. Most guys my age are too busy making thirst traps and banging their way through sorority girls to bring anything else to the table. With Theo, I can tell there is more, and the very distant, very tiny, part of me which is brave wants to be the one to unravel him.

*Sigh.* My track record with relationships is bad enough as it is. I don't need to add another failure to that list. My first serious boyfriend was a good guy, but I was young and hadn't figured out what I'd wanted. By the time I did, everything we'd built had been destroyed. From there, it only got worse with the next one, and since I wasn't born with the boldness I imagine is required for one-night stands, it's just been me and my little pink...

"SARAH."

*Tonight is the gift that keeps on giving. I'm being pulled out of a vibrator daydream by my boss.*

"Sorry! Yes, Karen?"

"Are you going to let our only customer sit there all night without being served so you can drool all over our clean napkins, thanks to whatever godforsaken thoughts are running through that juvenile, barren mind of yours? Or do you think you can bring yourself to do some real work?"

"You know what? Fuck you, Karen." Is exactly what I *should* say. That was the most insulting sentence I've ever had the displeasure of receiving.

The worst part? That darkness inside me *agrees* with her, tells me she's right.

My head hangs, realizing with utter horror that Theo hasn't left, but is actually sitting close enough that he would have overheard that, as I make my way over to take his order. "What can I get you?"

"Well first, I'd like to know what you were thinking about that caused you to drool all over those napkins?" Theo says with a naughty wink. "Because I'm hoping that it had something to do with me."

I groan, covering my face with my hands and notepad, before sure hands gently pull them away. I'm met by open green eyes, full of concern, tinted along the edges by anger. His hands linger on mine a moment too long before they slowly release my wrists.

"In all seriousness, who is that ogre who thinks she can treat you like garbage?"

"That's Karen, my boss, so unfortunately she *can* treat me like garbage."

"Her name is actually Karen?"

"Yep."

Theo cocks his head in amusement. "Fitting."

Dismayed over the fact that I don't feel all that embarrassed, a hint of a smile plays on my lips. "I say the same thing." Theo just witnessed an absolute slaughter occur, yet the moment I felt his presence, I felt *better*.

"No wonder she is such a cow. It's like the universe knows who will be a shrew and wants to warn the rest of us by naming them Karen."

I laugh. It's breathy and probably more like a gasp, but it's a laugh, my first one since Dad died, and Theo's looking at me like...like I've never been looked at before.

"So, do you actually want anything, or did you just come for the show?"

"I want to hang out with you."

Smirking, I comment, "I meant from the *menu*."

"What time do you get off?"

For some reason, unbeknownst to me, I tell him. "One AM."

"That's late." Theo blows a breath. "In that case, I'll take two shots of espresso. Black. Please."

*Hang on.* "I didn't *say* I would hang out with you."

"Well, I need to fuel up just in case you change your mind."

I give him a dry look. "Two shots of espresso coming right up. You're going to have a very lonely late night."

Karen blesses me with her presence once again as I type Theo's order into the machine.

"Surely that handsome young thing isn't a friend of *yours*." She looks her fill, eating him up, giving me the sudden and viscous urge to scratch her eyes out.

That is *IT*! I will no longer let this bitter, awful old woman disrespect me, knocking me down a peg every time she gets the chance.

Consequences be damned.

I'm. Done.

Having finished making Theo's coffee, which no doubt tastes like battery acid, I take it to his table, slamming it down with white knuckles. Theo's face falls at the sight of the to-go cup.

"I'll be sitting in the same spot where we first met at 1:05 AM. Bring a laptop. You're going to use those fancy writing skills to help me write a resignation letter."

Theo's answering grin would bring a lesser woman to her knees.

# CHAPTER SEVEN

## *Present - Ara*

Theo is already sitting outside my favorite terminal, laptop in hand, by the time I arrive after my shift.

"So, why are you hell-bent on getting in my pants?" I say in greeting. "Tinder not doing it for you?"

Theo chokes, literally chokes, sending a curl of sick pleasure through me. "Who said anything about your pants? Or Tinder, for that matter?"

"Why else would you be so intent on hanging out with me?" I shrug. "You should know it's pointless. I'm not putting out."

He laughs. "Do you always say exactly what's on your mind?'

This gives me pause because...no. In fact, I *never* say what's on my mind, even with the people I'm close to, but *especially* with people I hardly know. Dad was the only one I'd ever been able to speak my mind to besides *sometimes* Cameron, but that was a long time ago.

"I just wanted to let you know that if you think helping me with my resignation letter is going to get you laid, you're sadly mistaken, and if that's the only reason you're here, then you should just go now."

"For starters, I'm not here to get laid. You clearly need help dealing with that monster of a woman, and I'm just here to do a good deed."

"I don't need rescuing."

"That may be true, but you *do* need my laptop."

*Bastard.*

"As long as we are both aware that neither of us will be getting laid." The words are out before I realize the implication, as in I won't be getting laid at all. By anyone. I mean, I won't be, but he doesn't need to know that. "By each other, I meant. Not necessarily by others." My clarification is so cringey that it makes me want to shrivel up into a rock so I can never speak again.

"You made that clear." He's amused. Great.

"Good."

"Good."

"*Extra* good."

His amusement turns into an all-out smirk, and I wish I could stamp it out with my foot. "Since that's settled, I think it's safe to move on to the part of the night where we give Karen a giant middle finger, via resignation letter."

"Agreed. Have you ever written a resignation letter before?"

"Of course. Haven't you?"

"No." Anxiety rears its ugly head, preparing for the condescending comment that is surely about to leave his mouth.

Except, it doesn't.

"Don't worry, it was bound to happen eventually." He turns on his laptop. "Have you been in school up until now?"

Theo doesn't need to know that I'm a college dropout with no immediate family, no friends, and no direction in life. My job at the café is truly the only thing I have going for me, and he is here to help me bring an end to that, too.

Essentially I'll be a certifiable loser as soon as we hit 'Send' on the email.

"Listen, we aren't here to trade depressing life stories and cry it out. Let's just type this letter and move on. Separately." I tack on that last word so I don't set him up for one of his witty innuendos.

"Right." Sigh. "Okay, then. There is all the stuff a resignation letter is supposed to have such as the date, your full name, address, position title, standard two-week notice, etc."

"Wait." The world slowly crumbles underneath my Converse. "I have to see Karen *after* I tell her that I'm quitting?"

Theo gives me a bemused look. "Of course, you can't just quit and never show up again."

I groan. "Why not?"

Theo chuckles. "Don't worry, it'll be fine."

"There is no way I can write a resignation letter designed to make Karen feel like dog shit and face her the next day. I don't have the balls."

"At least that's good to know."

"What?"

"That you don't have balls."

A feeling which had become foreign until recently, starts to tingle around my lips as I fight the battle of my life right now. Losing, losing, losing...aaaaand *lost.* Either from the struggle, or the lack of use my facial muscles have received lately, my cheeks ache something fierce as I give Theo a broad, genuine smile.

While distracted with my internal battle, something caused Theo to lose his mental footing as if he's entered some sort of antechamber in his mind, where he's still processing his surroundings, but from afar. I wave my hand in front of his face. Nothing. Not a single reaction aside from his eyes turning into a dark, storming green.

I turn around, expecting to see Kate Upton running in slow motion in that skimpy lifeguard "uniform" (if you can even call it that) but I see nothing. Not. A. Soul. The airport is quiet, most of the flights having left hours ago. By the time I've faced back toward Theo, he is working studiously on his laptop as if I imagined the entire thing. *Weird.*

"Are you okay?"

"Huh?"

"You were just mentally frozen. Or potentially on fire."

Theo gives me a noncommittal shoulder lift. "My bad, I was just lost in thought."

"Yeah, *okay.* Let's just focus on the letter so you can go." And there it is. That tone. Accusatory. Ungrateful. Jumping to conclusions and giving the person in front of me a giant shove. Why does zoning out for a second instantly mean he wants to leave?

"Save the cold treatment for someone it'll dissuade." He brushes off my sudden impertinence like it's a gnat, and just like that, the creature puts away her claws, utterly dismissed. "So, where were we? Oh right, I was going to introduce you to a little term called passive aggressive."

"Explain." It's not beyond me that I should be more familiar with the term, proving how successfully I've alienated the rest of the world. Minus Theo, apparently.

"It's how you make someone feel like crap without saying anything outright, kinda like stabbing someone in the back while you give them your best smile."

"How the hell am I supposed to come up with something like *that*?"

"I'm not here just as your eye candy."

This guy is...honestly, I can't even pick a fucking word. "You're not my eye candy."

"Come on now, Ara. Let's not lie to each other," he says with a wink.

"You were saying?"

"I'm a writer," Theo explains, without mansplaining. "That means I have to get into the mindset of characters, even the bad guys. I need to understand them. *Be* them."

"Okay then, show me what you've got."

There is no point in telling him how much I admire his passion, his confidence in his work. When he talks about writing, he's got that fire in his eyes, similar to earlier, as if he's thinking about something magnificent.

Taking advantage of his focus being elsewhere, I finally grant my eyes the freedom to inspect every inch of him. I adore the way his curls tumble onto his forehead as he looks down, a contrast to how perfectly styled they were last month. It's almost as if he's been running his fingers through his hair, unable to figure something out.

His long, thick eyelashes cast shadows over his cheeks, leading to the rest of his features that are so chiseled, a master artisan must have carved him just perfectly. The only soft thing about him are his generously full lips. I just *know* those would feel amazing...

I look away when he starts to nibble on one in his focused state. *What the hell, Ara? Get your shit together and stop panting after this guy.*

I don't listen.

My eyes pick up where they left off, no longer under my control. The linen shirt he's chosen in the perfect shade of dark green, to match his eyes, is no accident. He knows how to dress.

With his light golden skin, green eyes and dark hair, he looks like someone waved a magic wand and brought one of my favorite book boyfriends to life. It gets even better, or worse depending how you look at it, when I notice a hint of defined chest, peeking out from where his shirt is unbuttoned at the top. Blaming curiosity, I drop my gaze slightly and find the outline of defined pecs. With his exposed forearms that are corded with lean muscle, all evidence points to the fact that Theo works out.

How have I never noticed this before!? Have I retreated so far into myself these past few years and recent months that I don't notice a hot guy even if he slaps me in the face?

My perusal continues over his shirt, which he wears casually untucked over white chinos, paired with brown leather sneakers. He looks classy, without coming across pretentious.

Though you could never tell from what I wear, I love fashion. I'm usually living in black leggings, oversized t-shirts and Converse. The only time it varies is during winter where I substitute my t-shirts for hoodies.

Having an entire wardrobe full of unique, self-made outfits that I never wear has become my specialty. Instead, I cycle through the same Target outfits day in and day out.

"Is there something on my shoe?"

I slam back into the present as gracefully as a jackhammer. "Huh?"

"I asked if there was something on my shoe. You've been staring at it for approximately two minutes."

Sending up a mental prayer to whichever god I have to thank for keeping him busy until I made it to his shoes, I slap him with the excuse he gave me. "I was just zoning out. Are you finished?"

"Besides the personal details, yes. It's ready for your approval."

As he sets his Mac down on my lap, his thumb brushes my inner thigh and I can't stop my soft inhale.

Theo instantly lifts his hands in surrender. "Not trying to get laid, just trying to put the laptop down where you can read the letter and make changes."

I clear my throat. "Didn't even notice the contact."

Not even remotely believable, but Theo is too much of a gentleman to call me out on my porno breathing. It's been so long since anyone has touched me, that all it takes is some accidental contact and I'm...I won't even say. You can use your imagination.

"Yep. Cool." Theo's answer is too delayed, he's holding his breath. Either to stop himself from moving, or to hide how hard he is breathing, I can't tell.

I mean, I'm not an eyesore or anything, but as my ex put it, my looks are an "acquired taste." His message was loud and clear, I'm not the type anybody lusts over. They want the blondes with massive tits, not a brunette B-cup covered in freckles. Cameron said he loved my imperfections, but the fact that he had to call them that says enough.

Then I remember the part where it doesn't matter if Theo finds me attractive because I'm not sleeping with him or plan on ever seeing him again. He's a means to an end, and I need to get my head in the game. Mentally bitch slapping the hell out of myself, I mean a *real* fucking smack, I begin reading the letter.

*Sarah (I don't know your last name)7th of February 2023(Add phone number) (Add Address) (Add position title)*

*Dear Karen,*

*Please accept this letter as my formal resignation from the position of (insert position title again here) at The Airport Café, and consider my final two weeks commencing upon receipt of this letter.*

*As I'm sure you well know, respect and compassion are very important qualities, and since working here, I've learned how important it is to have them in a professional environment as well.*

*As my supervisor, you've helped me develop valuable skills on how to handle extremely rude and abrasive individuals who seek to belittle others, starting with the realization that those individuals only treat others the way they do because they have nothing happy in their lives and want to make everyone as miserable as them.*

*I thank you for this knowledge and experience that you are directly responsible for. It has given me strength and the ability to recognize my worth, which I will carry with me into my career going forward.*

*All the best,*

*Sarah (Last name here)*

*Whoa.* He can wield words like weapons. Looking back to Theo with wide eyes, his gaze is already on me and I know it's never left.

"Well? What do you think?"

"Remind me to never piss you off."

He laughs.

"It's perfect." Just in case there was any confusion.

"I'm glad. All we need to add is your contact information."

"Yeah, nice try, stalker."

He chuckles. "At least give me your email so I can send it to you."

"Don't those snazzy MacBooks have AirDrop?"

"Well, I just thought maybe you'd share your number with a friend," Theo says as he copies it to his notes and AirDrops it to me anyway.

"Are we friends?"

"I'd like to be."

Friendships are like relationships. They never end well. Take it from me. Eyes near pleading, Theo waits with bated breath for my answer. I'm not sure why it matters so much to him.

At the end of the day, it's not Theo who caused that pain. I can't keep using the actions of individuals who live in the past to define my future. Dad wanted me to remember what it's like to live. Isn't part of that having a friend, at the very least, to share it with?

This could be the first step toward taking control of my life again.

"Okay. I'll try."

"Why do you make it sound like it's going to be hard?"

If he only knew. "Because it will be."

"If we're friends, the reason behind it is something you'd share with me."

Fine. Theo wants to run before we walk? Let's take that new leaf and fucking shred it, rather than gently turning it over.

"The only friend I've ever had ended up sleeping with my boyfriend behind my back for God only knows how long. Ergo, the destruction of all desire of mine to have close, trusting relationships again."

Theo blows out a breath. "That *is* rough. But I'll raise you from one 'cheating ex with best friend' to 'cheating ex with my own father."

"NO!"

"I wish I could cut out the section of my brain which stores that haunting memory."

"You SAW it!?"

"Unfortunately."

"How does that even happen!?"

"Well, when two people love each other very much..."

"Theo! I know how sex works. I want to know how your father had enough game to swoop in and steal your girl?"

"Is that a roundabout way of saying that you think I'm a catch?" he says with a little smirk.

A sound of frustration. "That's not what I was saying!"

He smiles anyway. "I think it was less about his game, and more about his money, something I don't go waving around."

"How could someone do that to you?" It makes me genuinely nauseous thinking about what Theo must have gone through.

"I used to ask myself the same thing every day, until I realized that she did me a favor. Imagine if I had ended up spending the rest of my life with someone like that."

I've never thought about it like that. It's so...healthy. Why bother missing someone who doesn't recognize your worth? "My sob story seems significantly less sob-worthy now."

"I'm glad my life has made yours seem a tad less tragic, but no need to pity me. Real-life trauma is great inspiration for fiction."

I could sit here and talk to Theo until sunrise. Maybe even longer. I want to ask him about his father, so I can learn about what kind of man could do that to their son, and this *awful* ex-girlfriend. I would also ask him about the fiction he writes and how he can imagine such things.

I find myself wanting to know *everything*. It's terrifying.

"On that cheery note, I should probably get back home and get some sleep. Turns out, I still have work tomorrow." I joke. *I JOKE.*

He nods. "I'll walk you to your car."

I should say no.

But I don't.

We make our way to the staff parking in comfortable silence, both of us processing how we ended up here tonight. My lime-green Volkswagen beetle comes into view when Theo finally speaks. "My phone died, and I should let my roommate know that I'll be home soon. I'm not usually out this late and he might be worried. Mind if I borrow yours?"

"Yeah, of course." I pull out my ancient iPhone and hand it over. I've never bothered with passcodes. Partly because I don't have anything to snoop for, but also because even thieves have higher standards. I watch him type in a number, but instead of making a call, he hands it back to me.

Confused, I look down and see a new contact under "Theo" with the two dancing girls emoji. I can't help my surprised giggle.

"That's us, because we are already on our way to being BFFs."

This weird feeling takes flight in my gut, as if I'm on a roller coaster looking over the edge of the next drop, full of anticipation.

"Sorry, but I don't know if you could work that leotard." I tell him with a little smile.

"That's number five."

Peering up, my eyes lock with his. "What's number five?"

Theo lifts his hand, guiding it toward my face so slowly, as if he's taking care not to spook me, but I couldn't move if I wanted to. He grabs a loose wave, having escaped my bun, and gently tucks it behind my ear. His fingers linger a little before he drags them away, slightly grazing my neck as if they've got a mind of their own.

I forget that he hasn't answered my question.

"I would have gone to a thousand cafés if it meant having you as my friend."

With that, Theo walks away, leaving me with my thundering heart as my only company.

*I am so screwed.*

# CHAPTER EIGHT

## *Present - Ara*

I got almost no sleep last night, but not because I was out too late with Theo. We were only together for an hour or so before I went home. Just last night felt...*monumental.*

When I got home, I was wired. Even giving myself a full mani/pedi, which looking at it this morning confirms that I did a terrible job, didn't tire me out. So I followed it up with a full skincare routine, complete with a face-mask that's been sitting in my cabinet for so long that I probably should have checked the expiration date, and applied a hair mask for half an hour and *still* wasn't tired.

By the time my head hit the pillow, I was sure I'd never smelled so good or felt so soft. Yet, I still couldn't bring myself to sleep. Instead, I laid in bed, unable to stop replaying what Theo had said as he left. It was something out of a fucking Nicholas Sparks novel.

*I would've gone to a thousand cafés if it meant having you as my friend.*

And the way his fingers grazed my neck just before he left...I groan.

When I'm not wrapped up in the memory of his touch, I'm busy wondering how Theo keeps showing up in my life. First the airport, then the diner, as if he knew exactly where I would be. Now he's found me where I work, and wants me to believe these were just coincidences?

A prickle spreads across my back as I stare at Theo's contact information in my phone, the way I have been doing since I woke up. Regardless of his reasons, I know in the pit of my stomach that I'm safe with him. I *think*.

Surely, he gave me his number because he wanted me to use it?

*Fuck it.*

**Last night was fun.**

No, that's lame.

**Officially resigned, as of this morning.**

That's stupid too.

**How did you sleep?**

What am I? His fucking mother?

I growl and delete it all, throwing my phone back on the table and return to my cereal. What is *wrong* with me? Last night didn't mean anything. We are just casual acquaintances now, as in, I have someone to call if I get a flat tire. That's it.

*Knock, Knock, Knock.*

Oh, my God. Dad's letter. It has to be that.

Shooting up from my chair, I nearly knock over my entire dining table and bowl of cereal with it as I run to the door and throw it open, not caring as it slams against the wall.

A deep gasp leaves the delivery man's throat as he clutches his chest in shock. "Good heavens, young lady, you scared the bejeezus out of me!"

"I'm so sorry! I've been looking forward to this for days." It's not lost on me that I could have been spending this man's last moments with him on my doorstep, had I given him a heart attack.

"Well, okay then," he says with a chuckle as he reaches into his bag and grabs the letter. "I guess I won't make you wait any longer."

The envelope is the same as the last, light gray, and Dad's handwriting scrawled across the front. My eyes instantly fill with tears. Though he's never let me down, part of me was afraid the next letter would never come. It's surreal, the sense of safety these letters bring after only having received two now.

I miss him so much that my *very soul* hurts, wishing for nothing more than to be able to sit down and speak with him in person. He would reassure me, tell me not to be afraid, even cheer me on at the decision that I made to quit my job. I would also tell him about Theo so he could warn me off men forever.

I would give anything to hear his chuckle and feel his calming presence one last time, but I never will. These letters were his last stand against the Universe that took him away from his daughter when she still needed him. It has to be enough.

Swiping at my eyes, they clear enough for me to make out the name embroidered on the pocket of his shirt. "Thank you, Dave. You have no idea how much these letters mean to me."

The last time he was here, all I noticed was that he was sweaty and out of breath, so lost in my devastation that I hadn't noticed his kind smile that's surrounded by lines which tell me he does it a lot, and rosy cheeks that are rather endearing.

"It's been my pleasure," Dave says with another happy grin. "Since you know my name, it's only fair if I know yours in return."

"I'm Ara." I point to my name on the letter with a cautious smile of my own.

"You have a nice smile, Ara, it's a shame I didn't get to see much of it last month."

I flinch. I was horrible to this adorable old man.

"Oh, I'm sure you had your reasons, just happy to see you've got some light in those eyes, sweetie. You're too young for it to be any other way."

"Thanks, Dave." Seeing as I'm about thirty seconds away from going full sobs on this unsuspecting man, I need to make a quick exit. "I better be going."

"You have a good day now, darlin."

"You, too," I say and shut my door.

This time, I don't wait to open the letter. I don't fear what's inside, I crave it. And that feeling is so far away from where I was a month ago.

*Dear Ara,*

*Remember that time those kids spread that awful rumor about you in school? Well, at the time you hadn't actually told me why you were upset, but I found out later on. I couldn't stand seeing you so hurt.*

*We stopped by the grocery store under the guise of needing to get something for dinner, but really I was only there to buy the nicest looking brownies and vanilla ice cream they had to offer in an attempt to cheer you up.*

*We went home, watched* The Iron Giant *for the hundredth time and found something to be happy about. The world could have been ending around us, but sitting there in that living room, saying the lines out loud when our favorite scenes came around, that was happiness.*

*You might be wondering what this has to do with anything. Well, I've been feeling pretty nostalgic lately, and I've been passing time by going through my favorite memories with you, just to make sure I don't forget a single one.*

*Besides that, I want you to always find something to be happy about, even if it feels like the world has gone to ruin, and sometimes when that's too hard, helping others find their happiness helps us find some of our own.*

*Which brings me to your task for this month.*

Help someone find something to be happy about.

*It can be big or small and for a total stranger. I want you to do something that brings a smile to their face and happiness to their life. It's a good place to start on the road to finding your own.*

*Oh, one more thing before I leave you to it. It's okay if you haven't got it all figured out. I believe in you. Remember to believe in yourself, too, even when I'm not there to remind you.*

*I miss you. Wherever I go, I know that will be true.*

*Now go find the someone for this task.*

*Love,*

*Dad*

I know he wants me to rush out into the world and start shitting rainbows for people's happiness, but I need a minute—or ten—with this tissue box. Potentially all day.

At some point, I stopped trusting myself to make the right decisions. Maybe it was when my choices started leading to so much hurt. I don't think I've ever gotten over what happened after I'd made the decision to trust, and before that, when I'd put in so much effort to get into college, just to throw it all away because it isn't what I wanted to do.

Once that self-assurance was lost, I granted this *thing* inside me more power than ever, and it greedily took over the wheel, not allowing me to make decisions for myself. I know it's why I've stayed at the café for so much longer than I should have, rather than working on something I genuinely care about. It's why I haven't let anyone in as a friend or more in...a while. That monster has been feeding me poison and I've let it.

How Dad knew exactly what I would need to hear this month, I have no idea, but he is right. I have been so focused on how I have nothing figured out, that I stopped aiming to figure them out. About two-thirds of the way into the tissue box, I come to terms with the fact that I can't keep living my life this way.

My thoughts drift to Theo and his grand gesture to be my friend. Underneath my trepidation and trust issues, I'm convinced that he's genuine. Although his cryptic explanations give me nothing but reason to doubt his motivations, he has experienced the kind of trauma which alters you for life, making damn sure you never put another person through that.

I still can't shake the look on Theo's face after he told me what happened between his ex-girlfriend and his father, as if he was leached of all his joy and charm for a moment. People are sick. I'd be hard pressed to admit it, but Theo's charisma has started to grow on me, and I don't like the idea of it being replaced by that detached look.

Moving for my phone before I even know the decision has been made, I shoot a text.

**Meet me after my shift. Wear all black.**

Just like that, I'm going to help Theo find something to be happy about.

• • •

"What did you do?" Joel asks me as soon as I walk in for my shift. I won't lie, I barely had the courage to show up, so this question has me putting my tail between my legs.

"What do you mean?" I ask nervously. "Dan, what is he talking about?"

They pause, having a silent conversation about how much they should say.

Finally, Joel is the one to speak. "We overheard Karen in the office. Something...wasn't pleasing. We heard your name followed by a string of curses, and we've been dealing with her extra foul mood ever since."

"Yeah, thanks for that," Dan tacks on with a teasing grin.

I lean against the counter and put my face in my hands. "I knew I shouldn't have done it."

"What did you do?" Joel asks.

"I sent in my resignation letter this morning, and she must have seen it when she got in. I don't know what I was thinking."

"Ara, we've never understood why you are working here in the first place. You're so young with so much potential. It shouldn't be wasted in this café."

Joel thinks I have potential? A little fissure begins to form in my rock-solid, arm's-length wall.

Dan continues where Joel left off, as usual. "You should be out there discovering what you want to do, what you *love*."

Joel opens his mouth to go on, but is interrupted by a screeching, acidic voice on approach from the seating area. "Have you been served yet? No? Let me get someone for you."

The three of us have never moved faster. I throw my bag into the break room, not caring where it lands. Joel launches back to the grill, Dave back to the industrial sink that's half the size of my living room. I desperately search for something to do to look busy, and come up empty, leaving my only option to stand up straight and weather the storm.

Karen's eyes instantly narrow when she finds me standing there. "Your shift has already begun, and I expect you to do something with yourself for the next fourteen days, or so help me God, I will make sure nobody hires you again."

"Sorry, Karen," I say as I grab a spare apron and chuck it over my head.

It's rare that Dan and Joel witness the full extent of the verbal abuse I receive from Karen. Both of them stare at her, hell in their eyes and steam coming out of their ears. I shake my head slightly to warn them off saying anything, I won't be here much longer, and it doesn't feel right for them to endanger their own positions on my behalf.

I plaster a grin on my face and walk out to serve our customers, noticing it wasn't as hard to do as it usually is.

Tonight's shift goes quickly, being a busy night, and by the time I'm locking up, a foreign feeling has taken over. It has my heart pumping and limbs feeling jittery as I look over my all-black outfit I've just changed into.

"Oh, now I see what's had you acting all keyed up tonight," Joel says with a smile.

"What do you mean?" I ask while I jiggle the door to make sure it's properly locked.

"I guess I should say *who's* got you all keyed up."

I whip around to find Theo, leaned up against a pillar, in all black.

I thought deep green had been complementing, but Theo in all black? Fuck. My. Life.

Where I might look like an awkward teen going through her first goth phase, he looks like a dark prince, sin incarnate. It's completely unfair and also, unsettling. Do friends normally make other friends have indecent thoughts?

The way Theo's eyes glitter tells me that curiosity has been eating him alive. *Good.* I can't help the grin that spreads across my face, and Theo responds in kind.

"Are you two robbing a bank tonight or something?" Joel asks.

I roll my eyes. "Or something."

"Joel, this is Theo," with a shy smile I add, "my *friend*."

"Nice to meet you, Joel." Theo doesn't miss a beat, extending his hand to Joel. "To be frank, I have no idea what we are doing tonight, I'm just along for the ride."

Joel laughs. "Well, you take care of her, otherwise I'll have something to say about it."

Theo looks me in the eyes, rather than Joel, and says, "I intend to."

It's a declaration to me, rather than an answer to Joel, his words invading my chest and wrapping around my heart, warming it with a gentle squeeze. The warmth sinks to my middle and I get the feeling that I've finally disappeared over the edge of that roller coaster.

"We better get going, I'll see you tomorrow, Joel!"

"See you tomorrow!" Joel gives us a little wave before walking toward his bus stop.

It saddens me that just as I finally let myself interact with those guys when in thirteen more days I'll be leaving the café. I put that thought where it belongs for now, the back burner, because tonight is about Theo.

I managed to get a spot right up front, my 2007 lime green VW Beetle greeting us front and center in a sea of white and black automobiles.

"Okay, I must know. Why am I dressed in all black?"

Certain very *loud* and very *distracting* body parts of mine seem to think it's for *their* enjoyment. "That's for me to know, and you to find out! The only hint you're getting is that our first stop is Walmart." I toss him my keys. "You drive."

"Are we robbing Walmart? If so, I feel like I qualify for a better position than just in-the-dark getaway driver."

I roll my eyes as Theo yelps, his knees driving straight into the steering wheel. "Who drives this close to the steering wheel?"

"It's not my fault that you're a giant." I plug in my phone to the aux cord which I had to get specially installed as he adjusts his seat.

When you grow up with your dad as your only hero and friend, classic rock easily becomes your favorite. I don't pick our playlist which took years to curate, knowing I'll end up in tears. Tonight is supposed to be fun, so instead I put on my "Best of the Best" playlist, featuring the best songs from across all decades.

Tina Turner comes on first, and Theo reaches down to turn it up, bringing a smile to my face, which he doesn't miss as he rolls down the windows, letting in the cool evening air. Before long we're sailing on the highway as he belts out the lyrics to "Simply the Best" and since his voice is as bad as mine, I join in too.

I stick my arm out the window as we make our way to Walmart, singing song after song. The roads are empty, giving the impression that time has frozen, it's just us, the music, and the wind. I look over and find Theo with a smile that could light up the city.

I dare to think my plan could work.

We pull into the Walmart parking lot, and I don't miss that Theo knew where to go like a Tampa local. Getting out of the car, I grab his hand to drag him inside, not letting myself think about what the touch does to me or how naturally it comes.

• • •

"Two black beanies, a pair of scissors, and enough toilet paper to supply a small country." He looks at me and laughs. "What the hell are we doing, Ara?"

"Come on, be a good sport!" I get this funny look on my face. "I promise to tell you our next destination after you use those big muscles of yours to stuff all of this into the car."

Theo raises his brows.

"What? I'm not blind," I say back defensively, having just admitted to checking him out. "Stuff. In. Car. Now."

Theo reaches for the first pack of toilet paper. "I'm definitely going to regret this."

The half-smile he fails to hide tells me that he regrets nothing.

Getting everything into the car is like a game of Tetris. I love my car to death, but it's not very practical. By the time we load it all up, every inch of my Beetle is packed, with the last package of toilet paper winding up on my lap.

It makes a perfect table for my next task, using the scissors to cut little holes for our eyes, nose and mouth in each beanie.

Theo looks at me with mock terror. "Is this where you take me to an abandoned field, kill me, and wrap me up like a mummy?"

"If I was going to kill you, I wouldn't have gotten you a mask, too." I roll my eyes but pause when I realize too late our next destination could upset him. "Do you trust me?"

Theo looks at me, *really* looks at me. His gaze reaches the depths of my soul, seeing everything I have to offer, good and bad. My fear that he won't like what he finds settles as his eyes soften. "I do."

I take a deep breath. "Then take us to your father's house."

Theo is dead silent, frozen in position long enough for me to start hating myself. He moves like a zombie and puts the car in drive, pulling onto the road without further question. This time, the car ride is silent except for the never-ending thoughts crowding into my mind.

I've known Theo for a month, hours really, and I'm currently asking him to drive face first into his trauma. Based on what? Some ridiculous notion that I could possibly know how to make him happy? What is *wrong* with me?

I could have taken him for ice cream. Ice cream always makes people happy, but no, I had to force Theo to drive straight up to his house of goddamn horrors.

I'm *such* an idiot.

Here I am again, making decisions that hurt others and hurt myself. The fear hooks into me and I begin to shut down. *This* is why I always second guess myself and don't ever *do* anything. Rightfully, so.

I sigh, covering my face with my hands, ready to apologize and beg Theo to turn around, to forget all about this, when I feel his hand lightly grab one of mine, pulling it away from my face.

"You are literally the only person on Planet Earth, capable of getting me to go anywhere near this place. Yet, the million-dollar question still remains."

His slightly lighter, teasing tone frees some of the weight from my chest. "Why am I driving to my father's house in the middle of the night, wearing all black, in a car full of toilet paper?"

I wait for it to sink in, as I try to kick toward the surface of my mind.

It finally clicks. "You want to TP my father's house."

*There it is.*

He looks at me and bursts into hysterical laughter. "Do you know who my father is?"

"A total douchebag?"

"Yes, that, too, but do you know what he does for a living?"

"The stalker tendencies are reserved for you, so no, I don't know what your father does for a living. That would require knowing your last name, I suppose."

"My last name is Carter." He smirks, as if it's *his* turn to watch something obvious sink in.

I rack my brain and come up empty. "I've got nothing."

"Well, then look up to your left."

A gigantic billboard looms across the road, plastered with some advertisement for that famous defense attorney, Bill Carter.

"Your father is that huge attorney, who is a known savage!?"

"The one and only," he says grimly.

This idea is somehow seeming even worse than it did five minutes ago. The potential consequences begin to dawn on me. "We could be fined for trespassing! Or littering. Or vandalism!"

"Or worse." Theo shrugs. "But it's too late to chicken out now, we're here."

The view from my window makes me instantly feel sick, when I see we may as well have pulled up to the White House. His father is clearly loaded, the entire place (I wouldn't call it a home) built from expensive white marble, carved into custom designs. It's beautiful, and yet it does nothing but make me squirm.

"Finally see the appeal?" Theo asks in a dead voice.

I'm not sure why I do it, but I slap him on the arm. *Hard.* "I wouldn't want to step one foot inside that mausoleum-looking...thing." I toss one of the beanies at him. "Now put your mask on and let's do this thing, before I start running in the other direction."

Thankfully, the light has mostly returned to Theo's eyes, and it gives me the confidence I need to don my mask. We decide to divide and conquer, Theo will take on the house itself and I will take on everything in the yard.

My mission is to blanket the wrought iron fence surrounding the front of the property, every shrub, object, and surface I can find, even tossing rolls over the trees. The driveway becomes my favorite, as I roll them down the length of it, covering the entire thing. By the time I'm satisfied, both arms become noodles, cheeks aching from my grin.

I finally stop to check on Theo's progress and come up speechless. He's got one hell of an arm and some fucking good aim. The house is *completely* covered. TP rains down from every corner of the roof, balcony, and front-facing part of the house.

The smile on his face is nothing short of hellborn, as he delights in his masterpiece. Seeing him back to his weightless, charming self becomes contagious. I haven't felt this happy in so long that I don't even want to acknowledge just how long it's been and ruin the moment.

Holding out the last roll that I saved just for him, "Care to do the honors of the last throw?"

Theo takes it with a smile and grabs my hand before I can pull it away, giving it a gentle squeeze. "Thank you."

There are so many layers of hurt, fear, and pain from the past wrapped up into those two little words, but there is also gratitude and recognition. Being on the receiving end of that look begins to mend something deep inside me, knitting pieces back together which were torn apart long ago.

Perhaps one day we can take the time to journey through the tiers of our pain together, but for now I squeeze back. "Anything for a friend."

"I think it's safe to say we are *best friends*." His thumb mindlessly drags across the back of my hand, sending waves of awareness up my arm. "We just TPed a house together."

I nod to the TP he still holds. "Okay, bestie, show me what you've got."

Theo launches the roll into the air, and as it crests into a downward curve toward the second floor balcony, my stomach drops. A small, potted plant ruptures into shards as it falls to the ground, the silence of night intensifying the crash. For a split second, we are both frozen in shock, or maybe the fruitless hope that nobody heard that.

The lights abruptly switch on exposing the male shape inside, shadowed against the light, moving at top speeds toward the balcony door to deliver our reckoning.

# CHAPTER NINE

## Present - Ara

"Shit!!!!!" Theo grabs my hand, dragging me into a run. I break for the car, but he hauls me past it. "I don't want him catching your license plate if he sees us drive away!"

I don't have enough air in my lungs to formulate a response, so I just keep running, relying on the pull of his hand to drive myself forward. We make it to the street corner and take a right before I realize we still have our makeshift masks on.

"Theo!" I can't breathe, pointing to my mask. "We look so illegal!!"

"Fuck! Good call." We rip off our masks and dump them down one of the drains on the side of the street. Sorry environment, I'll recycle extra hard this month.

Theo grabs my hand, hauling me back into a sprint. "We have to get far enough away in case he tries to follow us!"

*I.*

*Hate.*

*Running.*

*So.*

*Fucking.*

*Much.*

If I had known this night would result in my life riding on my ability to run a 5k, I would have definitely stuck with the fucking ice cream. We take another right, then left before a 24-hour Walgreens comes into view. Theo slows down to a speed walk, leading me toward the entrance.

"Thank God," I wheeze and heave. *I wheeve.* "I couldn't have made it another street."

We stand there panting, me more so than Lance Armstrong over here, our wide eyes fixed on each other. Theo's are alight with joy and exhilaration, no trace of the shadows from earlier. There's amusement, too, as he takes me in, and…something else. We burst into laughter and walk farther inside, getting strange looks from the cashier as we go by.

Grabbing an orange Gatorade, donuts, and an ice cream cookie sandwich, I hadn't realized how hungry I was until these amazing snacks were staring me in the face. Theo tosses some jalapeño chips on top of the mound of goodies already in my arms, before leading me to a small clothing rack.

"Here." Theo holds out an obnoxious pink shirt which reads "I'm a Clearwater B*ach".

The cheesy play-on-words makes me cringe almost as much as the pink flamingo shirt Theo presumably holds for himself.

I snort.

"It's the best they've got as far as disguises go."

"Disguises?"

"The last thing I need is my father catching me and my conspirator in his neighborhood dressed in all black. At least this way, he will be more focused on not throwing up at the sight of my shirt."

A laugh explodes out of me because, well, Theo is funny and also right. His shirt is horrible, and I need to permanently document it. Obviously.

Reaching into my pocket, I try to be sneaky as I grab my phone and move to open the camera.

Theo, not missing a thing, grabs my phone out of my hand. "The only way you're getting photo evidence of this is if you're in it with me."

"Over my dead body."

"I'm a criminal now, Ara," he says with a wink. "This life of illegal activity has hardened me. You don't know my limits."

Looking like a kid eating cotton candy for the first time, I smile up at Theo, having never felt this buoyant. Dad had always made me laugh, but with Theo it feels different. There is a pang in my gut at the thought, knowing there will never be a day where I don't think about my dad, but I know he would be happy to see me smiling now.

"Fine," I say.

Theo lifts his brows in surprise and I'm right there with him. I hate photos, even more than running, but here I am doing both tonight.

Theo flips the camera around so that it's facing us and lifts it up for a selfie. I look over to see what kind of expression he is making so I can match the vibe, and find him with a goofy face that brings another smile to my face.

*snap*

"I wasn't ready!!" I complain.

"Okay, let's do another one."

Hopefully, the absolute mess which is my camera isn't good enough to capture the embarrassing glee pouring from my expression.

"Wait, one more." I grab the phone from him and prop it up on one of the shelves. I set the five-second timer and dash back to his side. "Pose like a tourist!"

I grab my phone, dying to see the results, but Theo covers it with his hand. "Save it for later. I'll get us an Uber back to the airport and I can take you home from there."

"What about my car?"

"I'll drop it off at your place before you need to head to work tomorrow."

This is the part where I usually find a reason to put up a polite fight and insist we go our separate ways. His father would have no idea who I was if he passed me by on the walk to my car. Especially with my "disguise." I know I can figure out the car thing on my own. The thing is, I don't want to say goodbye yet.

So, for once in my life, I agree.

Theo covers the midnight snacks and disguises while I step outside to make sure the coast is clear. Doing my best to take a good, inconspicuous look around, once I'm certain there is not a soul in sight, I give the all clear to Theo and he joins me outside.

"What a night," he says with a bright grin.

"I know, right?"

"Can I ask you something?" His voice is a bit quieter now.

"You just did." I nudge him with my shoulder.

He nudges me back. "What made you get this idea of TPing my father's house?"

Ultimately, it was because of Dad's letter. He told me to help someone find something to be happy about, and I wanted that person to be Theo. Tonight has been liberating, that first burst of oxygen after being held under the surface by my grief. I know that I can trust Theo with the full story, but I'm just not ready for the liberating feeling to ebb when I dive into everything about Dad.

As if Theo followed my train of thought, "Another time, maybe?"

"Another time," I promise as the Uber pulls up to the parking lot.

Theo opens my door for me, closing it, before he joins me in the backseat from the other side. We arrive at the airport in no time, getting dropped off at his car, a dark blue BMW that's old enough to be considered special. It's classy, stylish, and old-fashioned, just like Theo.

"It was a gift from my grandfather when he passed away. He knew I would take good care of his favorite gal," he says with a loving pat on the hood.

"She's got charm. Just like her driver."

"Are you feeling alright?" Theo looks me over, concerned. "That almost sounded like a compliment."

"God forbid," I say with an eye roll.

Having to spend the entire drive giving Theo directions, I can't help but feel like our last remaining time has been robbed from us. When he pulls to a stop outside my place, I'm not ready to say goodbye, nor am I ready to see where inviting him upstairs would take us.

Instead, I become determined to avoid the severely awkward part of the night where he sits there waiting for me to invite him in and I'll *know* he's waiting for me to invite him in. But I don't want to invite him in (mostly because my house is a disaster). But I also don't want him to *think/know* that I don't want to invite him in, so instead we end up sitting there in never-ending awkward silence for way too long.

"I'll see you around, Theo," I pipe up quickly, keeping it straightforward and simple as I scramble out of the car.

As I'm walking away, I hear his door shut followed by sure footsteps.

I turn around just in time to see him close the last few feet between us.

"Theo–"

He does the one thing I don't expect and engulfs me into a hug, my body instantly relaxing into his as he wraps one arm around my upper back.

Cradling my head to his chest while the other wraps around my waist, in an annoyingly respectable way, he then rests his cheek on the top of my head.

Theo was built in a mold just for me, fitting my body perfectly. Taking a deep inhale, I'm instantly intoxicated, becoming wrapped in the scent of fresh greenery and cinnamon. Finally getting the hype of the pine smell I've read so much about, I could literally die and be reborn in his arms.

"I'm not sure what I was doing before you came along, but it sure wasn't living." Theo pulls back, playfully twirling one of my loose waves around his finger before tucking it behind my ear and walking back to his car. I'm stuck in a mental coma, staring after him the entire way, too dazed to even check out his butt.

Theo reaches his car, shooting me a confused look. "I don't want to leave until you've made it inside."

*For fuck's sake, Theo, please do something I can hate.*

Sending him a salute, I force my legs to carry me up the stairs to the front door of my apartment, focusing on the feel of my keys as I let myself inside. Giving Theo a final wave before closing the door behind me, I rush to pull out my phone and open the camera roll.

The first photo sends shock waves through me. It's a picture of me smiling at Theo, while he's being goofy and I look so…content. Flipping to the next one where we are smiling together, the breath is knocked out of me when I see Theo's eyes glowing so bright, they could rival the stars. Finally swiping to the last photo of us, posing like tourists, my heart erupts at the undiluted joy plastered across our faces. Neither of us were looking at the camera, too busy laughing at the other.

Once I'm done setting Theo's contact ID as the one of his goofy face, I sit down on my couch, examining our faces until the screen goes dark. I know in my bones that I made Theo happy tonight, he even felt *alive.* Reaching up, I grasp the wave Theo wrapped around his fingers, as if I can soak up what remains of his touch.

Dad was right.

Theo's happiness made *me* happy, too.

So I sit here alone in my apartment as I pretend like that's what friends are for.

# CHAPTER TEN

## Five Years Ago - Ara

Dad has been unusually quiet this morning. I know him well enough to know exactly what is on his mind, but curiosity has gotten the best of me, and I want to see how long it's going to take him before he finally coughs it up.

Slowly pouring us bowls of Honey Nut Cheerios, it takes strength to withhold my smile. It's already been about five minutes since I found him in the kitchen, intentionally running behind on his morning routine to get the chance to talk to me.

"How did you sleep?" He's stalling.

"Good! How about you?"

"Yeah, me too."

"Cool." I deserve an Oscar for keeping it together right now.

He pauses. "Any big plans at school today?"

"Just the usual."

Here it comes.

"Okay, did Chuck and Blair finally get together or *what*!?"

I howl with laughter and almost drop the milk in the process of grabbing my stomach.

"Come on, Ara! Just put me out of my misery and tell me what happened!"

Last night, Dad got bored of whatever National Geographic show he had on, coming into my room to bother me instead. I had *Gossip Girl* rolling on season four, where Chuck proposes, and then the thing with Jenny happens...

you know the one. Dad couldn't stand the angst any longer and bailed…and now he's paying the price.

My laughter becomes greedy. "You'll just have to come watch the rest to find out."

He grabs his bowl of Cheerios in frustration and walks out.

"I didn't raise you to be so cruel!" he calls from the other room, indignant.

I collapse on the floor, laughing until tears break free and I'm late for school.

# CHAPTER ELEVEN

## *Present - Ara*

The late morning sun warms my face, rousing me from sleep and with the way the light is falling, I realize that I might be glowing as much on the outside as I am on the inside. Last night was magical. Grabbing a pillow to shove over my face, the stupid grin feels permanently etched onto my face, too embarrassing for even the ceiling to see.

This funny feeling starts up again like I'm back at the top of the roller coaster. My room looks different, feels brighter. The colors stand out more, and for the first time in months, I feel like I could bring myself to create something today.

When I was six years old, I fell in love with textiles. My art teacher had the great idea of making Mother's Day gifts, not thinking there could be a few of us who didn't have one. She let me pick whatever art project I wanted, so I spent the entire class feeling the different materials in her collection, too enraptured to try and make anything. When she saw how fond I was of this particular pink lace, she cut me a big square and let me take it home.

I glued it to a piece of paper, doing the best job a small child is capable of to cut it into the shape of a dress, taping it around one of the Barbies I'd never bothered playing with until then. When I showed Dad, he looked at me with such love and adoration, and told me that one day if I wanted to, I could go to a special school to learn how to make clothes for all the women of the world.

As I got older, I started experimenting with different patterns and stitching, learning very quickly that I did not have the patience for embroidery, so I stuck with making clothing, watching videos on YouTube until I could create something on my own. Dad saw how much time I was spending on stitching, so for my sixteenth birthday he bought me my very own sewing machine. It became my favorite way to spend my free time.

It's something I've kept secret, strictly reserved for whenever the feeling strikes, like today. Dad is the only one who ever knew how much my designs meant to me, besides Cameron, the last person I told and instantly regretted doing so. Any time I've mentioned loving fashion, people take one look at my leggings and ignore the rest of what I have to say, as if it was a pipe dream. So one day, that's all it became.

Of course, I never stopped making clothes, I just stopped sharing it with others, not wanting their opinions to change how I felt. Thus, why I keep them nice and safe in their own little room. Most of what I've made are outfits you'd have to leave the house for something other than work to wear anyway, so there they remain, untouched.

It's not like I grew up a social pariah or something, I was bullied the standard amount, nothing too overboard. I even had "friends," I just didn't particularly enjoy hanging out with them since we had nothing in common. Birthday parties were even more awkward, with all the moms sitting together to talk about "mom things," while Dad stood on his own until one of the ladies took pity on him and left the hub to keep him company.

Dad never complained, but I hated seeing him look like he didn't belong. Pretty soon, the kids got meaner and the invitations stopped coming anyway. So instead, Dad and I would kick back and watch movies, new and old. Sometimes we'd go on adventures, driving to see race cars and horse shows. We even tried water skiing, neither of us managing to stand up a single time, so we opted to spend the day eating two-dollar grilled cheese sandwiches while watching the pros instead.

We developed our own unspoken language, never bothering to gush about our emotions, knowing each other so well we didn't need to. Personally, I kept it all to myself, good and bad, regardless. By the time I got out into the world, I realized that most people aren't like that. If someone made them mad, they would scream with rage. If they loved, they would yell it from the rooftops.

Cameron was one of those people. He used to say it was love at first sight, something out of a movie, the way fate intervened placing us both at the library that day. I never told him it was because I was at the library almost every day, and it would have been hard for him to miss me.

I liked that he accepted me for who I was, never forcing me to go to the parties he went to or on double dates with his friends, content with coming over to my house or meeting at the library. It was...nice Companionable. We never disagreed on anything, and it was easy.

Until senior year, when the time came to apply for college. I'd recently told him about my designs, and he didn't understand the big deal I'd made it into. I made clothes? So what? I could follow him to New York and take some "sewing classes" while he attended NYU's art program.

Full disclosure? It had terrified me, following him to another state, which seemed like more than a decision on where to go to college. In a way, I was choosing who to spend the rest of my life with, and I wasn't prepared to make that decision at seventeen years old. Plus, if I ever did find the courage to move to New York and pursue fashion, I'd want it to be for *me*, not because I was following someone else.

Dad saw these thoughts written all over my face for months. Cameron would come over with his applications and I would sit there, motion sick. Dad didn't say anything about it for a while, but I think eventually he got worried that I would follow another person's path just to avoid the confrontation.

Finally, he sat me down and said, "Ara, sometimes I think I might have let you become a bit too much like me."

As if that could be a bad thing.

"You need to tell Cameron that you don't want to go to New York for *him*. You still have time to decide where your life is going to take you and when. Don't rush it because someone wants you to."

I had asked him how he had known exactly what was on my mind and he said, "You're my best friend, it would be pretty lame if I couldn't read your mind."

After that talk with Dad, I attempted to tell Cameron how I felt but to him, it made perfect sense for me to follow him to New York regardless since I had nothing going on here. It's where he would be, after all. In the end, I didn't want to risk holding him back or becoming the person who gets left behind, figuring that if I was the one to end things, it wouldn't hurt as much. I told him we needed to take a break so I could figure out what I wanted, so we did.

I spent the remainder of senior year trying to figure out what I wanted to do, until just before graduation I finally came up with business school. It was a safe option. There would be a lot of job opportunities with a degree in business, so it'd be easier to find something I didn't hate. Once I had my degree, I could figure out what I wanted to do with it.

With the time apart from Cameron, I became lonely. Despite our differences, I missed him. He was the only person who had bothered to be in my life besides Dad, and I missed that. Eventually I came to the conclusion that I'd made the wrong decision in ending things, moving to New York for a few years didn't have to result in marriage.

I only applied to one college, ten minutes away via public transport from NYU. Small, not too overwhelming, and it had a great business program. The day I got accepted, I showed up at Cameron's high school, excited to share the good news, and spent the afternoon curled up in a bush hiding, while he made out with another girl less than five feet away.

Listening to someone suck face for an hour is gross enough. I mean, those sounds? *Ick.*

But what really made me nauseous was when he told the girl that it was *fate* that she transferred to his school for the last semester of high school. Fate must be his best fucking friend.

Looking back, it was wrong to expect that he wouldn't meet someone else during the nine months that we were apart, any healthy person would move on by then. It absolutely crushed me, but I don't fault him. Instead, I've faulted myself ever since.

*I* was the one who got scared and ended things. It was *my* fault for having no idea what I wanted, and it cost me not only Cameron as my friend, but also my boyfriend and future. Still, using the same line he used on me to some other chick? Dick move.

Arriving back home that evening, covered in dirt, leaves, and maybe even a branch or two, I had to experience the humiliation of knocking on the door for Dad to see me in my "nature state" having forgotten my keys.

Being the everyday superhero that he was, Dad managed to help me fix the college problem by calling in a favor with one of his clients who worked in the admissions department of the University of South Florida in Tampa. He convinced him to accept my application even though admissions had long since closed, and a month later, I found myself in college right here in Tampa.

Seeing what happened between Cameron and me had worried him. Dad wanted me to have more than one person in my life, which is what led to him insisting I have the real college experience. So, there I was, just me and my social anxiety moving into a dorm with a total stranger.

That's where I met Katie, my future best friend and evil cow, becoming friends by default. It's hard not to get to know someone when you're experiencing the same stress over exams while living together. We didn't have much in common outside of that, but it didn't stop her from dragging me to parties.

Which is also how I ended up meeting Blake, future ex-boyfriend and source of trauma. His name should have been the first red flag. I mean, has there ever been a decent guy in college named Blake? Try to think of one. You won't.

I was in a weird place, still recovering from the way things ended with Cameron, and wound up sleeping with Blake. I don't know why I did it, maybe because it felt like a rite of passage? But to be fair, even antisocial girls like me have needs. I'd expected him to ghost me the next day, but he surprised me by sticking around to ruin my life.

Blake was supposed to just be my comfort zone at parties when Katie ran off without me, but the regular hookups turned into him staying over when it got too late. Suddenly, he started dragging me everywhere that had a keg, started introducing me as his girlfriend and I never corrected him. Talk about a 21st century love story.

Next to the terms "gaslighting" and "red flag" there should be a picture of Blake, holding a big fish he caught. He was extremely jealous, which is comical when you think of how things ended. If I didn't text him back straight away because of a class that ran late, I would open my phone to sweet nothings like "cheating bitch" and "untrustworthy whore."

I had been so wrapped up in not jeopardizing another relationship, that I ended up jeopardizing myself and my happiness instead. It took walking in on Katie and Blake going at it like rabbits on *my* bed, in our *shared* dorm where her bed was less than *ten* feet away, to realize what I had with Blake was NOT it.

Rather than crying and running away, I stood my ground, told them to get dressed and get the hell out. I'm still proud of that tiny strength I showed in the end, watching them both scramble away, until the door closed and I let myself fall apart. In her haste, fleeing from her misdeeds, Katie left her phone behind. I took it as an invitation from the universe to create a group text to every male contact in Katie's phone saying she had contracted an STD and to get tested.

That was probably too far and I'm not proud.

That's a lie. I'm super proud.

At the end of the day, I didn't leave college and my business degree behind because of what went down with Katie and Blake. I had already been speaking with Dad about dropping out to get work experience until I figured out what I wanted to do.

When I showed up at this door with all my stuff, he wasn't all that surprised, having noticed the stress I was under for something I didn't care about. He *was* surprised to find out that I'd made a friend and found a boyfriend, the poor man looking like a fish out of water, opening and closing his mouth, as I told him how I'd discovered them. He was traumatized.

So how did I end up mentally revisiting that nostalgic trainwreck?

Right. I wanted to make something today.

**Me: Hey, don't rush with the car. I forgot to tell you that I have off today.**

Before I can set my phone down, it buzzes with a text.

**Theo: Your car is already outside.**

Something instantly happens in my stomach, but he can't know that.

**Me: Overachiever.**

**Theo: So if you are off work, what are you doing today?**

Does he want to see me again?

**Me: Why? Trying to get some more stalking in?**

**Theo: It's not stalking if you want me there.**

**Me: And when did I say that I wanted you there?**

**Theo: You didn't need to *winky face***

I roll my eyes.

**Me: I'm going to Jane's Material Store.**

**Theo: What a coincidence. I was JUST telling my roommate about how I needed some new materials.**

**Me: What a coincidence.**

**Theo: What time should I pick you up?**

**Me: Are you *also* planning to make something black and lacy?**

I wasn't planning to make something black and lacy, but now I'm feeling a special kind of inspiration.

**Theo: I wouldn't want to stop your heart.**

**Me: Pick me up in an hour.**

**Theo: It's a date.**

My heart drops to my feet.

**Theo: A completely platonic date.**

Right. Is he trying to convince me or himself?

• • •

Keeping my posture nonchalant as I make my way down the sidewalk to Theo's old BMW, I can't help but worry that somehow our easy chemistry from last night or from *any* day, won't be there again. My palms begin to sweat, my throat closes up. What if I've completely misread this situation?

Reaching his car, I pause a moment, taking a deep breath to steady myself.

*Just rip off the fucking Band-Aid and open the door.*

Three, Two, One.

*Car door is open.*

"Hey, bestie," Theo says in greeting with a huge grin.

"Hey, yourself." My unease was for nothing other than the sick pleasure of that monster below my skin, never missing an opportunity to convince me of the worst.

"So, even though I've been there a *thousand* times, for some reason I forget how to get there. You'll have to remind me."

Hiding my grin, "Take the causeway and it'll be on our left."

"How could I forget?"

I play along. "So, what kind of textiles are you looking for?"

"The really textil-ey ones."

I snort.

We spend the drive with the windows down, playing a beachy playlist which isn't normally my thing, but it fits this moment so well that it's impossible not to get lost in it. Since I rarely get driven anywhere, I take advantage of the situation and admire the view.

Florida is beautiful, even though I hate to admit it. I could live without the humidity and mosquitoes, but there is something calming about a wide expanse of water. Nothing in the world compares to driving down the Courtney Campbell Causeway, surrounded by blue skies, palm trees, and the salty breeze blowing in through the open windows.

Wondering how this moment can exist, I look over to Theo. How can my heart still want something this special, despite being ruined? It's been broken by betrayal and hardened by loss, yet here it sits, struggling to make room for one more.

There is no traffic today, and the drive is about to be over, too soon for my liking. Theo sees the sign, turning on his indicator to get over and lowers the music. "See? Been here a hundred times."

"I thought it was thousands?" I tease.

He winks. "So what *do* you plan on doing with your textiles?"

I hesitate.

"Why do you have that weird look on your face like you've been caught doing something embarrassing?"

Wow, he's really just gonna call it like it is. "I... make ...clothes?"

Not sure why it comes out as a question, but I'm considering it a win that I said it out loud. Not an ounce of judgment or condescension enters his expression, the same way it didn't when I told him I work at the café.

Instead, his mouth drops. "That's incredible. How did you learn to do something like that?"

A massive blush flushes my face. I'm not used to receiving compliments as it is, let alone about something I love. "I'm actually self-taught. Mainly just trial and error mixed with a lot of YouTube tutorials."

"You're telling me that you learned something as intricate as making clothes from YouTube?"

I shrug. With the first wall down, that ruined part of me opens one eye, ready to lock me down at the first hint of inquisition as to why I don't do more with it.

"Wow. The longer I know you, the better you get." Theo shakes his head. "It's settled, then…you're making me something pretty."

• • •

"What about this one?" Theo holds up another sample of black lace. I take a good look at his suggestion but shake my head. It's still just not *quite* what I'm looking for. I want something that's a bit more sheer, more revealing.

Theo has seemed to enjoy himself since we walked through the doors. I trail my fingers over the dozens of samples of black lace until I find the perfect one. It's black as ink, yet sheer enough to see skin underneath, detailed with stunning roses and ivy patterns.

"I found it."

Theo joins me to consider the one I've chosen, his eyes darkening. "What are you going to make with it?"

"Most likely something *not* designed for platonic eyes."

"Well, surely you need to sample the design on a test subject before presenting it to the intended demographic."

Is this...are we...*flirting*?

Theo steps a bit closer, facing me now, and I catch his eyes trailing over my lips. I'm locked in place, thoughts becoming absolute mayhem. The foreground looks something like "I will die if he doesn't kiss me right now" and in the background, they're trying to remember logic.

His eyes, having become nothing but stormy green depths, meet mine again as he takes another step forward, slowly dropping his head toward mine. He moves *so* slowly that I think…

"Ara? Is that you?"

Theo and I lurch back to an acceptable distance apart, trance utterly broken. My brows lift in surprise when I see that it's Susan standing beside Theo. I can't decide if I want to strangle her or hug her for interrupting what certainly was about to happen.

"Oh, hi, Susan. Good to see you!" Is it though?

Managing to keep my voice calm for a pleasant greeting, it serves as a total contrast to the pandemonium happening in my head.

"You, too, sweetie! I just stopped by to get some material for our Valentine's Day napkins. What a coincidence seeing you here."

My laugh comes out strangled. "Crazy, right?"

"Okay, you two! Have fun shopping. Tell your father that I said hello!"

Susan's innocent request hits me straight in the gut, a powerful cocktail of grief and guilt. She doesn't know about Dad and I'm too weak to tell her. A lifeless wave is all I can muster as she walks away.

My head sags until warm fingers gently touch my chin, guiding my face back toward the lights.

"You okay?" he asks softly.

It's now or never. "My dad died."

"When?" His eyes are so gentle, my vital organs turn to mush.

"A little over a month ago. His funeral was the day we met at the airport. It had all been too much for me and I ran."

"I'm so sorry."

"Me, too." I should say more. I should tell him how great of a man he was, how big of a disservice it was to this world, taking him away, but I can't get the words out. As per usual.

"Come here." Theo wraps his arms around me, pulling me close.

The tension-filled heat from earlier has vanished, replaced by this tender moment. His cheek rests on my head, while his hands make long, comforting strokes up and down my back. With each caress, I feel less broken. Less alone.

Theo gently pulls away but leaves his hands on my shoulders, ducking down to my level. "Come on, it's my turn."

"For what?"

"To pick out the material for what you're making *me*." Theo's trying to lighten the mood, and as some of the grief retreats, I realize that it's working. "I want to look pretty."

# CHAPTER TWELVE

## *Present - Ara*

By the time I get to the door of my apartment, the heaviness has completely lifted, replaced by nerves. Theo is about to enter my apartment with me. First of all, it's a disaster and completely humiliating. The remnants of my last laundry loads are still on the chair in the corner, not to mention the fact that I haven't made my bed in years, beyond throwing the bedding back on after a wash. The only impressive thing about my apartment is my wall of plants, and those are fake.

Second of all, we had a moment earlier, and I'm worried that it will happen again. Except this time, we'll be in my apartment with no one to interrupt us and *plenty* of surfaces. Third of all, I'm worried because I *want* the heat to return between us, and I don't know what that means. The inferno that I felt in that fabric store, when Theo had almost closed that distance between us, is something I've never even felt with a *boyfriend*. I *definitely* haven't experienced it with a friend.

"I love your place." Theo's voice is genuine as we walk through the front door. "It feels like a real home."

Leave it to Theo to find the perfect words to completely dissipate my anxiety. I expect him to nosy around the way most people do, but instead he walks straight to my couch and plops down as if he's done it a hundred times.

He lets out a long groan. "This couch is so comfortable, you might have to roll me out of here."

This makes me laugh, as a fuzzy, comforting warmth floods my veins, knowing that Theo loves my pride and joy. The couch isn't much of a looker, but it is arguably the most comfortable couch in the world. In fact, I would bet on it. New couches may look nice, but good luck sitting down to binge a good book on one of those. Your ass will be killing you by the end of it.

"You're being quiet," Theo says.

"Sorry." I give him a shy smile. "I was just in my head."

"Why don't you share what you're thinking?"

I shrug. "Because nobody asks."

"What were you thinking?"

Shit. I didn't expect him to *actually* ask.

"I'm happy that you like my place." That sounds too romantic. I quickly add, "Because it would suck if my new best friend never wanted to come over."

"Now, you're never getting rid of me," he says with a wink.

I hide my smile by walking into my creative room to deposit the supplies. In the end, Theo picked a gorgeous emerald-green velvet material and a black satin for the lining and lapel. Grabbing my stool and measuring tape, I head back out to the living room, closing the door behind me.

"What's in there?"

I freeze. I've never shown anyone my design room, not even Dad. It's always been my oasis to be as vulnerable as I wanted, without any fear, and as great as Theo is, I may never be willing to share it. Not wanting to offend him, humor is the best way to brush it off.

"That's just where I store all of my murder weapons and sex toys." I shrug. "Sometimes they're interchangeable, so it only makes sense to keep them in the same room."

Theo laughs. "I see what you're doing here, but I want it on the record that I'm not pushing you. You can show me your secret room whenever you're ready."

"You seem mighty sure that I will. Why is that?"

"I want to know you better than anyone else ever has."

His words, they *do* something to me, igniting something deep. I set the stool down beside the couch, doing my best to conceal the tremors.

"Up," I order.

Theo begrudgingly stands from his spot on the couch, moving to stand on the stool, but I stop him with a hand on his chest. "The stool is for *me*, giant."

Theo smiles down at me as I step onto the small stool, just reaching his nose.

I claim no responsibility for what leaves my mouth next. "Take off your shirt."

Theo raises his brow, and it's at this precise moment that I pray he has never been measured for a suit, because nobody *ever* does it shirtless. The question dances in his eyes, sending me on the defense.

"Do you want the jacket to fit perfectly or not?"

He smirks, slowly lifting his shirt over his head, muscles on full display as they flex with the motion.

*Shit.* Theo *really* goes to the gym, looking like a goddamn erotica cover model. The sound of panties hitting the floor echoes in my mind.

"Put your arms out." I keep my face all-business even though my blood sears a painful path through my veins. Where did my sudden brashness come from?

I stay silent as I go through the motions of measuring Theo, starting with his shoulders, the only sound filling the room being his soft inhales each time I graze his skin. Maybe it's because my hands are cold, but in my core I know it's more, feeding my boldness.

Finding excuses to touch him again on his chest, his biceps, I slowly graze him each time as I work my way down. When it's finally time to measure his waist, my mind goes dead as I brush my fingers down his abs, touch featherlight, feeling them clench beneath my tips. The noise he makes in the back of his throat snaps me out of my haze.

"Sorry, I'm just trying to find where your waist is." Heat rushes to my face. What the *fuck*, Ara? I know that gorgeous V at his waist is literally staring you in the face, but stop groping him.

Theo nods and doesn't say anything. By the time I'm done, I feel like I've tortured the poor guy. He looks like he is in *physical* pain, eyes so stormy they've changed color.

He moves to put his shirt back on, stepping close as he pulls it over his head. I look up just in time to see his eyes dart away from my lips, back to my eyes. A devious smile creeps up at the corner of his lips.

"My turn."

Pause. "Your turn for what?"

"To measure you. Shirt off."

My jaw hits the floor, he can't be serious. "You don't even know how to measure."

"I think I can figure it out," he says with a grin.

I can do nothing but stare, utterly floored.

"Where is this deer-in-the-headlights look coming from? You were mighty confident about two minutes ago."

Logically, I know that a small child could outrun me, and therefore there will be no escape. It doesn't stop me from fleeing to the other side of the couch, doing nothing for my sense of security as I realize he could probably *step* over it with his long legs.

Theo knows it, breaking into a laugh, fuller than I've ever had the pleasure to witness until now. "Where do you think you're going?"

I shake my head, panic entering my voice. "You'll never catch me."

"We'll see about that. I've seen you reach your top speed, and it's about as impressive as a basset hound." I don't have time to get offended, because with that he launches into a chase.

I take off squealing, hoping to get the dining room table between us, my socks sending me into a slide. My apartment isn't that big, but we manage to make a real game out of it. I'm laughing so hard that I can't breathe as I manage to fake him out and reach my kitchen island, except he launches himself over the island like one of those crazy Parkour people.

"Shit!" I take off toward the only room that would keep him out, throwing open the door to my creative space, stopping in the middle of the room to catch my breath.

Theo stops just outside the threshold just like I knew he would, his eyes not straying a centimeter, resting only on me. I'm barely getting any air down, still laughing and adrenaline pumping. My exhilaration is reflected back to me by the gleam in Theo's eyes and his splitting grin.

I'm not sure if it's the fact that he would rather give up a game than risk making me uncomfortable, or the fact that he's keeping his eyes only on me and not even looking at my designs without permission, but it has me saying, "You can come in" and *mean* it.

"You're sure?" he asks, giving me the opportunity to change my mind.

I nod.

A look of awe takes over his face as his eyes leave mine and drift toward my creations, walls covered in drawings of future projects. My stand-alone racks are filled with everything I've ever made, and the mannequins I snagged at a close-out sale are my personal favorites.

Theo walks up to my most cherished piece, a dress which took me over six months to perfect. I was feeling particularly inspired one day and bought some sparkly silver tulle just to see where it would take me, and ended up going back and buying every foot they had. Somehow, it became a gown that would rival that of a princess.

The bodice features a straight cut, strapless neckline ruched with the same glittery tulle as the skirt. With the built-in corset underneath, it allows just the right amount of decolletage to show. Below the neckline, I hand sewed bead after bead all the way down the bodice, letting it trickle over the skirt and disappear into the silver tulle.

Theo's fingers hover over the dress, as if he's dying to touch it but afraid to ruin it. "Ara, this is a *masterpiece*."

A blush from hell climbs up my neck, reaching my cheeks, my inexperience of receiving such compliments revealing itself.

"Women would go into *war* to wear your designs." He turns in a circle, taking it all in and shaking his head. "Every. Single. One."

I could cry right now. *Shit. I AM CRYING.* I wipe my face furiously, trying to hide the evidence.

Theo doesn't ask why I don't do anything with my designs, sharing this with him doesn't feel insignificant. I feel seen, respected, and for once, I feel like I've done my creations the justice they deserve.

"You can't find anything as beautiful as these out there."

That does it. The tears begin to fall freely.

*One blink. Two blinks. Three blinks.*

I make it to twenty-seven blinks before the tears finally stop.

Theo gives me a reassuring smile, before wrapping his arm around my shoulders and leading me back out to the living room. I'm deposited on my couch before he moves to my kitchen, opening the fridge.

"Tortilla chips...shredded cheese…ground beef...sour cream...salsa… guacamole…" Theo lists off the only items in my fridge. "Are you a nacho enthusiast?"

"There's nothing better in the world," I say matter-of-factly, and if Theo disagrees, he can find a new friend. "And don't question the chips being kept in the fridge, it keeps them from going stale."

"I couldn't agree more." He begins pulling out the supplies, making us a jumbo plate of nachos.

Once my apartment is filled with smells of Mexican heaven, he plops down on the couch next to me, setting the plate on a pillow between us. I cross my legs underneath me so I can sit facing him and he does the same. Neither of us wait to dig in.

"The good news is you can still be my friend," I say, feeling like I need to be the one to break the ice after my display of emotion.

"*Best* friend," he corrects. "And as a fellow nacho lover, I have to say I would completely understand. It would be nothing short of a deal breaker if you didn't like nachos."

"I'm glad we're on the same page." As usual, it's not awkward with Theo. Ever. It has me feeling brave again. "So, Theo, what's your story?"

"I want yours," he says simply.

"You know *way* more about me than I know about you. You've seen my design room. You know where I work and that I'm quitting. You know where I live." I pause. "You know that my dad died. My favorite breakfast place. My favorite spot at the airport. All *I* know is that you're a writer of some kind, that you drive an old BMW, and that you have a douchebag of a father."

He laughs. "I really do sound like a stalker."

"Yeah, you do." I smile. "So it's only fair."

"Fine. Which version do you want? The not-so-depressing abridged version, or the crush-your-soul overshare version?"

"Crush my soul. Definitely."

"Then I'm going to need alcohol and permission to stay on this couch tonight."

"I think that all I've got is vodka," I say in a silly attempt to not bring alcohol into this equation. Theo has me losing my mind even when I'm sober.

"It'll do." Totally unbothered.

Great.

Theo makes his way back to my kitchen, reaching for the only cabinet containing alcohol like he's done it a thousand times, and grabs the vodka leftover from God knows when and two shot glasses with cheesy souvenir writing.

"Here are the rules," he says, setting the glasses on my coffee table, filling them up in turn. "When it gets too depressing, we both take a shot."

This is such a bad idea. "Okay."

"And questions about the airport and the diner are off limits."

I hesitate. What could he be so secretive about that he's worried about me broaching the subject when he's got alcohol in his system? However curious I may be, this is a chance to learn more about him, and I don't want to miss out completely. "Deal."

The answers to my questions about how he found me at the airport and then the diner will have to come another day.

"I'm originally from Maine, but moved down here when I was about fifteen, after my father found out how much money was in getting trust fund babies out of DUIs in Florida. I don't want to know what other kind of people he's ended up defending to make the money he's made, but that's how he started." He takes a deep breath. "My mother died giving birth to me, on Christmas, and he's always hated me for it."

"Take a shot." Because that's fucking terrible.

"Taking shots already?" he says a bit darkly. "We're in for a long night."

We both knock one back before he continues.

"Childhood wasn't too terrible beyond the general shittiness of being an attorney's son, but especially an attorney who lost the only person he cared about. My father was demanding, overbearing, and a dick on a good day, but it was tolerable until we moved down here.

"Everyone in Maine knew him and my mother. It's a small town, so he could never go too off the rails without someone sticking their nose into his business. After we got here, the defense cases started pouring in, along with the money, and eventually so did the alcohol." He pauses. "I need another shot for this next part."

We both take one.

"Things got pretty bad after that. One night he came home extremely drunk. I woke up to him choking me, saying that I murdered my mother and deserved to die."My stomach churns and it's not because of the alcohol.

"After that, it was a pretty dark time in my life, I won't lie to you. For a while, I wasn't sure what I was sticking around for." Theo takes another shot and I follow suit. "One night, I was sitting out by the water for...what I intended to be the last time."

No. It can't possibly be. Someone this *good,* this *bright,* failed by the world and left to consider such a thing.

"I had done my research and I had a plan, but I wanted to enjoy a beautiful view before I went through with it. That's when fate stepped in, and I met Connor." He smiles to himself. "He appeared from the shadows and said 'Mate, what's got you by the balls so bad, the look on your face makes me think they're about to rip off?' I couldn't help but laugh because that's exactly how I felt. Connor sat down next to me, offered me a cigarette, and for some reason I told a complete stranger exactly why I was sitting by that water."

I stay silent, afraid he'll stop, my heart squeezing painfully.

"Connor had been living on the streets after getting kicked out by his parents when he refused to go to medical school and wanted to become a musician instead. Having recently moved here from Australia after his dad was recruited to one of the top hospitals, Connor didn't have anywhere else to go, so I offered him our spare room. I figured it was the least I could do for the guy who saved my life.

"Things were better for a while, and Connor became a friend. He encouraged me to find an outlet for what was happening in my head, and having someone else in the house curbed Dad's drunken anger for the most part."

"Is that when you began writing?" My voice shakes, heavy with the weight of everything he's shared with me tonight.

Theo nods. "The reason I had always loved to read was because I could escape to any world I wanted, so I decided to try my hand at building my own, and began writing short stories. Mainly thrillers, but other stuff, too, when it came to mind.

Theo pours us both another shot. Taking advantage of the brief opportunity, my eyes roam over him again, seeing him in a new light. He's been through hell, that I know. Yet, I can't help the hope which fills my chest. Theo stared the chasm of darkness in the face when it was just a step away, as his trauma, given strength by the words contained in it, encouraged him to take that last plunge into nothing.

Except, he didn't fall victim to the poisonous whispers of words once seethed, but decided to brave the journey back to the surface. Rather than letting his abuse become what would break him, he made it that which *empowered* him. The very words his father used to ruin him became the catalyst which shaped his kindness. In his creativity, Theo found a way to heal.

And maybe I can do the same.

"The night of my high school graduation, my father came home rip-roaring drunk, totally out of his mind. He came into my room, just like the many nights which came before it, but this time was different. My father came in with the end in his eyes and began beating me to a pulp, saying, 'It's your fault' over and over. I knew what he meant."

My stomach roils, with sickness in a way I've never known.

"Connor heard the altercation and came to intervene, pulling my father off of me and fighting back until he left us alone. He still has a scar over his eye from coming to my defense because of the damage my father did to his face for doing so. Since I was in worse shape, Connor drove us to the hospital so we could get stitches. The story was that Connor backed me in a fight with some other dude over a girl at a bar."

We both reach for another shot.

"The hospital kept me overnight after realizing that I was severely concussed, sporting several broken bones. Connor stayed with me the entire night on a crappy fold-out chair after telling the nurses that he was my brother. They released me the next morning, and it was the first time my father had left the damage in places that he could see once he was sober again. The first question out of his mouth was if I had given a statement to the police, not an apology or even checking to see if I was okay.

"As a thank you for not ratting him out for the domestic abuse, he got me and Connor our own place, paid for entirely until the day we decide to move out. To be honest, I never wanted to take anything from the man, let alone have any excuse to deal with him, but I wasn't too proud to miss out on a chance for my friend to be able to pursue his music for as long as he needed without worrying about life expenses. So, we took my father up on his offer and moved out the same week. Connor and I have lived together ever since, and he is the only person I truly consider family."

"He sounds like an amazing friend," I whisper, the biggest understatement.

"He pulled me out of the darkest time in my life. Twice. He reminded me that there are things on this Earth left living for, even if I hadn't found them yet." Theo looks at me intently, then. "No matter how dark things are now, if you just keep putting one foot in front of the other, you will come out on the other side. Even if we have nothing else left in the world, we still have ourselves, and *we* are worth it."

My eyes fill up with tears because I know exactly what he means. We both take a shot, this time in cheers to his victory.

"That's pretty much the last of the depressing shit. Not sure I can stay upright if I have any more of those anyway," he jokes, pointing toward the shot glasses.

I marvel at the fact that he can open up to me so easily, showing me all the pieces of himself, even the damaged and wrecked ones. He lays it all out for me to see and still finds it in himself to joke, to make me smile. Theo is the strongest person I have ever met.

It's that moment where I feel it. A crack, straight through the center of the thickest wall around my heart, along with a realization. Every time I told him to leave me alone, it was a silent plea, a challenge, for him to be the one to break down these protective barriers I've so carefully constructed. And here he is, answering my call, seeing the girl who's been hiding behind her ramparts for too long and coaxing her out.

Theo continues, "After moving out, I began taking writing seriously. I wrote my first full-length novel, which is a murder mystery. I believed in the piece so much, I sent it out to literary agents, publishers, and writing contests to try to get published."

I can't imagine having the kind of bravery to face that amount of potential rejection, hence why my designs are locked up in their little room like Rapunzel.

"I didn't have any success for the first two years or so. Then, I guess you could say fate decided to intervene and I was lucky enough to be in the right place at the right time and met someone who changed my life forever." He looks at me, pausing as if he's lost his train of thought. "God, you're beautiful."

A deep blush flows to my face, and I have to look away before the alcohol starts talking for me.

Theo clears his throat. "Anyway, this person was kind enough to call in an old favor and get my manuscript reviewed at a well-known publishing house for my genre. The moment they read it, they referred me to an agent they work with a lot and we drew up a contract. It will be released in a couple months."

The news of his achievement frees me from my embarrassment caused by his words, which I'm pretty sure I dreamed up. "You're a published writer!?"

"Well, technically it's not published *yet*."

"You found your happy ending." Wonder fills my words.

"I'm pretty sure I have." The way his eyes gaze into mine after brushing over my face, I'm no longer sure if we are still talking about his book. Warmth bleeds into me, along with the breed of confidence that brings trouble.

Those words of his, full of meaning and emotion, have me thinking all kinds of things, but I know myself, and this is not my bravery. If I act now, with the departure of this brave buzz will come the fear, the anxiety which will ruin this before it begins.

I ruin the moment the best way I know how, instantly hating myself for it. "You never told me about finding your dad with your ex-girlfriend."

Theo drops his gaze and pulls back, giving me a little half smile. "I don't think I've got it in me tonight."

I know the feeling.

"But I'll make you a deal, Ara."

God, I *love* the way my name sounds on his lips.

"I will tell you that story as soon as you tell me yours, the unabridged edition, that is."

I stand up, the full effect of those shots finally kicking in, leaving me a whisper away from spilling it all.

Grabbing Theo a pillow from my room and an extra blanket, I return to the living room and find Theo with his shoes off, eyes closed, lying on my couch with his hands behind his head.

"Don't hold your breath for that, Theo."

He opens his eyes. "I don't care how long it takes, but I want to know you, Ara."

I keep my mouth shut because I don't trust the words that are sure to come out, turning back toward my room.

"Ara?" he says just as I reach my doorway.

"Yeah?" I turn back toward Theo, gripping the doorknob behind my back for strength.

"Do you have plans for Valentine's Day?"

I give a dry laugh. "What do you think?"

He smiles. "Be my date then? I was hoping to have an excuse to wear my new jacket."

"How do you know I'd finish it in time?"

He shrugs, "I have a feeling."

"Are we going platonically?" I ask, not sure which answer I'm hoping for.

Accepting Theo's friendship was a lot for me. Going on a date on Valentine's Day, of all days, is even more. The truth is, I'm still raw with grief, not to mention my metaphorical closet full of trust issues. When Theo is around, things look brighter. I find myself wanting to take leaps, but when it's all said and done, would I be able to follow through?

He pauses, reading me as easily as if I were wrapped in tape labeled *Fragile: Handle With Care*. "Platonically, of course."

The vodka sinks into my stomach. "Then, it's a date. Platonically."

"Goodnight, Ara."

"Goodnight, Theo."

I close my bedroom door before I change my mind…and not just about the date, but about it being platonic.

# CHAPTER THIRTEEN

## *Four Years Ago - Ara*

Dad clears his throat, his tell for when he's about to address something we'd both rather die than discuss with each other.

"Listen, I know we've always kept the topic of boys on a need-to-know basis."

*Oh, shit.*

"As we should," I say in hopes of putting this conversation to an end before it begins.

He clears his throat again. This is going to be *bad.*

"You're going to college soon, and I just want to make sure that you're… *safe.*"

"Da-"

"Safer than what safe meant with...Cameron. There are other...things...to worry about in college that you probably...well, *hopefully*...didn't have to worry about with Cameron."

This is worse than I had even imagined.

"Dad, for the love of God, please stop talking."

"I've heard about this new Binder thing..."

"Binder?"

"You know, the app you kids use these days to find...um...dates?"

Someone shoot me. "Do you mean *Tinder*?"

"That's the one. I just want to make sure you don't take too many risks in that, uh, department."

"Consider me thoroughly warned."

"Good. Thank God that's over with." Dad grabs the remote, looking more like a tomato than a tomato itself, while I try not to combust from mortification.

# CHAPTER FOURTEEN

## *Present - Ara*

Today is Valentine's Day.

This entire week felt like time wouldn't pass fast enough, when in fact, I could have used a lot more of it, having called in sick in order to have Theo's jacket and matching tie done in time. Not to mention, I obviously had to have something to wear myself. Full of anticipation for our "date," I haven't even thought about the potential consequences of skipping out on a portion of my last two weeks.

Theo's jacket turned out amazing. He's supposed to come in black dress pants, a white tuxedo shirt, and leave the rest up to me, my sewing kit handy, just in case I need to make any final adjustments.

A moment later, there is a knock at the door, right on time.

My nerves go crazy, sending a tremor through my hands as I unlock the door, swinging it open to reveal the man on my doorstep.

*Wow.* Theo is an absolute vision and he's not even fully dressed yet. I'm speechless as I take my time looking him over, his hair styled to perfection, gelled into those old Hollywood-waves that I love so much. Face smooth, the fresh scent of his aftershave invades my senses and I hope it accompanies us for the rest of the night.

His tuxedo shirt is tailored flawlessly to his frame, unbuttoned enough that a smidge of toned chest peeps through. My jaw slackens as I take in how well his clothes hug him, stopping at his belt before I start imagining what's under *there.*

Theo notices the liberties my eyes take and grabs at the opportunity to do the same. His eyes rove over my hair which I styled into old Hollywood-waves myself, hoping he'd do the same. Theo has never seen me in anything but oversized t-shirts and messy buns, yet surprise isn't what I'd use to describe what I see in his eyes, as my hair falls to my waist even when curled. His gaze slowly drifts over my face, taking in every single detail, leaving a warm trail in their wake as they drift down to what I'm wearing.

"You look stunning." Theo's voice is rough, slightly breathless. Must be the stairs.

I snort. "Theo, I'm not actually going to wear a robe on our date."

"I wouldn't care if you did."

"No, Theo." I roll my eyes. "I just needed something easy to change out of so I can make sure your jacket is perfect before getting dressed myself."

I'm positively delighted as something close to wariness crosses his features, knowing that this isn't the final look. *Good.*

"Let me grab the jacket," I say, walking toward my design room, making sure to close the door behind me so he doesn't get even a *peek* at what I have in store. Exiting the room in the same fashion, Theo doesn't miss a thing. To distract him, I hold up his jacket and the matching bow tie with a huge grin. "What do you think?"

Theo moves toward me, taking the jacket into his hands, stroking the velvet with those perfect fingers of his. He meets my eyes again with a smile. "It's almost as beautiful as its maker."

Never graceful, I pretend like the compliment doesn't exist. "Okay then, let's make sure it fits."

Speaking of perfect fingers, the way they fiddle with the buttons, one by one, as he does up his shirt to the collar is… distracting. I clear my throat and Theo shoots me a smirk.

Once he's done with the torturing process, I help him slip into the jacket. A perfect fit. My measurements couldn't have been better. You can tell it was made for him, from his shoulders to the waist, he is a work of art.

"I've never loved anything I've worn as much as I love this jacket." Theo takes a long look in the mirror. "I guess measuring with my shirt off really does make the difference."

I can't help but giggle. "I should change, now that I know your suit is perfect."

His eyes meet mine in the reflection of the mirror, making me feel like a stone plunging into the depths of a green ocean, darker and stormier the deeper I sink. Something passes between us then, and he slowly turns to face me, his chest brushing mine.

"Should I be worried?"

"Probably." I don't know where this daring attitude is coming from, but I can't switch it off when he's around.

Entering my design room for the last time before the reveal, no way would I have the guts to wear this dress if it were anyone but Theo out there. I took the typical design of lingerie and converted it into a dress, making it from the black lace that I purchased with Theo.

Two cups fit perfectly for my breasts—giving them a generous lift into plump little half circles—is where the bodice starts. The rest is entirely sheer, showcasing my waist and leaving *just* enough to the imagination. My favorite touch is the illusion split that I created with nude mesh, which starts behind my left hip, curving around to the front of my leg and opening into a real split, mid-thigh.

My floor-length mirror shows me everything, and I know without a doubt I look sexy as all hell. I've never felt this way about myself—being able to look in the mirror and appreciate what I see—before tonight. Yet here I stand, in lingerie-turned-dress, on Valentine's Day, for my new best friend. And this platonic date. I'm not even going to *try* to make sense of any of that tonight.

I quickly grab the red pointed pumps and matching clutch that I bought just for this, and make my way to the door, taking a deep breath and swinging it open before I lose my nerve.

Theo startles from where he's standing, his jaw *literally* dropping when he sees my dress, when he sees *me*. He takes an unthinking step forward, the most basic part of himself unable to stand the distance between us.

Mission *fucking* accomplished.

This time, his eyes linger on my breasts as if he knows he should pull them away, but physically can't. My heart is pounding by the time he finds the strength to drag them to my almost-bare torso, taking in every bit of skin on display beneath the lace.

His eyes are ravenous by the time he makes it to the invisible material posing as an *insanely* high split. Once his eyes have traveled the full length of my body, he closes them and clenches his jaw.

Theo may be a gentleman, but I'm happy to know he is still a man.

Just because I'm feeling extra cruel tonight, after he finally opens his eyes, I put my arms at my sides and give him a slow twirl, showing off another feature of the dress: the back. I used the nude mesh again, giving it the illusion of dropping into a scandalously low 'V" until the black lace takes over again, curving around my small bottom.

I know the second Theo notices how well this dress hugs my ass, thanks to the sound he makes in the back of his throat. By the time I finish the slow turn to face him again, he's scarcely gotten himself together, looking like a man who's been through hell and is diving back in for the return trip.

"Well?" I ask innocently, as if I haven't noticed the onslaught of his attention.

Theo clears his throat. Once. Twice.

"You look…" He shakes his head and moves toward me.

I don't think I'll stop him if he decides to tear this dress to threads, right here. It would be a worthy sacrifice, but instead, he grabs my hand, bringing it up so I can twirl around again under his guidance.

"You look…*devastating.*"

Theo is helpless against this dress.

"Is it normal to want to have sex with your best friend?"

His question sets my body abuzz. I manage to keep my face neutral as I raise my shoulder in a slight shrug and say, "I've never had a male best friend before, but I'd guess that it's not normal."

"Well, it would be a lot easier if you didn't look like this." He motions toward me as if that's explanation enough. "I was kidding myself when I agreed for this to be platonic, because I am not looking at you—or thinking about you—platonically."

"So, then it's not normal for my best friend to be staring at my boobs?"

He lets out an embarrassed chuckle. "I don't believe so."

I step closer to him. "What a shame. I guess I better tell the rest of my best friends to stop, then."

Theo smirks. "I was under the impression that I was the only best friend looking at your boobs."

"That's one hell of an assumption, isn't it?" As I take another step closer, I see Theo's pulse thrumming beneath his jaw line.

"I'll make you another deal," he breathes.

I lift one brow in consideration. "What do you propose?"

"Starting now, we're not platonic for this one night, and at the end of this date, we will go back to being just friends."

"Not platonic? For one night?" I repeat.

He nods.

"What would that include?" My heart erupts at the possibilities.

"You get to decide, but I'd like to be able to look at you without feeling like I'm crossing a line." He gives me a little smile, always the gentleman. "I won't make a single move unless you ask me to."

I pretend to think it over, much longer than necessary. "It's a deal."

"Good, because you threw platonic out the window the moment you put on that dress." His eyes are dragging over me for what won't be the last time tonight, and he takes a deep breath. "If we're going to make it to our reservation, we'd better get going before I do something extraordinarily stupid."

As much as I would love for him to peel this dress off right this very moment and take advantage of our new deal *thoroughly,* I know I'm not ready to be that vulnerable again. It would inevitably lead to feelings, and every time I've cared about someone, I've lost them. Whether it was the fault of my own or a twisted game of fate, the ending has always been the same.

And I'm not ready to lose Theo.

"Lead the way," I say, gesturing forward.

"And miss out on that outstanding view?" He scoffs. "No way."

I smile again, taking the lead.

In the past, the guys I'd been with made me feel like they were doing me a favor by settling with what I had to offer. Not Theo. He makes me feel like I'm something to behold, something to treasure.

As I get to the bottom step, welcoming me back to the flat ground outside my apartment building, Theo ducks past me and jogs to his car. He opens the passenger door, bending down to retrieve something which he hides from my view as he walks back to where I wait.

"I got you something."

I instantly feel bad. "Theo, I'm so sorry, I didn't realize we were exchanging gifts."

"Ara, you made me the finest jacket any man has ever worn. That is *way* better than what I got you." He smiles and finally reveals the cutest teddy bear I've ever seen.

I take the teddy bear, having never felt anything so soft, squeezing it to my chest and relishing in the fact that it smells like him. "It's perfect."

"It's pretty much the only thing I could find that wasn't expressly for a significant other, and I didn't want to make it weird."

As if giving me a rose would have been more weird than dressing in pseudo-lingerie.

I link my arm with his. "Come on, Theo Carter. We have a non-platonic date to attend."

• • •

Eating at a restaurant this nice is completely out of my comfort zone. The place is beautiful, don't get me wrong. The architecture alone is a work of art, along with everything and everyone inside. I just have no idea what I'll do if I sit down and there's seventeen pieces of silverware.

Heads turn as we are led to our table, eyes widening as they roam over my dress. I'm not overdressed by any means, the other women in floor-length dresses as well, meaning it's definitely just *my* dress. A flush creeps up my neck as I start to wish I hadn't stepped this far outside my comfort zone.

Theo leans in, lips brushing my ear as his hand rests on my lower back. "You are the most exquisite thing I've ever seen."

My flush continues to spread, but for an entirely different reason than feeling self-conscious. "How did you manage to get into a place like this on Valentine's Day?"

"I just dropped the Carter name. It's not my fault they never confirm whether or not it's the Carter anyone cares about," he says dryly.

"Well, it's amazing. I don't think I've ever been somewhere this...fancy."

As we sit down, our waiter appears at the table, asking if we would care for a glass of wine or champagne. Our eyes meet as we both say, "No, thank you" simultaneously. We both smile, not needing to say out loud that neither of us trust ourselves enough to add alcohol to the mix.

Eyes twinkling, Theo says, "I blame the dress."

"I blame the jacket," I say with a smirk as I take a sip of my water.

*Are we flirting?*

I pick up my menu to distract myself from ogling at Theo and realize that I have no idea what the hell this menu says. "Theo. We have a problem."

He looks genuinely concerned as he leans toward me, "What's wrong?"

"There are no nachos on this menu," I deliver with a straight face.

Theo laughs and I can't help but join in. I don't know how to describe it, but I'm falling in love with the version of myself that I am around Theo. He brings out the real me. The girl who smiles and makes people laugh. The girl who knows she's *alive*. Dad would adore him.

My eyes get glassy at the thought, and Theo reaches over to take my hand. I try not to think about how natural the contact feels, or how just by stroking my hand with his thumb, he sends chills throughout my entire body.

"I was just thinking that my dad would have absolutely adored you. He would be so happy to see that I'm out doing things like this." I gesture to the restaurant around us with my free hand. "With someone like you."

Theo squeezes my hand, "I'm sure that somehow, wherever he is, he knows we're together, having fun."

I believe him.

With perfect timing, the waiter comes and asks for our orders. Theo allows me to go first, and I still don't know what any of these words means. I roll the dice and pick the item which looks the easiest to pronounce, though I'm sure that I still manage to botch it. Theo looks alarmed. "Are you sure? You don't want to get something else?"

I'm too embarrassed to admit that I have no fucking clue what I just ordered, so I just say, "I'm sure," with a smile and reassuring nod.

"Brave." Theo shakes his head and follows with his order.

I don't know what I've just done, but I'm positive I'm going to regret it.

We devour the bread and butter they start us with, and I'm on my second or third slice before I remember that I'm not supposed to *really eat* on proper dates. I put the slice back in the basket and look up to find Theo watching me.

"No way you're already full."

I shrug. "I already had a few pieces."

"It's bottomless bread, have some more."

"That's okay. I know we're just friends, but I still don't want to gross you out."

"Gross me out? What are you talking about?"

I instantly regret bringing it up. Not only am I feeling like an insecure idiot, but now Theo is going to *know* I'm an insecure idiot. "You know what I mean. I don't want to gross you out by eating a whole bunch of food."

"Um, eating a ton of food is the whole point of going to a restaurant. Why would you think it would gross me out?"

Theo never sounds condescending, he's asking because he genuinely wants to know. "Doesn't it gross guys out to watch their dates eat?"

"What kind of dirtbag told you that?" He sounds appalled.

Wow, of course it's just more poison from Blake, and I didn't know any better due to my lack of experience. I slap my forehead. "This is just embarrassing now."

"No, don't feel embarrassed. I just don't know why anyone would say such a thing to *any* woman, but especially to you."

"It was my ex who told me that. He liked giving me advice for my 'well-being.'" I shrug. "Things like counting calories to avoid passing my healthy weight threshold, but I just love food way too much to pick what I eat based on a number."

"He's an asshole."

I feel a blush coming so I look down. "I don't have a lot of experience with guys. I just thought my first boyfriend had been too nice to say anything, but I guess I'm realizing now that it's just another messed-up Blake-ism."

"His name should've been clue enough, he's a douche."

This brings a half smile to my lips. "I said the same thing."

"If you don't help me finish off every crumb in that bread bowl, I'm going to consider this a failed date."

And just like that, Theo takes a subject which has made me feel insecure and unhappy for years and retires it forever.

• • •

Even with the bread, I'm still starving by the time my food arrives, but I'm also certain I will *still* be starving even after dinner. The portion sizes are tiny, and I don't even know what I'm looking at on my plate.

Designs in variously colored sauces lead up to a dark, gooey-looking mound smaller than my palm, resting on a bed of vegetables that are so fancy I've never seen them before. To be honest, I'm not even sure whether they're supposed to be eaten or are there for decoration.

Judging by the size, I must have ordered an appetizer by accident, but in looking over to Theo's meal, which is roughly the same size, I realize this is what they consider a meal. Theo's ordered some sort of steak which is just as tiny, but looks edible which is more than what I can say about mine.

Amusement graces Theo's faultless features. "You have no idea what you ordered, do you?"

"Not a fucking clue."

He chuckles. "Come on, let's get out of here."

"But we haven't even eaten our dinners, and this looks expensive."

"I'm not letting you eat that. Honestly, this restaurant was a bad idea from the get-go; you don't care about stuff like this, so I'm not sure why I thought this was the way to impress you."

"Theo, I *am* impressed."

"But you'd rather have nachos, no? Or even a hot dog?"

I can't contain my grin, he already knows me so well.

"I thought so. Let's go." He stands, taking me with him. As we walk by the waiter, he pauses to talk to him. "I'm sorry, my girlfriend isn't feeling well. Please charge the dinner to the Carter tab."

*Girlfriend?* Theo mistakes my lurch for alarm.

"Just tonight, remember?" he says, reassuringly, cluelessly. Theo has no idea that it was only a mass eruption of butterflies erupting in my stomach that caused that reaction. Since when do I get excited at the prospect of something so terrifying?

"At least this dinner wasn't a total waste. At the very least it'll annoy my father to no end, having to pay for a dinner that wasn't his to enjoy, making that little field trip good for something."

"I'd never pass up an opportunity to help you annoy that asshat." Earning another smile from Theo, I feel like this night truly belongs to us, beginning and ending and traveling where we tell it. "Where to?"

"You'll see."

Not even twenty minutes later, we pull up to Taco Bell, sending another stupid grin to my face. Stopping for a crunch wrap supreme in a floor-length gown and tuxedo? A more perfect Valentine's date doesn't exist.

I glance over, finding Theo deliciously disheveled. He's removed his bow-tie, allowing himself to unbutton the collar of his shirt. An unexplainable heat shoots through me, despite the cool night air. I'm not worried about my hair being completely ruined from the wind, or that all my lipstick has probably been wiped off. I'm just… *present.* Enjoying this moment.

Theo circles the car to open the passenger door for me. I step out, bending down to twist my hair into a messy knot on top of my head. Since it's already windblown, I might as well get it out of the way.

Theo looks at me curiously.

"My hair is too heavy to put it in a bun the normal way."

"Your hair is beautiful. And… you missed one." I'm locked in place by his stare, as he grabs a loose strand and deftly twists it around the knot. I close my eyes as his fingers trail down my ear and across my jaw to my chin. "Now, let's go destroy our bowels."

I laugh, grateful to be extinguished from the heat that has the power and temperature to burn me to the ground. Theo grabs my hand, tugging me inside.

"Can you read this one?" Theo teases as we have a look at the menu.

I dig my elbow into his ribs with a smile as I order my usual with a frozen Baja Blast and extra hot sauce. Theo follows suit and we grab a table in the far back corner, Theo sitting across from me as we wait for our number to be called.

"I can honestly say that I've never taken a girl on a date to Taco Bell."

It piques my interest. I can't help it. "Where *do* you take girls on dates?"

Theo lifts a brow.

"*You* brought it up." I defend myself. "And as your non-platonic date, I'm allowed to ask."

He smirks. "I haven't been on a date in....a while. So, I suppose the answer to your question would be nowhere."

Interesting. "Where did you take girls before?"

"Someone is awfully curious tonight." Another half smile graces those lips as his eyes drift to mine, currently being chewed between my teeth. "Since most of them were usually more interested in the place rather than me, definitely not Taco Bell."

"Clearly, they had bad taste, because this is by far the best date I've ever been on, real or not real."

"Ara, this is very real." Before I can delve into what exactly he means by that, they call our number and Theo stands to collect our food. There is a pull forming between us, becoming so strong neither of us will be able to ignore it for much longer.

My thoughts are still wreaking havoc on me by the time Theo deposits our food onto the table. "I'm sorry, but this is so much better than whatever that squishy shit was on my plate."

Theo laughs. "Do you want to know what it was?"

"Hit me."

"It was essentially a sack of pig's blood, but they call it a sausage. It's considered a French delicacy."

Horror. That's undiluted horror that I feel. "That's the grossest thing I've ever heard."

"Why do you think I saved you from yourself?"

"I was committed, too."

He laughs. "I know you were."

"Well, thanks for saving my ass."

"Any time. That's what non-platonic friends are for."

• • •

After we come to a stop in front of my place, Theo opens my car door for me yet again. Both of us are quiet as we start up the stairs, my nerves off the charts. We're about to have a fucking doorstep moment. There is so much tension rolling between us, you could cut it with child-safe scissors.

The panic subsides as his eyes run over my face, my exposed neck, and land on the jacket I made him which still rests on my shoulders, where he placed it after my Baja Blast gave me a shiver. They turn to embers and drift lower, the fire in my veins following their path.

Theo's eyes make it back up to mine, and buried beneath the desire and want is a simple question. Captured by his stare, if he holds me hostage any longer, I will ask him to cross this threshold and take us straight to the finish line.

It's easy to set being platonic aside for one night to enjoy each other's company, but taking things to a physical level? There is no coming back from that. It could jeopardize what we've built. *I* could jeopardize what we've built. Where would it leave us? I open my mouth to ask him exactly that, but before I can get any words out, he closes his eyes, releasing me.

Theo leans in, kissing me softly on the forehead. "Goodnight, Ara."

He doesn't wait for a response as he turns to walk away.

I hesitate, not knowing what to do. This moment feels important. Every cell in my body burns for me to call out his name, close the distance between us and never let us come apart again. I can't shake the feeling that if I don't make the right move, here and now, it will sentence us to a future neither of us want.

"Wait!" I slip off my heels, leaving them discarded in front of my door. His gaze is hungry as he turns around, watching me close the last few feet remaining between us.

"You forgot your jacket." Slipping it from my shoulders to hand it over, the ferocity gleaming in Theo's eyes dims, but he still gives me a smile.

"Right, thank you."

"We had a deal." I don't know if I'm reminding him or myself, but we agreed to remain just friends after tonight.

"That we did. I hope it didn't scare you off."

I shake my head.

"Good. Me neither." He takes another look at me, and I can only imagine what he finds as he tells me again, "Goodnight, Ara."

"Goodnight, Theo."

I make it back to my door just in time to watch Theo drive away. As much as every piece of me was screaming to drag him inside and tear off his clothes, I know I'm not ready for what would come after. Which probably makes me the biggest idiot on the planet.

I don't want to rush what we have and wind up destroying it, the way I always do. Theo doesn't deserve to be a crutch. I want to be more than this broken person I've become, to put back those pieces that have been taken from me. This is the most precious feeling I've ever had, and I will protect it at all costs. Even though I've never given him an explanation, Theo seems to understand that I'm not ready.

I just hope he sticks around long enough for me to get ready.

# CHAPTER FIFTEEN

## Present - Ara

I never believed that my last day at The Airport Café would come. I can't imagine how unpleasant Karen is going to be today. She was more than disgruntled about the sick days I took, even going so far as to say that my two-week notice would need to be extended. I downright refused, seeing as though the only days I have ever taken off since working there was for the funeral.

I've been dreading the fact that leaving the café means I won't be seeing Joel and Dan anymore, right as we were starting to become closer. Nor will I be seeing Theo, apparently. He hasn't asked to see me since Valentine's Day, nearly two weeks ago, and I haven't pushed it either.

I hate to admit it, but I miss him like crazy. We texted the day after Valentine's Day, but we've mainly just been sending each other funny memes and random snapshots of moments throughout our days since. I'm not sure why he hasn't asked to see me again, but it worries me. When I should really be feeling thankful. Because not a single night has gone by without me having to use my little pink friend at least *twice* before going to sleep, accompanied by all thoughts of Theo. Theo biting his lip...Theo ripping my beautiful dress in half...Theo in my design room...on my counter...in my shower. It's safe to say I needed some cooling down time.

Speaking of Theo, I pick up my phone and search for the ugliest monster GIF I can find, deciding to go with one of Jabba the Hutt from *Star Wars*, holding Princess Leia as his slave. Captioning it with *Officially free from my keeper after tonight*, I hit send. A moment later, my special notification sound for Theo rings out.

Yes, I made a special notification sound for him.

Yes, I know it's pathetic.

But I was getting too disappointed when my phone would go off with notifications from apps I don't even remember downloading and it wasn't him.

My attempt at drilling my heart into not reacting when it was a text from him, a *friend,* hasn't been successful. It doesn't seem to be listening at all these days.

*Ding.*

Case in point.

Opening my texts with Theo, I see that he's sent back a GIF of Han Solo saying *May the force be with you,* making me cackle. I send him a few cry-laughing emojis and put my phone back down.

As much as I joke about it, quitting this job absolutely terrifies me, and I've been trying not to think about what it truly means. I'll have no job, which means no stable income, and I'll be relying on the little money I have saved until I find another one. I've been looking for another position, but absolutely nothing I've found has felt like an improvement.

I know Dad left me something, but I haven't bothered finding out how much, much to his attorney's chagrin. It doesn't feel right to accept money as a replacement for Dad. He had thought of everything, even going so far as a prepaid and preplanned funeral, and I know he would have wanted to make sure I was taken care of even beyond that. The letters are proof of that.

Another notification from Theo rings out and I unlock my phone.

**Theo: This is the first step toward figuring out the rest. You've got this.**

**Me: Thank you. I needed that.**

I take a deep breath and look out my window. Theo is right. I've got this. I'm going to figure it all out, but if I sit in this comfortable bubble forever, I never will. It's time I take the first step.

Grabbing my keys, I head in to face Jabba the Hutt herself, for the last time.

With a smile on my face.

• • •

Joel and Dan attempted to bake me a going away cake and I'm here for it. It looks absolutely terrible, which makes it mean even more to me. I engulf them both in a hug and ignore the look of shock on their faces at my affection.

I pull back and look around before whispering, "Where is the demon?"

The boys look around conspiratorially and whisper back at the same time, "We're not sure."

That's strange. I pull out my phone and see an email from Karen, reading it out loud.

Sarah,
It seems I must have caught your bug. I am unwell and won't be coming in.
The new trainee will be there for this shift, teach her the ropes.
No slacking.
-Karen

We look up at each other in disbelief, getting to spend my last shift enjoying each other's company without Karen breathing down our necks? It's almost too good to be true. The boys erupt with gleeful cheers, and I can't help but join in with a smile.

"So, guys? How's life?" Even though I see them almost every day, we've never gotten to know each other personally. Mostly due to my aversion to establishing personal connections, but also because of Karen acting like an ogre.

"Nope," Joel says. "We've been working with you for what? Two years now?"

Dan pipes up then, "And we know almost nothing about you."

"Then that boy shows up out of the blue…" adds Joel.

"And we want answers," Dan finishes.

I look between them both and can't help my giggle. "Did you guys rehearse that before I got here?"

"You're deflecting." Joel looks back to Dan. "This is what my teenagers do when they want me off their back."

I roll my eyes, and only because I've been dying to talk to anyone about Theo, I tell them. "His name is Theo, and he's nice."

They both raise their eyebrows, glancing at each other, telling me how nice they believe a young man can be.

"No, really. He's experienced real shit, so he treats people well and doesn't take things for granted. He's a published writer, intelligent... and sometimes I think that he can read my mind." I stop talking because I realize I'm *gushing*. I'm *fucking gushing*. And I could go on for much longer.

I haven't even mentioned the way his stormy green eyes feel as they brush over my skin, leaving me feeling as though I'm made of nothing but flammable materials, just waiting to be ignited. I could tell them about his smile, which leaves me disarmed and ready to offer up my heart, despite my greatest fears. I could tell them about his soul, so deep and honest, which grounds me in a way I've never experienced.

The guys look at me knowingly.

"You're in deep shit," Joel says with a waggle of his brows.

As if I didn't already know that. "We are strictly friends, nothing more."

Dan rolls his eyes. "You can say whatever you like, but you've got it bad for that boy."

"No one has it bad for *anyone*." I sound defensive even to my own ears.

"Dan, we better clear our calendars, there is a wedding in our future," Joel teases.

Just then, the new girl becomes my favorite fucking person on this Earth when she walks into the kitchen with a wave, shutting them right up with her southern accented words, "Hey, guys! I'm Lou. Karen asked me to come in tonight for my onboarding."

Lou has the clearest blue eyes I've ever seen, made more striking by her light blonde, ringlet curls and tanned skin. Her smile is infectious, and I find myself returning it instantly. She's wearing a graphic tee that reads "A yawn is a silent scream for coffee" and maybe it's her obvious sense of humor or laid-back demeanor, but I'm instantly at ease around her.

"I'm Ara, and I'll be showing you the ropes tonight. This is Dan, our dishwasher, and this is Joel, our cook. Do your best to ignore them."

They shoot me badly acted looks of hurt, but approval shines out from them.

"Nice to meet you guys," Lou says with an open smile, the kind of genuineness you don't see very often anymore.

"I'll show you where you can leave your stuff."

"That'd be great because I packed *way* too much shit into this bag, and I think my shoulder is about to fall off," Lou groans.

I laugh, the only encouragement she needs.

"You know those first-day nerves where you're like 'what the fuck do I bring' so you end up with like ten tampons even though you haven't started your period, a flashlight, and a hot pink highlighter JUST IN CASE."

"I consider myself lucky if I even make it to somewhere new." I snort, surprising myself a little with the honest interaction.

Leading her to the staff room, I move my stuff so she can use my old cubby (yes, I know that's a kindergarten word, but it's a goddamn cubby, there is no other way to describe it) and find her a clean apron. The cleaning closet is what I show Lou next, also serving as the laundry. The washing machine is ancient, so I teach her the right places to jiggle the toggles, hoping to save her from having to ask Karen.

"The guys seem cool." Lou makes easy conversation as I show her the rounds.

"They *are* cool. The *coolest,* actually." I might miss this café, just a little. "But don't tell them I said that."

Lou grins. "Your secret is safe with me."

And I believe her.

• • •

Tonight is proving to be a slow night, so I spend most of the shift teaching Lou what I do when there aren't customers. I feel bad for subjecting her to Karen when she seems like such a cool person, but I remind myself that Dan and Joel will be looking out for her. Plus, Lou seems like a hard worker, and she knows her way around a café. If Karen could like anyone, it would be Lou.

We are just finishing the napkin folding when Lou squeals and says, "We finally have a customer."

It's as if my body has already memorized the change in atmosphere that happens when he enters a room. My cells are instantly alive. My skin is humming. My heart is slamming. I don't need to turn around to know that it's Theo who just walked in.

"Do you remember what to say?" I whisper to Lou.

"Yep! I've got this." She grabs her notepad and heads out with confidence.

"Good," I say to no one, still lost in my body's reaction.

I take a moment to settle myself before turning around. This is the longest I've gone without seeing Theo since we became friends, and incidentally, it's right after we made that deal on Valentine's Day.

Although nothing physical happened, I know there has been a shift between us. The only way I'll find out if it's been a shift toward awkwardness, a shift toward tearing each other's clothes off, or a shift toward deeper friendship is by going out there and talking to him.

Once my breathing is even enough, I turn around, eyes landing on him instantly as if they know exactly where to look. Theo stops mid-coffee order, setting those deep green eyes on me, sending my stomach straight into my shoes.

"Hey, stranger," he says with a little half smile. I know Theo didn't intend for that to come out so sensually, yet here I am, a hair's breadth away from panting, as usual.

Lou looks between us. "Are you a regular here?"

Theo doesn't look away from me. "Of sorts."

"Actually, he's a friend of mine." I've *really* missed him.

That feeling of a puzzle piece slipping into place when he's around stirs that monster under my skin, sensing someone has gained some power over my feelings. I stay quiet, hoping it goes back to sleep, while Theo finishes his coffee order.

When he asks for a decaf to-go, my stomach sinks, knowing that he's not planning to stay. Lou gives me an amused look and leaves us alone to make his coffee. In her previous job, she was a certified barista, which means she's way more suited for this position than I ever was.

"So, what brought you to the airport this evening?" I take the seat across from Theo.

His eyes widen and shoot toward the back, looking for signs of danger.

"It's okay, Jabba isn't here tonight, and I've already shown the new girl pretty much everything. She's way more qualified than I am."

"Thank God, not sure I could have choked down another cup of battery acid," Theo says with a wink. "Actually, on second thought, that's offensive to battery acid."

"Hey!!!" I say with a scoff, reaching across the table to smack him on the arm.

His smile warms. "I guess I didn't need to come check on you after all."

"I still appreciate the gesture." I do. A weight I didn't know I'd been carrying with me lifts from my heart at the realization that we haven't lost... whatever this is. Something more than friends and less than...anything else.

Lou brings Theo his coffee, sporting a curious smile and he accepts it graciously.

"I should probably get back to work."

"Yeah, all good, I wasn't planning on staying."

We both stand, still facing each other. As his eyes meet mine, I momentarily forget that Lou is still standing here, watching us like she's at a live taping of *Jerry Springer*. My worries about things being ruined between us slip away. Everything is exactly as it's supposed to be.

For now.

"Friends?" Theo asks.

"Friends," I say with a relieved smile.

He wraps his arms around me, pulling me against him. Even if I had forever to hug Theo, it wouldn't be enough. Filling my lungs with his clean scent, I find myself wishing I could bottle it up for whenever I missed it, like a fucking serial killer.

We pull back, Theo playfully tugging on a loose strand of my hair before turning to walk away. "I'll see you soon, Ara."

Speechless, I turn back to Lou, a funny look on her face.

"If I don't get hugged like that before I die, then all of this was a waste of my goddamn time. Y'all somehow just turned a damn embrace into...I don't even know *what* that was, but it was hotter than hell." Lou fans herself with one of the napkins.

And I look for something to fan myself with too.

• • •

Since Lou is a fast learner and it's been a slow night, we decide to close a bit early. To my extreme embarrassment, the boys decided to throw a little going away party for me. Joel even managed to sneak in some beers, and I offered to split mine with Lou since I'd be driving home soon, and they were only expecting the three of us.

"Should we sing something?" Dan asks.

"I will turn around and walk out of here if you so much as open your mouth. Singing on birthdays is bad enough." I push away the thought of whose birthday, as well as my own, that I'll be celebrating alone this year.

Grabbing a knife from Joel's collection, I cut right into the disaster we are calling a cake.

*Chocolate.* My favorite.

"Okay, who wants a giant piece?" I offer.

Lou surprises me by swiping for it instantly, noting my reaction. "What? I love cake."

No shame. *I like her.* I cut myself an equally gigantic piece and hand the knife over to Joel. "You boys can serve yourselves."

Lou finally gives in to her curiosity. "So, what's the deal between you and that guy?"

"We're friends." Lou sends me a look, but leaves it alone. "I should give you my number in case you need any help and don't want to ask Karen."

"Why wouldn't I want to ask Karen?"

Dan visibly cringes.

"Listen, I'm sure it's mostly because I was terrible at this job, but she isn't the *warmest* person you'll ever meet," I say with a grimace.

"I kinda got that vibe during my interview, but I don't plan to give her anything to nit-pick."

"I'll give you my number anyway, just in case."

"I'll give you mine, too, just in case you ever want to hang out. I just moved here, meaning I'm always available." Lou shares a self-deprecating smile.

I type in my number with genuine hope.

"Okay," Dan says after polishing off another piece of cake, "it's time I get back to my wife before she starts worrying."

"I should also get going. I'd like to get a little sleep before my next shift," says Joel. He gives me a big hug and kisses me on the cheek. "Good luck with everything, Ara."

"Thanks, Joel," I say with a little sniffle, regretting that I waited so long to open up.

Dan wraps me up into a hug next. "We'll miss having you around here, but I can't wait to see where you go next."

I squeeze him even harder, before wiping my eyes as they walk away. How much fun have I missed out on these past few years by shutting them out? I vow to never make that same mistake again.

I look over to see Lou crying, more freely than any of us. "Oh my gosh, this is so embarrassing. I'm an empathetic crier, so I'm sorry, but I literally can't stop."

I laugh, genuinely, and I give her a hug, too.

I don't think I've hugged this many people... ever.

I'm turning into a hug-slut.

Why do I like it?

"I wish you weren't leaving," she says into my shoulder. "I feel like we could be friends."

I pull back. "Text me, we can still be friends."

"I'd like that." Lou sniffles.

"Come on, I'll show you how to lock up."

Yep...Dad would be happy.

# CHAPTER SIXTEEN

## *Four Years Ago - Ara*

A soft knock on my door lets me know that it's time to wake up for school. I haven't been getting up on my own recently because, well, I just don't want to.

The closer I get to my senior year being over, the closer I get to the future. And I think the future might just be the scariest thing in the world. You never know what's going to happen, and I'm not too sure whether it's in our control.

Dad slowly opens my door, and I think he's got his eyes closed too. Ever since he accidentally walked in on me half-naked after I didn't hear his knock, he takes pains to make sure it never happens again. The poor man probably would have bleached his eyes if he could.

"Ara?"

"Yeah, I'm awake."

"Can I come in?"

"Yes, Dad. I'm dressed."

"Okay, good." He lets out a breath. "I wanted to show you something."

He makes his way into my room, holding two rectangular passes in his hand.

"I know that you've had a difficult year, and you're a bit worried about the future." I'm quiet because he's right, and I don't need to tell him so. "I took the day off work so we could go check this out. It's the last day, and I thought it might be a good way to get your mind off things."

He hands me the passes, which are two entry tickets to a massive fashion expo here in Tampa. It's being held at the fairgrounds and will have all kinds of things to check out. I'd actually seen a flier for it but never thought I'd get to go.

"What about school?"

Dad looks at me a bit mischievously. "Surely your throat feels a tad dry?"

This makes me smile. "I'll get dressed."

"I'll make breakfast."

The fashion expo is more amazing than I could have ever imagined.

There are textiles everywhere, of all different patterns and thickness. People have little shops set up to feature their own designs and crafts. Everywhere I turn, there is something beautiful to investigate.

Dad is mostly quiet, but I think he's just happy to see me smiling and interested in something again.

Before long, I find this one booth that renders me speechless. Each material is something out of a fairytale, and each one is covered in different sorts of glitter. Some are two-toned sparkles, changing color in the light. Some are a beautiful sheer material, with only a hint of shimmer. Some are covered in crystals.

Then I see it.

A beautiful silver tulle, so glittery that it looks like it's made of diamonds.

I can only imagine the kind of dress I could make with that.

Dad offers to buy it for me, but I only take a little bit at first, not wanting to waste something so beautiful, but by the time I've made my second round of the expo, I know exactly what I'd use it for.

Dad buys me the entire roll.

MARCH
Dear Ara

# CHAPTER SEVENTEEN

*Present - Ara*

It's chilly for a March morning in Florida. I wish I could say I've made any sort of progress on my state of unemployment, but besides becoming a Starbucks regular with my new friend Lou, I've accomplished nothing, and I feel even further away from knowing what I'm going to do with my life.

Every morning I wake up, grab my laptop and go to the Starbucks down the street, spending the first half of the day searching and applying for jobs online.

My new ritual has two purposes.

The first is obvious: I need a job. I've only allocated enough funds from my savings to support myself for two weeks until I find another job. The second reason behind it is that I'm still trying to figure out what I want to do long term and I'm hoping that some listing will jump out at me, slap me in the face, and I'll have found my calling.

So far, both searches have been fruitless.

For the second half of my day, I spend it on the Internet researching all different kinds of careers. I've been learning that doing anything creative is risky, and never has a guaranteed paycheck, which is therefore *not* an option. I've also learned that I have absolutely no interest in careers which *do* have guaranteed paychecks. More often than not, I'm missing the qualifications required for those anyway.

What did I expect to happen after dropping out of college? Did I think I was just going to trip and fall into a six-figure salary? Obviously not. I just wanted to find something I didn't hate, but that something is seeming less and less possible.

Admittedly, it's been nice to have time to bond with Lou. We grab coffee pretty much every morning where I listen to her complain about Karen, whom she agrees is the literal devil, and she listens to me complain about not being able to find a single job that I would remotely enjoy. Then we drown our sorrows in caramel macchiatos and sweets.

I told her this morning that I would have to skip our Starbucks run, knowing another one of Dad's letters is due any day now. I'm pleading with the universe and Dad, wherever he is, that there will be something inside this letter to steer me in the right direction.

There's finally a knock on my door and I exhale with relief. Grabbing the donuts I bought for Dave, I open my door and he's as smiley as ever. I hold out the donuts in offering, making him light up even more, and I can't help but grin in answer.

Old people have always put me at ease. Somehow, I get the idea that they have seen so much of life, that even if I manage to royally embarrass myself, they've already seen it before. Plus, who would they tell? You don't see any of them uploading embarrassing content to their social media accounts. It keeps the usual fears which stop me from interacting at bay, and I find myself enjoying their company and doing nice things for them.

"You know the way to an old man's heart," Dave says as he graciously accepts the donuts. "I imagine that this is what you're waiting for?"

Dave extends the letter, and my heart seizes at the familiar handwriting. No matter how many letters I receive, I will always get emotional seeing a piece of Dad which is still left in the world.

"Thank you so much, Dave."

"I'll leave you to it, sweetheart." He turns to walk away, but after a few steps, he looks back. "Whatever it is you've been doin', I see some light in those eyes. Keep it up."

I let one tear escape and go back into my apartment, whipping up a cup of hot chocolate, and because I know I'll need the extra comfort, I pile on the marshmallows and whipped cream. So what if I'm also having two donuts. This situation warrants all the comfort.

As I sit on my couch, I take a massive bite of my first donut and try not to think about the fact that one day these letters will run out and I'll have to be my own lifeline. The thought is terrifying, and until that time comes, I will treasure every single one.

*Dear Ara,*
*I realized a few months ago that there is no return policy on fate. All we can do is claim it as our own and take whatever control we can with whatever time we have left. Ever since coming to that realization, I've been looking at the bright sides.*
*Here are a few of mine:*
*-I'll never have to go to the dentist again*
*-I'll never have to wait on hold with an airline*
*-I'll never have to wait in line at the DMV*
*-I'll never have to speak to Gladys from the IRS again*
*-Since I no longer have to worry about my health, I'll be having chocolate milkshakes with every meal*
*I want to make sure you're looking at your bright sides too. No matter how tough the situation is, you always have to find that silver lining. I know it's easier said than done, but it's the only way to find happiness.*
*When your mother left this world, I was shattered. I know that I never told you enough about her or our love, but believe me when I tell you: it was out of this world.*
*Your mother was larger than life, the opposite of me. I was reserved at best, only had a few friends. You know your old man well enough. Your mother? She commanded rooms.*
*She was the axis which social gatherings rotated around. Yet, she made everybody feel special because that sort of influence never went to her head. Her purpose in life was to inspire others to be their best self.*
*You're probably wondering how on Earth we ended up together. Well, I asked myself the same question every single day. I never understood why, out of everyone, she chose me. She could have had her pick, too, trust me.*
*The day we had you, I stopped asking. I finally realized that even though we couldn't be more different, we made magic when we were together.*
*After her car accident, I didn't know how I would survive it. I was only good at math. She was the one who was good at life.*
*I had no idea how to do it by myself, and YouTube didn't exist back then.*

*One night, I was feeling so lonely, so lost without her, and I decided to walk into your nursery. I'm not sure whether it was to feel closer to her, as if her memory was forever etched into those walls we painted together, or if I just needed the company. But there you sat, in your little crib, the silver lining. The only other person I could love more than the one who gifted you to me.*

*I decided right then that it was all worth it. I would experience the pain and loss another fifty times as long as I still had you.*

*So, there it is. The topic of this letter. The task for this month.*

*I want you to focus on that silver lining, that thing which brings you happiness. If you're a better person than me (which I know you are), your silver lining will be something you generate from yourself, rather than letting your happiness rely on another person.*

*I think I might have an idea of what it may be for you, that thing which brings you happiness. If I'm right, I hope you run with it. I hope you design and create as much as you breathe. Make yourself happy with it.*

*I hope one day, you'll share that silver lining with the world.*

*I love you so much, Ara.*

*Love,*

*Dad*

*P.S. Don't wait until tomorrow because tomorrow is never promised. Find your silver lining today.*

I set the letter down before I ruin it with my falling tears. Once again, Dad is right. No matter how much I screw things up, when I'm designing, it all disappears. The fears, that part which isn't really me that likes to take control of my life, the worries. Designing makes me happier than anything else in this world. It's my silver lining. My purpose.

I stuff the remaining donut in my teary face and grab my keys.

Job hunting can wait until tomorrow.

Today, I'm going to Jane's Material Store.

• • •

My heart starts racing as I walk up to Jane's door, truly not able to believe my eyes when I read the sign posted on her glass door, reading it over and over and over. So simple, yet potentially so monumental.

**Help Wanted**

I open the door so fast, the usually soft tinkling bells slam noisily against the hard glass as I rush to the counter, where a young cashier looks startled, probably due to the crazed look in my eyes.

"Who can I speak to about applying for a job?" I haven't even gotten an interview yet and I'm acting like a wild animal. Awesome.

"Jane is in the back unloading a delivery." She looks me up and down. "You can speak to her about it."

Taking off running down my favorite aisle, I know this place like the back of my hand, having come here since I got my first machine six years ago. I turn the corner and slow down as I approach the back door, which is currently propped open to the alley behind.

A woman who is obviously well into her sixties is standing at the back of a big truck, about to lift a box which is so big she can hardly get her arms around it. The delivery man is standing about fifteen feet away on his phone, and I realize that if I don't quickly step in, she is likely to hurt herself.

"Let me help you!" I run to her side, helping to lift the box from the truck. It's so heavy that even with my help, we struggle to get it to the ground inside the shop.

She wipes her hands on her thick jeans and lets out a breath. "Thanks, I don't think I could've done that on my own."

Surprisingly potent rage floods my veins, sending my usual anxiety in social situations to a screeching halt. Most of the time I find any route to avoid speaking to strangers, but someone needs to say something.

"Excuse me for a second," I say as I storm back outside. I stomp right up to the delivery guy and poke him straight in the chest. "What the *fuck* is wrong with you!? Didn't you see that old woman struggling to get a box out of *your* truck? Your *job* is to *deliver* the boxes!"

He has the sense to look nervous.

*Good.*

"I'm-m-m on my break!" He stutters. "I asked her to wait for me to take my twenty minutes, but she said there was too much to do."

"Then don't make her wait! Put your phone down and help her." The look on my face lets him know I'm one-hundred percent serious, and he quickly pockets his phone and gets to work unloading the rest of the boxes.

The old woman walks out with a curious look and approaches me. She probably heard me swearing, and even worse, refer to her as *old*, making me instantly regret my word choice. "I'm sorry if you heard all of that, I just couldn't believe his audacity."

"That's quite all right. It seems I've lost some of my fire, seeing as though I didn't think to tell him off myself." She smiles at me and holds out her hand. "My name is Jane."

*Shit.*

She's *never* going to hire me after witnessing that tantrum. All the same, I'm honored to finally meet the woman behind such an incredible store. I happily take her hand. "It's nice to meet you, Jane, I'm Ara. I've been coming to your store for a long time."

"And what were you doing all the way back here to witness that?"

Cue anxiety.

"I was actually looking for you." I look down sheepishly. "The girl at the front said you were the one to speak to about the job opening."

"Well, good. It's yours if you want it," Jane says plainly.

Coming in prepared to get down on my hands and knees for this job, her easy statement has me questioning if it's time to get my ears checked. "It is?"

"Yes, if you want it, the position is yours."

"Don't you want to ask about my qualifications? Or speak to references?" The only reference I have is Karen, and I have no qualifications to work in retail. I always find a way to shoot myself in my foot, and here I go again, safety off.

Jane laughs. "You just told me that you've been coming here for years, so I assume you have some affinity for the arts. You have no issue telling people what to do." She motions back toward the delivery guy who is now hard at work. "Plus, you knew your way around here well enough to find me, so it'll save time on having to show you around. Seems like all I need to know."

I'm shocked stupid, but I try my best not to show it.

Jane doesn't realize that telling off the delivery guy was a once-in-a-lifetime moment, spurred by anger, which was totally out of character for me.

But sitting here, listing the reasons why I don't think I'm right for the job isn't going to get me anywhere. If I end up sucking, she can just fire me. I'll make sure not to do irreversible damage while I'm here, no harm done.

"When would you like me to start?"

"How about right now?" She grins.

"What would you like me to do?" I want to get to work before she changes her mind.

"Let's unpack these boxes. I ordered a whole bunch of new textiles."

I smile so widely that the aliens can see it from Mars at the prospect of spending my entire day with textiles of all different types, colors, textures and calling it *work*?

Jane shows me to a storage room where I can leave my things, and she leaves me to stow them. I pull out my phone.

**Me: GUESS WHAT.**

I stare at my screen and hope that the first person I wanted to share this with isn't too busy. My phone vibrates before the screen even goes dark.

**Theo: WHAT.**

**Me: I got a job.**

**Theo: Fuck yes.**

**Me: GUESS WHERE.**

**Theo: WHERE.**

**Me: Jane's Material Store**

**Theo: OMG IT'S PERFECT.**

**Me: I KNOW, RIGHT!?!?**

I love that he knows what this means for me without having to explain it further to him.

**Theo: What time do you finish?**

**Me: I have no idea.**

**Theo: All good, I'll just google closing time.**

**Me: Why?**

**Theo: I'll be outside waiting when you get off.**

Play it cool, Ara.

**Me: What's on the agenda?**

**Theo: Obviously, we're celebrating.**

My smile widens and now the aliens can see it from Pluto.

**Me: See you tonight then.**

**Me: I have to get back to MY AWESOME JOB now.**

**Theo: Hey, Ara?**

**Me: Yeah?**

**Theo: I love this for you.**

Squeezing my phone to my chest, I spin in a little circle.

I want to send back an entire paragraph about how Dad's letter sent me here, and how I've never felt this excited about a job. I want to tell Theo that he was the first person I wanted to share it with, that he's become the first person I *always* want to share things with.

But all of that will have to wait.

I have a job to do.

Jane and I are utterly spent by the time we finish unloading the new material rolls from the boxes. There must have been a hundred of them. I welcome the exhaustion after having weeks of inactivity, but Jane looks like she needs to take a seat.

"Were you planning to do all of that yourself?"

Jane nods. "My store manager had to leave suddenly last week to go care for her ill mother. Of course, she had to go, but it's left me in a bit of a tight spot."

"That's terrible." Then one word, tucked into the rest of the sentence clangs through me.

*Manager.*

*Manager.*

*Manager.*

"Who is her replacement?" It can't possibly be, but Jane is looking at me like I'm missing something obvious.

"*I'm* her *replacemen*t?" I screech. So professional. So elegant.

"What did you think I was hiring you for?" Jane asks with a chuckle.

"Well, the sign just said 'Help Wanted' so I figured you needed someone to keep stock or something."

"Sweetie, one look at you, and that kind of job would be an insult. I can tell you're a designer of some kind. You've got a clever eye and you're brimming with potential."

Jane thinks I'm clever? That I have potential?

Like a nauseating montage, I can't help but run through all the times Karen spoke to me like I was little more than garbage. Jane has only known me for an afternoon and thinks more of my worth than I do.

For years, I've surrounded myself with people who belittle me, gaslight me, go behind my back, and worse. Somewhere along the way I started believing it was because of *me,* that I was lacking some ingredient, which made me undeserving of human decency.

*Fuck that.*

"You know what? You're right. You won't be disappointed," I say with the confidence of a boss bitch who believes it. I vow to start believing in myself right then and there.

"I know I won't." Jane smiles. "Now get to work, all the new samples need to be cut and displayed in front of the rolls."

"On it, boss," I say with a huge grin.

• • •

I've been so absorbed in getting the last of the new textiles displayed that I nearly jump out of my clothes when someone puts their hand on my shoulder.

"Ahhhh!!"

"It's just me!" Theo laughs.

Theo wasn't supposed to be here until after closing time.

"You're here already?" That's when I notice that most of the lights are off, which makes me even more confused.

Theo chuckles. "First day and you're already a workaholic."

He reaches over and playfully grabs one of my waves, which has escaped my top knot, giving it a little tug before placing it behind my ear. He's done it before, yet the novelty of the shivers it sends over my skin never dissipates. Every time feels like the first time, leaving me lost in the sensation.

Theo looks away from where he's tucked my hair back in place and meets my eyes. "It's almost an hour after closing time. I was waiting patiently in my car, but I wanted to make sure you hadn't been kidnapped."

I had no idea what time it was. "Theo, I'm so sorry that I kept you waiting, Jane gave me this task, and I really wanted to finish it."

"Do you want some help?"

I genuinely expect to wake up one of these days and realize that everything with Theo has been a sick trick of my imagination. "I don't have much more to do, but that would be great."

He nods. "Tell me where you want me."

I can think of lots of places, starting with him pressing me against these shelves, but that is NOT why we are here. "Okay, see those little squares I've cut and set in front of the shelves? They need to go into the little plastic frame displays in front of their matching rolls."

"Got it." Theo moves to get started. "So, how was your first day?"

"It was *amazing*. It was... a total fluke that I came by today. I got a sudden inspiration for another project, and came to get the supplies, and there was a sign on the door which said they needed help. Turns out 'help' was actually a manager position, and Jane wanted me for it."

"That's incredible."

"You're not surprised?"

"Surprised about what?"

"That she hired me as a manager?"

"I think it's the best decision she's ever made for this place. You'll love it like your own."

It must be because Theo wields words for a living, but damn is he good with them. His sincerity leaves me speechless, and a comfortable silence settles between us as we finish our work. With double the hands, it doesn't take long at all.

Once we wrap up, I grab my stuff and the bag of old material I asked Jane if I could keep. I'm about to head off with Theo when I realize that I have no idea how to lock up.

"I'll wait outside." Theo heads toward the entrance, giving me the space to sort through my first day.

"Okay, I'll only be a minute." Walking to the back, where I presume Jane's office would be. I find her with her glasses on, scrunching over some old beat-up notebooks, knocking softly to make her aware of my presence.

She looks up, shocked, and glances at the clock. "You're still here? You should have left over an hour ago!"

"I wanted to make sure I got all the textiles displayed."

"Ara, I didn't expect you to stay late to do it," she says in a sweet, but chastising, tone. With her silvery hair, soft eyes, and firm stance, she reminds me of the grandmotherly figure I've always wanted.

"I know, but I have trouble walking away from an unfinished project."

Jane smiles. "I understand that quite well."

"I'm heading out now, I just wanted to make sure there was someone here to lock up because I have no idea how."

"Of course, darling. I'll close up on my way out."

"Okay, then. See you tomorrow, Jane."

"See you tomorrow, Ara."

Walking back through the store, I admire everything in a new light. This is all mine to manage and care for. *My* responsibility. The most beautiful place in existence has been entrusted to *me*.

I give it one last look and step out into the cool evening air, finding Theo propped against the passenger door of his car, patiently waiting. A modern Prince Charming. He smiles so wide, I'm back at the top of that roller coaster, waiting for the fall.

"What's in the bag?" he asks, always curious.

I look down thoughtfully at the giant bag full of material. "My next project."

Theo waits.

I know Dad didn't mean it in the literal sense, but in the end that's what came to mind. A beautiful piece, made from dark material, sheer enough to see the silver lining beneath. A physical representation of being able to find that bright side despite whatever darkness tries to conceal it.

"I'm simply making something with a silver lining."

# CHAPTER EIGHTEEN

*Present - Ara*

Theo takes us to a cute little town about fifteen minutes from Jane's. I pestered him throughout the entire car ride to find out where we were going, but he insisted on keeping it a surprise. He pulls into the first parking lot we come across and finds a spot immediately.

The gravel crunches beneath my feet as I awkwardly lift myself out of the car. We've parked in a free city space, which means it isn't particularly well cared for. Instead of cement, it's laid with rocks and there's overfilled dumpsters along one side. I look around for any clue as to where we are going, but don't find any.

"My surprise is an empty parking lot?" I tease, shutting my door.

"You're hilarious." Theo wanders over to my side, getting closer and closer. His warmth permeates my right side as his breath caresses my ear. "Walking down Main Street, to *get* to your surprise, is part of the experience."

Theo is close enough that with a tilt of my jaw and lift of my toes, I could kiss him. The edges of his clothes graze mine, as he braces his right hand on the car next to my head, leaning in a bit more. I close my eyes for a moment, wanting to be covered in his incredible scent. A distant part of myself wonders if that's how dogs feel, right before they roll in shit.

My eyes open, wandering over his perfect lips, down his throat and muscled chest. They travel to his wide shoulders and corded arms, to the hand resting next to my head. One look at that hand, and it's impossible not to imagine what those fingers could be capable of. I clench my jaw, swearing not to make a sound.

Theo's breath picks up, grazing my lips, as if I've announced my thoughts with a megaphone.

That part of me, which isn't really me, suddenly opens its eyes. The mental panic crowds in, claws sinking into my flesh, telling me to shy away. This is real. This is dangerous. This could result in irreparable pain.

Looking up, I try to reason with it, try to push it out. This is Theo. It feels *right*.

Theo is nearly panting now, and whether it's from desire or restraint, I'm not sure. His eyes are locked on my lips, and I'm using everything I have to overcome the anxious beast who is trying to steal this moment from us. While I silently will him to close that tiny distance, and give us what we're both craving, the beast reminds me of everything I have to lose.

Always the gentleman, Theo's eyes slowly climb up to mine seeking permission. A torturously long second crawls forward, indecision touching his eyes, my heart slamming against my ribs. Unsure of what outcome I'm hoping for, I hold my breath and wet my lips.

Except whatever he finds in my expression has him pulling back.

Like a douse of cold water, chill night air rushes back in and bursts our little bubble. I want to tell him to wait. I want to grab him and slam him against the car. I want him to pick me up so I can wrap my legs around his waist, while I press my lips to his and see how we fit. I want his hands all over me, feeling every inch of my body which burns for him.

Instead, he clears his throat, reaching down to yank my cardigan from where I didn't notice it'd been caught. "Your sweater was stuck in the door."

Lit on fire by his eyes alone, I don't know what will happen when he finally touches me, but a voice in the back of my head stops me from asking him to. Whatever his reason for pulling back, Theo has always given me the space I need, and I trust him.

So, I close the distance between us once again, but instead of dragging my nails down his back, I hook my arm around his. "Lead the way. I want my surprise."

His smile, accompanied by stormy eyes which haven't quite sobered and the sound of our crunching steps, are his only answer.

After a few minutes of walking down Main Street, I start to recognize where we are. Blake used to drag me here all the time to one of his favorite restaurants, which is just across the road from where we are now, and I silently plead that it's not where we're going.

I personally didn't love the place. The menu changes every night, never giving me something to look forward to, which is hard for me, being an emotional eater that chooses my meals based on my mood. Blake said it was because I'm uncultured and immature, but I just prefer knowing a restaurant will have something I like, or at the very least, chicken tenders to fall back on.

Okay, maybe I am a little uncultured and immature.

Theo indicates for us to cross the road, and I work hard to keep my cringe internal. Aside from not particularly enjoying the food, I don't want to spend a night with Theo in a place where bad memories of Blake will inevitably shadow us. Plus, there is always the unlikely, but still possible, risk of running into Blake. Maybe even Katie, too, if they're still hooking up.

"We're here," Theo announces. Dread seeps into my stomach as I look up and see that we're standing right outside of Blake's favorite restaurant. "It's the best Mexican food I've ever had aside from the food *in* Mexico, so I promise that it's worth the wait."

Relief washes over me as I realize we're waiting in a small line for the restaurant next door, not entering the one we've stopped in front of, and I chide myself for doubting him.

"This is perfect." I want to squeal and jump into his arms, but I settle for the appreciation I can show without stepping too far outside my comfort zone: a warm smile and gratitude shining.

Theo grins. "Just wait until you take your first bite of their loaded chicken nachos."

"I'll probably have the most intense food-gasm any girl has ever had. I'll probably have to get down on my knees for you after." The words are out before I notice the innuendo.

Theo's mouth drops open, literally *drops* open as the words which just tumbled from my mouth turn into a flashing neon sign in my mind.

*Get. On. My. Knees.*

"I, I, uh, I meant getting on my knees to *thank* you, like a *worship*...okay, I'm making it worse. I didn't mean it like that."

A blush creeps up my neck, covering every inch of skin up to my scalp before Theo finally frees himself from his stupefaction and bursts into laughter, giving me a little wink. "Of course not."

It doesn't escape me that Theo didn't seem to mind the suggestion *had* I meant it, but I'm in dangerous waters, toeing this line of friendship with him. A mental affirmation is in order, and I make one. Or four.

I won't take it any further tonight. No more teasing. No more touching. No more innuendos.

This ever-present pull between us has gotten stronger. Theo has been a good friend to me. I *should* trust him, and maybe it seems ridiculous that I'm still not sure if I do. But beyond that, I don't trust *myself*. I *want* to let him in. I *want* to trust him. Then, that voice in the back of my head pipes up.

*What if it turns out to be just another bad choice in my portfolio of bad choices? What if taking this leap becomes the thing that breaks me beyond repair?*

The voice is silenced when we finally get a table, and wow, he was not over-selling this place. While we wait for our food, I admire the authentic Mexican décor and live music which emanates from a band in the corner. Fresh tortilla chips and pico de gallo are placed on our table, my mouth instantly watering.

Our food arrives just as I've reached the bottom of the basket, and it's a moment that alters my very makeup. The nachos are nothing short of *fucking* phenomenal.

"Theo. You've ruined my life."

He stops chewing his burrito. "How?"

"Now that I know this place is here, I'm going to spend all my money on gas and food to have it."

Theo smiles around his mouth full. "We can carpool."

After another bite layered with the perfect amount of toppings, I moan so loudly that other tables send us curious glances. The better version of me, which comes out a little more each time I'm with Theo, takes over, as I lean in. "You'd think a girl could get some privacy for her food-gasm."

I'm awarded with another laugh. Not sure where this person has been hiding, but I love her. Having never made anyone laugh besides Dad, every grin and chuckle becomes something novel for me, a gift for the girl who isn't afraid to put some of her humor into the world.

"Maybe if you take your nachos to the bathroom, you'll have some more privacy to *finish*." Theo's eyes dance, flirtation laced through his words.

A clever comeback (which sends my earlier affirmation about innuendos straight to the back of my mind) burns my tongue just as my phone starts to ring.

Saved by the bell. "Sorry, let me just check who it is."

*Do Not Answer*

Dad's lawyer, again. I've been dodging his emails and letters for weeks, so I guess he's resorted to calling me at all hours of the day in an attempt to get a hold of me.

"Do you need to take that?"

"It's just a lawyer who's been calling me."

"About your dad?"

"Yeah."

"Why don't you answer?" Theo's tone is so full of gentle concern, the question doesn't grate my nerves like it normally would but softens me.

"It just makes everything feel a bit...final." I glance up and find sad understanding in Theo's eyes, giving me the courage to share the rest. "I don't want his money or his things… I want *him*. And I don't think I'll ever be ready to go through his things and decide what to deem as garbage."

"That makes sense." Theo takes my nacho-crusted hand in his.

I grimace, noticing my fingers are covered in cheese and sour cream which will surely rub off on him, momentarily stopping me from descending into the depths of grief which I remain just millimeters away from at any given time.

Theo doesn't mind when I eat my food like a cave person, but this is another level. Rather than recoiling, he lifts my hand up and slips the tip of my index finger into his mouth. His lips are velvety soft, his warm tongue grazing my finger, up and down.

My body ignites. Every cell from my face to my toes becomes a painfully aware, burning inferno. Theo sees it in my eyes, as he guides my entire finger into his mouth, sucking until every minutia of cheese and sour cream is gone, leaving me absolutely fucking... something. He releases my finger, resting my hand back on the table as if it was nothing of consequence.

Theo brushes his jaw with his impossibly clean hands as a smirk takes over. "Sorry, I noticed you had something on your finger."

Toeing the line of friendship? More like an Olympic long jump right fucking *over* the line.

Trying and failing to collect myself, I refuse to excuse myself from the table like I want to, the way I *need* to. Theo raises his hand to call over the waiter, still smirking. "I think we're ready for the check."

I'm ready for much more than the check.

When I almost say the words out loud, I declare that I need space.

"I need to use the restroom to… ummm, to wash my hands."

Theo's laugh follows me all the way to the bathroom door.

• • •

Between the ice-cold water that I spent five minutes splashing on my face, and the brisk night air, things have cooled down enough that I can act like a normal individual on a walk.

Theo breaks the silence first. "There's still more to the surprise."

"Really?"

"Part two is just a few doors down." Theo nudges me with his arm. It's usually innocent, minus the finger situation at the table, but he always finds ways to keep physical contact.

Eagerly looking around to see if I can spot the next part of the surprise, I smile when I find a giant cartoon cow, holding up a sign which reads "Homemade Ice Cream." It's the perfect way to end the night.

Unwilling to wait another minute, I grab his arm and drag him inside. We decide to go with waffle cones since the weather is cool for once, and we'll have a standing chance to finish our ice cream before it drips down the sides. Theo surprised me by being a strawberry guy, and I very predictably went with chocolate.

Once we're back on Main Street walking in the direction of where we parked, I'm so wrapped up in this perfect night and the feel of my arm wrapped around Theo's, that I almost don't notice the familiar figure approaching.

No matter how much I'd like to, I'll never be able to forget that spiked hair and arrogant posture. Ice shoots through my veins as recognition strikes, the blood draining from my face.

I want to melt into the fucking concrete right now.

"Ara? What's wrong?' Theo asks, noticing the shift in my demeanor.

"It's Blake."

"The dickhead who said eating was unattractive?"

"The very one." I'm trying not to cry. "Oh God, I don't want to see him. Maybe I can just–"

Theo cuts me off by grabbing my free hand, lacing his fingers through mine. Feeling completely helpless, I look up at him, vulnerability on full display.

"Do you trust me?"

I do. I trust him with everything I have.

I nod.

"Good, then follow my lead." He keeps hold of my hand, gently brushing the back of mine with his thumb.

My panic rises, having no idea what to do or how to act, when Theo starts laughing and pulls me closer, dropping my hand so his arm can circle me around my waist.

Theo's hand moves up my back, reaching my shoulder before ascending to my neck, leaving goosebumps in its wake. His fingers stroke my neck, making me forget everything from why I wanted to disappear, to my goddamn name. I can only think of how his fingers feel on my skin as he begins to trace my jaw.

Theo cups my cheek and glides his thumb over my freckles with a reverent stroke. The lift of my chin happens naturally as I bask in his touch. This moment, despite being fully clothed on a public street, becomes the most intimate moment of my life.

It's as if he can see straight to my soul and wants every part of it, yet all I see is darkness. It takes me a second too long to realize that it's because I've unwittingly closed my eyes. They shoot open, not wanting to miss a single second.

It makes him smile.

As Theo's eyes lock onto my lips, I answer his with a smile of my own. He moves even slower than he did at the car, slowly leaning in until the anticipation becomes unbearable.

"Trust me?" he whispers one last time, close enough that his lips brush mine with the question.

"Always."

Before I can breathe, Theo's mouth is on mine. His lips are gentle, taking it slow at first, polite even. He's holding back, not wanting to overstep or use this situation to take liberties, but apparently, it's not him we have to worry about.

Kissing Theo is something I can only compare to drinking a forbidden elixir, taking me to heights I've never known, making me dizzy and breathless, unable to imagine coming down from this altitude. Down to my bones, I know that I'll never be able to live without it again.

How good something feels tells you in an exact ratio how bad it will hurt if it ends. Alarm crosses my mind, but my brain is no longer connected to my body, which has taken control of itself. I can only sit back and see what it does while reaping the rewards.

My hands travel up Theo's taut arms, memorizing the feel of him. I register that I must have dropped my ice cream at some point when I sink both hands into his wavy hair, not surprised to find it just as thick and luscious as I imagined. What *does* surprise me is the little noise he makes in the back of his throat, somewhere between a moan and a purr.

More. I need more.

My mouth opens for him, and thankfully he deepens the kiss, but rather than ease my need, a viscous chasm of craving opens within me.

Theo wraps his arm around my waist, pulling me closer, as his tongue slides into my mouth, no longer polite but hungry. For once I'm not stuck thinking about the mechanics of it all, his mouth becoming my beginning and end. I let my body do what it wants, taking what it needs.

Theo moans again, letting me know I'm not alone in this. He tastes like strawberry ice cream and feels like everything I have ever desired. My body didn't make sense being with anyone else because it was always waiting for him. My jacket suddenly feels too bulky, my clothes too rough.

Theo moves his hand to cradle my neck so he can deepen the kiss once more, and it's not lost on me that even in this moment of passion, he takes measures to ensure my well-being. His level of thoughtfulness is my undoing. I'm going to rip off his clothes and let him know just exactly how much I–

The sound of a clearing throat halts my thoughts. "Ara? Is that you?"

Mocking. A knife barely concealed by jabby humor.

Only Blake could be so self-absorbed to interrupt his ex from a clearly enjoyable make-out session. A normal person would have walked past and left me alone, but God forbid he misses out on an opportunity to make me miserable.

I begin to pull back, but Theo doesn't give me an inch of space, his lips remaining hungry against mine. He takes his time, witnesses be damned, as if he's not ready for this moment to be over. As if he isn't ready for us to remember that this isn't our norm, for us to go back to where I feel safe, back to being friends who don't kiss. For now.

With this kiss, though gentle once again, Theo is trying to tell me something, something important. I want to take the time to understand, to find out what this kiss means, but Blake has other plans.

Not put off in the slightest, he clears his throat again and adds, "I haven't seen you in forever!"

Bastard. He is a fucking bastard.

It's time I confront him, and Theo's kiss has given me the fire I need to do so. As if Theo feels my determination lock into place, he finally frees me.

Looking at Blake after all of this time, I can't help but wonder what I ever saw in him. Compared to Theo, his looks are average at best. Not to mention, his insides are full of the kind of poison which survives on bringing people down. Nothing but someone who's peaked in college, desperate for it to last just a little longer.

I take my time scrutinizing Blake, finally seeing him for what he truly is.

"You're right! It has been forever," I say, my voice coated in Stevia. It seems sweet, but yuck. "I think the last time we saw each other must have been when I found you buried inside of Katie."

Theo snorts beside me, but I know he doesn't find it remotely funny. He extends a hand toward Blake, all confidence. "I'm Theo, Ara's boyfriend."

I try to keep the shock off of my face at the unexpected title as Blake takes his hand. "Nice to meet you, man, I'm Blake."

"I know who you are." Theo doesn't bother concealing his venom, it's laced in his words and written all over his face.

"Where's Katie?" I will not cower around this asshole anymore.

"Oh, we aren't together."

"Shocking. You seemed *really* into each other."

Blake shrugs, finally having the sense to look a bit uncomfortable. "It didn't work out."

*Good.* I want him running away with his tail between his legs.

"So? Still in school?" I don't know how he does it, but Theo makes college sound like an insult.

"Yeah, I'm just about to wrap up my bachelor's degree." Blake struggles to find his footing, but I won't allow it.

"So you managed to pass geometry?" I ask, knowing how deep it will cut.

"Yeah. I did. So, what do *you* do?" Blake directs at Theo, changing from defense to offense, finally seeing that he's in unwelcome territory and that I'm not going to take his shit anymore.

"I'm a writer," Theo replies, matter of fact.

"What do you do for work then?" Blake is trying to sound cunning and condescending, but in competition with Theo, he sounds like a put-out meat-head.

"Writing *is* my work. I'm a published author." Theo glides. "Though, you don't strike me as the reading type, so I'm not offended if you haven't heard of me."

I snort, never wanting to be on the opposing team against Theo.

Blake, not satisfied with missing his mark, turns on me. The easier prey.

"What about you, Ara?" The sick twist I know too well enters Blake's voice. "Still living the dream as a college drop-out, working in a run-down café?"

I'm in shock for about three whole seconds.

Blake is resorting back to his old means, targeting my insecurities in an attempt to make me feel like I'm worthless. Getting me to question everything I want to accomplish. Showing me that I'm inferior. Making me malleable.

Out of the corner of my eye, I see Theo already in motion, but I beat him to it.

This is *my* fight.

I take every single ounce of hurt, grief, anger, and self-doubt that I've kept bottled up because of this gaslighting monster, throwing every single shred of pent-up emotion into the hardest, and only punch I have ever thrown.

# CHAPTER NINETEEN

## *Present - Ara*

My fist collides with Blake's nose, using all my might. Blake used to spend lots of time in the mirror, obsessing over his slightly crooked nose left over from a sports injury, saying it ruined his face. So I know how to hit him where it hurts, too.

There is a small crunch, and I have no idea if it came from his face or my hand, but it's the last thing on my mind as his nose starts to bleed. A cruel satisfaction spreads through me, having stood up to my bully and finally feeling powerful.

As pain lashes through my hand, I start to think the crunch may have come from my hand. I keep the hurt off my face, caused by both the punch and the sight of my dropped ice cream melting on the ground, ensuring all that Blake sees in my eyes is victory. "You don't affect my happiness anymore."

I look over to Theo, who's sporting the widest grin I've ever seen on him. He bursts into laughter, wrapping his arm around my shoulder and pulling me in to kiss me on the cheek. "You are my fucking hero."

Blake is too busy trying to stop the bleeding to form any real response.

With that, Theo turns us away, but before we get very far, Theo turns back around to face Blake. "Thanks for messing everything up so that I could meet the love of my life."

I need to remind myself that this is pretend, but my heart refuses to listen as it sticks to Theo's words with every beat.

"Theo…" I whisper, just in case Blake is still within earshot, as another bolt of pain runs through my hand. "I think I might have broken my hand."

"Shit, are you serious?"

"I heard a crunch, and it was either my hand or Blake's nose."

"Let's get around the corner and I'll check it out." He keeps his arm around my shoulder and our walk casual. "But my bet is on it being Blake's nose, you threw that punch like a badass."

I shrug. "It was time I fought back."

"I'm glad you did."

We turn the corner, and it seems there is a guardian angel watching over me as we spot a twenty-four-hour CVS directly on our right. We hurry across the road, and once we're in the light, Theo's fingers are gentle as they grip my wrist to hold up my hand for inspection. There is some slight bruising starting to form across my knuckles, but nowhere else.

Theo gently squeezes around my palm, lightly at first, and increasing pressure as he goes. Thankfully, it doesn't hurt, and he does the same to each of my fingers. They *are* sore, but the sharp pain from the initial contact has seemed to ebb.

"Can you try to bend your fingers for me?" Theo asks in that calm, reassuring voice that doctors use with their patients.

I go through and bend each one without too much difficulty, knowing it's a good sign from when I broke my finger playing dodgeball as a kid and I couldn't bend it at all.

"Okay, that's good. Can you move them all together?"

I bend them all together in a slow clench of my fist, the movement a bit more tender, but without too much trouble or pain.

"Okay, that's also good. I don't think you broke anything, but the only way to be sureis to go get an X-ray."

I look at the clock on the wall, which tells me that it's too late to go anywhere besides the emergency room. I shake my head. "No, thanks. I'm not paying an ER bill for something that's most likely not broken."

"Fair enough, but we should at least wrap it up for the night to make sure you don't injure it further. If it gets worse by the morning, you should get it looked at."

"Thanks, Dr. Theo, will do," I say with a smirk.

He smiles. "Come on, let's get what we need to wrap it up."

Theo places his arm around my shoulders once again, but I don't have it in me to tell him that we don't have to pretend anymore.

• • •

I boost myself up onto my kitchen counter with my good hand and get comfortable. Theo insisted on being the one to wrap my hand, even though I told him I could manage it on my own. Admittedly, I probably *couldn't* manage it on my own, but I was just worried about having more time for him to bring up certain subjects. Such as fake kisses and what friends do after such things.

Theo comes to stand in front of me, and I have to part my legs for him to get a good angle. Always the gentleman, he turns to the side so his hip lines up with my lady parts, rather than anything else. I'm not sure if I appreciate it or want to throttle him.

Why the *hell* did I pick the counter!? This is like the *hottest* surface…

Theo slowly removes the tiny bag of ice (manufactured from a CVS bag and stray cubes that escaped the big bags in the ice chest) which he had taped around my hand for the car ride. My hand is so numb that I wouldn't be able to tell whether it's gotten better or worse, but the swelling is still very minimal, which is another good sign.

Theo takes the elastic bandage and begins methodically wrapping my hand, starting with the palm.

"So, Dr. Theo, how did you learn to wrap a hand?"

He grins. "YouTube. I punched a few things as an angsty teenager."

This makes me laugh. "I will admit, this is the first time I've punched anyone or anything."

He looks up at me then. "It seemed like it was long overdue."

I know what he's asking. Theo came to my rescue without a second thought, and the least I can do is give him an explanation.

"Katie was my roommate in college. She was also my best friend." Theo's brows lift in a mixture of surprise and disgust as he connects the dots, but he doesn't interrupt. "Truthfully, she only became my best friend by default. We shared a dorm room and classes together, but that's about as far as our similarities went. She used to drag me to parties, and that's where I eventually met Blake.

"I was still hung up on my ex-boyfriend from high school, and I figured Blake might be a way to get him out of my head. I never planned on dating him because to be honest, I didn't even really *like* him.

I sigh. "After that first time, he became a familiar face at parties which I started to rely on, not being the most *extroverted* person. One thing led to another, and he started sleeping over, and Blake sort of assumed that meant we were boyfriend and girlfriend. I never corrected him.

"You know everything you need to know about the between. Our relationship was extremely unhealthy, but I was too much of a pushover to stand my ground and get out of it. Plus, I genuinely believed I was to blame for all our issues, and felt like I constantly owed it to him to be better.

I groan. "It makes me cringe thinking back on it, now. The red flags seem so obvious, but back then I didn't really acknowledge them. I messed up my first relationship, at least I always thought I did."

I don't tell Theo that he's the reason I stopped regretting my breakup with Cameron. I'd always thought he was the one to get away until Theo walked into my life, making me feel more alive than I'd *ever* felt with Cameron. Realizing that things with Cameron had been lukewarm, at best, showed me that ending it with him had always been the right choice.

"Anyway, I was so caught up in thinking that I made a huge mistake by ending onerelationship that I ended up making the biggest mistake of them all: staying in a toxic one." I had already been thinking about leaving college. I was miserable, having less than zero interest in what I was studying and not knowing what I would do with it. The only thing that had been keeping me there was the peer pressure from others to stay and the stigma of being a dropout.

"I thought Dad would be disappointed in me if I left college, but when I finally got the guts to tell him I wasn't happy, he told me he was so relieved that I was finally talking to him about it. Dad knew me better than anyone, and he could tell I had been miserable since my first day.

I smile, missing the way Dad knew me and accepted me. The thought cuts deep but doesn't incapacitate me the way it would have last month. "Once I had his blessing, I was planning to wrap up the remaining semester and then drop out. About a week later, my professor was ill and canceled our class at the last minute. I came back to the dorm early, only to find Blake and Katie in *my* bed.

"I told Blake to get out of her, my dorm, and then my life, packing my stuff right then and blocking them on everything. I never got the explanation of why or how long it had been going on, but to be honest, I didn't need or want it. I stayed with my dad until I got the job at the café and stumbled upon this apartment, and I've been trying to figure out what to do ever since. Until today."

"Until today." Theo smiles, sharing in the happiness which the night began with. A celebration for finding a job that I love. Theo is quiet as he finishes the wrap on my hand and starts with the tape. "That douchebag is even worse than I initially thought."

My laugh is dry, void of real humor. "Yeah, now you know why I haven't itched to get close to people." Until recently, that is.

He nods.

Desperately in need of changing the subject, I decide to tell him about Lou. "I made a friend."

"Oh?"

"Yeah. You were my first friend since all of that, and you made me realize that it's not so bad to let people in, as long as they're worth it." I look up and meet his eyes, hoping he knows just how worth it he is. "Remember my replacement from the café?"

He nods. "Yeah, the bubbly blonde."

I smile. She is the bubbliest of all blondes. "Her name is Lou, and she just recently moved to Florida. We started hanging out, and we've become friends. Real friends."

He smiles, brushing his fingers across the areas of skin not covered by the bandage. "I'm happy for you."

Seemingly satisfied with his work, Theo lays my hand gently on my thigh and slowly turns toward me. This is *exactly* why I should have sat on a chair at the table.

Theo grabs one of my loose waves, giving it a tug before he tucks it behind my ear, fingers lingering a while longer than necessary.

He finally speaks again. "You're screwed."

I have no idea where he is going with this, but I don't like it. "What do you mean?"

Theo takes his time as he reaches up and brushes my cheek. "This is the part where you inevitably fall in love with me."

A jackhammer has replaced the organ previously known as my heart.

He smirks. "I'll take your silence as confirmation."

"You're clearly mistaken. My silence was induced by how far *off* the mark you are. I'm not falling for *anyone*."

Theo chuckles. "Haven't you ever read a romance novel? We fake-dated tonight. Then we kissed and I cared for your injury."

Shit, he is so painfully right. "You're the one who's been stalking me since day one."

"I had my reasons."

Reasons he has yet to share. I need to play this cool as a cucumber. "It was *your* idea to fake-date. *You* kissed *me.*"

He gives me a shrug, all confidence. "I was doing you a favor, and don't act like you didn't enjoy it."

"Your moans told me that it was more of a favor for yourself."

"I'm surprised you could even hear that over the sounds *you* were making, right up until the point where you practically undressed me right there on the street."

My cheeks are flaming. "Were you also doing me a favor when you reached over and sucked on my finger during dinner?"

"Yeah. I told you that you had something on your finger."

His unaffected act sets me off. I stab my finger into his chest. "I will not be admitting *anything*."

Theo covers my hand with his and leans in closely. I hadn't realized how close we had gotten during our little battle of wills. He's pressed up against me and his breath is tickling my face. "At least you agree there *is* something to admit."

He pulls back, leaving me stunned as he walks to my door to let himself out.

"I didn't say that!" My voice comes out flustered, bothered, blatantly obvious.

"Let me know when you want to do something about it." He tosses over his shoulder.

"I have nothing to admit!" I yell as he closes the door.

I jump off the counter and swear.

How did today go from receiving Dad's letter, to my first day at an amazing job, to celebrating with Theo, to running into my ex, to losing myself in

Theo's kiss and punching Blake in the face? All to end with Theo calling me out for feeling something…more?

I don't acknowledge the double-sided revelation.

Theo has yet to see how stubborn I can be, but he is going to learn.

Though, I'm not stupid enough to think that after that kiss I will be able to keep resisting temptation on my own. I will need reinforcements, someone to keep me strong.

With a quick text to Lou, we make plans to meet in the morning.

Because nobody wins a war without strategy.

# CHAPTER TWENTY

## *Present - Ara*

"Okay, repeat it back to me again. We need to make sure you're solid on this." Lou must have been a drill sergeant in a past life.

We got up at the ass crack of dawn to meet at Starbucks before my shift at Jane's starts. Lou is currently drilling me on the new protocol to avoid all Theo-related temptations. I haven't told her the full story yet, just enough so she can help me get my head on straight.

She didn't even remember who Theo was by name, and I hate that it put me at ease having to remind her that he was the friend who visited me at the café. I guess part of me was still worried about having a female friend again, no matter how much I've grown to like her during our little Starbucks rendezvous.

"If Theo enters my personal space, do not put my hand up to stop him. This could lead to touching and further distractions. Instead, sidestep him and change the subject," I rattle off.

We've thought through every single scenario where Theo could tempt me into admitting feelings. I don't know what feelings I would be admitting to, seeing as though I haven't even admitted them to myself, but nonetheless I will not allow myself to get into a situation where desire gets me talking nonsense.

"Good, you're getting it, but I do see why you're struggling. Men don't do it for me, but if they did…*damn*." Lou glances up at me, slightly wary, gauging my reaction to her revelation.

She must think there is a chance that I won't be accepting. The best way to prove that her sexual preference doesn't make a difference to me is to move right along, so I do.

I groan. "I can't believe I'm outside of Starbucks, resorting to memorizing protocols against getting laid."

Lou visibly relaxes before wagging her brows indicatively. "Theo strikes me as the type of guy who sticks around until he gets what he wants."

Essentially what she's telling me is that this is hopeless.

"I'm screwed."

Lou winks. "There is *always* that option."

"Lou!!"

"I'm serious. I don't understand why you're so against having a good ol' tumble in the sheets and working it out from there."

Sigh. "I can't."

"Why? Is your vagina broken or something?"

I give her a pointed look. "No, my vagina works just fine, thank you."

It's because of so many other reasons. At the top of the list is probably fear. I'm not delusional enough to pretend I don't have *any* feelings for Theo. It just terrifies me how strong they are when they haven't even been given the chance to blossom further into a relationship. If I put myself in such an intimate place with Theo, I know that there will be no point of return.

Then there is the matter of stubbornness. It's not a trait I've been able to apply toward things like chasing dreams or pushing through hard times. It's more of a skill I use to get in my own way, stomping my feet over things that don't matter.

"I just can't. End of story."

"You two have the kind of tension that brings the damn world to war. Good luck holding out."

I frown. "That was oddly poetic."

"It's the truth." Lou looks at her watch. "Now, get your ass to work and make sure you finish on time. I want to come over before my shift starts."

"Only if we swear off all Theo-related topics. I can't have my world turning on its axis."

"Deal."

I kiss her on the cheek and jog to my car. "Thanks for the coffee, Ms. Love Therapist!"

Lou gives me the middle finger.

• • •

Work goes by too fast, making me wish that there were more hours in the day. I spent the entire morning with Jane, learning the inner workings of the store. Since I already know my way around the supplies, art forms, and layout, she taught me about accounting, stocking, staffing, and the million other things that go into running a business.

I've spent my entire life underestimating the people that own businesses. It amazes me how much they've had to learn, and what they manage on a day-to-day basis. Jane says that she will still oversee most things but wants me to get the understanding of what goes on behind the scenes, so I can better improve the public front.

My main function is to keep the store running in such a way that Jane has the means to stay on top of expenses. Since we are a small group working here, it also involves me juggling the responsibilities below me when needed. When we get big deliveries, it's all-hands-on-deck. If the register girl needs to break for lunch, then I'll take over for her to do so.

My favorite part of my new role is that I have the freedom to create. Jane says she wants me to treat this store like it's my own. I'm supposed to share any ideas on how we can better improve the store and bring in more customers. I never thought that running a business felt like an art form, requiring endless creativity. I don't know what they were teaching in my college business classes, but it wasn't this.

Over lunch, I sat down and made a list of all the different ways I think we could get more customers in. One of them really stuck out to me as a great opportunity, and I'm about to propose it to Jane. Even though I know Jane is the sweetest person on Earth, I can't fight the nerves which drum up in the face of potential rejection.

This fear is too familiar. I know the route it takes through my mind and my body. Usually, I sit back and watch as it takes over, making me freeze. Except, today is different. It is my *duty* to tell Jane my ideas, and I can't let her down this early on.

I wipe my sweaty palms down my pants, practicing my proposal over and over, as I pace outside her door. I reassure myself that she is a good person, that she will let me down easy and not go out of her way to make me feel worse. All

I have to do is tell her the idea, take the gentle refusal without crying, and my job will be done. I can go back to my comfort zone.

Taking one more final breath in an attempt to push my anxiety away, I knock on her door.

"Come in!" Jane calls.

I open the door and take a seat in the chair across from her, forcing my legs to be still and my hands to remain folded in my lap.

"I took what you said earlier to heart, and I have an idea to run past you."

She smiles. "I'd love to hear it."

I'm in the door. Mini victory. "I'm not sure if this is the case for other artists, but in order to learn how to sew, I spent countless hours trying to learn from YouTube, but it can only get you so far, wasting a lot of time and material on trial and error. I'd tried looking up classes for design, but could only find universities, no local classes which taught the basics."

"Interesting. I'm sure other budding artists run into similar trouble."

I nod. My anxiety settles slightly at her agreement, giving me the strength to press on.

"That's what brought about this idea." Deep breath. Wipe palms. Sit still. "I'm proposing that we start to hold basic workshops here in the store. We can ask some of our more advanced customers to come in and teach the fundamentals for beginning artists."

Jane nods quietly, encouraging me to plow on. "If that takes off, I was thinking we could also branch out into holding workshops for fun. We could hold classes for people who aren't artists, but want a fun day of activity. For example, we could arrange a simple painting lesson and provide the supplies and an instructor. They just have to show up and have fun."

Jane starts shaking her head and I halt, trying to figure out where I went wrong. She was nodding in the first half. Was it the suggestion of workshops for fun? Did I overlook something? Maybe she thinks it belittles the store to entertain non-artists? My anxiety pools in through every crack in my mental blockade, washing away all confidence I'd started to build.

Jane finally speaks. "I'm in shock and disbelief, Ara."

This is *so* not good. This is what happens when I put my ideas out in the world when I should've known better.

"In all my years of business, I've never come up with something so... *innovative*. This is going to take our store to the next level."

Wait, *what!*? She *likes* it?

"Really?" I say, way too surprised.

"Yes." She conceals a grin. "I want you to write down the proposal and submit a budget to get it off the ground. Whatever you need, consider it done."

"You trust me with your money? For one of my ideas?" I hadn't even thought that far ahead. Never in a million years did I think I would run with this. I planned to tell her, as part of my job description, and move on.

Jane laughs. "Sweetie. What you've thought of is nothing short of genius. I think it's the big push that this old place has always needed." She considers me for a moment. "I believe in your idea, and I believe in your ability to make it into a reality. You should, too."

I'm in shock.

Jane *likes* my idea.

Jane would pay *money* for my idea.

I didn't get rejected.

I put aside my fears, and it *got* me somewhere.

Somewhere *good*.

"Thank you so much, Jane. I won't disappoint you." I swear it to myself, most of all.

"I know you won't. Now get to work on that proposal so we can start on these workshops immediately."

I head out of her office high on adrenaline.

I fucking nailed that. I can't wait to tell Theo. And Lou.

But more than anything, I wish I could tell Dad.

It's the double-edged sword of loss. Harder times become harder, not being able to rest your head on their shoulder and seek their advice. But potentially worse than that is not being able to share the good times. Your successes. Your achievements. Your breakthroughs, after years of struggle. All I can do is imagine the way his eyes would fill with pride, how he would smile at my joy and wrap his arms around me in celebration.

I have to settle with the hope that somehow he knows.

• • •

After a lot of consideration, I've decided to make the workshops free until they gain some traction. It's a bit of a risk, meaning the return on investment would be dependent on the students becoming customers, but offering the classes for free will encourage more attendance. Once it becomes more popular, we can charge a small entry fee to keep them going.

The main things I need to figure out is how to get instructors and how to get attendees. I can figure out the when, where, and what later. The most straightforward way is to start advertising to the customers we already have, who are either already experts in their field, or people who want to learn. Plus, I don't need any money from Jane to do it. Just a laptop and printer.

I grab my phone.

**Me: I need to borrow your laptop.**

**Theo: Need some new material to work out the tension from last night?**

Theo will be the death of me, my poor underwear being collateral damage.

**Me: *eyeroll***

**Me: Are you free or not?**

**Theo: Jane's?**

**Me: Yep.**

**Theo: On my way ;-)**

I need to buy my own goddamn laptop.

The bell dings about a half an hour later, indicating that someone has entered the store, and my stomach drops to my feet. Every cell in my body spikes with awareness, as if my body is already so attuned to him that it can *feel* his proximity. I don't have to look to know it's Theo.

Closing my eyes, I try to clear my thoughts. I simply need his laptop. Nothing else.

"Imagining all the interesting things we could do against these shelves?" Although his tone is teasing, there is no stopping the shiver it sends down my spine.

"Theo!" I scold, slapping him on the arm.

Not thirty seconds in and I'm already touching him.

He gives me an apologetic smile, a ceasefire. "Weapons down?"

"Weapons down." I sigh in relief. "I need your help with something important."

"I'm all yours." His simple words send me straight to the top of that roller coaster, stomach flipping out of control as I hang just over the edge, ready to fall.

"Let's go next door, they have Wi-Fi and coffee."

I leave Jane a note, saying that I'm working on the proposal next door in case she comes looking for me. We grab a table outside, enjoying the last few weeks before the Florida weather turns into the fiery rings of hell.

Theo orders a hot black coffee, and I get my usual iced coffee with extra cream. I don't waste any time, diving straight into an explanation about my project. For some reason, I don't feel as nervous explaining it to Theo. I'm not sure if it's because I've already been reassured of its validity, or if it's because I'm always a little bit braver when he's around.

"Ara, you realize this is incredible, right?"

I blush. "You really think so?"

Theo nods. "You should share your ideas with the world more often."

I'm bad at taking compliments, so I wave him off and continue with business, though his words remind me of what Dad used to say. I never listened, but maybe he was right. Maybe people *would* like what I have to offer if I ever become brave enough to do the offering.

"I needed the laptop because I wanted to make posters and put them up in the store, one seeking instructors, and one to let our customers know that the workshops will soon be available."

Theo nods his agreement. "You should also ask Jane if they have any sort of an email list or social media profile. If they don't, you could start one to reach new people that way, maybe even set up a live stream of the workshops."

"I can't believe I didn't think of that."

"We make a good team." Theo powers up his laptop, opens a free graphic design program, and turns it my way. "I use it to put together book cover concepts, but they also have tons of flier templates."

"This is amazing, thank you." I start scrolling through the different templates, and find so many good options that I instantly dive in, starting on the first one.

"Take your time, I'll just enjoy the view," Theo says with a smirk.

I snort. "What view?"

There's nothing around besides a beat-up Toyota Corolla, empty parking spots, and storefronts. I look up to see what he's talking about and find that he's staring at me. His eyes have that sparkle to them, that special look reserved just for me that I haven't been able to decipher.

I can't resist the grin that fights its way to my lips. "Weapons down, remember?"

He puts his hands up in surrender. "No weapons, just my thoughts to keep me company while you work."

Theo let his dark waves do their worst today, with no hair gel in sight. I've come to adore this version of him. He's got a navy blue Henley on, with light blue jeans, both perfectly fitted, paired with white Converse that are impossibly clean. I can't decide whether his clothes are unusually well-made, or if he's just so wonderfully put together that everything looks better on him. How did he ever find his way into the chair across from me?

"Penny for your thoughts?"

I don't shy away this time. "I was just thinking that I'd never believed in fate before."

"And now?"

I shrug. "Dad always said that we are the masters of our own universe, but I never really believed that either."

"And yet?"

"And yet, neither explanation seems to help me figure out how you found your way into my life. Or why you decided to stay."

Theo gets this look on his face, as if he's torn between happiness and pain, remembering something that is as beautiful as it is tragic. "I think that sometimes there are many universes at play, not just our own and I think they find a way to overlap, changing our trajectory."

I mull this over and decide to ask what I've been too afraid to. "Which universe sent you to the airport that night? Why did you decide to talk to me?"

Theo swallows hard. "In all the time that you'd been sitting there, you had looked lost, devastated even, as if you were looking for someone in the crowd but couldn't find them. I was planning to get up and leave you to it, but then you smiled, and I felt my trajectory switch in an instant. I lost contact with everything else, needing to know what it was that made you smile."

His words...his *confession...* reach the deepest parts of me. "I wish you could have met my dad, somehow I just know that you would have *loved* him." My voice wavers, but I've wanted to share this for a while. "I know he would've liked you, too. Dad didn't normally establish much affection for people other than me, but something tells me it would've been different with you."

"Something tells me that you're right." Theo's eyes glass over, voice cracking as if he *understands* what the world lost when cancer claimed Dad. As if Theo mourns him too. He must feel exactly the same way about his mother.

Seeing his emotion is almost enough to keep me from realizing that I'm on uneven footing yet again. I've told Theo why I was at the airport, and Theo still hasn't revealed why *he* was there. "Why were you at the airport?"

Theo looks down for a moment, seeming to gather himself. When he looks back up, the twisted emotions from a moment ago have been replaced with a mischievous smile. "Maybe fate exists after all."

He stands to kiss me on the cheek, sending shock waves through my body, my cheek being the epicenter. "I've got to run. I promised Connor that I'd help him set up for his gig tonight. You can keep the laptop as long as you need." Theo walks away, leaving me floored and full of more questions than I have answers to.

What's bothering me the most is that I can't shake the feeling that he isn't telling me everything and I can't understand why he would have to keep his reason for being there a secret.

# CHAPTER TWENTY-ONE

*Present - Ara*

Lou bursts into my apartment, nearly dropping our pizzas everywhere. "Help!'

I rush to grab the giant bottles of soda and whatever is in the smaller boxes, garlic bread judging by the fucking amazing smell, as she stabilizes the pizzas just in time.

"I'm glad I had the right apartment. Can you imagine if I busted in, screaming at a naked old dude?" Lou laughs and looks around, setting the boxes on my counter. "I like your place!"

I think of poor old Melvin who lives across from me and cringe. "Why didn't you just call me to come down?"

"Um, hello?" Lou sends a puzzled look my way. "I needed to get it all in one trip, by myself, or die trying."

"Right, of course," I say with an eye roll.

I move to grab us some plates for the pizza as she opens the boxes, the aroma of carbs and cheese filling my kitchen. Talk of Theo is banned tonight, saving me from having to mention that I saw Theo today, and the fact that I broke our no-touching protocol in under a minute.

"So, how is it going at the café?" With everything that's been going on in my life, I feel like I haven't checked in on her enough.

"Honestly, I don't mind it. Dealing with Karen isn't a walk in the park, but I manage. I come from the South, which feels weird to say now that I'm in Florida, which is technically *more* South, but way less *Southern,* if you know what I mean."

I laugh because it's true. "Florida is its own country."

"That's what we say in the South! Anyway, where I'm from, people are both the nicest folks you've ever met, but also tough as nails. Teachers, bosses, parents...there's no messing around or room for disrespectin'."

"Well, I'm glad you're handling Karen much better than I ever did. I was worried I was sentencing you to something terrible."

Lou waves me off. "She's nothing I can't handle. Plus, I enjoy meeting so many people from all over the world."

"Why did you move down here anyway?"

"I needed a bit of change. *A lot* of change, actually." I can tell this is a sore subject for her by the shift in tone. "My family are amazing people, but they have very strict views on certain things. Love and *who* one should love is one of them."

I reach over and squeeze her hand. "You don't have to dive into all of that unless you want to, but I'm ready to listen if you do."

She smiles at me. "It feels good to talk about it, for once. I've never had a friend I could share my *true* self with."

"That must have been really hard." I wasn't big on friends either, but I always had Dad, who made it a point to be the best friend someone could have.

She shrugs. "At first, nobody suspected anything was different about me. I threw myself into school and activities, so everyone thought I was just a smart, ambitious young woman. And I was, but it started so I'd have an excuse not to go on dates with the boys who asked me out.

"About two years ago, everyone in my graduating class went to college, which I opted out of. My parents weren't happy and couldn't understand why I'd worked so hard in high school if I wasn't planning to continue my education. I told them I wanted to learn business through practical application instead.

"By that point, all my peers were in serious relationships or getting engaged. My mother, having pretty much the only daughter not spoken for in our community, started trying to set me up on dates." Lou lets out a humorless laugh.

"Even if I *was* straight, no way in hell would I have gone out with these guys. They were the *literal* leftovers. I told her that I wanted to get my life more established before letting someone else take such a big part of it, and it got me off the hook for a while…but last year the façade came crumbling down.

"We went to a big community brunch and this girl, Becca, who hated my guts since kindergarten, had had one too many. She ran into me and ended up spilling her drink all over herself, but of course, she blamed me. To get back at me, she made a big announcement in front of everyone accusing me of being gay. Once the words were out of her mouth, there was no denying it.

"In a way, I was mortified for having my secret come out, but not because people knew my secret, that was a relief, if I'm honest. I was mortified for giving that power to someone else. Even worse, to Becca. I should have been brave enough to say something on my own, years before.

"That night, my mother *begged* me to go on a date with a man, to quell the rumors. She wanted to make it all disappear." Lou sighs. "I know she regrets asking me to do such a thing, but I haven't been able to look at her the same since. She asked me, her *daughter*, to set aside what made me *happy*, rather than asking the community to be more accepting, all to avoid being a spectacle.

"I worked three jobs for the rest of the year and saved up enough money to relocate on my own. People were looking at me funny until the day I left town. My plan is to keep working for a couple more years until I've saved up enough to open my own café."

There is so much layered into what she just told me: fear of judgment, fear of rejection, loss of family, loss of friendship. I realize Lou and I aren't very different. Though I could never claim to know what she's gone through, I understand her. I want to remind her that she's made it. That she has me, and I love her regardless. The best way I can do that is to show her it doesn't change anything for me.

"Okay, but why the hell did you pick *Florida*? You could have gone *anywhere*!"

Her laugh is weak, but there is more light in her eyes than before. "Honestly, it seemed like the only place weird enough that didn't require a passport. I thought if there are people who choose to live in swamps and naked people getting eaten by alligators, I wouldn't stick out."

I burst into laughter. She joins in, until tears shed from our eyes. At first, they are the tears that have worked their way out after what she's shared, but they are soon replaced by tears of humor and happiness at the realization that despite everything she's been through, she can still laugh. We laugh and laugh and laugh until our stomachs are cramping and our cheeks ache.

When the hysteria finally starts to ebb, Lou continues, "I also read that Tampa Bay has one of the worst coffee cultures in all of America, and I figured I could start a coffee revolution."

"Lou, you might very well be a genius. There are like *two* real coffee shops…and seventeen Starbucks."

"I know." She's quiet for a moment. "Ara, I don't want what I've told you to make you think badly of my family. They tried their best to accept me. I think it's hard when you're faced with someone you love going against everything you've been taught about right and wrong. I think we all just need time."

"It's okay, Lou. I don't think they're bad people."

"I really did try, you know? To live up to what people believed was right, but after a while, I realized it's not something you get to wake up and choose, no matter how hard you want to."

"Don't ever try to change who you are for others." I grab her hand and can't help but think about all the times I should have taken my own advice. "You should also know that I'm a total hypocrite, and every time I say something wise, I should be talking to myself."

Lou cackles. "How are you a hypocrite? You dropped out of college to find work you love instead. You went against everything people expect. That takes bravery."

"That's not exactly what I'm talking about." Lou has been so open, so honest, so raw about her fears, it's only fair that I show her mine. "It's easier if I show you."

Lou follows me to the closed door, looking curious until I open it, revealing my designs. The first thing Lou notices is the dress I wore for Theo on Valentine's Day.

"*SHUT UP*!? *This* is the dress you wore on Valentine's Day? No wonder Theo lost his goddamn mind!!"

I snort. "Yeah, I guess."

Lou's voice is nothing short of awed. "Where did you find something so… sinfully elegant?"

Her word choice is perfect. Sinful elegance. "I made it myself."

Lou looks at me, silent.

Still silent.

More silence.

"You *made* this? Like came up with this idea and physically created it?"

I nod.

"*WHAT THE HELL!!*" Lou is screeching now. "Why is your stuff not *everywhere?* This is red carpet shit!"

"Uh, I wouldn't go *that* far."

"Oh, I get it now," Lou says, nodding her head. "You *are* a total hypocrite. I still love you, but you're just as chicken shit as me."

"Correction: I'm *more* of a chicken shit. If anyone put my designs out in the world before I was ready, I think I'd rather curl up in a ball forever than face anyone ever again."

I feel the beast below my skin start to rear its head at the sheer thought of it.

"You *do* realize that you need to make more of this, right?"

"More of what?"

"More of everything, but especially *this*. You need to make an entire wardrobe like this, toeing the perfect line between scandal and class."

Whoa. "This was just a crazy stupid idea I had one day to get under Theo's skin."

"And you think you're the only woman who's ever desired to get under someone's skin?"

I'm stunned into silence. Could Lou be right?

"I'm going to need my own version of this."

"You'd wear something I make?"

"Are you kidding? This is the only kind of outfit I want to wear from now on." Lou looks around my room some more. "Your other designs are just as incredible. I would invest with you, you know. Give you some of my savings to get your line started. I'm that confident."

Her confidence in me, the fact that she would share what she's worked so hard for with me sends my heart swelling. "Lou, stand on that stool right now."

She hops up without a single question as I begin to take her measurements.

I won't be taking Lou's money, but I will be making her an outfit that will bring people to their knees.

• • •

Lou left about an hour ago for her shift at the café and I've been working on the sketch of her outfit ever since. I cracked open a bottle of wine, got my favorite Fleetwood Mac album going, and lost myself to creativity. It's nearly finished. A few years back, I fell in love with this beautiful cyan material, but I couldn't explain why because it is *so* not my color. It's been sitting with my other unused supplies ever since, waiting for the perfect project.

Lou is that perfect project.

As I sketch out the design, I know exactly what it was meant for. Cyan is the perfect color to bring out Lou's eyes, and I have just enough to make her a three-piece matching power suit.

The material is one of the most unique I've ever seen. It's a thick, yet soft satin, featuring delicate floral jacquard designs throughout. The jacket will be tight fitting and tapered at the waist to accentuate her generous shape. The pants will be fitted around her waist and backside, flaring out mid-thigh to enhance her curves and small waist.

However stunning both those pieces will be, the bustier top will be the main event. Made from the same material as the other pieces, the cups will be perfectly sized for her generous breasts, keeping just enough to the imagination. I will add the boning in a V-shaped pattern to make her waist look even smaller and add structure to the top. It will end just above the waistline of her pants, leaving just about an inch of skin on display. Sinful, yet elegant.

My phone alerts me from the other room with my favorite sound. I drop my pen and dash to retrieve it. No point in acting cool when there's no one else to observe me acting like a love-sick schoolgirl.

**Theo: I better not be getting any new pop-ups when you return my laptop.**

Ha.

**Me: New?**

**Theo: ;)**

**Theo: Sorry for taking off earlier. How did it go?**

**Me: Really well. I already got the fliers up around the store.**

**Theo: Now you can add graphic design to the list of your many talents.**

**Me: Ha. I'm not sure how long that list goes.**

**Theo: I'd love to find out ;)**

**Me: Lots of winky faces recently. Trying to tell me something?**

**Theo: I believe that it's you who needs to tell me something.**

**Me: Why is it one-sided? You haven't said much at all.**

**Theo: I don't need to.**

**Me: And why is that?**

**Theo: Because I went to one-hundred-and-sixty-three places that serve coffee and food. And I don't like coffee *that* much.**

**Me: Stalker.**

**Theo: You're deflecting.**

**Me: I am not.**

**Theo: Textbook denial.**

I'm trying to figure out what to type that won't sound like more denial when I get another text from Theo.

**Theo: It won't hurt to tell me, I promise.**

See, that's where he's wrong.

**Me: You can't predict the future.**

**Theo: No, but we can write whatever version of it that we want. Together.**

His words feel like a promise. That if I decide to give him my heart, he will care for it. But that fear I know too well begins to roar. What if he is taken away, too? I wouldn't recover.

So, I do what I do best and kill the mood.

**Me: This conversation just got so deep that it's tickling Earth's core.**

**Theo: Deflecting. Again.**

**Me: GTG! Need to water my plants.**

**Theo: Your plants are fake.**

**Me: Need to feed my cat!**

**Theo: You don't have a cat.**

**Me: My neighbor's sisters' second cousin needs a ride to Greece!**

**Theo: Goodnight, Ara.**

I groan. I'm even disappointed with myself.

# CHAPTER TWENTY-TWO

## Four Years Ago - Ara

"It's Saturday night. Shouldn't you be out with friends, getting drunk, so I can lecture you about being more responsible?"

Dad is always worrying that I'm missing out on things that normal people do at my age. "First of all, I'm not old enough to drink."

Dad makes a face which tells me it never stopped him.

"Second of all, I don't like anyone enough to go out with them. They're too busy climbing social ladders that I couldn't give two shits about."

Dad nods, admitting it to be a fair point.

"Third of all, tomorrow is your birthday, and I want to bake you a cake."

He grimaces. "Are you sure you don't want my help?"

"I'm following a recipe. How hard can it be?"

Very hard, as it turns out.

After a few spills, mixing ingredients out of sequence which I thought wouldn't matter, and a fire alarm being set off, I run into Publix, making it inside *just* before they close, with Dad waiting outside in the getaway car.

I hate to be that asshole who dashes in five minutes before closing, but I almost burned down our house and still don't have a cake for Dad. By some miracle that can only be explained by fate, there is a pre-decorated cake, themed with *Ice Age* characters, and it couldn't be more perfect.

My greedy little hands latch onto it and run to the nearest checkout lane, getting glares from every staff member I pass.

*I'm running, assholes. What else do you want from me?*

APRIL
Dear Ara

# CHAPTER TWENTY-THREE

*Present - Ava*

It's April and today is Dad's birthday.

The first of many that I'll have to celebrate without him. I know that it's going to suck regardless, so the least I can do is to celebrate properly for him, starting the day off exactly how he would want: getting the usual from the diner.

Pulling open the door, I already feel comforted by the smell of freshly baked biscuits and coffee, as I find my usual spot and take a seat at our booth. Dad wouldn't want me eating at home by myself, and while I can't stomach spending this day with anyone other than him, I needed to get out of the house.

The booth across from me snags my attention and I smile. If it weren't for this diner and their amazing waffles Theo had mysteriously heard so much about, I probably would've never seen him again after the night we met. I would've never gotten to know this version of myself, the one who wants to find it in herself to be brave. The one who kissed her best friend and has spent the last month reliving the memory of what it felt like.

This diner holds something just as precious as the time I spent here with Dad. It holds my present, and what I'm starting to think could be my future, since the morning it sat in the booth across from me. Looking back to the seat Dad used to take in front of me, I reach over and stroke the table lovingly. It's time I stop living in my past, otherwise, the fears and failures which live there will prevent me from having any kind of a future.

"I'm not leaving you behind, Dad, I'm just accepting my new future," I whisper to his empty seat.

Moving across the aisle, I take my new seat opposite from where Theo first sat, taking a deep breath. It feels right.

Susan makes her way to my table with a friendly, but confused, look. I'm going to have to finally tell her. "Good morning, sweetheart! Are you guys changing it up for today?"

I give her a reassuring smile, just to make sure she knows I haven't lost *all* my marbles. "Actually, I think I'll be sitting here from now on."

"Well, okay then, darling! When is the birthday boy arriving? I'd love to sneak some candles into his waffles again." The memory makes my heart constrict. Susan manages to remember his birthday every year, despite him begging her to forget.

This is what Dad loved about this place. He felt the world was getting so fast-paced and commercialized that people forgot to slow down to remember people. Not Susan. I mentally prepare myself to deliver the news.

"Susan, I know I should have told you earlier, but I hadn't accepted the truth of it myself... even now." Her smile falters the slightest bit, but I force myself to get it out. "Dad... he, uh... he passed away. Cancer."

She presses her hands over her mouth with a small gasp.

"I'm so sorry I didn't tell you earlier, I was struggling to deal with it on my own and I didn't want to upset–"

I'm cut off by Susan scooting into the booth next to me, wrapping me into a hug. Something about Susan's embrace is surprisingly comforting, so I hug her back, realizing how much I needed it.

"You have nothing to apologize for." She pulls back after a minute, and her watery eyes look straight into mine. "Your father was a great man, you must miss him so much."

Eyes brimming and voice not working, I nod furiously as the tears start to fall and I'm hit with an undeniable truth.

Today is going to fucking suck.

Every day that he's not here is going to fucking suck.

"I'll be right back, honey. Please don't go anywhere." Susan gets up, heading over to the order station, and after a while, I see her coming back with two plates of food. She sets a plate in front of me, and then puts the other plate in front of herself as she sits across from me. "Mind if I join you?"

Surprisingly, I don't. "I could use the company."

"When did it happen?"

"New Year's Eve."

She shakes her head. "I had no idea that he was fighting cancer."

"Neither did I." Susan rightfully looks confused, so I explain. "Dad never told me about the cancer. Supposedly he found out just a few months before he passed, and there was nothing they could do. He didn't want our years of happiness to be tainted by the months it took for it to end."

A sad smile graces her face. "He always was such a willful man, wasn't he?"

"He really was." Stubborn ass is maybe how I would have put it, but it doesn't change the fact that he will always be my favorite person.

"How are you holding up?"

"I mean, I'm functioning, but I guess it depends on your definition of okay." I grimace. "I have a friend who's been helping me fill the time. You met him, actually."

"Is that the handsome young man who showed up here that morning?"

"The very one."

"He looks like James Dean."

"He does," I say with a smile, having always thought the same thing.

"You'd never forget that face, or that hair, or those eyes," Susan says with a little blush.

Something in the back of my mind stands up and dances, demanding my attention after flying under the radar for too long. Theo told me he heard the diner had great waffles, yet the morning he found me here, he'd said he already ate. He didn't eat a thing at the diner, but especially not any waffles.

What reason would he have to mislead me for his reason for being at the diner? Because I am certain that he wasn't here for the waffles.

"Otherwise, are you managing things okay by yourself?"

Susan's question reminds me that a world still exists outside my Nancy Drew moment. "I am, actually. Things were a bit tough at first, but I quit the café and found a great job."

"That's great news, but I hope you know that if you ever need work, you know I'd take you in a heartbeat."

"Thanks, Susan. I appreciate that, I really do." At least I have a backup plan should I manage to mess things up at Jane's. "But I really hope I'll make it on my own."

"Your dad was already so proud of you."

"I know, but I still want to do it for myself." I need to know that I can make it on my own.

"Ah, yes. That is the most important thing." Susan grabs my hand from across the table, giving it a squeeze. "You remind me a lot of your dad."

Bittersweet gratitude begins to fill some of the emptiness I woke up with in my chest.

Maybe today doesn't have to be as bad as I thought.

• • •

I was delusional.

Today is horrible.

Tied for the worst of all time, actually.

I've just finished an entire box of tissues and ugly-cried throughout the entire running time of *The Iron Giant*. We used to watch it at least once a year together, followed by *Ice Age* and *Shrek*. They were the only movies that entertained me as a kid, but were hilarious enough that Dad didn't mind watching them over and over. It became our tradition, even into adulthood.

We would sit down with a bowl of popcorn and say our favorite lines when they came on, never failing to make us smile. Today, they make me cry. Hard.

The kind of sobs that wrap you around a toilet and wrack your bones, leaving you sore from exertion. Yet no matter how much your muscles ache from the endless hours of grief, it will never come close to the ache in your soul.

The deep, festering wounds with no cure, no off-button, and no relief in sight. Just the terrifying truth that the hollow, excruciating emptiness which was once filled by someone you love, will never be whole.

I grab another box of tissues, hit play on *Ice Age,* and brace myself for the memories, the sad realization hitting me that they are the only things I have left.

• • •

Looking at my phone I realize that it's nearly 7 PM.

Time has seemingly ceased to exist, yet didn't pause its torment, the growing pile of snotty tissues the only indication it was passing at all.

Deep down, I know I won't survive if I stay in this apartment for the rest of the night. I decide to do something I've never done before, something that any normal person my age would do, but for me it's a cry for help ringing loud and true.

Finding the least detestable looking bar that Google has to offer, nestled into a rich area of St. Pete where the well-off trust fund kids hang out, I copy it into Maps to get directions. It's got a hipster vibe, and surely hipsters don't date-rape.

Let's give it a whirl. The night couldn't get any worse after all.

The bar is pretty far from my house, but I was right, it's nice. Everything appears to be vintage, and it gives off such a classic vibe that I can't imagine anything seedy going down here. It's not the sort of place that the riff-raff would frequent; though, after making the bathroom my first stop to clean myself up, I see that I could pass for captain of the riff-raff judging by my appearance.

Luckily, I wasn't wearing any makeup today, so there was nothing to streak down my face. I brush out my hair with my fingers, blow the remaining snot out of my nose, and hold my face in the cold water that I've cupped in my hands in hopes that it will reduce the swelling around my eyes.

I'm not really sure why I came here. I guess it's because Dad used to tell me these crazy stories from his youth, doing unthinkable things in unsupervised pastures scattered around Iowa. His stories were always entertaining, playing the part of a different person, before he had responsibilities that came with falling in love, becoming a widower, and ultimately being a single dad.

He wanted me to live my life while I was young and enjoy every moment and somehow, tonight in my grief-addled brain, that translates into going to a hipster bar.

*I'm an idiot.*

I might as well get some food and have a drink before going home. At least that way the drive would be worth it. The bar is mostly empty when I exit the bathroom and spot an open stool in front of a male bartender.

"What can I get for you?"

It's funny because a few months ago, I would have salivated over this guy. He's emitting bad boy danger without even trying, making it all that more attractive. His black hair is straight, so perfectly disheveled that it must have been done on purpose. His features are almost too striking, refusing to conform to what is believed to be beauty, and from the bits I can see peeking out from his sleeves and collar, he is *covered* in tattoos.

Full sleeves and a large chest piece at the very least. His pale white skin creates an even starker contrast against his black nose piercing and dark features. You can tell he'd rather use his body for expression, rather than what may appeal to others.

Yet here I sit, none of this doing *anything* for me, because a certain set of green eyes belonging to a witty gentleman have thoroughly ruined the appeal for me entirely. "Do you have food?"

"Yeah, but it's mainly just appetizers." I can tell he's bored here, hoping an interesting customer comes in to provide some entertainment.

*Sorry, dude, it won't be me.*

"That's the best kind." He passes me a menu and I look over it for a moment. "Can I have the boneless wings, fried pickles, and tater tots?"

He raises his brows.

"What?" I've had a shit enough day, I don't need someone questioning my choice in comfort food.

"Anything to drink?"

"Not yet, I should get some food into me first."

"Sure thing." He grabs the menu, leaving me alone.

Always alone.

Squirting hand sanitizer into a papercut would be a better idea, but I open my phone to pass the time by looking through my pictures of Dad. It took quite a lot to collect the few I have. Neither of us were into having our photos taken, but thankfully we still managed to get some good ones over the years.

It's crazy how a moment is captured, and as that shutter snaps, preserving the memory forever, you never know how much it will come to mean one day. Being able to look back and see the gleam of mischief in their eyes or the lines from their smiles.

My phone slips from my hand and I accidentally tap the top of the screen, sending my camera roll to the very beginning. A blurred video close to the top catches my eye, so I tap on it.

Tears flood my eyes as the unmistakable sound of Dad's laughter fills my little spot at the bar. Covering my mouth, I hold the speaker closer to my ear, letting the sound consume me. I had recorded this one night when he wasn't looking as he watched one of his favorite TV shows. Another moment I'd once thought insignificant, now meaning everything.

Tears begin to fall, and I know that I can't do this in public. Swiping out of the video, I open a picture of Dad as a young man in Australia, his 80's mustache never failing to make me smile, even now through the leftover tears.

"Who's in the picture?"

I glare up at the bartender. "You realize that it's beyond inappropriate to look at a stranger's pictures?"

He shrugs. "I would've looked away if it was your tits in the photo."

"How considerate of you."

"He's a good-looking guy, isn't he?" His question manages to slightly quell my irritation. Something tells me that this bartender has learned not to care what anyone thinks, and you either love him or hate him for it.

I haven't decided where I stand.

With a sigh and swipe at the lingering dampness on my cheeks, I turn my phone for him to see the photo better. "It's an old photo of my dad, and he *was* good-looking, though he probably never noticed."

"Was?"

"Yeah. *Was.*" I hate that word.

"Shit."

"Today is his birthday."

"Bigger shit." I look up and find his eyes softer than before, just slightly. Looking less bored and more empathetic, as if there could be a whole other person under that exterior, just waiting for the right person to lure it out of him.

He studies me for a moment and then reaches out his hand. "I'm Ryder. How about I get that drink started?"

I shake his hand and nod.

"What do you usually drink?"

"Wine." My mouth starts salivating as someone from the kitchen brings out my appetizers, placing them in front of me like my own personal feast.

"I think you need something a little stronger."

"Then what can you recommend?" I've never had a *proper* drink beyond wine or random mixtures at college parties.

"Leave it to me." Ryder walks toward his fancy drink station and leaves me to dig into my food.

By the time he brings back my drink, I've scarfed down both my fried pickles and boneless wings. The drink looks more like a piece of art than something you could consume, and it's so strong I can smell the alcohol from where he places it on the bar.

"Sex on the beach," Ryder says, a slight intonation on the word beach so I don't know whether it was a question or not.

"Excuse me?"

"The drink." He smirks. A tattooed hand runs over his chin, making a pass over his lips, almost like he's unaware of it. "It's called Sex on the Beach."

I'm a social invalid. "Right."

Ryder chuckles, but it lacks mirth. "Let me know if you need anything else."

And then, I start having Sex on the Beach, alone, courtesy of Ryder.

I can tell that he was *very* generous with the amount of alcohol in this thing. I've heard that bars tend to water down the alcohol to increase profits, but Ryder has done no such thing. I'm only about five sips in before the lines between my grief and worry start to blur.

Six more sips and suddenly I notice there is music playing, *good* music.

Seven more sips, and I'm swaying to the beat.

I've made it to the bottom of my drink and I'm quietly singing along, even though I don't know the words.

Ryder appears in front of me with a pleased smirk, but it's not *the* smirk I've come to love from a certain someone. "I see that you liked the drink."

"Yep, it was sooooo good." For some reason, I giggle. I mentally register that nothing was funny, but I feel too far away to care. "Can you make me something else you think I'll like?"

"Sure." He makes me another one, but I give him a little pout when he places it in front of me. "Why are you pouting?"

"That glass is *way* smaller than the last one."

"Try it and let me know if you're still disappointed."

I take a sip. This one is equally as strong and delicious as the last one, and not remotely disappointing. "What's this one called?"

"Cosmopolitan."

I take another sip. "Make sure you put these on my receipt so I can remember what they're called for next time."

"Sure thing."

You know, Ryder isn't so bad. With his looks, he probably has to act like a dick to everyone in this place to keep them at bay, male or female. And he seems to be watching out for me tonight.

"My name is Sarah, by the way, but most people call me Ara. You can call me Ara, too, if you want."

"It's nice to meet you, Ara." The typical words sound strange coming from him in his slightly monotonous voice, but I still think he means it.

"To be honest, I wish I wasn't so sad that I ended up in a random bar meeting you, but here I am!" A hysterical laugh escapes me, and I know this Cosmopolitan is packing a punch.

"You enjoy that, Ara." Ryder lets a small grin escape, just a twitch of his left lip as he walks away to serve another customer.

I'm finishing my fifth cocktail, courtesy of some random person, when I notice how busy it's gotten at the bar. I have to pee *so* bad, but I don't want to risk losing my seat.

"Ryder! Are you avoiding me?" I start laughing. Everything is so freaking hilarious right now, even though Ryder started playing hard to get after I finished my third drink.

I'm surprised by how many strangers have bought me drinks tonight, instantly becoming my friends. A group of guys even let me take Jell-O shots with them earlier. We sang "Happy Birthday" for Dad as loudly as we could and got the entire bar to join in.

Ryder gives me a disapproving look. "How many have you had? I know the last few drinks haven't gone through me."

"I haven't had *enough*, if that's what you're asking!" I'm yelling because I'm so happy that I met Ryder and I want him to know. Even though he doesn't smile much, I know that he's a good one.

"That's the last one for you. I'll be keeping better tabs, too, so don't try asking anyone else for drinks." Ryder's attention is snagged by a group of kids who don't even look old enough to be here who have just come in the door. They're the kind of brats I always see around the rich parts of Tampa Bay, in their pastel-colored Ralph Lauren shirts, and their Sperry shoes, as if it's the official uniform.

One of the boys nods to Ryder, and I follow his gaze to see Ryder's jaw tic, just before he leans over to push a button underneath the bar. The kids slip through the crowd, and push through what I didn't even realize was a door.

"Ooooo, what's back there? A secret party dungeon?"

Ryder gives me a sharp look. "It's a limited-access lounge."

"Sureeeeee, it is. I've seen enough *Law and Order*." I giggle. "Now, come on!! Whip me up something fancy, Ryyyydderrrrrr!!"

"No."

"Looks like fun Ryder has left the building," I say in a mock announcement. "It's not even the last call yet! It's only like 9 PM!"

"It's 11:30 and no, it's not the last call for the bar, just for you." Ryder sighs. "Come on, I'll call you a taxi."

"Um, I'm *not* drunk. I'm just having a *reallly* good time tonight...OMG! I love this song!!!" I know I was just saying something important, but Britney Spears just came on and I absolutely *must* sing this with my new friends.

"Paul! Steve!" I can't find my friends. "DEREK!!!"

Is that even their names? I truly don't know. Slowly standing on my chair to see if I can find someone whom I recognize, everything starts to spin.

"Shit," someone mutters from behind me.

Suddenly, I'm heading toward the floor, all limbs, as someone gracelessly interrupts my lying down time by catching me in midair. "Let me go!! I need to lie down and then find my friends!"

"Either you call a taxi right now, or I will," Ryder says in a no-nonsense tone.

"I thought you were supposed to be a bad boy, with all that stuff you've got going on." I groan, waving up and down. "You're more like a mother hen."

"Bad boy?" Snort. "That's funny."

"Oh, as if you don't do it on purpose. You've got all those tattoos and piercings, trying to scare everyone away." I have never felt honesty escape out of me like this. I want to try it more often. It feels...*good.*

Ryder's amusement disappears, replaced by a stern look. "Taxi. Now."

"Fine." I grab my phone and start scrolling through my contacts all the way down to "T" for taxi. There is only one contact starting with a "T," so I push the call icon.

"Hello?" They pick up after only one ring, which is impressive, but I'm not sure why they sound confused. Don't people call taxis all the time?

"You shouldn't be on the phone while you're driving," I chastise.

"Um....I'm not driving."

"Well, you better get off the phone and *start* driving, taxi man, or I won't be tipping you." I start laughing again and this time, I'm about one laugh away from peeing my pants. "Shit. I forgot to pee!!!! Hurry, taxi man!!! I'm at the hipster bar."

"Ara? Are you drunk?"

Wait. How does the taxi man know my name?

Someone grabs my phone from me and looks at the screen. "Hey, man, the bar is called The Swan and we're on 30th street in St. Pete."

I don't wait for them to finish talking. Instead, I run for the bathroom because I can't hold it any longer, almost ripping my jeans in half while trying to get them off in time. The relief is better than an orgasm as I lean my head against the toilet paper dispenser and close my eyes.

Everything starts spinning again, so I keep them shut. It doesn't get any better, so I groan, telling the bathroom to stop moving. It *finally* listens, right as the nausea starts to rise. Time disappears for a moment, leaving me feeling peaceful, until I'm woken up by my head dropping forward and I lurch upright.

*Shit, how long have I been in here for?*

*What if Ryder thinks I'm pooping!?*

I can't remember if I already wiped, so I do it again just in case. Making quick but efficient work of my hand washing, I walk back out to the bar a moment later. I was planning to head straight for Ryder to tell him it was only a pee, when I feel the beat of the music again, pulling me toward the dance floor. Just before I reach the crowded bodies slick with sweat, someone steps in my way.

"Good, you're alive. I was just about to come in there to make sure you weren't drowning in your own vomit."

"I want to dance." I go to push Ryder out of my way, but send myself flying backward instead. "What are you made of? Cement?"

I can't believe I've gone my entire life without dancing when it looks like so much fun.

"I think we should get you home." Oh my God. I know that voice.

Theo stands right behind Ryder, trying to hide his amusement. I start walking toward the dance floor again, but strong arms wrap around my waist pulling me away.

"Hey! I want to get my groove on."

Theo's breath brushes my ear as he lets out a warm chuckle. "Nobody says 'groove' unless they are certifiably wasted."

"I'm not wasted!" I still find it in myself to sound indignant, despite the chills he's sent over my entire body with his touch.

"Someone saying they aren't wasted is the biggest proof that they are, in fact, wasted."

"That doesn't even make sense!" I growl.

"It would if you weren't wasted," he whispers in my ear, close enough that I feel the softest caress of his lips, barely even a touch.

The arms around my waist loosen just slightly, so he can drag his hands to my hips. I'm not sure whether it's because he's afraid to let go in case I make a run for it—or pass out—or if he just can't stop himself from exploring my body with his hands. Either way, a trail of desire is being left in their wake as he brings them to my hips, gripping me harder.

*Oh.* This is *so* much better than dancing.

Just as I lean my backside into him in appreciation, I'm lifted straight up and plopped onto a barstool like a toddler. Part of me wants to unpack how hot that was, but I'm too disgruntled about the lack of personal dignity to focus.

"Ryder? Can we get some water over here?" asks Theo.

"What are you guys friends now or something?" I say in accusation.

"I'd be friends with *anyone* who helps me get water into your system, but yeah, he's an old buddy of Connor's, actually."

"What a small world," I mutter.

Of course, I managed to pick the *one* bar in St. Pete where the bartender would be connected to Theo. The number of coincidences where he is concerned are starting to add up. Technically, this time I had to call him to tell him where I was, but still, I'm going to be really pissed if he ends up being a guardian angel or something stupid.

Theo grins, knowing my mind has gone to weird places. "How much have you had to drink?"

"Only a couple."

"Probably about ten if I had to guess. I only served her three, but she managed to snag drinks from others. Not to mention the Jell-O shots." It's like bro code instantly trumps any kind of camaraderie I'd established with Ryder.

"Sell out," I grumble.

Theo tries to hold back a smile and fails, setting those twinkling eyes on me once again. "Jell-O shots?"

I roll my eyes. "I was celebrating."

Ryder grimaces.

"Ah, I see," Theo says.

"Aren't you going to ask me what I was celebrating?"

"No."

Well, I'll tell him anyway.

"It's Dad's birthday." Somewhere distant, I register that I should feel sad, but I don't. I hope this weightlessness never ends. "And you can take your pity and shove it where the sun doesn't shine. I'm having the best night of my life!"

I yell a loud whoop toward the dance floor and they give me a loud whoop back. "See!"

Theo picks up the cup of water Ryder brought and puts it in front of me. "Drink."

I've never seen Theo in such a no-bullshit kind of mode. It makes me wonder why on Earth I haven't slept with him yet. I know it would be good.

"Why haven't we had sex yet?"

Theo loses his composure for all of two seconds before putting the caretaker face back on, like he's dealing with someone mentally unsound. "Because we're friends."

"So, you don't want to have sex with me?"

Theo looks at me meaningfully. "I didn't say *that*."

"Then what *are* you saying?"

"I'm saying that we are just friends, for now at least, and I can't wait to see your face in the morning after you remember how many times you've said the word 'sex' to me tonight."

"In the morning? Does that mean you're asking me to stay over?"

"I'm not asking."

"Does that mean you're bringing me over so we can have sex?"

"Jesus Christ, Ara. No, we are not having sex tonight." He stands up from his barstool and offers me his hand. "But we are getting out of here."

I finish my cup of water and it brings a sort of heaviness with it. Darkness begins to seep in at the corners of my mind, wanting to drag me under. "I have to pay."

Ryder appears again after making another round of drinks. "Don't worry about it. Tonight's fun was on the house."

"Thanks, man. I really appreciate you watching out for her. I didn't know she was coming out tonight," Theo says and reaches across the bar to bump knuckles with Ryder.

They should get a room.

"Of course, bro. Getting the girls into a taxi safely is part of the job description, as far as I'm concerned."

"It's good they have you then, I guess." Theo's comment is ever so slightly disapproving, and Ryder's jaw tics in response.

"Can you tell Connor I said 'hey?' That cunt never comes around anymore."

Theo laughs and I cringe at the use of such a crude word. "I'll tell him, man. Thanks again."

"Have a good one, guys." Ryder gives us a nod and makes his way back to the demanding line of customers.

I've gotten enough of myself back to appreciate the care that Theo has shown by coming here. He dropped whatever he was doing just to come to my rescue. This isn't the first time, either. Every time I call or text him, he shows up. Every. Single. Time.

The truth of it hits me with the force of a cannon.

I *like* Theo.

One minute I'm gazing at Theo, trying to get a handle on my gooey grin, and the next I'm heading toward the ground at record speed for the second time tonight. Instead of the hard impact of a dirty floor, I'm saved by solid arms that still manage to soften the fall. A wave of nausea crests as I'm hoisted up, cradled against Theo's dark green shirt, the only thing separating me from his bare chest.

Taking a deep inhale, I try to memorize the crisp scent I've come to crave. It goes straight to my head, acting like a truth serum.

"I like you," I say, tracing little circles over his chest with my fingers.

Theo's soft gasp tells me he's very aware of my gentle touch. "Tell me again tomorrow when you are sober and I'll do something about it."

I wish I wasn't so nauseous. I want those words to hit my core like they should. I want to feel the race of my heart and the heat he brings to my skin. Yet, all I can do is close my eyes and try not to throw up. The motion of walking is making it progressively worse. The bile starts to rise up and...*oh. Oh no.*

I want to warn him, but I'm afraid that if I open my mouth it won't be words which shoot up. Tapping him furiously and pointing to the ground with as much alarm as possible, Theo gets the message and sets me down just in time for me to hurl my guts all over the parking lot.

Instead of backing away in disgust like I expect, like he *should*, Theo gently wraps my loose knot around his hand to hold it away from my face. Another wave hits me, and Theo starts soothing circles over my back. After what feels like hours but is probably only a few minutes, the nausea begins to subside.

"You think you're done for now?" he asks gently.

I nod my head, not knowing where to wipe my mouth. He scoops me up despite the vomit, and gets us to his car.

"My car."

"Don't worry, we'll get it tomorrow." He shifts me so he's supporting me with just one arm, opening the passenger door with the other, and maneuvers me into the passenger seat without a single bump to my head.

"You're like a book boyfriend."

"A what?"

"Like Rhysand, or as close to him as a mortal can get, no offense. Don't feel inadequate or anything, he's just in another league."

"Who is Rhysand?"

"Or Thomas Cresswell, he's human, so that's more fair."

"I don't know who these people are."

"You remind me of them."

He sighs. "Okay, then."

Theo clearly doesn't understand that this is praise of the highest magnitude.

Once we're on the road, and I think he won't catch me, I let myself gawk at him. How does someone like him exist in real life? The longer I look at him, the more painful it gets. The tight, constricting pressure pushes harder and harder on my chest. I can't tell whether I'm on the brink of a medical emergency, or if this is what it feels like to realize you're falling.

I need to tell him.

He *needs* to know.

"I *like* you."

He looks over at me, smiling when he meets my gaze. "So you have said. But I hope you remember to tell me again tomorrow."

Maybe I'm still a little drunk, but I couldn't be more honest. I've been lying to us both every day until now, but *especially* to myself. Tonight, I've found clarity, but if he wants to hear it tomorrow, then I'll tell him tomorrow.

I'll say: I like you, Theo. *Do* something about it.

I repeat the words over and over in my head, just to be sure that I won't forget…at least I do until unconsciousness drags me under.

# CHAPTER TWENTY-FOUR

## *Present - Ara*

Paradoxical.

*Dictionary.com* defines it as: "A statement or proposition that seems self-contradictory or absurd but in reality, expresses a possible truth." It's a word I've never been able to wrap my brain around until now. I have, undoubtedly, the worst migraine anybody has ever had, and yet I've never felt more serene.

*Paradoxical.*

My bed feels entirely different. Softer. Bigger. My sheets smell different, too, yet still familiar, pulling at a memory far back in my mind. I'm wrapped up in this amazing scent somewhere between green woods and baked cinnamon goodies. I peel back my eyelids with considerable effort and startle, realizing two things very quickly.

First, this is not my room.

Second, I don't know who this room belongs to.

It's admittedly very nice, to the point where I'm worried that I've left a trail of poor in my tracks. The floor-to-ceiling windows let in the amount of daylight that I thought I could only dream of being surrounded by each day. There is a perfect cushioned bench in one corner of the room, making it the perfect spot to curl up with a book.

The walls are painted a beautiful light gray, setting the perfect tone for the black-and-white-themed décor and marble floors. My favorite feature, aside from the possible book nook, is the ambient lighting installed between the levels of the panned marble ceiling, lighting the walls and creating a stunning amount of depth.

It could be worse. I could have woken up in someone's basement... or a ditch. After surveying most of the room and deem that I'm not in immediate danger, I prepare for the worst and look down to survey myself.

*Shit.*

I'm wearing only my bra and underwear, which is standard uniform for post-hookup mornings, based on what I've seen in the movies and read in books. My entire body aches and throbs with the tiniest of movements. That's not a reassuring sign of innocence, either. I'm about to mentally retrace my steps from yesterday to figure out how I got here, when someone releases a gentle, contented sigh.

*Code fucking red.*

Holy shit. I'm not alone.

There is someone else in this mammoth of a bed, whom I hadn't even noticed until now because it's so massive. This is so, so not good news. I have no recollection of who is lying next to me, and per evidence at hand, lying together is likely not all that we did.

It's bad news all around when I realize that I will be walking the red carpet of shame in my Fruit of the Loom, strawberry print undies that don't even match my wireless bralette, which does *nothing* for my boobs. I should at least be allowed a morsel of dignity and get to sneak out with the illusion of big tits.

The fact that I have zero recollection of how I got here is beyond unsettling. When I slept with Blake for the first time in college, was I buzzed? Yes. Was I so drunk that I didn't know exactly what or *who* I was doing? Absolutely not.

What if we didn't use protection? What if I was bad in bed? Is there some sort of *protocol* for this? I don't even know where my phone is to google it.

I close my eyes and focus on my breathing. The last thing I need to do is wake up my... bed mate... because I'm hyperventilating and in need of CPR or resuscitation. I need to breathe, and I need a fucking plan. A *good* plan.

*Okay focus, Ara.*

The good news is that this bed is massive and probably expensive, just like those mattress commercials where the lady can jump on it without spilling her wine. I can probably just slip out of this bed, and my roomie would be none the wiser.

*Good, this is good, Ara. Keep planning.*

Next, I will need my clothes. I tip my head up and wow, this room is even bigger than my initial survey made it out to be. It's probably going to be a nightmare to find...oh. My clothes are right there, folded neatly on a... sofa? A sofa that's part of an entire lounge set, beautifully placed together in front of a flat-screen TV so massive, it must have been made just for that wall.

*At least drunk me has standards.*

*mental high-five*

Mysterious-bed-person is so loaded they have nothing better to do with their money than to put a living room inside their bedroom, because can you imagine having to actually walk to another room to get to the couch? The horror.

*Focus! I need to focus.*

*Where was I?*

*Right. My clothes.*

After I'm dressed, shoes will be a bonus, but not wholly necessary for escape. If I find them, great, if not, I'll live. It'll make it easier to run anyway, which I hate doing even with the best of shoes.

If I was as drunk as I must have been to lose my memory entirely, the next necessity will be a phone, praying that I didn't drive myself here. I'll call both a taxi and an Uber, taking whichever shows up first. Douche move, but also the most efficient way of escape.

It's a solid plan. It only requires each move to be made flawlessly. I can do this. I just have to slip my leg out from under the covers and take the first step toward my pile of clothes in the bedroom-living room...

"I can practically hear your mental gears turning in what is surely the largest freakout of the twenty-first century." His familiar voice is wrapped in a sleepy gravel that sends a warmth flowing through my body.

*Oh, crap.*

Suddenly, I'm begging for it to be a stranger in this bed instead. I'd even take Steve Buscemi right about now. In fact, I'd take *anyone* else besides who I now know is lying on the other side of the bed.

I had sex with Theo!? And I don't remember it? Fuck. My. Life.

Is the universe so cruel that our friendship could come to an end with a one-two-pumperoo and I can't even recall a single firework!? We should've *at least* gone out with a bang (pun intended) and the memory of it being my consolation prize.

"Zoosh...zooosh...zooosh..." Theo mimics the sound of machine parts turning and chuckles.

I let out a miserable whine and cover my face with my hands. "We did, didn't we?"

"If by 'did' you mean go to sleep without anything sexual preceding it, then yes, we most certainly did." Pause. "For the most part."

"We didn't have sex?"

"Of course not." He seems appalled and it hurts my feelings more than it should. Theo, ever aware, continues. "I'm not turned off at the idea of having sex with you, just the part of having sex with you when you are so drunk that you wouldn't remember it is one gigantic absolutely not."

Oh.

"I *don't* remember anything," I admit sheepishly, waving my hand over my body still covered by the fluffy blanket. "I was just basing assumptions on the evidence at hand."

"Ah, the undies."

I allow fifteen seconds to utterly curse myself for owning anything which isn't a sexy laced thing, and for *ever* choosing to wear something with fucking strawberries on them. "How did I end up with my clothes off?"

This question makes him smirk, as if he's remembering something. "You have yourself to blame for that. After we got here, you insisted on practicing a strip tease, with me as your 'choice demographic.' You said that if you messed it up at Jane's, stripping may be your only option, although you admitted how you have no stamina and how those poles look more difficult to navigate around than one would think. But you still asked me for pointers in case they make you audition."

If only a bolt of lightning could strike me from this planet and this conversation. I can feel myself spiraling, and sadly it's not into a vortex of water or anything else which would stop my breathing. Strawberry undies feel like a bragging right compared to this level of embarrassment.

Theo clears his throat. "You didn't need them."

"What?"

"The pointers. You didn't need them." Pause. "Your clothes were covered in vomit, though, so I figured letting you take them off yourself would be less weird than taking them off *for* you. For obvious reasons." He glances at me sideways. "By the time I came back from putting them in the wash, you had started vomiting again, so I got you to the bathroom and changed the sheets."

I cover my face and groan, silently pleading for this story not to get any worse.

"I was planning to sleep in the guest room, but I was so worried that you might vomit in your sleep, I sat here to keep an eye on you." He gestures to his position on the bed with a chuckle. "I must have fallen asleep instead."

"You are definitely the hero of this story—and I'm obviously the villain," I say in absolute mortification.

"That's what friends are for," he says quietly.

"Are you sure you still want to be friends with me after last night?"

"Are you kidding? I would be an idiot not to stick around until I get to cash in on the massively torturous favor you now owe me," he says with a wink.

"Whether it's cleaning toilets or taking you to the doctor while you're having explosive diarrhea, I'm yours."

"I'm obviously kidding." He's quiet for a moment. "I liked being the one you called, the one to help you."

"You're always that person," I say quietly, low enough I'm not sure if he even heard it.

He sits up, eyes searching mine.

It's not lost on me that I'm in bed with Theo, in only my bra and underwear, with him looking at me as if I didn't spend the entire night spilling my guts over his expensive belongings. His stormy green eyes bore into mine, the tension building with every second that passes, as if he's waiting for something, something that will put him into motion.

Adrenaline fills my veins, heart pounding in anticipation. The sensation is mirrored in Theo, as his chest begins rising and falling. His entire being seems to be urging me...begging me to *say* something.

I just don't know what.

When he sees the confusion pass over my features, Theo clears his throat and looks away. "You can have a shower if you'd like. Your clothes are clean and just over there, Connor must have put them in the dryer. Towels are in the bathroom closet."

It's not a dismissal, but there is something I'm missing, and I can't shake the feeling that I'm forgetting something important. I take a moment, racking my migraine filled brain, trying to figure out what it is. I look back to Theo, hoping the sight of him will stir up a memory while willing myself to remember.

But I come up empty again.

"I'll give you some privacy," Theo says as he sits up and turns his back to me.

He spent the entire night caring for me, while I was in my strawberry underwear, but gives me the courtesy now of turning around as if he hasn't seen everything already.

I can't fathom how someone with his upbringing can be so incredible. It's all him, too, having a horrible example growing up and being treated worse than any human being deserves. He could have allowed domestic violence and loss to shape him in destructive ways, but he just kept choosing to be a good person instead.

A feeling bubbles up in my heart, shooting all the way down my stomach and through to my toes. It's followed by four little words that jump up, raging at me to let them escape, to use my hands to express them physically.

It takes every amount of willpower I have to resist their onslaught. I don't know where they've come from, but they've risen with a vengeance.

What if Theo doesn't feel the same way? What if we end up so happy together for fate to viscously rip it away from us to no fault of our own? The truth is, the kind of pain I've only known after losing the person closest to me is still too raw to risk that kind of hurt again.

It would break me.

So, I close the bathroom door behind me as I push the words down, down, down, down until they're just a faint whisper in the back of my mind.

*I like you, Theo.*

# CHAPTER TWENTY-FIVE

## Present - Ara

There is nothing sexier than a guy having a spotless bathroom accompanied by products for a complete hair routine and skin care regimen. None of that 3-in-1 bullshit that Blake used to use. I mean, who in their right mind would use the same product for shampoo, conditioner, body wash, and in Blake's case, also face wash. My skin hurts just thinking about it.

I grab one of the fluffy towels from Theo's bathroom closet after exiting the shower.

*Shut the front door.*

How is this towel so warm?

I take a better look inside the closet, and realize the shelves are not just shelves, but warming plates. That is some rich people shit that I can *definitely* get behind. Installing this magical appliance is the sole acceptable thing Bill Carter has contributed to this world since having Theo.

As I get dressed, I have to pretend that my undergarments have also been washed, so I can get them back on without having a mental breakdown over the lack of hygiene. I towel dry my hair as much as I possibly can, but it's probably going to look like I've been stranded on a jungle-covered island despite my best efforts.

Whatever. Theo's already seen me mostly naked and puking on myself. What's a little rat's nest to round out the entire picture?

I emerge from the bathroom a few minutes later to a glass of water and Advil capsule on the little table next to where my clothes had been sitting. I graciously chug the entire glass and swallow the Advil, praying that it helps with the slammer occurring in my head. Hangovers will *not* be going to the top of my list of experiences. I'm talking zero stars on Yelp.

Walking out of Theo's room, I find myself in a massive hallway with about seventeen doors. Since I don't know where to go, I follow the luring scent of coffee because coffee is one thing that has never steered me wrong.

Turns out Theo used the term "apartment" very loosely. His room should have been the first indication, but as I step out of the hallway and enter what must be the actual living room, I am speechless. This is definitely a penthouse, and probably the most expensive real estate that Tampa Bay has to offer.

The obscene amount of natural light coming from the *two-story* windows sends a new wave of thundering through my head, but the uninterrupted view of the bay is so amazing I hardly notice. I register a staircase so modern that it appears to float, leading up to a large loft of some sort, taking up only half of the space above. The rest is left open, aside from a glistening chandelier, which could only be made from real crystal.

The furnishings are simple, modern and timeless, just like Theo's room. A formal dining room sits off to the side, with a table so long I can't even see the end of it. The other half of the living room leads up to the kitchen, and another hallway beyond.

I'm so caught up in the beauty of it, I almost don't even notice the dude standing in the kitchen with his back to me, presumably cooking breakfast based on the mouthwatering smell. He turns around just as I notice him, his face opening up into a genuine grin.

"Oi! You must be Ara." His thick Australian accent confirms exactly what I suspected. This is Connor. "Theo will be out in a few minutes. Do you want some coffee? Tea?"

"Yes, thank you. I'll have a coffee."

"I'm Connor, by the way. Theo's roommate, bestie, brother, whateva'."

Connor. The person who saved Theo's life. Even though he is a total stranger to me, I'm already so grateful that he exists.

"Nice to meet you," I say with a genuine smile. "I've heard so much about you."

"Bloody hell, I can only imagine what you've heard."

"I've only told her the worst." Theo appears from the second hallway closest to the kitchen. He's running his hands through his wet, wavy hair, fresh from the shower. I can tell he was in a hurry getting dressed because his gray shirt has wet spots on his chest leading down to his stomach from not being fully dry before putting it on.

Connor snorts, bringing me back to the present. "I'm whipping up some brekkie, want some?"

I'm glad he changed the subject because I can't even remember what we were talking about a minute ago. I was too busy gawking at Theo like I've never seen a man before. My stomach practically answers for me as it lets out a loud grumble I'm sure the boys can hear.

"Oh my God," I say as I cover my stomach, embarrassed. "I'd love some breakfast, thank you."

"Anything you don't eat?"

Theo answers for me. "She eats like a frat boy. You can make her what we're having."

"No worries," Connor says, turning back to the stove as I shoot Theo a look.

"Don't act like it's not true." Theo nudges me with his elbow as he passes to take a barstool at the kitchen island. I follow, taking the seat next to him.

Connor is about to set two coffee mugs in front of us before Theo stops him. "You need to pour about half of our milk jug into Ara's coffee, otherwise she won't drink it."

My heart warms at Theo's teasing tone, and the fact that he already knows so many small details.

Connor startles me with a gagging noise. "Mate, you Americans liking drip coffee and Starbucks is bad enough, but adding milk to it when it's already half water? A fucking blasphemy." He shakes his head in disgust. "Don't even get me started about the muck you call half & half..."

"I never realized Australians were so passionate about coffee." I try not to giggle.

"It's part of the culture," Connor says, dignified, righteous. "Your coffee is shit water compared to back home."

Theo leans over and whispers in my ear, "Why do you think I started drinking black coffee? I couldn't take this speech every time."

This time I can't hold in my giggle.

"Shut up, cunt. I'm not deaf," Connor says while pointing a spatula at Theo, as if it's a weapon with one hand, and holding my milk-doused coffee in the other.

Connor finally puts down my mug and I greedily reach out to take a sip. It's stronger than I'm used to, but the taste is incredible. Maybe Connor isn't totally wrong about our lack of coffee culture. Lou should pick his brain when she's ready to start her coffee revolution.

"So, based on the fact that Theo showered in another bathroom, I guess you guys still haven't sealed the deal."

It happens so fast, there is nothing I can do to prevent it. The coffee sprays out of my mouth, covering the counter and scarcely missing Connor. He jumps out of the splash zone with a maniacal laugh, clearly enjoying my reaction.

"Shut up, man. There is no deal to be sealed." Theo gives his friend a warning look, but Connor keeps laughing and puts his attention back on me.

"Is that true?" Connor raises his eyebrows, daring me to say otherwise.

If I'm honest with myself and everyone else here, I would love nothing more than to seal whatever deal Theo offers me. However, this is neither the time nor the place to say so. I look to Theo for guidance, but he's staring into his coffee.

I'm on my own here. Awesome. "It's true. No deal to seal."

From the corner of my eye, I see Theo relax, creating this weird sinking sensation in my heart. I shouldn't be surprised. Last I checked, throwing up your guts for an entire night doesn't get anyone hot and bothered. I just thought this morning, maybe he *had* wanted something from me. Did I read it completely wrong? The thought shouldn't scare me as much as it does.

Connor shoots me a disapproving look as he finishes wiping up the coffee and turns around to flip our breakfast. I look back to Theo, and he's still focusing on his coffee. It would be nice to have some experience socializing with fellow humans about now.

"So, Theo tells me you're a musician. What kind of music do you play?" They both notice my awkward change of subject with no relevant segue, but thankfully Connor takes the bait and launches into a detailed description of his art form.

When Connor turns around to scoop the food onto plates, I shoot Theo a hesitant smile to make sure I didn't totally ruin anything. He smiles back, and from what I can tell it's genuine.

I go back to listening to Connor and learn everything I can about Theo's friend. He's originally from Sydney, plays the guitar and has an alright voice (his words). A little rough around the edges and way too honest, but he has a heart of gold. I can tell.

• • •

After breakfast, Theo drops me off at the bar to pick up my car. My mortification still weighs heavily, but I seem to be the only one aware of it as Theo turns to me with a half-smile that has my heart racing and head pounding.

"Can we never speak of this again?"

"I'm definitely not handing over my license to reference this night." Theo slowly raises his right hand into the air, followed by the left, so slowly it looks sensual. When he slowly rotates his torso and head as if he's tossing long hair, I realize he is mimicking a strip tease.

"You asshole!"

He laughs. "I'm sorry!!"

I scramble of out the car, slamming the door behind me. His window lets out a soft whir as it rolls down and he yells, "Come on, Ara! I'm just teasing."

I turn back toward him for a moment, allowing him a glance of my blush and the hesitant smile, knowing he hasn't written me off forever. He grins and I struggle to keep my pace even, as the sensation of falling consumes me. I toss a middle finger over my shoulder before I get into the driver's seat and pull out my phone to text Lou.

**Me: I have a level fucking TEN girl emergency.**

**Lou: I'll meet you in 5 minutes. Where?**

**Me: Starbucks?**

**Lou: Girl, if this is a level 10, we are going to need mimosas, not coffee.**

**Me: I don't want to touch alcohol with a 15-foot pole right now.**

**Lou: Starbucks, it is.**

**Me: Oh, and make it 20. I'm not at home.**

**Lou: Oh God, this is going to be so good.**

**Me: I assure you, it is so so bad.**

**Lou: Stop, you're making me drool all over my screen.**

This makes me laugh out loud.

**Me: I genuinely just LOLd.**

**Lou: Bitch, get in your car and drive before I die of suspense.**

**Me: OMW**

**Lou: You better speed.**

• • •

I get out of the car, Lou already waiting for me with two coffees at a table outside, bouncing in her chair. There's no doubting that she understood the assignment, picking a table far enough away from others that nobody can eavesdrop.

"Okay, spill!!!" she squeals as I approach.

I drag the metal chair from under the table, making a sound that sends another wave of throbbing through my head.

"I don't even know where to start." I groan, taking a sip of my coffee to stall and gather my thoughts.

"I'll help. How about you start with where you just drove from and why you look like death warmed over?"

"I had to pick up my car from a bar in St. Pete."

Lou doesn't miss a beat. "Who dropped you off at your car?"

"Theo."

"Is this a puking trainwreck story, or a hot steamy sex story?"

"Definitely a puking trainwreck." I try to hide my face with my coffee cup.

Lou pushes it down. "What happened?"

"Back story, but please don't let this make everything depressing. Yesterday was my dad's birthday and I didn't have the best day, as you can probably imagine." Lou sympathizes, but not an ounce of pity crosses her features. I could kiss her for it.

"Shit, you should've called me so you didn't have to go through that on your own." Lou means it, too. She's the type of person who genuinely cares and wears it all over her face.

It shocks me to realize that I *could* have called her. I could have called Theo, too, before I let myself get to such a bad place. Instead, I tried to face everything on my own, like usual, and wound up in a less than ideal circumstance.

Is this the root of my problems? Not letting people in and therefore trying to face things nobody can face on their own and considering it a failure? "You'll be my first call next time."

"Good. Now hurry up and get to the puking part, because I'm praying that your story will be more embarrassing than my own."

I love her honesty. "No way that yours is worse."

"Well, spit it out so I can decide."

"After a whole day of crying, I decided to go to a bar in St. Pete and have a drink, except one drink turned into...I don't even know how many. Enough that I don't remember the rest of my night except for little tidbits. Plus, what Theo filled me in on this morning.

"I do know that I got to the bar and ordered some food. The bartender, who I weirdly remember was covered in tattoos and named Ryder, made me a couple drinks. He seemed like an okay person, despite his best efforts. After that, it's mostly a blank. I remember almost falling once and worrying that Ryder might think I had been pooping..."

A loud, snorting laugh from Lou cuts me off and I grin. Even drunk off my ass, it's such a *me* thing to worry about someone jumping to conclusions about my bowel movements. I laugh with her until she waves me on to continue the story.

"After the pooping thing, Theo shows up at the bar, and I think it's because I called him. I checked my phone history this morning and it showed that I called him just before midnight and we talked for about two minutes. I remember him holding my hair while I puked my guts out in the parking lot and then the rest of the night went fully black, like I do not remember a single thing."

"Okay, so he saw you puke in a parking lot? That's totally recoverable."

"I haven't gotten to the worst part." I will myself to keep going. "This morning, I woke up in my bra and underwear, which were not even remotely sexy, by the way, having absolutely no idea whose bed I was in or how I got there. No slut shaming here, but it freaked me out not being able to remember *anything*."

"Yeah, total date-rape vibes."

"Exactly! I'm sitting there having a near panic attack when I realize IT'S THEO IN BED WITH ME!"

"Nooooo!!" She gasps, utterly riveted. "And you can't even remember if it was good? One look at him and you can tell he would be an absolute fiend in the bedroom."

"Right!?"

"Right."

"I have no idea how long Theo was awake while I laid there losing my mind, but he knew how much I was freaking out. Can you imagine how awkward I would've made it if we had *actually* hooked up?"

"Wait. So, you *didn't* sleep together?"

"Slept together? Yes. Had sex? No."

Lou pouts with disappointment at first, but must think better of it. "I guess it's a good thing y'all's first time wasn't while you were drunk."

"It's a *very* good thing because get this: I puked all over my clothes and in Theo's bed, forcing him to clean it up while I was curled over the toilet." I rub my face aggressively as if I can scrub away the memory.

"Okay, yeah. That is disgusting."

"And Theo is such a good guy that he didn't even make me feel bad about it, he just took care of me and said he was happy to be there." Until his parting gesture, that is.

"The dude is a saint, I'll give him that, but it could have been worse. I mean, everyone has been so drunk they've puked."

"But," I say, cutting her off. "Not everyone has asked for pointers on becoming a stripper."

Lou freezes. "I'm sorry, *what*?"

This conversation is worse than when Dad tried to have the sex talk with me.

"I guess I've been a little stressed about my new job. I've never loved a job the way I do now, and I've been worried about messing it up, having to do something I hate again." I sigh. "It must have been worrying me even while I was drunk, because I told Theo that stripping might end up being my only career path if I do screw up, and I started taking all my clothes off to practice my strip tease audition."

Lou stares at me, silently shocked before breaking into howling laughter. We get looks from the people at every table outside, and even the people sitting inside stop what they're doing to see what the noise is about. I can't help but join in until I have tears in my eyes, screaming with laughter and stomach aching.

"You asked him... how... to be a *stripper*!?" Lou laughs so hard she almost can't get the words out.

"Yes!! I... *hate*... myself!" I can't breathe.

Lou is wiping at her eyes and trying to catch her breath. I've never had this kind of relationship with another female, and I feel a little more of my walls break away.

She finally gets her laughter under control, just as I think a few people might file a complaint about us disrupting their meetings. I take deep breaths, trying to fully sober up.

"Okay, I definitely understand why you never want to touch alcohol again," she says, wiping her eyes while trying to hold in another fit of laughter.

"The only thing that stopped me from shriveling up and dying on the spot was when he said I didn't need pointers." I widen my eyes indicatively.

"Didn't need pointers? As in, it was sexy? Even after puking?"

"I was too embarrassed to ask for confirmation."

"I bet that's exactly what he meant." Lou waggles her brows.

"I don't think I'll ever know," I say, recalling the weirdness at breakfast.

"How did you guys leave things?"

"We had breakfast with his best friend and roommate, Connor, at their, er, apartment." I decide to leave out the details about the penthouse that the HGTV hoe in me is dying to share. "Connor asked why we hadn't 'sealed the deal' and it got awkward. Theo said there was no deal to seal, so I just agreed with him. And...part of me still fears he's not into me."

"Girl, are you blind, deaf, or dumb? Theo nursed you all night with no expectations." Lou pauses for dramatic effect. "He's in it for the long haul."

"Yeah, but is he hauling as a friend or... more?" Why am I even worrying about this? I'm the one who has locked down any sort of feelings for fear of getting hurt.

Lou ponders this over a sip of coffee. "Does he seem like he's attracted to you?"

I think back to Valentine's Day when I exited my design room in my corset dress. Theo's eyes left a burning trail all the way down my body, and we made a deal just so that he could look at me as much as he wanted. I mean, the room had felt like it was about to combust if we didn't–

"What are you thinking about right now?" Lou asks with a raised brow.

I'm so busted.

"Oh, it's some juicy shit, isn't it?" Lou says with a grin. "That's all the confirmation I need. I'm grabbing another coffee for us both, and this time, you're telling me *everything*. I mean every single, *sweaty* detail since day one."

"Wait!" I grab my debit card. "The next round is on me."

Lou smiles and takes my card.

As she jogs in to get us more coffee, I recognize that this is the first time in my life where I've done the talking during girl talk and adored it. Of course, it's largely because of Theo, the star of the show, but it's also because of me. And Lou.

If I hadn't met Theo, I would have never had the guts to quit, which means I would have never met Lou. I have two whole people in my life now. The best people, whom I can call when I need them. I have *friends,* and maybe even one who's a little bit more. So I pick up my phone to send a quick text of appreciation, despite him teasing me about something that will haunt me for the rest of my life.

**Me: Sorry again for last night.**

**Me: You're my hero.**

He texts back before I even lock my screen.

**Theo: Anytime.**

"What are you smiling at?" Lou asks.

*Busted.* Again.

"You got a text from Theo, didn't you?"

I nod sheepishly as she sets down our coffees and hands me my card.

"Start from the beginning. We have exactly one hour before I need to get ready for work. How *exactly* did you meet Theo?"

I think back to that night at the airport when Theo was just a stranger. There I was, completely shattered from the loss of Dad, and Theo walked into my life as if he's always belonged. Despite my best efforts, he's never left.

As I describe our story to a captivated Lou, realization crashes through me, soothing scars from the past as it goes. I can't shed the feeling that Theo was sent into my life by some guardian angel. It's as if somebody knew how badly I would need him, and put him on the path directly to me.

I'm *not* alone. I've *never* been alone.

I hope Dad knows.

# CHAPTER TWENTY-SIX

## Present - Ara

The box of freshly baked cookies is sitting patiently on my counter. Unlike me. My leg is wiggling uncontrollably as I watch the clock move, minute by minute, as if the harder I stare the faster it will go.

*Knock.*

I'm moving before he has time for the second knock.

"Hi, Dave!!!"

"Hi there, Ara." He reaches into his bag with a smile, pulling out the light gray envelope.

I reveal the cookies from where I'd tucked them behind my back, Dave's smile widening as we make the trade. "You have a good one, Ara."

"You, too, Dave."

This month feels different as I close my front door behind me. Not quite contentment, but something like it. I no longer rely on this letter to be the thing which pulls me back from the trenches of despair. Instead, I can look forward to this moment with Dad with a small smile on my face. I brush my thumb over his handwriting, treasuring this gift he's left me.

"I miss you." My voice is a whisper as I clutch the letter to my chest, imagining that he's here. I can almost feel the safety of Dad's arms as I take a deep breath, remembering the smell of his favorite aftershave. One single tear falls before I take a seat on my couch and gently open the letter.

*Dear Ara,*

*It's probably too optimistic, but I'm hoping that this month hasn't been too hard on you. Don't feel bad that I missed a birthday. To be honest, I don't think I ever wanted to see the day where I started losing my hair and looking like an old man anyway. Starting a life in diapers is bad enough, I never wanted to go out the same way.*

*Although, it would've been a fair price to pay to get more time with you. Did I ever tell you that I've always wanted to go to Greece? Your mother is the one who got me to fall in love with the idea of going. There is an island there named Rhodes. They sometimes call it "Knight's Island."*

*The beaches are beautiful, and history is etched into everything. There is a castle and cliffs and views that I'm sure the pictures haven't done justice. We wanted to drink cocktails on the warm sand and swim in the crystal waters.*

*We'd always planned on going together, but things came up which seemed more important. After your mother passed, I'd always planned to take you. You'll have to go visit for all of us one day.*

*Looking back, I see that there was never going to be a right time. There is never a right or easy time for anything. You have to make time for it, even when it seems difficult. That goes for relationships, following your dreams, a trip, or even something simple that you've always wanted to do.*

*The point of this letter, Ara, is don't let those things build up. Don't put them off. Take advantage of your time and do <u>all</u> of those little things. I want you to do the big things too. Cross them off your list. Life is too short to keep putting them off.*

*That brings me to the task of this month. My only birthday wish.*

*I want you to go out and do something which you've always wanted to do but haven't.*

*I want you to cross something off that list.*

*I'd guess it's been roughly four months. It's weird to think that I won't be able to see the changes. You may have cut your hair by now or changed your wardrobe. I think it'll be those little changes as you grow that I'll miss the most. Just please promise me you'll never try to go blonde again.*

*I'll admit that today has been a bit of a rough day for me. I'm not feeling very inspiring or eloquent and I'm sorry for that. But I want you to know that I'm being cared for, and I don't feel alone. I've still been*

*managing to find joy in most of my days.*
*I hope you are doing the same.*
*I love you so much.*
*I miss you every day.*
*Love,*
*Dad*

His words are bittersweet, and I want nothing more than to comfort him despite the struggles he faced that day. Knowing that he was cared for eases some of the worry I've buried these passing months, and he's right. There *is* something I've been wanting to do and today I'm going to do it.

**Me: What are you doing right now?**

**Theo: In a meeting with the publishers. What's up?**

**Me: Is it an important meeting?**

**Theo: It's a meeting that definitely could have been put in an email.**

**Me: In that case, tell them your pet fish's cousin fell and broke their hip and urgently needs your help.**

**Theo: Where do I meet you?**

• • •

I get out of my car and make it inside. We aren't off to a good start when the snotty receptionist makes me feel like more of an inconvenience than a customer.

*Sorry for existing, bitch face.*

I take a seat on the comfy leather couch to fill out the necessary forms and wait for my turn. I'm a bit worried as to whose hands I'm about to lay the fate of my body into. My social ineptitude is bad enough, so I have no idea how I'm going to relate with someone wild enough to do this for a living. All my fears are put to rest when the tattoo artist turns out to be a big teddy bear, covered in ink. I mean, I literally want to hug the guy.

Fishing my phone out of my bag, I show him the few pins I added to my Pinterest board this morning before coming over. It hadn't taken long for me to decide what I wanted. He takes note of everything I show him and disappears into the back to make a few designs for me to choose from.

Finally, feeling brave enough to take in my surroundings, I look around. My attention is instantly snagged by a group of girls a few stations down. There's five of them and they all look so different, not the typical group of girls you'd see, but you can tell they'll be together forever just by the way they interact. The way they seem to speak in their own language, and how everything outside of their moment doesn't seem to exist. I'd bet money that they would bury bodies for each other.

The one lying on the table looks like she's doing everything in her power to hold back a laugh and remain still, as the other four girls howl with laughter and squat like they're trying not to pee. Even their artist is laughing.

They've got a little bar of milkshakes and a spread from Chick-fil-A courtesy of Uber, which tells me that they must have been here for a while already. I turn my gaze away before they notice me encroaching on their moment. My mind wanders to Lou, Theo, and even Connor, wondering if we could have our own found family one day, too. I spare the girls one last glance and their wave of laughter fills me with hope.

A black-and-white drawing on the wall captures my attention as I look away, clearly an original design by one of the artists that I imagine is waiting for the perfect person to etch it onto their skin forever. The design is done in a silhouette style, showing a couple in a passionate embrace.

Looking away before I get a blush from a drawing, my thoughts immediately go to Theo. The way they've instantly done for the last month, any time something gets me thinking about sex, kissing, friendship, nachos, or literally fucking *anything* if it has some *tiny,* microscopic thread that connects me to him.

The tell-tale warning that someone is entering the shop (not a bell, but a ringtone of an aggressive "Fuck You" in a Brooklyn accent) rings out and Theo walks in. It would be nice if I could remain breathing for once. Theo still has no clue what is going on, but his green eyes brighten when they land on me, melting me straight down the middle.

My mission to remain calm, the face of unaffected and cool as a cucumber flies out the window when he smiles. I blame it on his eyes. I blame it on his stupid smirk. I blame it on the way one curl has escaped the others and droops over his forehead. I blame it on how his clothes always fit him disgustingly well. I instantly become a very uncool cucumber and run to him.

Theo steps forward to catch me as I launch (okay, more like small bunny hop) into his open arms. I hook my arms around his neck as he clutches me around my waist. His cheek presses on top of my head and we both take a deep inhale at the same time, which is nice, so it's not just me and I don't feel like a serial killer.

"You going to tell me what we're doing here?" he whispers into my ear.

"I'm doing something I've always wanted to do but haven't."

"You're getting a tattoo?" He doesn't say it like it's gross, just confirming the reason for being here.

I nod.

Right on time, I see the tattoo artist coming back with the design.

The artist, who I find out is named Everest, shows me what he's designed, and it stalls the breath from my lungs. Theo reaches over and clasps my hand as my eyes pool with tears. If I didn't know any better, the artist himself seems choked up. If Everest starts crying, I'm going to start crying and leave this place buried in tissues and banned for life.

I sniffle. "We better get started."

My inked teddy bear chuckles. "I'll get set up."

I look over to Theo, the feeling of cardiac arrest which has become the telltale sign of his presence is strong. I've got shallow breathing, constricting in my heart, pressure in my chest. Google would tell me that I'm dying.

He looks over, reading my thoughts. "Same."

Refusing to acknowledge his uncanny ability to always know what I'm thinking, I try to throw him off. "You're also planning on knitting a sweater with seven cats?"

He winks, not fooled. "All the time."

• • •

I did cry. Not from the pain, and not until the end, when I found myself looking at the curve and flow of the script, the words brushing my soul. Admittedly, I don't have much of an idea about the afterlife, or if there even is one, but I can only hope these words now forever marked on my forearm, follow me wherever I go and lead me to the person I miss the most.

*May we meet again*

"Do you have more time?" Theo surprises me with his question.

"Yeah, man. I do."

Theo lets out a breath. "I have this design in mind. It was inspired by someone I cared about." He looks at me for a moment before looking back to Everest. "I want an antique timepiece with new life growing from it, almost like it's a seed sprouting new blooms of petunias."

Botox becomes a guaranteed future as my brows shoot up, while I fight the endless questions barraging the walls of my mind. Is it a coincidence that he's picked the same spot as mine? I settle with just one question.

"Why petunias?"

He's quiet for a moment. "I read somewhere that they symbolize hope."

This tattoo isn't just something spontaneous, it's something with a meaning so deep, his answer hasn't even scratched the surface. I put a sock in my mind's mouth, clutch Theo's hand, and don't release it until the end.

• • •

Florida's bright, April sunshine hits my face as I step out of the tattoo shop. Thankfully it's not too humid today, so I have an extra thirty seconds before I'm pooling with sweat.

"I should be going," Theo says, realizing the time. "My meeting mates weren't too happy about my pet fish's cousin breaking their hip."

I chuckle. "Thank you for coming."

It takes physical restraint to stop the questions from pouring out of me.

Theo reaches up, grabbing one of my waves, giving it a little tug. I close my eyes as he tucks it behind my ear, his fingers leaving a hot, delicate path. I expect him to pull away as he usually does, but my eyes flash open as he slides his palm across my cheek until he's gripping me softly.

Theo slowly leans down, resting his forehead against mine. "It's not my secret to tell, but hopefully one day I can tell you everything." His hands slide up my hips to my waist and he presses me against the window.

A trickle of sweat drips down my spine as I think about all the people inside watching this. Watching *us* and the way his body is pressing against mine. Today is turning out to be a day of self-discovery as I realize the idea of strangers being able to see sends its own thrill and heat through my core.

Nose to nose, with his lips only a breath away, he continues. "I plan to make this slow burn so goddamn worth it."

"Are you referencing another trope?"

He chuckles. "The best one."

Theo's lips are millimeters away, waiting patiently to see what I will do about it. War breaks out within me between everything that I feel for him, everything my body wants, and everything that monster who rules me fears. She needs to be slayed and put to bed forever, but I don't know *how*.

*I like you, Theo.* The words are on the tip of my tongue, my heart a beating drum, all I have to do is tell him how I feel, tell him what I want.

Theo's chest begins to rise and fall with his heavy breaths.

I open my mouth.

"Once you say it, there is no going back." His eyes hold an intensity I've never seen before.

I close my mouth.

"Once you're mine it's for *good*, but you need to be ready for that."

*Am* I ready? My mouth remains shut as I begin to panic, to run through every scenario in which I could ruin this. Gone are the games, the tiptoeing around it, the pretending. It's no longer a question of *if* between us, it is only a question of *when*. As much as it lights me on fire, it equally terrifies me.

As usual, Theo reads my mind and pulls away, giving me my space. Surely there will be an end to his patience one day, I just pray that this isn't it. If I don't get a handle on my fears, they will be what ruins this before it begins. Theo is understanding, respectful, and tolerant, but still a man.

With that, he walks to his car trying to hide the hint of disappointment, and I don't see him for another month.

# CHAPTER TWENTY-SEVEN

## Last Year - Theo

I blow out a breath.

I'm not in a hurry to get back. Connor is going to be waiting around to see how it went. As my best friend, well, *brother* I should say, I think it hurts him just as much as it hurts me when I get rejected. Possibly more.

The concrete step at least isn't digging into me as I sit here feeling sorry for myself. It's one of those weirdly soft, porous, kind of curvy ones, and it's all I can really ask for. The news needs to soak in so I can make a new plan before I face Connor and inevitably crush his hopes for me.

Somehow, I thought this one was going to be *it*. I'd had this weird feeling this morning, convinced that *this* was the day. I'd *felt* it, or thought I had.

It *was* something, I guess.

Something that consisted of me not getting my foot past the receptionist desk before security showed me out. They left me outside the office door, plopping my manuscript onto the ground, as if it wasn't my life's creation, its words resting across the pages.

I can't look at it right now. In a way, it feels like the pages and the characters who live within are upset with me for not having figured out a way to share them with the world yet. So, it remains in the spot next to me, where I had gently set it before dropping my head in my hands.

"You okay, there?" A reserved, but friendly voice says, encouraging me to lift my head from my hands. I watch him eye the manuscript laying to my side and look back to me. "That yours?"

I nod. To my surprise he leans down, gently picking it up, and takes a seat next to me.

"Is it any good?" There is a kindness about him which is authentic and genuine. I haven't gotten to experience much of it in my life, so I could recognize it anywhere. *Kindness.* I cherish the bits and pieces of it that I have received and try to put more of it into the world every day.

I nod again. Normally I would say more, get up and shake this man's hand with respect and introduce myself, but he doesn't seem to mind.

"Mind if I have a look?" You can tell that he was especially handsome in his day. He's got light brown hair without a lick of gray, and a hairline my father would pay millions for. The way this man dresses though, simple and practical, tells me he would never be the kind to pay for such vanity.

His hazel eyes are still on me, and I shake my head because I don't mind at all. I know my manuscript is good, I only need it to be seen by the right person. Until then, at least I can share my characters with this man.

"You must be Theo?" It shocks me for a second, until I remember that he's peering at a manuscript that I wrote under my own name, bolded below the title.

"Yes, sir. It's nice to meet you." I reach out my hand, preparing for the tight manly squeeze to no doubt show me who is in charge. Instead, he takes my hand gently with quiet confidence.

"My name is William and it's nice to meet you, too." He releases my hand and casually flips to the beginning of my manuscript. He's quiet for a while, and I relish the feeling of someone finally getting to meet the people I've come to love so much: my characters.

"Are you trying to get Puffin Press to have a look at this?" His question is intelligent, connecting the dots fast as to why I'm here, sitting on the steps as a broken man after failing yet again. The cleverness would have surprised me had I not already seen it in his eyes.

"Yes, sir."

"Call me William." He waves his hand. "Don't bother with that *sir* crap."

This makes me smile, and for some reason I begin to imagine what it would be like to be this man's son. I imagine him to be wise, giving sound advice whenever you need it. Logical, yet warm, understanding and patient. He wouldn't yell or even raise his voice. He would be an amazing cook and an even better baker. Really all that anyone could want in a father. All the things I never had in mine.

"I've been trying to get my manuscript looked at for a while now, but it's been...challenging."

"Are you going to give up?"

"I think about it sometimes, but I don't think I could even if I wanted to." He's quiet, waiting for me to explain, so I do. "This story, it kind of exploded out of me. I couldn't keep it in even if I wanted to."

He smiles at that, and I keep going.

"I'm not sure I can explain it without sounding crazy, but it's as if these characters chose me and I'm their messenger, helping them tell their stories which need to be told." I shrug. "What I'm trying to say is that even if I decided to give up, they would keep haunting me until I tried again."

"Hmm..." he says in agreement, as if what I said sounded remotely normal. William has almost perused to the end of the first chapter when he sets down my manuscript. "You're right, though. This *is* good."

"Thank you." If there is one thing I'm certain of, it's the fact that this story needs to be out in the world.

He sighs. "This is probably going to be weird, but I have an offer for you."

I raise my brows.

William clears his throat uncomfortably. "I, uh, need a... favor. It's kind of a big favor, so I'm prepared to make it worth your while."

I'd be lying if I said I wasn't intrigued. What could this man possibly want from me?

"Phil, the head of Puffin Press, happens to owe me a favor." He nods toward my manuscript. "I'll get you and your manuscript in front of him. He's not stupid enough to turn you away once he gets a look at it."

The ground seems to fall out from under me in that very instant. Could I possibly be this lucky?

"I will ask him either way, but if you're willing, there is something you could help me with in return should you wish."

"Anything," I say too quickly.

He chuckles. "Maybe you should hear what it is first before you agree."

"Sir, sorry—I mean, William, this is a huge moment for me. There's not much I wouldn't do, besides maybe hurt someone."

He looks at his watch. “I was planning to take the rest of the day off from work anyway. You hungry?”

“I am, actually.” I haven’t eaten all day due to my nerves and the uneasy stomach they left in their wake.

“Well, let’s go. I know a place that has great waffles.”

MAY
Dear Ara

# CHAPTER TWENTY-EIGHT

*Present - Ara*

Opening the door to my apartment, the warm May air being the first thing to greet me, I take a deep breath and smell the new life which has sprung into existence, savoring the little time that remains before the heat and humidity take over.

Theo leans against the wall opposite where my front door is nestled, holding purple flowers, petunias by the look of them.

My heart swells, because that's just the kind of guy he is, showing up on our first real date with flowers that *mean* something.

I finally found the courage last night to tell him how I feel, leaving my fears in the dust after realizing that the only thing that mattered is us, and not wasting any more time.

Theo is the perfect gentleman, slowly approaching me, as if he time traveled from another age to pick me up. My admission of feelings has set me free.

Theo stalks the remaining distance at a hurried pace, taking my face into his hands, strongly and gently all at the same time, as he brings our mouths together. The feel of his lips on mine turns me into a raging inferno. Our kiss is rushed, hurried, hungry.

My apartment door bangs back open. We are going to miss our reservation, but I'm not thinking about that. Suddenly we are standing in my living room, my hands working on the buttons at the front of Theo's shirt. My dress is already off.

I can't remember if we closed the front door, but now we're in my bed, and I don't stop to question it. Both of us are too hungry to take this any slower.

*Bang, bang, bang.*

"Ara!!!!"

That's not Theo's voice.

*Bang, bang, bang.*

Theo suddenly vanishes from where he was on top of me.

*What the fuck?*

I lurch into an upright position finding myself fully clothed and in my room utterly alone.

*Shit.*

Another goddamn dream about Theo. Growling in frustration, I slam my head back against my pillow.

"It's Dave! I have your letter!!" My favorite delivery man calls in his booming voice.

"Coming!!!" I jump out of bed and grab my robe.

Dave is waiting outside, all smiles and cheer.

I let out a woosh of air and pray that whatever is inside this envelope helps me figure out what to do about my life. Well, correction. I just need to figure out what to do about Theo. The rest of my life seems to be going in the right direction for once, but Theo? I haven't seen him in weeks and we've barely texted.

Ever since that day where I turned him away, yet again, he's been pretty much MIA. He always answers my texts, but his responses are more reserved than usual. I even resorted to asking him to collect his laptop as an excuse to see him, but he's been too busy, working on his next novel. Apparently, he doesn't need it in order to keep writing.

Although I've been just as busy with my day-to-day work and the workshops, I can't shake the fear that Theo has really given up on me this time, and it's no one's fault but my own. I don't know what the protocol is here. We're technically just friends, but I'm an emotional wreck over the thought that he may not want to be in my life anymore. Ironically, it was my fear of losing him which caused me to push him away in the first place, but now it seems that I may have lost him already before ever getting to really have him. And there is still this voice in the back of my head, yelling at me to fight for it, to risk *everything*.

"I'd love to stay and chat, but I've got a long list of deliveries ahead of me." Dave's voice startles me, pulling me out of my thoughts. "You have a good day now, sweetheart."

"You have a good one, Dave," I say with a smile and close my door as he walks away.

Despite my sour mood, I'm more than relieved to have a moment with Dad among all the change that's been happening in my life. His advice and comforting words are exactly what I need.

I open the letter.

*Dear Ara,*

*In my last letter, I told you to do something you've always wanted to do, and I hope you did. I hope you continue making time for those things. That's all I want for you: A life well-lived, full of happiness and fulfillment.*

*There is another thing in life which is so very important, and that is pushing yourself outside of your comfort zone. I know, I know, if you try to think of a time where I pushed myself out of my own comfort zone, you'll come up empty.*

*That's because this isn't my lesson, but something I know that your mother would have wanted me to impart to you. She is probably going to kick my ass for not stressing it more, if I'm lucky enough to find her again, that is.*

*You were always so brave already, sometimes it was a lesson that was easy for me to overlook. You were the one teaching me what it was like to run straight into the arms of life, and it always reminded me so much of your mother.*

*So, this month, your task is something she would have given you if she'd had the chance to write you a letter. This month's task is to do something outside of your comfort zone. I'm sure very little of these last few months have been comfortable for you with me being gone.*

*This task though, is for something different.*

*Whatever it is in your life that you're shying away from right now, I want you to tackle it. I want you to hit it head on no matter how far outside of your comfort zone it takes you. I want you to do that one thing which seems terrifying right now.*

*We have always been so much alike, and it's made us the best of friends. Except, on this one thing, you've got to be different than me. Be like your mother, instead. You've got to be brave, and I know you can be brave, Ara.*

*I know this, because you have your mother in you. I've seen it in the set of your jaw when you get stubborn. I've seen it when you decide to hunker down and get something done. I saw it when you walked away from college because you believed you were capable of more.*

*So go out there with that bravery and throw yourself into whatever is scaring you.*

*I don't know what it could be, but I know you already do.*

*I shouldn't have to tell you, but I will.*

*Do it today.*

*No chickening out.*

*Love,*

*Dad*

No chickening out!? *Is he serious?*

Newsflash: I'm a massive fucking chicken.

For once, Dad has been completely unhelpful. Surely he wrote this having no idea that it would have something to do with my friend whom I may or may not be falling for. Dad's letter essentially means that I'm supposed to show up and tell Theo that I'm miserable without him.

This letter was supposed to tell me that I don't need to tackle anything if I don't want to. It was supposed to tell me to stay away from boys. He was meant to say that protecting myself comes before all else, and not risk my feelings getting hurt. Instead, I get this inspirational crap about being brave and running into the arms of life?

No, thanks.

I won't be running into anything but the cushions of my couch, Dad.

I lift my middle finger up toward the sky and plop down.

• • •

Unsure if I'm just feeling guilty about sending my dead dad a middle finger, but after spending half the day watching Elena and Damon overcome the destiny of the universe so they can be together, I feel like doing something epic. Getting my friend back doesn't mean I have to be *completely* vulnerable. I can take this one step at a time. Theo never pushes me further than I'm comfortable with anyway.

Now that I think of it, it's kind of frustrating how much of a gentleman he is. Sometimes a girl just wants to be thrown against a wall when they're least expecting it, you know? Maybe all this back and forth could have been avoided if he did that months ago.

A peek into my closet reminds me that I've only dressed for something epic once, on Valentine's Day, and I settle for something a little less homeless before grabbing my keys. I take off in a little jog toward my door but stop after five steps, which is enough to remind me that I would prefer to *walk* into life's arms. Running is reserved for life and death situations only.

The plan forms in my head as I finally reach my door and lock it behind me. I'll show up at Theo's penthouse, knock on his front door, and explain *everything*. I want him to understand *why* I'm so afraid and convince him that he can't give up on me just yet.

I can't get the driver's door of my Beetle unlocked fast enough, making me feel like one of the idiots in the horror movies. That's the issue with driving an old Beetle. Lots of charm and absolutely no helpful features.

Finally, I get it open and let out a frustrated growl. She takes a few turns to get going but finally grumbles to life. I'm about to peel away when I realize a tiny little detail: I don't remember how to get to Theo's penthouse.

Damon never has to *ask* Elena for her address. He simply shows up and makes our panties suffer for it every time. This is why grand gestures never happen in the real world. Nobody can get around anymore without GPS showing the way.

I close my eyes and try to remember everything I can from the morning Theo drove me from his place back to the bar. I had been so wrapped up in my embarrassment that I hadn't paid attention. All I can remember is a few glimpses from when I came up for air between thoughts.

The bar was in St. Pete, so I know we came from the Tampa area. His building was extremely modern, and there's only a handful of places in Tampa with buildings like that. I'm sure I could recognize it from the outside if I managed to at least get on the correct street.

I mean, how many giant blue, window-paned buildings exist?

I'll start where the most modern, high-rise buildings are in Tampa.

• • •

After barely managing the one-way streets and traffic of Downtown, all I have to show for the first hour of searching is an army of angry drivers who would like to see my license revoked.

• • •

Another hour of searching the buildings nestled by the Causeway proves entirely fruitless. Davis Island and Harbour Island are next on my list, having the kind of properties rich lawyers would buy. I keep my eyes peeled for anything else I might recognize as I drive.

• • •

More searching and more nothing has me convinced that we came from an entirely different direction. With nothing to lose, I make my way to Clearwater where a handful of tall buildings were built in the tiny downtown area.

• • •

After two more hours in, I'm about to give up when an idea strikes me like lightning. The stupidity of not thinking to do this *before* driving all around Tampa Bay may counteract my current genius, but whatever. I have a good feeling about this.

Pulling over and whipping out my phone, I open Zillow and type in "Penthouse Tampa Bay" and skip all the ones listed for sale, looking only for those that are off the market. There are a lot more than I expected, and after a few pages of scrolling, I switch to Google and type in the same thing.

I scroll and scroll and scroll until I find an article from *The Real Estate Times* from a few years ago with the headline reading, "Big Shot Tampa Bay Lawyer to Purchase the Most Expensive Penthouse Tampa Bay Has To Offer".

This *has* to be it. I open the article, and Theo's building looks exactly as I remember it. Clicking on the address I realize that I'm even *more* stupid than I thought as pieces begin clicking into place. It makes total sense why it was so easy for him to drop my car at my place, how Theo seems to know his way around my area, and suggested carpooling to the Mexican restaurant, where we celebrated getting my new job.

I drove all around Tampa Bay and didn't think to check the ridiculously luxurious neighborhoods *down the street* from where I live. Even though it's within walking distance from my own building, I've never explored that area and wouldn't have recognized it. The little strip right by the water always seemed a bit plastic for my taste, so I stuck to my little Hyde Park Village with trees and greenery.

I toss my phone into the passenger seat and put my car in drive.

This time, I don't need navigation to get to my destination.

# CHAPTER TWENTY-NINE

## *Present - Ara*

Not sure why I thought I could just walk into the most expensive building in Tampa Bay, but after fifteen minutes of pointless attempts of convincing, the doorman hasn't budged an inch. His job is way too important to him to risk letting an unwanted stranger into the building, which is fair enough.

Clive, the doorman, offers again to call Theo and get permission to let me up, but I refuse. Nothing epic starts with a call from a doorman. There is also the risk of standing here for so long that Theo himself comes by, catching me outside his building like a weirdo.

Walking back to the car with my tail between my legs starts looking better and better when I spot a sandy brown head with the top of a guitar case sticking out from behind it.

*Connor!*

Maybe the universe *doesn't* hate me. I try to look as casual as possible as he approaches.

Wait, what if he doesn't remember me? I only met him that one incredibly awkward morning. Or what if Theo told him that he no longer wants anything to do with me? Just as I start to panic and consider jumping into a bush, Connor spots me.

He breaks out into a grin of recognition. "Are you here to see Theo?"

"Yeah! I was just about to call up, actually." I can feel Clive's eyes digging holes into my back.

"Don't bother, you can take the lift with me." Connor's accent and no-drama-persona makes him begrudgingly likable. I feel slightly more at ease, knowing that he's the kind of person whom you could have a full-scale meltdown in front of and he'd brush it off without a second thought. The only unsettling thing about him is his complete lack of social filter, and the fact that he has zero reservations when it comes to sticking his nose *straight* into my business.

"Thanks!" As we go by, I send Clive a look that says 'See, I told you I'm not a weirdo stalker'.

"I'm really glad you finally rocked up. Theo has been moping around for weeks." Connor shakes his head. "Maybe this will finally perk him up."

Theo has been moping? "What do you mean, moping?"

"You know, *moping*. Walking around like a sad puppy who's just lost his balls?"

I roll my eyes. "I know what moping *means*, but I don't understand *why* he would be moping. Did something happen?"

Connor pushes the button for the elevator and shoots me a look that says I'm missing something obvious. "*You* happened."

"*I* happened? He's the one who's been sending me one-word texts!"

The elevator opens with a ding. Connor scans a fancy fob and punches the top floor number. "Probably because my poor mate needed to take some steps toward self-preservation. He's never been this into someone."

"You must be mistaken." In my gut I know that he isn't.

"I don't know why you two haven't hooked up already." Connor sighs. "Blow each other's minds, maybe some other body parts, too."

I blink. "We are *just* friends."

"And? Is there some law against friends hooking up? Friends hook up all the time."

"Well, not me and Theo. It's not like that between us."

The elevator suddenly seems to get smaller. Warmer.

Connor laughs. "Oh, it is like that. You think I didn't notice you undressing him with your eyes when he came out of the shower?"

Okay. It's not the elevator getting hot, it's my face, which is currently enflamed and the color of a tomato.

"I thought so." Connor smirks. "Just can't wrap my mind around why the two of you are hell bent on making yourselves suffer."

"It's not that simple." I try to push my thoughts away to reduce my flush. It doesn't work.

Connor rakes his hand through his messy musician hair. "It could be. You obviously want him. Just say so. I'm sure my boy would be happy to oblige."

"But then what happens after?" I have no idea why I'm entertaining this conversation right now, but maybe Connor will have some insight.

"Normally one would throw away the condom."

Never mind. Absolutely no insight.

"Oh my God, that's not what I meant." I drag my hand down my face. "I meant with the emotions and the relationship."

"If you ask me, you're better off without any of it. No emotions. No relationship. Just sex. It's easier that way."

"Clearly you've never read a romance novel, because those arrangements never work. Usually someone still gets hurt and then they end up finding a way to fall in love anyway."

"Sounds like a bunch of romanticized crap to me. It's not like that in real life."

And I thought I had issues. "Someone's been hurt."

"You don't get hurt if you don't give someone the chance to do the hurting." He shrugs. "Besides, you're the one who's afraid."

"Don't quit your day job, Connor. You'd make a terrible therapist."

He smiles mischievously. "But I'm perfect for a musician. I stand by what I said."

"Thank you for your input, but it isn't necessary."

"I think it is necessary. I'm just trying to do my part as Theo's wingman."

"Wingmen are for picking up chicks at a bar, not convincing his friends to hook up with him."

"Friend. Singular. You're the only one I'm trying to convince to sleep with him, and like I said earlier, I don't think you require much convincing," he says with a wink.

The doors finally open and release me from this godforsaken elevator ride right into their penthouse. I forgot that their place is so fancy that they don't even have a front door. My plan seems so stupid now. The grand gesture will be me showing up outside his bedroom like a creep. Jumping out of their highest window starts looking like a better option.

"His room is the last door on your left."

"Yeah, I remember." Apparently, the location of Theo's bedroom is the only thing I haven't forgotten.

Connor shoots me a smug look as he walks past "I hope you shaved."

I decide that I didn't hear his parting comment, because if I did hear it, I would die on the spot. Part of me is uncomfortable with Connor's forwardness, but deep down I know he's right. Plus, that forwardness is what saved Theo's life. So I can never be mad about it.

I have no choice now but to show my face. Connor knows I was here and is surely going to mention it. The only thing weirder than showing up at Theo's penthouse unannounced is doing it and then leaving without saying anything.

It's time to remember what that letter from my dad said and buck up.

I make my way down the hallway with walls that are lined with pictures of Theo and Connor. My heart throbs at the effort these two young men went through to make themselves each other's family. Even down to the black-and-white portraits, they are brothers in every way that counts.

I finally approach the last door on the left and knock softly.

"Why are you even knocking? Come in!" Theo calls from the other side of the door.

I guess Connor sent him a text to warn him of my arrival.

Opening the door with as much courage as I can muster, my body stops dead. Theo has moved all of his furniture which took up half the room the last time I was here. He's pushed it all against a far wall, next to a desk with an iMac that I hadn't noticed before, leaving a big open space between his bed and TV.

I'm pretty sure that's a Wii remote in his hand as he lines up to bowl. There are just enough of my brain cells in operation to register that the last Wiis on Earth seemed to have disappeared ten years ago, but here he is, playing Wii.

Theo is all focus as he hurls the virtual ball down the lane. It must be a good throw because Theo raises his fist in the air, not even acknowledging my presence. Yet, none of this is what has caused my brain to officially detach from the rest of my body.

*That* is because Theo is standing in nothing but his underwear.

Of course, I'm not lucky enough for it to be a pair of ugly plaid boxers, no. If it were ugly plaid boxers, my brain may still be intact.

Theo is in none other than light gray Calvin Kleins, fitted to his every curve. I now realized that despite his clothes being wonderfully tailored, they have done his lower body no justice at all.

These briefs, though? Wow. The waistband is low enough that I get an eyeful of happy trail leading right down to...*oh.* Somewhere in the distance of my mind, I'm yelling at myself to look away because I'm being a completely indecent friend.

One thing is certain, if there is a God, Theo is definitely his favorite.

"Bro, why are you just standing..." Theo cuts off. "Oh. Ara."

Theo has now spotted me, while I have my eyes currently zeroed in on his bottom half. He definitely thought it was Connor knocking on his door, not me, and I'm capable of nothing except standing here like a fish out of water, open and closing its mouth.

This is awesome. I absolutely love going out of my comfort zone, Mom and Dad!

I hope they're witnessing this fucking trainwreck they're responsible for, which might be even worse than puking on his bed. The thought is jarring enough that I somehow manage to shut my eyes.

"Ara? Are you okay? What are you doing here?" I feel Theo's hands gently grip my shoulders.

Oh boy.

"Fine!!!" I shout hysterically, cracked voice and all, even though Theo is standing less than a foot away from me. Maybe I can laugh it off, so I try, but all that comes out is a high-pitched shriek.

This is so bad.

"What's going on? Why are your eyes closed?" He's got his sweet voice on, which tells me two things.

One, he still cares about me. All is not lost. At least it won't be if I can get my brain connected again. Two, he doesn't mind that I've just seen him in his underwear. Three, I don't mind that he doesn't mind.

"I have something in my eye." Super convincing as I make no move to get said 'thing' out.

Theo lets out a soft chuckle. "Do you want some eye drops?"

I hate eye drops.

My eyes flash open. "All better!!"

He's still shirtless and only in his Calvins, and somehow even closer, so I take a large step back and turn around. "I'm so sorry!! You said to come in, so I thought it meant you were decent."

"It's fine, you've seen me shirtless before." Pause. "It doesn't bother me."

Play it cool, Ara.

"Right, totally." I turn back around and make a very clear effort of not looking below his chin. "I came because I was worried that a robot had taken control of your phone and I was beginning to worry about your well-being."

He sighs. "I was just giving you space."

"Don't play stupid. You were showing me what life would be like without you, and it worked, dummy. Now put a shirt on so I can explain myself."

Theo steps closer again. He's only three inches away. "Why? Something bothering you? His voice takes on a seductive tone that he has *never* used on me before, and my stubborn—and very turned-on—streak takes over.

Fine. I'll show him. I lift my hand and start to delicately trace his muscles with my index finger. When I hear his breath catch, I flatten my palm against his chest and shove him back. "Not bothered at all. It's up to you if you want to traipse around Tampa with me in your underwear."

With a shrug, I walk out of his bedroom door without a backward glance, mentally begging him to follow.

• • •

Evening has already descended, and the sky has gone fully dark by the time we arrive. We finally make our way up the last ramp, approaching the chained-off staircase and I gesture for Theo to go first.

"Isn't this considered trespassing?"

"If they really wanted to keep people out, they'd do a better job at blocking it off. It's been this way for years."

He gives me a wary look and steps over the chain.

"I don't know why this place exists, there's nothing around to indicate the purpose it served when the parking garage was in use," I explain as we emerge onto my little square of respite. "Maybe someone else needed an escape, too."

Theo is quiet as he takes it in. Admittedly, the space isn't much to look at. Between the plain cement walls and gray rocks which line the ground, that's pretty much everything there is to see. But the view?

"It's beautiful," Theo says, his voice filled with awe.

He turns slowly, appreciating the sights from my little space atop the world, starting with the downtown Tampa skyline. The buildings are lit, sending glowing colors into the night sky and reflecting off the water. I'll never get tired of the mirrored effect created on the calm waters, which doubles the beauty and colors.

"I found this place by mistake in high school. I was wandering around, avoiding a tough conversation." I glance in Theo's direction. "I stumbled upon this garage and thought maybe getting above my problems in the physical sense would help clear my head."

Theo turns to his right, taking in the cars and people that are no bigger than the size of toys from our vantage point. They've always seemed less threatening from up here, as they hurry by, unaware of my gaze and thoughts.

"Thank you for showing me."

I turn my back on Theo, looking out across the dark expanse of peaceful water as a reminder that the world is *not* caving in around me. "It's an olive branch, of sorts. I've never shared this place with anyone.

"An olive branch for what?"

"Have you ever felt like you're floating a foot behind your head? Almost like you're a separate entity, just watching while your anxiety takes away all of your power?"

Theo is quiet a moment. "Yes."

"Every time it happens, I feel like I'm just there, watching myself while *something* or *someone* else calls the shots. When I encounter a situation which could be deemed dangerous territory, this thing rears its head and takes control." My voice is raw with emotion and frustration as I describe what I fight against every day of my life.

"I know what that's like," Theo says gently.

"I know you do." I take a deep breath, willing myself to keep going. "Usually, I can feel the anxiety just lingering, waiting for any excuse to sink its claws into me. When it finally does, I always fight. I tell myself that I am strong enough to overcome it. Then, this feeling of being stuck underwater takes hold. I can't yell, I can't speak, I can't breathe, and I can't reach myself. It drags me down, down, down until I stop fighting. That's when I lose."

We're both quiet, needing a moment to recover from my truth. I'm unsure whether I'll have the strength to continue, until the balmy night breeze carrying the scent of the ocean brushes across my face like a comforting caress, as if someone sent it to tell me to keep going.

"Once I come back to the surface, I have to witness the damage this other *thing* caused while I was away, and the people who got hurt because of it." I turn to face Theo once again. "Even right now, I'm *battling* to tell you. *Battling.* This was the only place I had a chance of overcoming it, the wide-open peaceful space. As long as I can see far enough in front of me, I have a chance to outrun it."

A tear slips from my eye, sending Theo into motion, three furiously long strides before he can finally reach me and engulfs me with his arms. One hand comes to the crown of my head, pressing my face into his chest, while the other wraps around my waist and tugs, pulling me closer.

Theo's strong arms and intoxicating scent keep me grounded, keep me strong in this battle of wills. I'm tired of the fear of failing. I'm tired of the fear of loss. I'm tired of losing control over my own life. I'm tired of it and I'm done.

"I understand, Ara," he whispers into my ear, following it with a kiss to my hair. "Goddamnit, I understand."

My very being knows that he speaks truth. The anxiety Theo must have had to fight every night just to get to sleep, terrified that his father would come to his room, is unimaginable. How the physical and mental abuse had driven him to such depths that Connor had to remind him that there were still things worth living for.

"Please don't give up on me." Another tear escapes with my request.

I hurt all over. It's as if I had to shred through layers and layers of self-constructed walls designed to protect my deepest darkest parts, before offering it all to Theo. Gone are the reasons to push him away. Gone are the fortresses created to keep him out.

"Never. I will *never* give up on you." He declares it to me, to the stars and to the universe.

I believe him.

Theo holds me tighter, as if he knows that he's the only thing keeping me from falling apart entirely. I don't know how long we stand there, but after a while the pieces of myself that were torn apart tonight begin to feel less raw, as if something filled with healing magic weaved through and fused them back together. I feel whole again. I feel like myself.

Theo begins to loosen his grip, as if he too feels it. He pulls back and brings his hands to my face. Theo leans down so he is perfectly eye level with me, wanting me to see his soul while he says his next words. "I. Am. Not. Going. Anywhere."

"Not even Dad could fight fate, Theo." One more tear escapes. "You say we can write our own future, but some things might be out of our control."

Theo wipes away the moisture, not retreating an inch.

"I don't care," he says firmly. "I. Am. Not. Going. Anywhere."

Theo's words, his promise, soothe the kind of wounds that aren't visible from the outside. He sees everything, he sees every broken piece of me and refuses to look away or retreat.

"Can I tell you something?"

"Anything," he says, still looking into my eyes.

"My dad writes me letters."

Theo freezes, eyes shuttering ever so slightly. He must think I'm delusional.

"He *wrote* me letters, I should say. Past tense. I don't know how, but he gets them delivered to me once a month."

"What do they say?"

"Before he died, he apparently wrote a letter for every month of this year. They get delivered on the same day, at almost the same time each month, containing a little window into his soul and his wishes for me."

"He sounds like an incredible man." I don't miss the genuine emotion in Theo's voice when I speak about my father.

"He was, and in a way I think he wanted me to be there with him, sharing his last thoughts." I smile for the first time tonight. "And within each letter is also a task."

A hint of surprise marks his features. "What kind of tasks?"

"At first, it was just getting me out of the house and into the world again." I snort. "He didn't want me sitting around feeling sorry for him."

"Is that why you were at the diner that morning?'

I nod. Curiosity gets the best of me. "How did you find me there, by the way?"

"I didn't know you'd be there that morning, I wasn't *actually* stalking you."

Theo, despite his talent with words, is a terrible liar. Rather, omitter. There is something that he isn't telling me, I can feel it. "But how did you end up at that diner?"

He shrugs. "I told you before, I heard they had good waffles."'

Interesting. Theo isn't budging on this and changes the subject.

"What else does he give you in your tasks?"

Since he has been extraordinarily kind to me, I allow it.

"My second task was to help someone else find their happiness, knowing I would've shied away from feeling happy myself." I look over at Theo. "That's when I took you TPing."

He laughs. "I'm not sure that's what he anticipated."

"But did it make you happy?"

Theo looks down at me. Despite everything I've told him tonight, he looks at me like I still have everything in the world to offer him. He reaches up and grabs one of my wild waves which has escaped my bun yet again, giving it a playful tug before tucking it behind my ear. No matter how many times he does this little ritual, it always leaves me feeling worshipped.

"You always make me happy," he finally says with a brush of his fingers over my ear and down my neck.

This. This right here is what every woman deserves.

I don't hide what I want, what I've been so afraid of until now.

My eyes drop to his lips, every cell in my body screaming for him to close the distance between us. Theo's eyes, darkening at my attention, drop to my lips in return.

Anticipation shoots through me.

Theo slowly grazes my bottom lip with this thumb. 'Soon, but not tonight."

I reach up and trace around his new tattoo. Maybe it's because there has been something burning between us since that fake kiss and my body has finally reached its limit, but I drag my finger over his upper arm and jaw line.

I blame it on the sound Theo makes in the back of his throat, and the words are out before I can clamp my mouth shut. "Why aren't you going to kiss me?"

"You know why." His throaty whisper sends his breath tickling my face.

Shivers break out despite the warm air. "I do?"

"Mmmhmm…" he says as he moves to nuzzle the hollow beneath my ear.

"What do I know again?"

"That I'm waiting, and that once you say the words there is no going back." His nose drags down my neck, tracing my collarbone, feather light. "You need time."

"What if I hate time? What if I said that I'm done waiting?" My confessions tonight have freed me. Now that I've braved it once, I feel a million feet tall and want to claim my victory.

He chuckles. "I'd say that I wasn't."

"Why not?"

He groans. "Because my characters have taken over my life. I can't go anywhere or do anything with them plaguing my thoughts."

"*So?*"

"*So*, I want every brain cell and burning iota of attention on you when I *do* kiss you." Theo glides his thumb over my lips one more time before dropping his hand. "I want nothing else on our minds. Nothing else on our schedules. Nothing that is going to pull you out of my bed before I'm ready."

I wait for the humiliation of rejection to sink in, but I realize it won't. I can see how much not kissing me right now tortures him, and despite him giving me the courtesy of not saying it out loud, he knows how vulnerable I've been tonight, and above all else, he respects it. Standing here with Theo, nothing bared but our souls, he won't risk moving too fast and have this night be responsible for anything other than healing.

Theo sits down on the gravel a moment later and sprawls out on his back, rubbing the spot next to him so that I join him. I place my head right next to his, so we are cheek to cheek, as our feet fan out in opposite directions.

The midnight sky takes away my words and Theo's too. Every time I'd come here before, I was so wrapped up in my issues, I'd never looked *up*. With the stars above as our only witness, we sit in comfortable silence for a while, the sound of traffic from below our only intrusion.

"Do you think they're up there? Your parents and my mother?" Theo asks.

"Ever since I saw *The Lion King* as a kid, I've wondered the same thing. I've always felt like there may be truth in that."

He chuckles. "Could each new star represent a lost soul?"

"I think the scientists of the world have said enough on that."

I feel, rather than see his smile. "True enough. I have my own theory."

"What's that?'

"I don't believe we live just one life. I believe that we are reborn after death."

"Like reincarnation?"

"Sort of."

"That would suck. Having to do it all over again."

"It could be another chance for those who messed it up the last time." He shrugs. "Or more time for those who didn't get enough."

This gives me pause. "Do you think my dad is living another life somewhere?"

"Wouldn't he prefer that than sitting around watching others live a life he can't be part of anymore? Or not existing at all?"

I consider this. "I think he would."

"But I do wonder if we'd get to pick where we go."

"Dad would pick Australia."

"Really?"

"I think so. He visited once when he was a young man and always talked about going back."

"Where would you pick?"

I don't hesitate. "Canada."

"Canada!?" Theo laughs. "Why *Canada*?"

"Don't laugh!" I reach up and smack him on the shoulder with a laugh. "I think Canada is underrated. It's stunningly beautiful there, and the people are lovely. It seems like a good choice."

Theo just laughs.

"Okay, Mr. Laugh-About-Canada, where would *you* go?"

"Hmm. I would have to really think about it. Consider all options."

I roll my eyes. "Just pick one for now."

"Probably Japan."

I groan and sort of...laugh? I *graugh*. "Of course, you'd choose Japan."

He nudges my shoulder, laughing. "And what is *that* supposed to mean?"

I giggle. "Nothing. Nothing!"

"What's wrong with Japan!?"

"There is *nothing* wrong with Japan, it's just unexpected. Most people would choose somewhere in Europe."

"You chose Canada."

"Touché." I turn my head toward Theo. "I guess if I'm in Canada and you're in Japan, we'd probably never meet?"

Theo turns his face toward mine, only a few inches away. "I would go to every continent. Every country. Every state. Every city. I would knock on every door to find you again."

It's so quiet, Theo can probably hear how hard my heart is pounding. "Would we recognize each other? In different bodies?"

Theo's eyes bore into mine. "I think souls have a way of remembering each other. Even after death."

I've never been a very spiritual person, but here in this moment, I know that I would recognize his soul anywhere. "I'll be the one with the red flags, crippling anxiety, and giving my trauma an outlet with misplaced humor."

Theo laughs. "I'll check Canada first."

I smile. "Sounds like a plan."

# CHAPTER THIRTY

## Last Year - Theo

The drive with William was quiet, yet comfortable. I've never met anyone like him. He never seems strained, but he's not super talkative either. He looks at everything with a fond gleam in his eye as I wonder why it's tinged with sadness.

"Where is Susan today?" By his familiar address, I assume that William comes here often.

"She took a day off, believe it or not," the waitress says with a smile.

William returns it. "About time. I'll have the waffles with a side of bacon and eggs."

He looks to me and I follow suit. "I'll have the same."

The waitress leaves and I become very aware that I'm sitting in a diner with a man I hardly know and somehow, I'm already looking at him as if he could be my second father. Like I can already depend on him. William is the kind of person you meet for five minutes, and those five minutes just might change your whole fucking life.

"I apologize for the strange manner I'm addressing this with you, but unfortunately, I don't have any other options at hand." He brushes his brow, full of concern. "Please know that there is no obligation, you're welcome to walk away anytime. I will just need to know now. My offer in regards to Phil will still stand either way."

"Okay, well, I appreciate that. As I said, there isn't much I wouldn't want to help you with."

William begins to look uncomfortable for the first time. "There isn't an easy way to say this, but… I'm dying." He laughs, humorlessly, and it comes out more like a sad rasp. "No matter how many times I say that out loud, it never gets easier."

I should say something. I should respond. I shouldn't remain silent, but that's all I'm capable of. I'm supposed to be a master of words, yet here I sit, utterly wordless.

"It's cancer. I won't bore you with the details, but it's not the type that I will survive." The waitress walks up and sets our food down. He finds it in himself to grin and thank her, making sure she feels appreciated despite the dark cloud which has descended on our table.

A good man, even in the worst of times, that's what William is.

"I have a daughter." The way his voice cracks sends emotion swirling in my own eyes, and I look hard at my waffles, trying to contain it before I can't. He pauses, collecting himself. "She's all I have in the world, and I'm the only one she has, too. Being that for someone feels good, until the day you find out that you have no choice but to abandon them."

*Utterly. Fucking. Wordless.*

"She isn't ready for this, and I'm not too sure she can weather this storm without me. She's already lost too much as it is." He clears his throat and looks out the window. "I can't leave knowing that. Knowing that I haven't done everything in my power to make sure she is okay."

"Does she know?"

"No, she doesn't." He looks at me, intent. "And she won't."

"It's none of my business, but can I ask why?" Wouldn't he want his daughter by his side? Wouldn't he want to say goodbye? Give her the chance of saying goodbye as well?

"I'm going to suffer. Hopefully not for long, but I'm going to suffer. I'd like to think that I'm strong, someone who would go through it with their grace and dignity intact, but I won't delude myself into thinking that I will be the same.

"If she finds out, there is not a distance far enough that would stop her from being there for every moment. And that would mean that she would have to lose me little by little, every single day. It would mean that when she remembers me, she will remember how I looked frail and in pain as she watches more of myself disappear into the misery and fear of death.

"At least this way, when she remembers me, it won't be wiping my mouth, getting me out of bed, or seeing the light go out. She will remember the best parts. The most important parts."

I can do nothing but listen and marvel at the love this man has for his daughter as my heart cracks for what they stand to lose.

"You see, I've seen something in her recently, the ideas spinning in her head and the budding bravery. I've been waiting for this day for her entire life, and I can't be the thing which throws her off course just before she gets started. I need to be there for her, help her through this, and I hope that wherever I go, I'll get to watch as she thrives." He smiles affectionately and wipes his eyes.

Here I am, a total stranger glancing into this life, this *beautiful* fucking life, and I know with absolute certainty that I would gladly offer to trade places with this incredible man, so his daughter, whoever she is, gets to keep him.

Since life doesn't always work how we'd want it to, the only option is to help him, help her. To keep their love alive. The kind of love that not even death can overcome.

"I'll help you. Whatever it is, you can count on me. I will help you."

He smiles. "Thank you, Theo."

And with that admission, I take a bite of my waffles.

JUNE
Dear Ara

# CHAPTER THIRTY-ONE

## *Present - Ara*

A knock on the door rouses me from bed. Dave doesn't usually come this early, and I'm not expecting any deliveries. It's hard to believe it's now June and it's been almost six months since I lost Dad.

Zombie-walking my way to the front door, I leave my hair down to do its wild worst. Not only can I not be bothered to wrangle it into a bun right now, but it also covers the fact that I'm not wearing a bra, not that there is much to conceal.

I rub my hands down my face, urging it into a humanoid expression, glancing longingly at my coffee machine as I pass by. The right move would be to look through the peephole and make sure it's not an assassin, but I throw the door open to reveal who has come to bother the troll under the bridge.

Theo stands well dressed, hair styled, holding a bag of wonderfully smelling breakfast in one hand, and coffees in the other. My insides are instantly at war over whether to feel embarrassed or ecstatic. His eyes drift over my sleepy state and smiles. Ecstatic wins.

Moving aside to let him in, Theo's arms brushes my chest as he passes and heads to the kitchen to grab cutlery.

"I'll be back in two seconds." My bladder is about to burst, and fuck if I'm letting my morning breath anywhere near him. I mean, gross.

After that night on the roof, I'd somehow dreamed up that the next time he saw me, my clothes would be incinerated in seconds with just his eyes. Except nothing happened. Well, not *nothing,* but nothing which involved getting naked.

The thought of it has me splashing cold water on my face, yet again, as if I'm a thirteen-year-old boy who just found a magazine at the height of puberty. It's embarrassing.

The last month we've both been busier than ever. Managing the store has become everything to me. With each passing weekend workshop, I've been building my self-confidence back, as I see how valuable my work has become. I've proved to myself that I'm worth something and have learned how to start believing in myself again along the way.

My workshops have had increasingly higher attendance, having filled every chair, bench, and nearby standing space. They have become something our customers and community members look forward to.

Meanwhile, Theo has been spending all his time hunched over his computer, creating magic in the form of written words long after dark and before morning light. During the few hours of the day in between, he's with his publisher in various meetings.

Having been signed on for an entire series now, the contracts have taken a lot of back and forth due to Theo's efforts to protect his artistic freedom. He's become inspired lately, and when it hits him, there is nothing he can do but ride it out and write it out.

Despite our busy lives, Theo has never let me feel forgotten. Every day I wake up to a good morning text and fall asleep to his wishes for my sweet dreams. He sends me cute selfies of him just waking up or brushing his teeth, sending me back to the top of that roller coaster.

Our stolen moments here and there are everything, where we can undoubtedly feel that something shifted between us after last month. On his way between his favorite writing spot in Clearwater and meetings, he likes to drop by and leave me little gifts. Sometimes it's a cake pop, a coffee made just how I like it, or a napkin with a little note.

The logical part of me knows that this is a crucial time in our lives, and we need to finish building ourselves before we can properly build with each other. But damn do I sometimes want to listen to the very loud, *team-spontaneously-throw-me-against-a-shelf* part of me and say fuck it.

By the time I get back to the living room, I'm salivating at the breakfast spread Theo has laid across the coffee table. He brought waffles, pancakes, eggs, bacon, assorted danishes, fresh fruit, and there's even whipped cream.

"What's the special occasion?'

"I wanted to see you." He holds out my coffee, marked extra cream, which I graciously accept. "*And* tell you that we've completed the contracts. I'm officially signed for the series."

I squeal, but before I can figure out an outlet for my excitement, he continues.

"There's more."

I dramatically sit down next to him, making sure he notices that I'm on the edge of my seat.

He smiles. "I'm going on tour to promote my book's launch."

I have enough of a mind to set my coffee down before wrapping my arms around his neck and pulling him in for a hug. "I'm so happy for you."

He nuzzles my neck. "There's still more."

"Oh?"

"I've finished the rough draft of book two."

"Wow." I know that's supposed to mean something, but the way he's nuzzling my neck is too distracting for me to try and connect the dots.

"Which means…" His hand comes up, brushing over my cheek. "My characters are leaving me alone…for now."

His words from last month hit me with a clang. I pull back just enough, seeing the confirmation in the way Theo nods, looking at my lips intently.

*Holy shit.*

His eyes have darkened to a stormy green, jaw flexing in what must be his last show of strength as he leaves the decision up to me. My mind drifts to the first time that I saw him at the airport, and what I'd assumed of him then: nothing more than a Tinder boy looking for a stray flight attendant. Over the last five months, he's proven to be so much more.

Through TPing his father's house and fake-dating in front of my ex, Theo has become the person I trust most in this world. Somewhere between Valentine's Day, getting the first job I've ever loved, and throwing up on his bed, I started to recognize that giving my heart to him wouldn't be so dangerous.

And last month, finally, I did.

Perhaps I gave it away long before I knew I did, but he's held it close, guarding it from everything which could threaten it, including myself, including time, until I was ready.

The depths of his eyes meet mine, the way they've done a handful of times before, searching. Except this time, what he finds tells him just that.

I'm ready.

Theo doesn't hesitate, bringing his mouth to mine. The kiss is feather-light, clearly too gentle for both of our liking as we move in unison. He twists to grab my waist just as I move to straddle him, my fingers diving into his stupidly perfect hair and pulling on the strands to bring his lips down harder on mine.

Theo groans as he slowly moves his hands to my ass and squeezes, pulling me impossibly closer. He hardens beneath me, and my hips decide to have a mind of their own as they grind down, rubbing against his length.

His hands move to my waist, dipping under my shirt, and sounds start escaping out of me. We are pouring every ounce of built-up need into this kiss. Every lick of fire which has been building in my veins finally has an outlet, and it just may burn us alive.

"*Fuck*." His rough, gravelly voice somewhat muffled by my lips and my tongue sends another wave of need through me.

His hands keep making the ascent until his thumbs reach the bottom curve of my breast. I tip my head back, unable to focus on moving my lips as he rubs his thumbs back and forth, tracing the small swell. Theo takes advantage, leaning in to kiss my neck.

He pulls away and I clamp my mouth shut, stopping the complaints, when I can tell by the look on his face that he's not done with me yet. His eyes are focused as he slowly begins to raise my shirt. Goosebumps spread over my skin as it passes my navel, the air kissing my ribs…

*Knock, knock, knock.*

I close my eyes in defeat, knowing what's on the other side of that door, the only thing on this planet important enough to get me to walk away from this. My body protests as I say softly, "I have to get that."

Theo slowly brings my shirt back down, smoothing it over with his hands, leaving me like a dejected child who's been conned by those county fair games and just lost my chance at a giant stuffed animal.

It's written all over my face as Theo chuckles and traces my bottom lip. "Don't worry. We have all the time in the world."

I slowly lift myself off of his lap, instantly feeling empty and too far away.

Theo's hand grabs mine and gives me pause. There is something so goddamn sexy about how he stands, gently tucking me into his side as he comes to open the door with me, as if I'm not the only one who can't stomach the small distance. Theo reaches for the door, opening it like he owns the place, and I almost burst right there.

"Oh! Hey there, Theo! Ara!" Dave's pleasant surprise leads into a smile. "I didn't know you two were friends."

Old man. *Friendly* old man. *Friendly old man who also knows Theo.* My body finally registers that it is not about to get laid and starts to simmer down.

I raise my brows, looking back and forth between Theo and Dave. "You two know each other?"

Theo smiles smoothly. "We're practically neighbors, Ara. I'm Dave's favorite on the route."

"That wouldn't be possible because *I'm* definitely his favorite. I give him treats."

"I don't have to resort to bribery." Theo looks down at me and winks. A little teasing and a single solitary wink and I'm ready to finish what we started on the couch.

"Here-here, you two," Dave says amicably, humor in his eyes. "I could never pick a favorite."

I remember why he's really here when he reaches into his bag and pulls out the envelope. My eyes lift to Theo's and gone is the dark, sexy look from a moment ago. His eyes are swimming with emotion as Dave hands me the letter, having probably connected the dots that I was receiving one of Dad's letters.

"I'll give you a minute." Theo turns, but I catch his arm and shake my head.

"Stay."

So, he does.

He stays right by my side as we say goodbye to Dave, make our way back to the couch and I open the letter.

*Dear Ara,*

*This one, well, I'm not sure if you're going to love me or hate me for it, but I've got a gut feeling that it will be the right time. That could also*

*be indigestion from the Mexican I ate, but let's go with a gut feeling.*
*I'll never forget the first time you brought home that little cut-out of material which you made a dress out of for your paper doll, knowing right then what you were going to be when you grew up.*
*After years of seeing how hard you were working to learn, I decided to help as much as I could, and that was the year I got you the sewing machine. I heard that little thing going and going and going. It brings a smile to my face whenever I think about it.*
*Later on, we went to that fashion expo, and you took home all of that amazing material and I'd always wondered what you'd make of it.*
*Then I saw it. It was an accident, but it rendered me speechless.*
*You were still getting ready to go when I arrived at your apartment and you had me wait in the living room. The door to your design room was cracked open and it stole my breath away when I saw that silver dress.*
*I always knew you were talented, but Ara, that dress? It was real-life magic.*
*I know it's scary, making the transition from doing something you love for fun to doing something you love with the intention of sharing it with others. But you can't let that stop you.*
*You have pure, raw talent and the ability to create such beauty.*
*The world needs more beauty.*
*I remembered that pamphlet you had up on your cork board next to those pictures of New York City. I googled it. They take applicants at this time of year, and now you're probably shitting bricks (as you say) thinking I'm going to tell you to apply.*
*Well, you'd be right. That's exactly what I'm going to tell you.*
*That's your task this month. Apply to that fashion school in New York that you've always dreamed of attending.*
*In fact, don't stop there. I want you to make it a moment. I want you to go to New York and explore the possibilities, really see if it's something you'd like to do.*
*I want you to have everything this world can possibly give you.*
*Whatever happens, know that I'm proud of you and that will still stand true regardless of the outcome, but they'd be crazy not to take you.*
*You're going to change the fashion of the world one day.*

*I'm not just saying that because I'm your dad, either.*
*It's the truth.*
*I love you so much, Ara.*
*Good luck.*
*Love,*
*Dad*

"Theo?"
"Yeah?"
"How do you feel about going to New York?"

• • •

It was an amazing feeling, arriving at Tampa International Airport, being one of the people to walk through my favorite terminal as someone with an adventure awaiting, blood rushing in anticipation.

Theo hadn't even questioned it when I asked him to take the first flight to New York with me. He'd told me the only seats remaining for today were first class and booked it, but getting onto a somewhat empty plane, I now know that hadn't been true.

But he wanted to make this a moment.

An hour into our flight and we haven't spoken about our extracurricular activities on the couch this morning, but he's held my hand and touched my waist, making sure I know that he hadn't forgotten.

The flight attendant approaches. "Champagne?"

I glance at Theo with wide eyes and he smiles. "Yes, two, please."

The plan is to work on my application on the plane with the help of the officially professional writer sitting next to me, find a hotel, and get settled in. Tomorrow morning we will go to The Fashion Institute, and see if we can swing a tour. If we can't on such short notice, we'll just walk around the grounds ourselves. Most people would probably be more prepared, but I don't want to wait. The more time I have to think about it, the higher the chance of me getting in my own way.

Taking a sip of champagne, I imagine what Lou would think of all this fancy plane stuff. I make a mental note to take her somewhere first class one day. She had *flipped* when I'd told her about the spontaneous trip.

**Me: I'm going to NY**

**Lou: WTF when?**

**Me: Now.**

**Lou: Uh, okay Ms. Spontaneity. Who are you and what have you done with my best friend?**

**Lou: Wait. By yourself?**

**Me: ...with Theo...**

**Lou: Don't come back until you've had at least seven orgasms.**

That last one had made me snort water out of my nose.

Since we'll only be in New York for one day, we won't be doing much sightseeing. I have to be back at Jane's, and Theo, I assume, has to be back for his book tour.

Speaking of… "So, when do you go on tour?"

He sighs. "Soon. I leave in a few days, and I'll be gone for a month." My chest hollows out at the thought of being apart for that much time. "It's an amazing opportunity, so I can't complain, but I could have done with more notice and a shorter trip."

"Well, I'll still be here when you get back." I duck my head down, not able to believe that I said something so cheesy out loud.

Theo gently tilts my chin up, kissing me softly. "I'm banking on that."

# CHAPTER THIRTY-TWO

## *Present - Ara*

It was cute how we thought we could just show up in New York and get a hotel room that we didn't have to share with a cockroach on such short notice. I cross my fingers as we walk into the last hotel that came up on our search near The Fashion Institute. It's much nicer than the others, which also means more expensive, but it's got good reviews, and we won't have any tiny roommates.

Despite the hotel being on the smaller side, it really is beautiful. With floors so shiny that I can almost see my reflection, and a chandelier hanging from the ceiling whose crystal shards send stunning light fragments throughout the lobby, it's something out of a dream.

The man at the front desk is dressed in a suit with more pieces than I can count, my stomach sinking when he says they are completely booked up. At this rate, we're going to be sleeping on the street.

"Isn't there anything you can do to help?" Theo's eyes are pleading. I would jump off a bridge when he asked if those eyes were pointed at me.

It looks like the man feels the same way because he looks down again, indecision and a slight grimace weighing on his features. "Well…there is one room. It's a queen suite, but the bathroom is under renovation, and therefore not technically available. You'd have to come down to the lobby or visit the pool during opening hours to use the bathroom or shower."

Theo glances at me and I nod. It's a bed. "We'll take it."

"Great. Let me just call up to someone to get the room ready. Perhaps you'd like to get some dinner first and explore the amenities?"

"Sure, how long do you need?" I'm relieved that Theo naturally does all the talking.

"A couple of hours."

"No problem at all, we are very appreciative." Theo gives the man his details and reaches into his wallet to tip him.

"Thank you very much," the man says. "Oh, and Mr. Carter, I'd really appreciate your uh, *discretion*. As I said, the room isn't supposed to be occupied."

Theo smiles. "What room?"

The man grins back and nods.

• • •

A couple hours later, I'm slipping the key card into the reader and opening the door so Theo can carry our bags in. The room is simple but elegant with a queen bed in the middle and the door to the bathroom taped off. We'd both decided to hit the bathroom before coming up here where I'd brushed my teeth. Five times.

I'd usually be tired by now, but my body is alive.

Theo sets my bag on the luggage rack in the corner of the room and puts his bag on the floor. It's the little things he does without thinking, the courteous gestures which show I'm at the forefront of his mind at all times, that drive me out of my mind for him.

I wander around, checking out what the mini bar has to offer, not that anyone in their right mind would take something from it with how overpriced it all is. Following it up with a perusal of the in-room dining menu, I'll be reading the phone directory in no time. I'm stalling and I know it.

"There's probably a Bible in one of the drawers if you want to check that out, too." Theo teases, a sensual lilt to his words.

"Gotta keep myself entertained somehow." When my tone comes out as suggestive as his, I know that I'm about to introduce my cautions to my good friend: the wind.

Theo walks over to me, puts his hands on both sides of my face with the tips of his fingers slipping into my hair and kisses me. It's not overpowered by our urgency like it was this morning. It starts out slow yet demanding, getting to feel every dip of his lips. He drags his tongue across my bottom lip, and I open for him.

One of his hands goes to the back of my neck for support, as he tips my head back and deepens the kiss even more. My hands come out of the frozen state they've been locked into, ready to trace every inch of him.

They find his jaw first, that chiseled line which is unfair to the rest of mankind, before heading down his neck, broad shoulders, and muscular arms. As I make it to his hands, he grabs mine to rest them against his chest before reaching down, grabbing my thighs and hoisting me up. I squeal with how easy he lifts me up, and he captures the sound with his mouth.

Theo sets me on the dresser, as I spread my legs so he can get closer and my hands drift down the muscular planes of his stomach. I've officially gone mad from frustration or desire when I slap his abs. "How can you look like this? It's completely unfair."

Theo kisses down my neck, before dragging his nose across my collarbone. "I could ask the same to you."

I snort.

He freezes.

I freeze.

*Why are we freezing?*

Theo pulls back. "Why did you snort like I said something ridiculous?"

*Oh.* "Uh, because you kind of did."

"What *exactly* was ridiculous?"

*Cool. Cool. Cool.* He's going to make me explain it. I look down at my fingers which I'm now wringing with the embarrassment that comes with ruining an incredible moment, for no other reason than feeling insecure.

"Ara. Look at me."

I do.

"No, I mean *really look* at me."

I *do.*

Theo's thick, dark hair is mussed in a wild, untamed way that sends heat flooding through me. His chest heaving, lips swollen, jaw feathering with restraint, and eyes full of dark need.

For *me.*

And I suddenly get his point. I drive him crazy in the way that he drives me crazy. He finds me beautiful, maybe even…*sexy.*

Theo's thumb brushes over my freckles, my nose, my lips. "You have the kind of beauty that people will try to pick apart because it's everything they want. They'll tell you its flaws when all they really want is to have what you have. And they never will. Your beauty is *unobtainable.*"

My insides, I swear they… sparkle.

Theo leans back in and kisses me, his lips proving that he meant every word and then, much to my horror, he pulls away, smoothing down my hair. "We should get to sleep."

My body is not remotely convinced, still feeling as if it's one touch away from exploding.

A moment later, instead of unzipping his pants, I'm unzipping my suitcase, trying to find the least ugly pair of pajamas that I brought. When I turn around, Theo is standing there having done the same thing. We stand there looking at each other, clutching our pajamas, with nowhere to go.

"You go first." He clears his throat. "I'll, uh, turn around to give you some privacy."

I'm grateful for him as he turns around and does just that. Getting stripped down while he's focused on kissing every inch of me is one thing, but getting undressed in front of him with the lights on and no other distractions is another thing entirely.

For whatever reason, I keep staring at his muscular back as I set my pajamas down on the bed to my right and begin to get undressed. I slide off my pants, laying them across the bed, and that's when I notice he's *fidgeting*, trying to focus on anything besides the fact that I'm standing right behind him, almost naked. Grabbing the hem of my t-shirt and pulling it over my head, my nipples harden as the awareness of being almost naked right behind Theo hits *me*.

*Unobtainable.* The word he used to describe my beauty brushes over me, caressing every single insecurity from top to bottom, until there lies nothing but the overwhelming urge of wanting him to see what's left in its path.

I take a step forward and tap him on the shoulder.

"You fini…" Theo trails off as he turns, eyes roaming over the deep red, lacy bra. The underwire gives me some lift, but with the sheer lace material and no padding, it's all me, and if he looks closely, he can see everything that waits for him underneath.

Theo's greediness glazes over my stomach and for the first time I don't have the urge to cover it. It's not perfectly flat, but it's mine. His gaze reaches my hips which I've always wished were wider and curvier, but the way he's looking at them, I realize they are everything and more. As he continues over my softest place and all the way down my legs, I fall in love with every inch of myself as I see the fire it ignites within him.

He sees all of me. He wants all of me. And I'm going to give it to him.

"Ara, I need to know something."

I nod, incapable of words but willing to tell him anything he wants to hear.

"I need to make sure we are doing this as *us*, I don't want this to be merely the thrill of leaving our lives behind and being different people for a day."

"Theo."

"Yes?"

"Sometimes a girl just needs you to *not* be a gentleman."

I don't even have time to blink between the words leaving my mouth and Theo's mouth meeting mine, as he forces me against the wall, cradling my throat before dragging his hand down my front. If I thought he was unleashed this morning, I don't even know what to call this.

*Utterly unhinged.*

We're both panting as he trails his fingers up my arms to where my bra straps sit on my shoulders. One by one, he gently pulls them down, off my shoulders. My heart pounds, his gaze branding me as he slips his hand up my back, unclipping my bra with a flick.

Theo groans and bites his fist. Hard. "I fucking knew you'd be perfect."

His hands slide down to my ass, giving it a squeeze, his fingers come dangerously close to where they meet. Just as I feel myself about to unravel, he brings his hands up my back and to my front, palming my breasts, eliciting a response in my body I have *never* fucking felt. Nobody has *ever* touched me this way.

My eyes roll back and the sound that leaves me is both a gasp and a groan, my head swinging to the side like it's sitting on a broken axis. He growls and takes my nipple into his mouth, sucking and tugging on it, mimicking the motion on the other side with his fingers instead. We won't even make it to the bed before I…

The pressure building between my legs is so intense it's almost painful. If he doesn't touch me *there* soon, he's not going to have to.

"Theo." I warn. "I'm going to explode."

He begins kissing down my stomach as if I haven't said a word, and I can't keep still as he reaches the seam of my underwear and slips his fingers just under the edges. Starting at the apex of my thighs, he drags them along the seams, teasing up and around to the back.

I don't know what to do with my hands and they roughly run down my face, as if that's going to release what is building up so strong within me. My legs begin to tremble when he leaves my panties on, but gently moves them to the side so that I'm on display.

He groans. "You're so beautiful."

I can't. I can't take another single fucking second. His fingers dip inside, sliding in easily, and that sensation alone nearly sends me over the edge.

"I'm…." I can't even get the words out, but he knows. Theo fucking knows. He pushes his fingers farther inside, placing his hand on my hip, guiding me to ride his fingers, this man who waited so patiently. Who reminded me that I'm something to be treasured. Who convinced me that I was worth believing in.

It's my undoing. The first wave crashes through me, and Theo grips me harder, guiding me to keep moving as wave after wave crests, until my legs give out and he catches me before I hit the floor.

"I can't believe I just…I mean, you barely even…." I groan, covering my face as the blush spreads at how quickly that went, until I become focused on something much worse. A familiar lash of pain whips through me, knifing its way through my insides.

*No. No. No.*

I mentally calculate, the reality of it sinking in and leaving me ready to throw up. In all the excitement, I didn't even come prepared.

"What's wrong?"

"I think I'm about to…" Another gripping pain lashes through and I'm mortified. "I think I'm starting my period. Any second now."

Theo is quiet, but he wraps his hands around my waist, pulling me to him. "Do you have cramps?"

I nod.

"Okay then, let's get you dressed." I forgot I was just standing here, basically naked and surprisingly, it doesn't bother me.

"Wait, what about you?" I can see him still bulging beneath his pants, permanently dousing the worry that he finds me disgusting.

"You don't feel well." He seems to think that's enough of an explanation.

"Yeah, but I…and you…*didn't.*"

"I'm not ready for the firsts to be over, anyway." With a kiss to my forehead, he walks over to our suitcases before digging around for a minute.

Pleasure surges through my body as he kneels in front of me with fresh underwear and fuzzy socks to help me dress, hands grazing my body as he stands up.

He shakes his head. "I just can't help myself."

A little shiver escapes me as he holds one of his shirts up, so I can stick my hands through the sleeves as he pulls it down over my head.

Theo walks over to the bed and pulls away the sheets for me to get in, just as the pains start to pick up. He tucks me in before calling room service to order a chocolate sundae.

"I'll be right back," he says, kissing my forehead. "I'm going to gather reinforcements."

I raise my brow.

"Don't worry, I'll be back soon." He leans down and kisses me on the lips. He meant for it to be a quick peck, but I deepen the kiss, showing my gratitude with my mouth.

"I don't know how I'm going to ever be able to leave you."

"Then don't."

"I'll be back soon." He kisses me one last time, and three words begin to climb their way out of my throat, but I remind myself that I need to walk before I can run.

"Theo?"

"Yeah?"

"I like you."

He smiles. "I know."

What can I say? Power walking is still walking.

• • •

A while later when I'm already halfway through the sundae, Theo comes back into the room, clutching his so-called reinforcements.

*Red wine.*

*Heat packs.*

*Three different brands of pads and tampons.*

*Chocolate.*

After Theo pours me a glass of wine and applies a heat pack, he's there curling around me, left arm circling my front, and his right hand rubs everywhere that I hurt.

Just after I've lost the battle to unconsciousness, perhaps in a dream, I think I hear Theo whisper those three little words I was so afraid of, which changes us forever.

And together, we run.

# CHAPTER THIRTY-THREE

## Present - Ara

I almost don't even notice my uterus trying to murder me from the inside out. Thanks to the kind of comfort only a hotel bed can give, paired with the warm, heavy arm draped around me, I could stay here forever. It brings me back to when I woke up similarly in Theo's bed after he rescued my drunk ass. Realizing how far we've come, how far *I've* come, I smile. I'm in New York, in bed with Theo, on purpose.

A little blue liquid gel and glass of water beckon from the nightstand, surely put out by my knight-in-Henley-armor. Normally I would let myself suffer through it, but I don't have time for that today. I've got a task to complete.

It's a weird feeling, that this task isn't sending me to the corner of the room to collapse. Five months ago, I couldn't bring myself to get out of my apartment, let alone fly to another state to pursue a passion of mine. That familiar monster who lived so close beneath my skin hasn't sunk its claws into me in... a while.

I slowly lean forward, reaching for Advil to get it into my system as fast as possible, when the arm squeezes around me, pulling me back to where I started.

*Yes, please. Trap me, I beg you.*

A warm breath tickles across my face with a sleepy little sound. "Where are you going?"

"Ideally nowhere."

"We have to." Theo chuckles. "Today is about you becoming the next fashion icon."

I snort. "I don't know about that."

He nuzzles my neck. "How are you feeling?

"Like death, but comfortable. Really comfortable death."

He sighs, content. "We should get going."

"We should. Doesn't mean that we have to."

He playfully smacks my hip and sits up. "Come on."

Theo comes around the bed, handing me the Advil which I graciously accept, hoping my salvation comes soon. I swish the water around my mouth in hopes that it does something to minimize the stank, just in time.

Theo leans in and kisses me.

I will never get used to this feeling, his lips against mine and his hands around my waist. His words from last night seem as though they came in a dream, but I know the truth. Theo shared them with me in a way which gave me the freedom to hold them close for a while, until I was ready.

Everything with Theo feels natural. Here I am, standing in nothing but his shirt and some underwear, wearing a pad he bought for me. Not even a lick of me feels self-conscious as I lift the shirt and begin getting dressed as he watches.

"What?"

He shakes his head. "I so badly want to touch you, but if I do then I'll never stop."

The things he says? They will be the death of me.

Yesterday when I was packing, I went to grab my most "fashiony" looking outfit I owned, something I bought and never wore which still had the tags. In the end, I didn't want to go about this day as anyone but me. If they didn't want me how I am, then I wouldn't want them.

In the end I went with my high-waisted jeans, my clean pair of Converse, with the first wearable shirt I ever made. From the front it looks like a plain, white crew-neck t-shirt, but the material is higher quality than what you can buy. The back is open, tying in a beautiful bow at the bottom. It's simple, me, but fucking cute.

Throwing my hair up into my usual bun, I mess around with the pieces so it looks a bit more tamed and less crazy. I dab some concealer under my eyes, then apply mascara and a bit of blush and highlighter to accent my bone structure (a little trick I learned from Lou).

Theo comes up behind me, looking as devastating as one can look in a Henley, as he wraps one arm around my waist, and the other comes around to brush my face.

"You look so beautiful." He runs a finger down my bare spine. "Did you make this?"

I nod.

He smiles. "I love it."

Not able to resist for a second more, I turn around to pull him down for a kiss. Theo slips his hands into the back pockets of my jeans, nearly sending me to the morgue.

*Here lies, Ara Scott, who died the way we'd all want to go: adorable as shit.*

"Thank you," I whisper against his lips.

"It's the truth."

"Not just for the compliment, but for everything." I need to get this out. "Theo, I don't know how you managed to walk into my life when and how you did. I've stopped questioning it because all I know is how right it feels. If you can't ever share how or why…I've decided I can live with that. But you've changed my life. You were the first person besides my dad to believe in me, and that means something."

"You made it easy." Emotion stirs in Theo's eyes.

"When I found out he was gone, I didn't know if I was going to survive it. It was the kind of darkness which sucks up everything around it, where you can't even see your own hand out in front of you, and I didn't know if there would ever be a way out." I pause. "With those letters, my Dad lit the path, but you guided me through. You were a flame in the dark, and I will never forget it."

"It's been my pleasure." Theo's eyes fill up with everything he wants to say, but can't. He settles for reaching up to tug a little strand of escaped hair and tucks it behind my ear. "Now, let's go see if this institute deserves you."

• • •

The place is beautiful, I will give it that. Its old architecture and brick façades are very New York. Every hall is picturesque, and I imagine how amazing it would be to spend my time here every day, walking through these halls, doing what I love.

The application in my hands feels heavy as we make our way to the admissions office. The lady at the desk is pleasant, but matter of fact, letting us know that tours are scheduled ahead of time and are done in groups. It makes sense, though, being impersonal. She gives us two visitor passes and says we can have a look on our own if we'd like.

The woman notices the application in my hands and lets me know the drop-off box is right outside. For some reason, I decide to hold on to it and Theo doesn't question me, wrapping his arm around my shoulders to lead me back outside.

We hold our coffees and take in the sights.

"It's beautiful." Theo breaks the silence first.

"It is." We're quiet for a while longer until a big group of students break out of class and head off in various directions. I remain quiet, picking up on conversations as they go by.

*"Honestly, I'm not too upset. Nobody has been able to impress Mr. Dequa. Nothing is ever good enough."*

*"Bianca poured her coffee on my project, but she did me a favor because my deadline was extended thanks to her. And she only did it because she knew mine was better."*

*"If I have to look in the mirror one more time after staring at a model all day, I might never touch another croissant for as long as I live."*

We walk by another classroom and I peer inside as the conversations that I overheard haunt me. Each station is set up differently, probably belonging to various students. The mannequins are dressed in various weird creations, really edgy stuff that lands somewhere between dress and trash bag. I would never be able to make anything like that. I'm not edgy or high fashion, I just want to showcase the *people* who wear what I make, not cover them up with something hideous.

We walk around a little bit more. Another classroom I peer into has things that appeal to me much more, but I can tell it's just basic textiles. Learning how to cut and piece things together. Attending this school means I may have to sit through several of those before I can move on. Since I'm self-taught, I'm sure there is room for me to improve in that area, but I'm not particularly interested in learning how to make something cookie-cutter.

We walk back through the courtyard and I take in the students. Nobody looks at ease. Some are stressed, some look *too* sure of themselves. After more than an hour of exploration and contemplation, we head back toward the admissions office to turn in our visitor cards.

As I stand in front of the box with my application in hand, I remember everything that I saw here. Is it possible that being at Jane's, helping budding artists flourish with creativity makes me more happy than a fancy fashion institute?

Theo gazes at me curiously. "A penny for your thoughts?"

"I'm feeling generous today." I smile. "I'll give them to you for free."

"Such a selfless creature."

I smile, then pause. Somewhat more serious. "Would I be letting my dad down if I decided not to apply?

"I think it would depend on your reason."

Theo lets me consider. What *is* my reason for walking away?

It's no longer fear. Standing here in front of this admissions office, application in hand, I know I could if I wanted to. There is no monster waking up inside of me, ready to shred and take this away from me. I don't want to dash into a corner or hide from sight. My palms aren't sweating with the knowledge that I'll never be good enough.

The simple fact is, I don't think this institute will make me happy.

"I'm not afraid," I tell Theo, meaning it. "But I don't think this institute is where I belong."

"I can say with certainty that your dad wouldn't want you doing something that doesn't contribute to your happiness," Theo says. "And being willing to walk away from something you've spent your entire life imagining because you can recognize it's not for you after all? I think that takes more bravery than applying."

I smile, walk over to the trash, and drop my application.

"Your dad would be proud," Theo tells me.

The cool thing is, I know he's right.

# CHAPTER THIRTY-FOUR

## Last Year - Theo

William did not oversell these waffles.

"Have you seen that movie? The one where the husband dies and leaves letters to his wife?"

I shake my head. "I haven't, actually."

"Well, good. At least one of us has his manhood still intact."

I chuckle. I get the sense that if I got to know him a bit better, I'd spend the majority of my time with him laughing.

"She made me watch it with her." Pause. Throat clear. "It was...well made."

I cover my smile with another bite of waffles.

"I plan to do the same thing. I'm going to write letters to Ara."

"That's beautiful." I ignore the sudden quickening of my pulse at hearing her name for the first time. *Ara.*

"I'm no poet, so don't give me too much credit." Longer pause, and he tilts his head in that way that shows he's considering something difficult. "It hinges on the fact that I manage to write them."

Even in death, his thoughts revolve around his daughter, making sure that she will be okay. It will take strength to write those letters, and I can't begin to imagine what he is going through, especially having to face it alone. I can't stand the thought of it, William dying alone.

"I plan to write her a letter for each month, the first delivery being just over a week after the funeral. I want her to have the time to process it all."

"And after the first week?"

"The letters will need to be delivered in order, each month. The address will be on the envelopes. Probably via the postal service or courier. If it's done as a mystery, she will turn into Nancy Drew and bust us."

The postal service isn't the most reliable, but I can think of one man, rosy and joyous enough to take this on. "I could work that out."

"I also want to write her a letter for her wedding day." William gathers himself. "You know, the one day above all others that I'm supposed to be there for."

I nod.

"I'm not sure how you'll stay up to date with how to get the letters to her..."

"I'll get them to her. Whatever it takes."

He nods. "Thank you, Theo."

JULY
Dear Ara

# CHAPTER THIRTY-FIVE

## Present - Ara

It's weird. Every month, I'd expected the letter to be delivered differently, but month after month it's always been delivered the same way. July's letter is no different. Dave knocks on my door with a smile full of joy. I open the door and he gives it to me, allowing me another precious moment with Dad. I thank him, sometimes with special treats, and then I close the door.

This time, though, I wasn't expecting it today. Or this week. Nor did I expect it to be accompanied by a big box, wrapped in paper. In fact, I'd become worried that I wouldn't be getting a letter this month since the usual delivery date had come and gone.

I should have known better.

Of course, he would send it on my birthday. It'll be different, not being with my dad this year, but knowing that I will have a good time with Lou makes it easier on my heart. It's a gift on its own, having such a beautiful friend to help me feel celebrated. I know Theo will want to do something when he gets back in a few days, too.

Life has gotten easier, which means that I'm healing. Both from the loss of my dad, but also from all the things that came before it. Sometimes, the grief still hits me with no mercy when something reminds me of him, but I don't think that will ever change. And sometimes that ugly monster who wants me afraid tries her hand again, too. It will be a battle every day to fend them off, but I'm winning.

The letters have played an important role in getting me to this place. If it weren't for my dad, guiding my path, I don't know if I would have ever made it out of that dark hole.

I will always miss him, and it hits me at all different times. It's when I take a bite of popcorn that's perfectly buttered and just a bit too salty, or imagining what he would say if he was watching the movie with me. There will never not be a place where he should be in my life. But I know, the only reason I could go on living was because he figured out a way to convince me that it was worth it.

My phone buzzes and butterflies come with the notification when I see the sender.

**Theo: Happy birthday, beautiful. I wish I was there.**

I smile.

**Me: Thank you <3 I miss you. When will you be back?**

**Theo: Before you know it.**

**Me: *skeleton gif indicating how long I feel like I've waited***

**Theo: I'm counting down the seconds.**

I still haven't brought up what he said that night, but it almost feels unnecessary. There is no question about how we feel for each other.

My phone buzzes again, this time it's from Lou.

**Lou: Happy Birthday, Bitch *one thousand emojis***

**Me: Haha ilysm.**

**Lou: Let's get tipsy tonight. The less we remember about getting older the better.**

**Me: Couldn't agree more. Pick me up whenever.**

**Lou: Anything before 5pm would be cringe.**

A moment later…

**Lou: I'll see you at 5:01.**

I snort.

**Me: See you then.**

Looking back to the letter from my dad, I take a deep breath and open it.

*Dear Ara,*

*Happy birthday, my girl.*

*Twenty-three this year. (I can't believe it either.)*

*Just yesterday, I was trying to figure out the right temperature for a bottle and learning how to braid your hair, then suddenly I was teaching you how to ride a bike. Before I knew it, it was your first day of junior high, and I thought I might keel over when I remembered the ages of the boys who would be in your class. Although, nothing was as bad as us sitting in front of the computer weeks later, trying to figure out from YouTube how one uses a tampon.*

*When you turned eighteen, I somehow managed to keep it together but I spent the entire night looking at your baby pictures, trying to figure out where the time had gone. Then you turned twenty-one. And twenty-two. I never thought it'd be the last birthday I would see.*

*Whether I'm there to celebrate or not, you deserve something on this very special day. I've spent hours researching, trying to find the perfect gift. You've never been one for material things such as expensive bags or shiny jewelry, and I didn't want my gift to you to be as fleeting as a moment. In the end, I decided to choose something that I hope will give you joy for years to come. Something that makes you feel happy, each time you bring it out. Something, which could possibly imbue your love into whatever you create with it.*

*I want this letter to be short and sweet. This month is about you. Nothing else.*

*So, your task this month is to celebrate your life.*

*Have fun.*

*I want you to feel as young as you are and appreciate every moment of it.*

*Happy birthday, Ara.*

*I miss you with my whole heart.*

*Save me a slice of chocolate cake.*

*I'll have the perfect ratio of vanilla ice cream ready.*

*Love,*

*Dad*

I can't tell you when the tears started, but they continue to flow freely as I read his last line and close my eyes, wishing for all that I'm worth that he was here to share this day with me.

Gently laying the letter down on my coffee table, I ensure there are no stray liquids waiting to ruin it at the first sign of contact, and reach for the big box. It's slightly too heavy to slide it toward me easily, so I wiggle my way to the very edge of the couch and begin pulling the paper away.

My hands meet my mouth in a gasp as I take in the picture on the box. It's not just *any* sewing machine. Not only is it the best brand on the market, but it's equipped with every feature I'd ever need, but my dad didn't stop there. This is one of the special editions, a beautiful hand-painted baby blue with colorful paisley.

It's beautiful. A work of art on its own.

Taking a moment, or maybe thirty, I let myself absorb how much his letter and gift mean to me. I soak it up, let my heart swell and crack before standing from the couch, pushing the box toward my design room and unpacking my new machine.

I've just finished setting up my new baby on its throne when I hear a knock on my door.

This time, I check through the peephole having genuinely no idea who it could be, and instantly wish I'd decided to parade around my house in nothing but lingerie that I don't own. My stomach erupts and the breath whooshes out of me as I open the door and see Theo for the first time in over a month.

For a moment we just stand there, looking at each other. His eyes are bright, one side of his mouth is pulled up in a smirk. I can tell he's just come out of the shower, still smelling of shampoo and body wash. My heart begins slamming against my ribs, like it's a prisoner begging someone to open its cell door.

Theo looks me up and down. *Ready.*

His smirk turns to a grin. *Set.*

"Surprise." *Go.*

*I launch into his arms.*

I'd always wished to be tiny, short, and petite. Not that I was considered particularly tall at my 5'7", but I always *felt* tall. Taller than the boys in my class. Not skinny. Not curvy. But in Theo's arms, fitting him perfectly, I don't wish to change a thing.

Theo's arm comes down, cradling my ass and carrying my weight as the other slides up my waist, my ribs, my neck, my cheek, and pulls my face to his.

I've worried that I'd forgotten how to kiss since the last time I saw him at the airport, saying goodbye before he took off to his first destination, but I know how silly I've been when he moans, as if he's finally taken a breath after near suffocation.

Theo pulls back, kissing over my freckles, my nose, my chin, my neck. "You couldn't possibly know how much I've missed you."

"I think I do." My voice literally squeaks, full of giddiness. I didn't think I was going to get to see him for another few days.

Theo trails kisses back up to my mouth, taking my bottom lip between his teeth, before kissing me again and pulling my hips tighter to his. I'm about to ask him to take me right here, not bothering to enter my apartment, when poor old Melvin clears his throat aggressively.

"This is common property," he scolds.

We break away from our kiss, and I smile against Theo's lips as he doesn't bother acknowledging my neighbor before he carries me inside, kicking the door shut behind him. We make it to the counter before he sets me down, pulling me up against him so my thighs are spread as far as they can go and his hands are under my shirt, gripping my ribcage.

*Why is that so hot? My ribcage? Lady parts, explain yourself.*

This is my favorite version of Theo, the one where he doesn't ask permission. There will be no reasoning as Theo lifts my shirt above my head, letting out a groan as he gets a view of the goods. Little goods, but they're there.

A moan escapes my mouth, and he swallows it whole. I pull back, leaning on my elbow against the counter, and pressing one hand against his chest as he tries to close the distance between our lips again. Theo's eyes darken as I push him back and sit up with him, pulling off his shirt and leaving it discarded somewhere on the kitchen floor next to mine.

I want to look and touch and feel everything I've been craving.

Starting at his cheek bones, I trace them and the rest of his beautiful facial structure, which was one of the first things I noticed about him. I go over his jawline, cut like marble yet soft to the touch. Theo swallows as my fingers come down the column of his throat and chest.

My hands become determined as they roam every inch of his frustratingly dip-filled stomach. I lose count as I trace over muscle after muscle, leading down to the V on each side, as they tense and retract. My eyes memorize every inch of his skin, a few shades lighter than my own, as I go down, down, down.

"You done?" His voice is raspy, impatient.

I nod.

Theo scoops me up so fast I don't have time to catch myself. At first I think we're headed to my bedroom, but he veers to the right and sets me on my feet in front of the couch.

"What–"

Theo silences me with another kiss, his hands trailing down my sides as he slides my pajama pants down my legs. My heart starts beating faster, increasing the pressure that's pulsating between my legs. I will never get used to the dizzying haze of having my breasts bared under Theo's agonizing gaze.

Not to be outdone or more naked, I reach to start on Theo's pants. He captures my hands before they can, "Tsk, tsk, tsk." He makes the tiny, teasing sound so quiet I can hardly hear it over my breathing. "It's your birthday. I came to give you your first gift."

Goosebumps spread across my body, and I need him. I need him *now*.

"But, in order to get your gift, you have to do as I say."

I'd jump into a volcano with nothing but a flamingo pool floaty if he used that voice to ask me.

"Can you do that?"

I nod.

"Good." He smiles against my neck, as he slides my underwear down, then whispers, "Sit."

I do.

He shakes his head. "That way."

I move to where he wants me, head resting on the arm of the couch, my legs stretched toward the other side of the couch. I'm not presumptuous enough to bend my legs myself, but thankfully, Theo kneels on the couch, near my feet, and takes matters into his own hands, *literally.*

He picks up my right foot, kissing my instep, before trailing kisses up my calf. Theo's lips reach my inner thigh and I nearly combust right there as he places my foot on the couch so my knee is bent, before moving to my next foot and following suit. My eyes roll back into my head as I'm bared for him and he licks his lips at the sight. My hips begin bucking of their own volition, begging for contact.

Eyes darker than the blackest depths of the ocean, churning with rough weather, I realize I am caught in Theo's storm. Lightning flashes through me, thunder rocks my body and it rips away my inhibitions, my fears, my worries, leaving nothing in its wake.

I see stars as his mouth makes contact with my center and begins tasting and licking like it's his reason for being on this planet. It's pleasure in a way that I've never known, letting me finally understand how pain and pleasure get their wires crossed, because right now it feels *torturously* good.

Theo savors the moment, tasting me the way you taste fine wine. The pressure builds and builds, with every movement of his tongue and circle of his fingers. I'm helpless against the synchronized motion sent from heaven, or maybe hell, because I am *burning* alive.

"Theo." I moan his name and slip my fingers in his hair, grasping at the wavy strands. He moans against me, and the vibrations followed by the knowledge that his sounds are muffled by *me,* that he's tasting *me*, sends me falling over the edge.

My arms dangle at my side. I can scarcely think, let alone move as I come down from such a high.

"Get ready." Theo hovers to kiss me. "More awaits."

I'm beyond words. "Huh?"

"We're going out."

"Where out?"

My eyes are closed, but I can feel his smile. "To a concert, out."

"Tonight?"

"Yes."

"Shit. I'm going to need a minute." On second thought, "Or sixty."

He chuckles. "Take as long as you need."

"I was supposed to go out with Lou, we were going to get tipsy."

"Bring her."

• • •

"Whatever we're doing tonight better be good. We had reservations at the hottest lady bar in Tampa Bay."

"You can make reservations at a bar?"

"Well, normal people can't, but I called and let the bartender know what I'd do to him if there weren't two seats open for us by the time we got there."

I snort. "He probably hung up and went straight back to work."

Lou looks at Theo, moving around the kitchen like he owns the place and looks pointedly at me, saying all she needs to with her eyes.

*"Something happened. You need to spill."*

*"I told you what happened in NYC." My eyes say back.*

*"No. You're flushed, he looks mighty proud, and it smells like sex. Something ELSE happened, and I'd wager it was right before I got here."*

*I grin.*

*"I knew it." Her eyes confirm.*

Switching back to communicating out loud, I decide now is as good a time as any. "Lou, I know it's my birthday, but I have something for you."

"Oooo, did you get donuts?"

I snort. "It's better than donuts."

She stops dead. "That's high praise coming from you."

"I made you something." I grin and lead her to my design room, opening the door in a dramatic swoop. "I've been working on it for… a while."

Tears form in Lou's eyes as her mouth drops into a silent gasp. The suit I spent months perfecting for her is now on the mannequin, its full power and beauty on display in the center of the room. She takes a tentative step forward.

"Can I touch it?" Lou whispers in awe.

I smile. "It's yours. You can do whatever you want with it."

Lou brushes her fingers delicately over the matching three-piece-suit now fully brought to life, just for her. Though she is only standing next to the cyan-colored suit, her eyes are already shining brighter than I've ever seen them. The color couldn't be more perfect.

"This is the most beautiful material I've ever seen," Lou says in quiet wonder. "What is it made of?"

"It's called jacquard, which is the design you see, made with a special loom." I love that she noticed such fine details. "It can be made with different types of materials, but yours is made with a soft, thick satin."

Lou's tears begin to fall as she embraces me in a tight hug. "Thank you, Ara."

My heart squeezes and I feel the moisture starting to pool in my eyes. "Lou, you better stop getting sappy or we'll be showing up to this concert all red and puffy."

"Okay, okay." She laughs, wiping her tears away. "You're going to have to keep this for me until I have somewhere to go that is deserving of this. No way am I giving someone the chance to spill their drink on it tonight or stuffing it into my closet."

I smile. "I can do that."

Lou looks back toward her gift, shaking her head. She runs her gaze over the tapered blazer, the bustier top and flared pants. "Sinful elegance," she repeats in a whisper. "But, Ara, it's your birthday, how will I ever get you a gift as incredible as this?"

I realize in that moment how amazing it feels to create something that makes another person feel empowered; to design something which speaks to their soul; to make something which makes them feel like their best self; toeing the line between scandalous and classic.

"You already have." Her friendship is the only gift I'll ever need from her. "You're going to bring people to their knees."

She grins. "Fuck yeah, I am."

• • •

We'd asked Theo what the dress code was for tonight, which is a stupid question to ask a guy. Despite him being one of the most well-dressed ones I've ever seen, it's either "nice" or "regular" with him. His mind doesn't process the endless sub-categories such as cute-but-we-didn't-try or cute-but-we-definitely-tried. When we began badgering him if it was a bikini and fishnet kind of concert, or one you wear clothes to, he finally relented and told us to dress like a chill rocker.

Turns out that meant the same thing to both Lou and me, which was nothing, and we both stand here in jeans and plain black tops. With Theo in a black Henley and jeans, we look like the three of us did it on purpose.

Lou slowly looks between us. "Someone has to change, otherwise the rockers are going to mosh pit us into the ground for being lame as fuck."

"It's not going to be one of those concerts," Theo says, amused. "Besides, I don't have any other clothes here."

"We shouldn't risk it." Lou looks at me. "Ara, go change."

"What? Why me?"

"You have a closet full of amazing things you've made and never worn. Go pick something from there." Lou winks at Theo.

That's when I figure out her agenda. She doesn't care that we match, she just wants me to wear something that I made.

Understanding lights Theo's eyes and he jumps on the train. "The birthday girl definitely has to look better than us."

I roll my eyes and walk toward my design room, not bothering to fight them since I know I'll never win. And maybe, just maybe, I can't help but feel a little bubble of excitement over getting to wear something I created.

The day I went to The Fashion Institute, I felt proud wearing the simple blouse I'd made. It's never been fair to shut away these beautiful pieces, hiding their personalities from the world for no other reason than fear. Because they *are* beautiful.

I decide to go with a lilac bodysuit that I made out of some beautiful, soft lace. It's one of the most recent designs I made, shortly after creating Lou's scandalous suit. It features a sheer bodice with nude underlining, that way you get the bare look without feeling too exposed.

Boning starts below the bust, dropping in a V to the waist. The built-in padding gives the girls a little push, and clips connect the seamless bottom, making it into a body suit that can be paired with anything, but I'm sticking with my jeans.

I take a look in the mirror and smile. I'm not the most confident person around, but I've always believed that if you could wear the right thing, it'd make you feel so beautiful that you'd forget to pick yourself apart.

I send a silent wish up to the stars that I can help women all around the world feel that way someday.

# CHAPTER THIRTY-SIX

*Present - Ara*

We arrive at the concert, my skin buzzing with excitement.

Having never been to any sort of a concert before, I hadn't known what to expect. An empty field still being set up wasn't at the top of my list, but understanding hits as I see a familiar head of sandy blonde hair. They're still setting up, and only the bands and their crews have arrived.

Connor doesn't spot us at first because he's busy looking down the shirt of a stagehand as she pushes her boobs together and sticks out her chest, batting her eyes so hard she's going to cause permanent damage to her corneas.

Lou scoffs. "Who is that insult to the male gender?"

Theo sighs. "That's my brother."

"You have a brother?" Lou isn't the person to backpedal. She says what she means and is unapologetic, which is how she's made the word *brother* sound like an accusation.

"Yep. Wait here."

I wrap my arm through Lou's and we watch silently as Theo sneaks up behind Connor and slaps him upside the head. We hear his Aussie howl all the way from here, and can't help but laugh as he rubs the back of his head in disbelief. The girl disappears back to work and leaves Theo and Connor alone to…hug.

Connor looks toward us and waves, pulling out three red lanyards from his back pocket and handing them to Theo. They have VIP written in such a big font I can read it from this distance.

"Holy hell. Who is that delicious cup of troubled bad news?"

I follow Lou's gaze and see someone leaning against the side of the stage looking like he'd rather be anywhere else. He's familiar, someone whom you couldn't forget no matter how drunk you got. "Holy shit, that's the bartender. Ryder."

"You mean that bartender who made sure you got home safely after you got wasted?"

"The one and only."

Lou whistles. "Where do you find these guys?"

"I wonder what he's doing here. He looks even more broody than the last time I saw him."

The girl who was just drooling over Connor walks up to Ryder, and the feeling I get is similar to being unable to look away from a car accident. She walks up, tits out, and Ryder looks directly at her, not bothering to hide his disdain as he takes in her posture, rolls his eyes, and walks in the other direction.

"Ouch," Lou swears. "Gotta admire her hustle, though."

I open my mouth to agree when warm arms wrap around my waist, Theo's scent invading my senses as he pulls me against him, placing a quick kiss on the crown of my head.

"Thank fuck *this* is happening." Connor drawls as he waves toward me and Theo. I don't know why, but I already love the idiot. He reaches over, musses my hair with an almost-noogie, and I silently hope it doesn't become our thing. "Even *my* balls were about to burst."

"Good to see you again, too," I say playfully. "This is my best friend, Lou."

"She means sister," Lou corrects as she puts her hand out to Connor for an introductory shake. "I'm from the South."

Connor smiles at her and shakes her hand. "I'm from Down Under."

Theo squeezes me, and I know this moment means the world to him.

Us. Together. With our friends.

It means the world to me, too.

Curiosity eventually gets the best of me. "What's Ryder doing here?"

"My lead singer is MIA, probably on some sort of bender. It wouldn't be the first time." Connor shrugs. "This is our biggest opening set to date, and there was no way we could back out. I wouldn't let this opportunity be ruined for the rest of the band. They deserve it."

This side of him is one I haven't seen before. He's passionate, responsible, caring, and a leader. This is the Connor who saved Theo's life.

"Ryder is sort of my mate, and the only one with a voice good enough to step in on such short notice. Turns out he has a good memory, too, because he learned our songs within a night. Granted, neither of us slept." Connor takes a sip of his energy drink at the reminder. Then he adds, almost as a quiet afterthought, not meant for everyone to hear, "He could benefit from having another focus anyway."

I don't miss the look Connor shares with Theo, but I let it go.

"Oh, and Happy Birthday, Ara," Connor says with a grin.

"Thank you. It's been a good one." A blush rises to my cheeks at the thought of the letter, the new sewing machine, and especially the couch activities which have made it so fantastic.

Connor's eyes sparkle with a subtle knowing. "I bet it has."

I punch his shoulder and realize then that Connor may become like *my* brother, too, one day. Looking at the four of us, I try not to get my hopes up, but I can't help but think we could be on the way to having something like those girls in the tattoo shop.

A family by choice.

Connor looks over his shoulder seeing that Ryder is no longer where he was, and looks slightly worried. "I'd better get back to the band and make sure Ryder isn't trying to make a run for it."

"You're going to kill it, bro." Theo slaps him on the shoulder and pulls him in for another hug.

I make to give Connor a little wave, but he pulls me in for a hug. Low enough so nobody else can hear, Connor says just for me, "You make him happy. Thank you for that."

My eyes are already watering by the time he pulls away and looks at Lou. She pins him with a little glare as he holds his arms open wide with a mischievous grin.

"I'm not going to catch anything, am I?"

"You can give me a full body exam if you'd like," Connor says with a wink.

"You're disgusting," Lou says with vehemence, but she cracks a smile as he pulls her in for a hug anyway.

Those two are going to provide years of entertainment. I'm sure of it.

• • •

Strangers' bodies are pressing against mine. I'm already sweating in the Florida humidity, which means they are, too, but somehow I can't find it in myself to care. There is an electricity and an excitement in the air at a level which I've never felt before.

Connor's band, *Immoral Support*, is coming on any second. If I'm honest, I'd never heard of a single one of these bands that's playing tonight, but this massive field, packed with people, tells me that a lot of people have.

Our VIP lanyards got us straight to the front. Not like the general front, but the front-front. Based on where the mic stand is, Ryder could sneeze and it would hit me in the face.

Finally, a guy runs out onto the stage holding a wireless mic. I deem him the hype man as he runs to both sides of the crowd, then to the middle getting the crowd to scream as he goes. Even I join in, screaming as loud as I've ever screamed before, voice getting lost in the rest.

"Please welcome Immoral Support!"

My stomach plunges as the crowd screams. Connor and Ryder make their way onto the stage, followed by the rest of the band. Women everywhere lose their minds as Connor smiles and gives them a wave. Ryder remains broody and unaffected, and I think that works its own magic as another round of ear-piercing screams fill the air when he grabs the mic and pulls it toward him.

I look at Theo and Lou, eyes wide. "This is *crazy*."

Theo chuckles. "Connor has worked his ass off, using whatever means necessary, to build his band to this low level of fame."

"I didn't realize they were so well known." Even Lou looks impressed. "I've never seen a crowd go this wild for the opening set."

Theo's eyes shine with the gleam of a proud brother."Most of these people are here for them, despite them only being the openers. If the right person discovers them, they will be headliners before we know it."

I don't have an ounce of doubt as Connor's drawl sounds through the mic, accent thick. "G'day." He laughs when the crowd instantly starts screaming again, and I'm pretty sure a girl next to me is about to pass out over it.

I smile up at Theo. "Thank you for taking me here tonight."

"Happy Birthday, Ara." His hand glides over my cheek which has started to ache from the constant grinning. "I wish your dad could see this smile."

I don't even know how to form the words in response, so I just pull him close and kiss him until we're both gasping for breath.

"Go get a porta potty or something." Lou complains from my side, but it lacks venom and I catch her smile.

Connor's guitar notes start to pour from the stage, and I'm instantly spellbound. Somehow, the crowd quiets, utterly entranced by the way he plays the instrument. I close my eyes, loving the feel of the music flowing through me as Theo holds me close.

Someone starts singing, and I'm astonished to open my eyes, finding Ryder with his lips pressed into the microphone. He wants to seem unfazed, wholly unaffected, but I can tell that the music speaks to him and it's captivating, the way his voice weaves through the crowd leaving goosebumps in its tracks.

I turn to Theo again, eyes wide once again.

"Now you know why Connor asked him to fill in."

"He's…unbelievable." Chills spread up my arms and a shiver racks through me. The way his voice comes out gravelly and whiny and smooth all at the same time, wraps around your soul like he is something *else*. Something not human.

"Part of me hopes that Ryder can get out of his own way at some point and do it for real. It's what Ryder needs, and it's what the band needs, too, but Connor won't ever admit it."

Ryder carries a note, belting it with the kind of emotion that punches the air out of your chest. The crowd is at his mercy as he rips the microphone away and the band stops, only the echo of Ryder's voice playing out. They begin to play at the exact millisecond he whips the microphone back to his mouth and belts it again. You'd think they'd been playing together for years. My heart beats as their music carries me away to another place.

Lou shakes her head. "That must be *some* person."

"What?" I yell over the sound of the screaming crowd, now chanting the lyrics of the chorus with Ryder.

"Whoever made him feel *that*, has to be *some* person." She shakes her head in wonder.

Ryder continues to pour everything into the lyrics as Connor steals the crowd's hearts with his guitar and back-up vocals.

And I lose myself as I sway and sing and let the music take me with it.

• • •

After Immoral Support's set, I tugged Theo's sleeve reminding him with my eyes that there was one more thing I needed before calling this the perfect day.

Connor had asked what the rush was, inviting us to an after party, but Theo gave him one look and Connor offered up a car that was supposed to be his ride so we didn't have to Uber back. Bro code and all that jazz.

But it's what happened on our way out which has kept rolling through my head on our ride back to my place, where Lou picked up her car and I grabbed my overnight stuff, before heading to Theo's.

We had almost reached the exit when a girl about my age stopped me with a tug to my arm as I passed her. "Oh my God, girl. I LOVE your top. Where did you find something like that?"

"Oh. Er, I didn't. Well, I did, but I didn't. It's not someone else's. I mean, I didn't find it, but it is mine?" The last bit had come out as a question, and I can say with certainty nobody knew what the fuck I meant.

Thankfully Lou came to my rescue. "Ara means that she *made* it. She came up with the idea and created it from scratch. By herself."

The girl's eyes widened. "You *made* that?"

I nodded.

"I need your Instagram." She pulled out her iPhone, strapped with a glowy circle thing and wrist strap. "What's the name of your brand and how do I order one?"

"Oh, uh–"

"Here." Lou took the girl's phone and typed in my username. "You'll be her first customer. Actually second, because I'm already her first, but you can be her first one who isn't family."

Theo had stood there with not an ounce of surprise, just pride, as he held my hand for strength. The girl followed me instantly, following it up with a DM request for a custom piece for some occasion she had coming up. One question has haunted me all the way through Theo's front door.

Could I really do this?

"You're quiet," Theo says as I set my stuff down next to his bed.

It will never not be surreal, walking into an apartment this nice and not being at risk of being escorted out by a fancy set of security. "I'm just in shock."

"Because that girl wants you to make something for her?"

I nod.

"I'm not. Your designs are going to be coveted by anyone who's unlucky enough not to have a piece."

"You have such confidence in me." My voice hitches a little.

"So did your dad, and he was a smart man."

It's all I needed to hear.

Opening my Instagram, I accept her follow and DM request before sending her a message of my own, requesting more information about her party theme, and to send some photos for inspiration.

I *can* do this.

Something else from tonight still bothers me. "What do you think of Connor's way with the ladies?"

Theo sighs. "I can't say I agree with his…way of life…but he has his reasons."

"He was hurt?" It's the only thing that would make sense. Connor isn't someone who doesn't have a heart, and I get the feeling he is just trying to protect himself in the only way he knows how.

"Not in the usual way, but yeah, he was hurt. *Bad.*"

"Do you think he'll ever find someone who will be worth the risk to him?"

Theo considers this. "I used to think so, but now I'm not so sure. I'm a bit scared of the kind of woman it would take to reel him in at this point."

I snort. "He could use a good punch to the nuts."

"It's true." Theo laughs. "The only quality of his that is potentially redeeming is that he doesn't leave a trail of broken hearts."

I think back to the girl he played with before the show, definitely not someone who screamed broken hearted.

"Can we stop talking about my brother now?" Theo's change in pitch goes straight to my core.

"What did you have in mind?"

He walks toward me, slowly. "So much."

I smile, feigning innocence. "Like what?"

"This, for starters." Theo kisses my lips.

My heart takes off, pounding in time with his movements.

"Then, some of this." He kisses down my neck, gently sucking as he goes until he reaches my collarbone and drags his tongue across.

"Maybe even some of this…" Trailing off as his hands lift my shirt above my head.

This time he lets me slide off his shirt and unbuckle his belt, removing his disgustingly tailored clothes until only his gray Calvin's are left. I kiss my way down his stomach, all the way to his navel, running my lips and tongue over his happy trail.

He groans and pulls me up as I begin to stroke his length through his underwear, something I've wanted to do since I walked in on him bowling, in nothing but his underwear those months ago. How far we've come since then.

We can take our time tonight, relishing in the fact that we can finally touch each other. We can celebrate my walls coming down with our mouths, with our hands, with our bodies. I can soak in his warmth and touch every surface of his skin, as I revel in his gaze.

Theo lays me down on the bed and hovers above me, holding himself just far enough that his bare skin grazes mine everywhere, sending a raging desire through me. If he doesn't touch me soon, I will be nothing but a burning ball of need that was once a person.

"Tell me what you want," he breathes into my ear.

"I want...I want." *God.* I want so many things. "I want it all."

"I need to hear you say it."

"I want you inside me."

Theo lets out a strangled moan and finally, after a rip of foil, I watch him push into me, the way I've craved for so long. He's gentle at first, letting me adjust to his size as he sinks deeper inch by inch.

I gasp at the feeling of fullness. Of completeness. Of healing. Of knowing we belong.

Theo rolls us, putting me on top. I expect to feel nerves, having never done this position before, but as his hands cup my breasts and roll my nipples, it's the last thing on my mind.

As I move, the world slips far away. The only thing I know is Theo. It becomes a chant as he leads me to my salvation.

*Theo. Theo. Theo.*

He sits up, bringing us closer, deeper so he can take my breast in his mouth. His hands grip my hips, guiding me into an unrelenting rhythm that sends the first wave of pleasure beckoning. Theo's mouth frees me as his eyes meet mine, before drifting to where we join.

"Fuck," his eyes close with a groan. "You feel..."

Theo trails off as he becomes consumed with gratification. Gone is the considerate gentleman, replaced by one of need. He's a man who has lost all ability to think as he looks down on me with undiluted desire, pleasure, and claiming. I am his and he is mine.

Lost in sensation, I don't know where he begins and I end. All I feel is our bodies and our souls as they join in a way that can never be undone. It's as if the world's pressure has pushed and pulled for billions of years in preparation for this moment, where we become one for eternity.

The feeling is everything, and though I don't want it to be over, I'm driven over the edge to a blinding release. As I call Theo's name, he falls over the edge right along me, my name a prayer on his lips.

We pant, coming down together.

"Wow." He breathes.

I smile. "Me too."

We lie there for a while, until Theo pulls me to the shower and we do it again.

And again.

And *again.*

And with that, my birthday is simply perfect.

# CHAPTER THIRTY-SEVEN

## Last Year - Theo

"I have one more favor to ask."

"Sure." If I spend a moment longer with this man, I'll be unable to deny him anything.

"The funeral is going to be hard on her." He looks guilty as if this is his doing. "Can you check on her for me? Afterward?"

I nod. "How do I find her without giving it away that I'm the one behind the letters?"

He takes another bite of waffles. "I have a feeling she'll leave early; go to the place where she likes to think."

"Where does she like to think?"

"Besides this diner, in this very booth, she likes to sit outside the busiest terminal at Tampa airport." William considers a moment. "There is another place, which Ara doesn't think I know about, but she won't pick that one. She won't want the quiet."

I don't live far from the airport. It'll be a quick drive. "What does she look like?"

"I'll show you a picture." William pulls out his wallet, followed by a photo, and it makes me smile that he keeps the real thing. He gently brushes his thumb over her face before holding it out to me. I wipe my hands on the napkin I've placed on my lap, just in case there is a drop of syrup somewhere, before taking the picture. "It's an old one, but it's still my favorite.

She was just a teenager here, but I'm instantly taken. His daughter is beautiful in this natural, unassuming way, smiling like crazy with her long, dark hair falling out of the top knot she'd tried to contain it into. Not a brush of makeup over her tanned skin, splattered with freckles under her striking chocolate eyes and full brows.

William sighs. "I should warn you, though, she isn't a fan of strangers, or people, in general. If you decide to talk to her, that's on you."

I can't help but smirk.

William lifts his drink in salute and mutters, "Good luck," so low I almost don't hear it.

We take a moment, scarfing down the last bits of food on our plates. I can't stomach the thought of that joy being ripped away from that beautiful girl. How she will feel alone in the world and not get the chance to say goodbye. I understand William's choice and ultimately, I will respect it. He wants to preserve her memory of him but still, he shouldn't go through this alone.

"Ara is twenty-two now, probably about your age. She isn't unobservant. I'm going to have to figure out something clever to throw her off the trail, so she doesn't know something is wrong."

"We." I correct.

He glances up at me, confused.

"*We* are going to have to come up with something clever."

The decision is made before I have the chance to think it over.

William won't be alone.

AUGUST
Dear Ara

# CHAPTER THIRTY-EIGHT

## *Present - Ara*

August came, the monthly letter with it, and yet another task from Dad.

Maybe it's just the effect of the letter, but with the delivery of each one, I can feel his presence for just a little while. It's in the silent brush of sunlight and moments where I feel the comfort which being around him always brought. His body may be gone, but I know in my bones that *he* is eternal. I close my eyes, welcoming it, until it's just me and the letter again.

Opening my eyes, now filled with moisture, I read his letter.

*Dear Ara,*

*There's no way to get to know yourself better than becoming responsible for another. Being the person that something or someone depends on to keep them alive. It can be slightly terrifying at times, but extremely rewarding.*

*I realize that because I'd never gotten you a puppy or a pony, and all your plants are very much fake after killing all the real ones, I've never assisted you in experiencing that feeling.*

*So, your task for this month is to keep something (and I mean literally anything) alive.*

*I was thinking you could try again at a cactus. I know you managed to kill two of them already, but third time's the charm, right?*

*Anyway, whether it's a cactus or a lucky bamboo or a peace lily (I google searched and that one came up as something that's easy to keep alive) or*

*you decided to run before you can walk and get a puppy, I want you to love it. Really love it.*
*It's time you learned that feeling and the joy you will have from taking care of something. The joy when that something starts to love you in the case of a pet, or when that something grows in the case of a plant.*
*I believe in you. I know you can do it.*
*And remember, choose with your heart.*
*Love,*
*Dad*

I know just what to do, but I'm going to need some help. Running into my room with the intention to gracelessly belly flop onto my bed, I pause when I see Theo still peacefully asleep on his back.

My chest squeezes as I take in his sleep-mussed hair, his beautiful features, and the delicate shadows his long lashes cast on his face. The way the sheets tangle around his waist have my thoughts going to less artistic places. It should be criminal, looking like that first thing in the morning. One arm is tucked behind his head, with his face tilted toward me, his other arm extended to where I had slept, as if it had been in search of my warmth.

I've had the pleasure of waking up to him every morning for the past month, whether we're at his place or my much smaller, less glamorous one. Sometimes he wakes me with his head between my legs, or his hands running down my body, and I've decided there is never a bad wake up when it's with him.

Theo was up late writing last night, which is why Dave's knocks didn't rouse him. I guess I should take this as my turn to wake him, seeing as though I have *never* been up before him.

I kneel onto my cheap mattress, trying my very best not to jostle him, and bring my fingers to his hair, running them through the thick curls. He makes a pleased, sleepy grunt, and I can't help but capture it with my lips. Theo's arm circles around my waist as I kiss my way down his neck. I'm rewarded with another sleepy grumble as I make my way over his chest.

"We need to get up soon," I say as I reach his navel.

"Why?"

I smile at the protest in his voice. "We have somewhere very important to be."

"Where–" His sentence breaks off as I pull the sheet away and take him into my hand, pleased to find he is more than ready.

"We have a date with the Humane Society."

"I–" Before he can get another word out, he moans as I take him into my mouth, relishing in how lost in the sensation he becomes. I take my time, making sure he knows just how much I love waking up to him every morning.

• • •

"You don't want to start with a plant?"

I pour milk over both of our bowls, full of my favorite cereal, and also the only food in my apartment.

"Go hard or go home." He doesn't look convinced. "If I can get over my fears and make something for a stranger to wear to their influencer-filled birthday party, I can do this."

I'd accepted the commission from the girl, Ivy, whom we'd met at Connor's concert to create a design for her birthday party. Knowing I had to please a specific person and let them wear it in front of probably fifty people was a big enough move for me to accept. Good thing I'd already accepted her deposit for material before I found out it was going to be a party with a guest list in the *thousands*.

See, if I was any sort of an actual person who knew how to work social media, I would have seen that she had over three-hundred-thousand followers on her page. I would have known that this party would be attended by people whose job it is to wear interesting things that garner attention, and I may have shied away.

I was a mess until Ivy sent me a text to say that everything went off without a hitch, everyone obsessing over her outfit, along with a few snaps from the night. Ivy offered to share my number with the "tons" of people who were asking where they could find something like it for themselves.

I'd asked her to hold off for now, until I figured some things out, like how much to charge, for starters. Ivy only paid for the material, being my first, and she offered full permission to use her content once I was ready. What I would do with it I had no idea.

Lou helped me change my Instagram handle to AraDesigns and that's about all we've come up with since. She's been working double shifts at the café for the past few months, trying to reach her savings goal to open her own place. I haven't seen her much, but I know that I'll get to visit her whenever I want next year, in her *own* cafe.

Theo brings me back to the moment, reminding me of how this started, "I'm not doubting your *ability*, I'm just asking if you *want* that level of commitment."

"If I find the right one, I think I will."

• • •

For someone who arguably lacks the qualifications to adopt one pet, I'm not sure how I'll make it out of this place without taking all of them with me. I took one look down the dog hallway and started crying. Thankfully, Theo was fast acting and pushed me in the other direction before my emotions got really out of control and ruined the day.

We come up to a young, smiling volunteer holding a cute little orange tabby kitten.

"Oh, hello!" I'm not sure what voice comes out of me, but it's high pitched, squealy, and embarrassing. I'm not particularly social with strangers on the usual, but hopefully she doesn't get offended that I'm speaking directly to the little one in her hands.

Thankfully, it seems par for the course when she responds with, "Hi!!" in a little voice, giving the little dude a bob as if he's the one saying it back. I give his head a little scratch and keep walking.

"What about that one?" Theo asks, gesturing to the little guy we just met.

In our pre-mission briefing, I'd told Theo his position in this is one thing and one thing only: damage control. It includes (but is not limited to):

1. Make sure Ara cries as little as possible, preferably under ten times. If Ara sees a sad animal and begins the descent into depression, point out one that looks happy. If there isn't a happy one, it's "Code Red." Exit the premises immediately.
2. Do not let Ara adopt anything that is high maintenance, needs potty training, or anything besides food and water.
3. Do not let Ara bring home more than one furry friend. Don't listen to anything that comes out of Ara's mouth to convince you otherwise, and especially don't let her tempt you with sex.

4. If there is talk about not being able to leave something fuzzy behind, it's time to go home.
5. If there is ugly sobbing, it's time to go home.

Theo knows it's in both of our best interest to get in and out of this place as quickly as possible, hence his question as to why I'm not picking the first kitten I laid my eyes on.

I shrug. "Keeping my options open."

Theo mutters a prayer and snakes a hand around my waist. Most would think it's a cute gesture, but I know he's taking his role seriously and is preparing for a very possible Code Red.

We come up to another young, cheery volunteer standing in front of a door to the cutest room to ever exist. "Hi, are you interested in adopting one of our kittens today?"

I nod, smiling.

"Come on in!" She opens the door to a little antechamber that ensures nobody escapes, and we slip inside. Once she closes the other door behind us, we open the door to heaven.

I take up a criss-cross applesauce sitting position and watch the kittens play for a while. Most of them don't seem particularly interested in us at first, happy to be snoozing or playing among themselves. They are all adorable and also pretty similar. I mean they are tiny, fuzzy, playful little things making the cutest noises.

Grabbing a toy, I start to interact with the few closest to me. One of them launches and misses, rolling away. That one becomes my favorite of the group, but nothing about it hits me in the chest. They're all just *cute*.

As always, Theo seems to know exactly what I'm thinking. "If you don't think you've found the one, we can always come back another day."

Sigh. "I really wanted to bring one home today, I just.. don't feel *it,* you know."

"That's okay. We can ask the attendant when they are expecting more kittens."

I say goodbye to my new little friends and Theo helps me up. We say our thanks to the volunteer outside and are just about to head back to the front office, when I see a lone, portable cage at the far side of the hallway, emitting little hisses.

"Wait." I peer inside, and a little growl, which is arguably the most adorable and non-threatening sound I've ever heard, is my only greeting until a little paw darts out. I can tell it's not one of the "please pet me" paws. It's definitely a "fuck right off" paw.

I bend lower to see who's making such a ruckus. Cowering in the back of the cage is a fluffy gray kitten, older by a few months than the other kittens, whose hair is standing straight up in the spots where it isn't missing big chunks. One of his eyes is a bit squinty, and he is growling for all he's worth.

He's got this one tuft of long hair on the top of his head, making him look like an angry old man who's yelling at me to get off his grass, and I can't help but chuckle. He looks away, clearly annoyed and trying to keep a semblance of dignity.

"Er, Ara, I don't think that one is available. He's probably over here for a reason." There is caution in Theo's voice, who is justified in his concern, but my feet remain rooted to the ground in front of this angry little kitten.

"Excuse me!" I call the volunteer, who momentarily forgets to hide her grimace after I wave her over. "Why is this one by himself? Is he sick?"

"Oh, no, uh, not exactly."

"Then why do they keep him alone where nobody will see him?"

She looks at a tag on his cage, marked with a big red "X" and cringes. "Er, um. Well, you see…"

Theo catches onto something before I do because he puts a comforting hand on my back and whispers, "We should go."

"No, I want to know why he is over here." I look back to the volunteer. "Nobody will adopt him if you don't give him a chance."

"We've tried." Her eyes are sad. "He's been with us for several months now and he has some behavior issues which have been deemed…unresolvable and dangerous."

I snort. "Dangerous? He's a kitten."

"Yes, but we can't adopt him into a home, knowing that after our best efforts he was still showing aggression even as a baby." She sighs. "We think it started as a self-defense mechanism. He was the runt of the litter and born with six toes. The other kittens picked on him, they would beat him up, and kept him from eating.

My heart breaks into tiny little pieces for this kitten, knowing exactly what that feels like, being deemed flawed and getting picked apart until you don't trust anyone. You start to hate everyone for the actions of a few.

"I know it's sad," she continues, "But he is unhappy, and if he stays here, he would live his life forever in a cage."

"What will happen to him?"

Theo squeezes my hand.

She pauses, choosing her words carefully. "He will go to a better place."

Not believing my ears, I look into the cage just as the kitten looks back at me. It's something about his eyes, something like a challenge, maybe even a little hope, that has me declaring, "I want him."

Theo's soft swear tells me he knew exactly where this was going.

"I'm sorry, ma'am, but he's been tagged. I can't process an adoption, no matter how much I'd love to see him get a second chance."

I look at Theo, eyes pleading. I'm not sure what I expect him to do, he's as helpless as the rest of us, but we can't do *nothing*. "Theo, he's like me."

My voice cracks at the end, and I know I don't need to say more. Theo understands. Connor gave him his second chance, the way Theo has given mine to me.

Theo takes a step forward, grabbing the tag and yanks. *Hard.* A loud snap sounds, startling the kitten into a fit of hisses and growls. He walks to the nearest trash can and drops the tag inside. He looks at the volunteer, straight faced, "What tag?"

A slow smile forms on her face, replacing the shock as she reaches for the cage. The little guy goes ape shit, screaming and hissing. She pulls back, almost on a trigger-response basis and alarm enters her eyes once again. Before she can rethink her decision, I step in.

"Here, let me." I grab the handle and lean down so the kitten can see me. "Listen, I'm getting you out of here. Once we're out those doors, you can howl to your little heart's content, but until then you keep quiet. Got it?"

I take his little growl as confirmation and pick up the cage. Theo offers to take it from me, but I shake my head. "Me and the little guy have an understanding."

He smiles. "Okay, then."

We're about to turn into the reception area when the volunteer curses and backs up.

"What?" I ask.

"The manager is back." She bites her lip, sadness filling her features again. "She will never let you take him."

"What's your name?" Theo asks her.

"Terra."

"Terra." He smiles. "It's nice to meet you, Terra, I'm Theo, and this is Ara."

She smiles at us and glances over her shoulder worriedly.

"We are taking this kitten," Theo says matter-of-factly. "So if that exit is *unworkable,* then please point to one which *is*."

I hold the cage tighter as Terra looks at us, and then back to where her manager stands in the other room with her back to us. She finally shakes her head, "Follow me."

And that's how I stole a kitten from the Humane Society.

• • •

The kitten, which is how I will refer to him until I've thought of a name, didn't stop hissing the entire way home. All through the pet store as we bought him a scratching tree, a litter box, food, toys, and a collar (which is currently blank on the name side but engraved with our numbers). It was any kitten's dream, but he didn't stop protesting it for a minute.

We took him to Theo's house, deciding it was probably best to pick one place, rather than moving him back and forth. Neither of us mentioned what that meant for the future, but it became a silent agreement of sorts.

I've been lying on the floor next to Theo's couch for over an hour, where the kitten darted the second we opened his cage, trying to lure the kitten out to eat and hopefully get his collar on.

"They just didn't like you because they were jealous," I tell him, wiggling my fingers. "You have more ingredients."

*Hiss.*

"Fine. Be that way." Indignant, I retract my hand, stand up, and make my way to the kitchen where I flop down into a chair at the island.

Connor and Theo go quiet, until the former takes in my huff and snorts. "Pussy playing hard to get?"

Thankfully I don't have to get up because Theo slaps him upside the head before I have to.

Connor rubs the back of his head. "Ah, come on, it was a joke."

"Your whole life is a joke." It's a cheap burn, the obvious answer. I look up and Connor is grinning, but letting me have it. "I saved his life and all he does is yell at me."

"He just needs time." Theo makes his way around the island to sit with me. "How much time did you need?"

I hate when he's wise. Looking back toward the couch I sigh, making a mental affirmation to give the little dude as much time as he needs. Even if he hates me forever, I know I did the right thing by saving his life.

"In other news, I need to ask you a favor." Theo's voice is hesitant, piquing my curiosity.

Theo rarely asks me for anything. "Oh?"

"There is a yearly charity fundraiser held in Tampa, designed to help struggling artists. A while ago, I asked my father to attend and donate. He agreed, shocking me at the time, because he rarely does anything for charity." He sighs. "Except he refuses to donate unless I attend with him every year. I've come to realize it's less for the charity for him, and more about having a guaranteed evening to torture me. Anyway, I was wondering if you would come with me?"

His father is such a dick.

"Your father is such a dick." Connor takes the words right out of my brain.

"Of course, I'll go with you. When is it?

He hesitates. "The first weekend in September"

"That's around the corner!!" I shout.

Theo grins. "You're the only person I know who has a ballgown fit for a charity event sitting in a little room just waiting to be let out."

I blanch. *No.* He couldn't possibly be referring to–

"Ara, it's time to break out the silver starlight dress."

I wait for the anxiety to crowd in. I wait for the moment where I lose myself, over the fear of my favorite design out for the world's eyes to judge and pick apart.

But the anxiety never comes.
Instead, I grin so hard that my cheeks ache.

# CHAPTER THIRTY-NINE

## Last Year - Theo

William decided it was a good idea to start getting rid of things. He wants to leave the valuables and sentimentals for his daughter to decide what to do with, but he didn't want to leave her with the junk. His words, not mine.

I wouldn't say any of this even qualifies as junk. William's house is simple, homey, and doesn't have an ounce of clutter. Even his garage is neat, tidy, and organized. I mean, how many Americans can say that?

Regardless, we started the dekluge today, beginning in the living room. He sits in his chair as I go, directing me as I open drawers and sort through things. Everything he doesn't want is going in boxes, which I will drop off to a charity for military veterans.

William comes in from the kitchen and hands me a glass of water. I've only taken a few sips when he swears.

"What's wrong?" I ask, instantly worried, looking him over for any signs of discomfort.

"My daughter just pulled into the driveway." William looks at me pointedly. "She can't meet you."

A car door opens, and I don't even glance at the figure stepping out before I dash to the closet closest to me. It's tucked right between the living room and kitchen. I take a deep breath, clutching my glass, secretly enjoying every moment of this.

Who hasn't dreamed about being forced to hide in a broom closet? I certainly never imagined it would be by a man twice my age, but hey, beggars can't be choosers when it comes to broom closets. The front door opens a moment later, and I hold my breath.

"Whoaaaa." She drags the word out as she takes in the state of the living room. "*What* the *hell* is going on?"

William clears his throat. "I'm just doing some spring cleaning."

"It's fall." Her dry, sarcastic tone brings a half smile to my face.

"So?"

"So, it's weird. You're being weird." William no doubt is about to land a retort, when a cough steals away his voice. I wince, noticing it sounds wetter than it did even days ago. "What's wrong with you?"

The dry humor in her voice is quickly replaced by alarm. She asks the question like it's an accusation, daring him to break the news that he is not invincible.

"They found mold in my office. I'll be getting some check-ups while I'm in New York for that conference, just to make sure I don't develop anything." I can tell William is searching for more words, needing to put her at ease, but he comes up empty.

Pause. "But you're okay?"

"Yeah, I'm okay."

"Okay." Uncertainty rings out in her voice. What he's saying sounds illogical to her, she knows it is, but when it's your hero, do you really want to know the truth?

"Okay."

I hold my breath as footsteps pass by inches from the door which I'm hidden behind. Some rustling comes from the kitchen. "I'm going to eat these."

"Have at 'em."

"Where did you get these?"

*Shit.* My jalapeño chips. My go-to. My staple snack.

"Someone at work gave them to me."

She misses nothing. "But you don't like spicy stuff."

"Who says an old dog can't learn new tricks?"

Snort. "That was lame."

"*You're* lame. Now stop bothering me and come sit down."

She walks by again and I fight the urge to leave my hiding spot just to get a look at her face in real life. From the picture he showed me of her as a teenager, she must be stunning as an adult. Paired with dry humor? I shake my head. I could stay here all night, trapped in this closet, listening to their bicker with no bite.

"Dad?"

"Yeah?"

"Do you *have* to go to New York?"

I close my eyes and rest my head against the shelf behind me. This is going to be a tough one. How William gets through this conversation without crying, I will never know.

He'd told his daughter that he would be going to New York for a work convention and staying for an over fifties retreat throughout the holiday season. He told her that his boss gave it to him as a gift, and since it was so expensive, he couldn't turn it down.

"Yeah. I have to go to New York."

"Can't I come with you then?"

William chuckles. "No, you can't come with me. You're not over fifty."

"Hear me out. I saw this video, of this young girl dressing like an old lady to get alcohol…"

"Ara. Not this time."

"I just don't know how I'll ever be able to get through Thanksgiving to New Year's without you." I hear emotion in her voice for the first time. "You're my best friend. I don't want to be by myself."

William tries to take the humor route, but it falls flat to us all. "It will be good practice for the future, when you're too cool to hang out with your old man."

"Like that day will ever come."

It won't be because she's too cool, but soon, she won't be able to hang out with her old man at all. She is going to lose him for good, and she has no idea. The thought sends my gut twisting.

"I have to go to work." Her voice is more reserved again.

William sighs. "I hope it's not miserable."

"Ugh, you're telling me." I can practically hear her eye roll from here.

"I love you, Ara." William's voice cracks ever so slightly. "I'll miss you so, *so* much."

Pause. "You sure you're fine?"

"I can't tell my daughter that I love her without there being something wrong?"

She's quiet again. Then, "I love you, too, Dad."

I hear the door shut and my heart cracks for the girl who is about to lose her entire world.

SEPTEMBER
Dear Ara

# CHAPTER FORTY

*Present - Ara*

Lou lets out a low whistle, slowly shaking her head. "If I wasn't already lesbian, I sure as hell would be now."

I grin. "That good, huh?"

"Good is an insult to what I'm looking at." She props her hands on her hips and looks me over, all business. "You're fucking surreal."

I can feel a blush rising, and I want to make it to a mirror before my redness ruins everything. Standing up from my spot at the makeup station that we fashioned in my living room, I make my way over to the full-length mirror on the far wall.

Lou insisted that she come over to do my makeup after I told her about tonight's charity ball, and that I would be wearing *THE* dress. She said that I could go bare faced and rock everyone's world, but why not add a little frosting and knock them *dead*. Turns out, she wasn't asking permission.

I take a deep breath and look at my reflection. I don't know what I was expecting, but it wasn't this. I thought makeup was used to cover up, to transform yourself into someone new, someone better. More perfect, even.

Lou hasn't covered anything up. She has taken my features and applied the makeup in such a way that they are their best selves. The eyeshadow is bright and glowy, coordinating perfectly with my dress, and simultaneously making my eyes pop.

Nothing is too thick or cakey. My skin is still my skin, but she's dusted and highlighted my face in a way that I'm seeing myself in a new way. I notice my strong bone structure for the first time, my full lips. I even take a moment to appreciate my eyebrows, which she's only enhanced.

More special to me than anything, Lou didn't see my freckles as blemishes to conceal. The way she's dusted over them puts them right on display, the main event, as if they are something to be treasured.

I feel...*beautiful.*

I feel like...*me.*

I don't let myself think too hard about the other glow about me, coming from the inside. After three months with Theo, it's becoming harder and harder not to acknowledge what I feel for him.

"Lou, this is incredible." I'm breathless. "How did you ever learn to do this?"

"My mom forced me into every 'Little Miss Southern' beauty pageant until I was sixteen. The tips and tricks have been permanently etched into my brain." Lou shrugs. "I just make sure you can still see the person underneath."

"You could do this for a living, you know?" I look in the mirror again, taking in my reflection one more time, as if it might disappear.

Lou scoffs. "I would rather stab myself in the eyes with toothpicks soaked in lemon juice than have to play nice with bridezillas and prom queens."

I laugh. "That's fair enough."

Lou has given me something special tonight. It's not just a friend doing another friend's makeup, she's reminded me that I'm beautiful.

Lou leaves me to get dressed while she packs up her weapons, the curling wand and makeup, I should say. I walk to the rack which currently holds the dress I will wear tonight. Theo's name that he gave it is fitting. My silver starlight dress is something out of a fairytale. I'm my worst critic, but even I can admit that it's the most beautiful dress I've laid my eyes on.

*My* dress.

I know it's a masterpiece. I've only seen such things in my imagination, ignited from the books I read of faraway places. Places of magic. Places of royalty. Every inch of the dress sparkling, even under dim lighting. My favorite part of this dress is the fact that it was indeed made just for me. That way the length is just long enough not to trip, not to have to carry the layers of the skirt, but long enough that no one can see the black-and-white Converse which I'm wearing underneath.

I slide off my robe and lift my piece of art that I never *dreamed* of actually getting to wear one day. As I slip into it for the first time, I feel myself transport into that magical universe where I can be anybody I want.

I don't have to be the Ara, who once warred with anxiety and loss more than she lived. I can be Ara, the designer. Someone who is proud of their work and brave enough to let the world see.

I take one final look in the mirror. Since I wear my hair up most days in a messy bun, Lou thought doing a formal updo wouldn't "knock Theo's dick around in his pants" enough. She wanted it to be spectacular.

She succeeded.

Lou started by straightening my hair, then curling it into perfectly spaced ringlets. I couldn't refrain from remarking on why someone would straighten their hair just to curl it, but she swore that it's a thing, and I can't argue after seeing the results.

My hair is delicately braided around my crown, with strands coming loose to fall perfectly in place with the rest of my hair. Throughout the braid, Lou has somehow fastened silver crystals in the shape of celestial stars from the night sky all throughout. She wanted it to look like I was hit by a ball of starlight, having it trickle from my hair down to my dress.

The rest of my hair is left mostly down, letting the curled lengths fall over my shoulders and back like a dark waterfall. Lou, whether a psychic or just a genius, left a few perfectly curled strands out to frame my face in just the right way, that will have Theo wanting to tuck them behind my ear.

I grab my phone to check the time as I walk out to the living room. I've still got time before Theo is supposed to pick me up. I open our text chain and shoot him a message to say that I'm ready whenever he is.

"I can see that," Theo says aloud, voice a notch lower than usual.

The air whooshes out of me as I look up to find Theo, standing behind my couch, arm propped against the back as if he needed the support. He is absolutely devastating in his suit. I can't withhold the smile crossing my lips the moment I realize he's dressed to match me.

Theo's jacket is the blackest of blacks, providing a stark contrast to his vest and tie, both of a silver silk that appear to have been spun from the stars themselves. Even his pocket square is made from that beautiful material I would likely give a vital organ to get my hands on.

Theo doesn't say anything as he gazes at me, eyes dark, mouth open in a silent gasp, throat working. I feel his gaze like a warm buzz over my skin, drifting over my face to my chest, pausing a little too long before moving down the rest of me ever so slowly.

Theo finally lifts his eyes back to mine and shakes his head, still holding the back of the couch in a death grip. His body is taut, like a wound coil. I can't help but wonder at his restraint.

Lou doesn't miss a thing. "I'm putting twenty bucks down on you guys not even getting out this door tonight."

Theo, still dark and dazed, can only smirk.

I can't control my laugh as Lou mouths from behind Theo, "His dick" and proceeds to undulate her entire body in chaotic rotations to mimic Theo's dick going crazy.

"Have fun!!" Lou says in a sing-songy voice as she makes to slip out the door.

"Wait!" I yell after her. "I need your help to tie my shoes!"

Lou grins conspiratorially at me. "I don't think Theo would mind an excuse to get under those skirts. Love ya!" She doesn't wait a second more before disappearing out my front door.

I look back over to Theo, still feeling the weight of his gaze. I softy run my fingers over the shimmery tulle of my skirt and ask, "Are you sure this is okay for tonight? It's not too much?"

Theo shakes his head and finally releases his death grip on my couch, taking slow, torturous steps until he is only a breath away. "*Okay* isn't even remotely close to a word I would use to describe you."

"That bad, huh?"

Theo puts his fingers under my chin, gently tipping my face back up to his. I can feel his eyes absorbing every detail of my face. "Saying that you're beautiful doesn't do an ounce of justice."

My heart takes off, pounding at his words.

Theo keeps my face tilted as he brings his other hand up, tracing my freckles with a featherlight touch. "Saying that you look perfect would be an insult because it's too generic."

I swallow.

He traces my nose. "Saying that you're gorgeous would be unfair, because then nobody could ever be considered gorgeous again."

He traces my lips. "Saying that you're stunning, would be the biggest understatement of the century, and quite possibly the millennium."

I'm not sure I'm still breathing.

He traces my jaw. "There are no words, because you're something of another world."

Theo finally releases me, taking a step back, as if he needs to the distance to clear his head. "Now, what is this nonsense about tying your shoes?"

I can't speak, my body and entire being are so thoroughly hung up on his words and gentle touches. So, I just point toward my feet and lift my skirts.

Theo doesn't hesitate and drops to his knees before me, suit and all. I close my eyes and try my best to think of the least sexy things in the world to counteract what seeing him on his knees and dipping under my skirts does to me.

*Elephant shit.*

*Granny panties.*

*Getting a pap smear.*

Theo chuckles when he spies the Converse hidden beneath my layers of skirt. I feel his fingers graze over my ankle and make quick work of the shoelaces. Thank the fucking Lord that I shaved my legs this morning.

"All tied up," Theo says, emerging from beneath my dress with a smile.

Theo straightens, eyes meeting mine once more. They're a dark, stormy green, no doubt from imagining what else he could be doing underneath my skirts. If I'm lucky, it won't be too long before I get to find out exactly what that was.

"Shall we?" he asks while offering me his arm.

"We shall." I take Theo's arm in mine, and we walk to my door.

• • •

Peering out of the door to the shiny black stretch limo that Theo's father insisted on us taking, I might as well be peering out of a portal into another world. I can hardly see through the chaos of flashing lights, which I shortly realize are camera flashes…from paparazzi.

*Papa-fucking-razzi.*

My stomach drops as I notice the color of the carpet I'm about to step onto. *Red.*

I pray no one is looking as I stick my Converse out of the car, coming down on the red material, which isn't nearly as soft or plush as I would have imagined. I send up another prayer that there is no mud on the bottom of these bad boys.

Theo is at my side, wrapping my arm back through his as he begins to lead the way into the fancy Downtown Tampa hotel which is hosting the ball.

"What. The. Fuck," I mumble without even opening my mouth.

"Surprise!" Theo says weakly from his spot next to me. If it wasn't for the endless eyes and cameras on us, I would make damn well sure that he knows how I feel about surprises. That is until I see his face, sucking the irritation right out of me.

Theo looks paler than I've ever seen. His usual care-free attitude has been replaced by a worried brow and stiff posture. There is no easy smile or smirk to drive me insane. For once there is no banter. Theo is standing next to me as a solid shell.

*Right.* Theo's piece of shit father is somewhere around here, waiting to terrorize his son. He will no doubt be holding the donations over Theo's head the entire night to generate his own sick pleasure.

I sidle in closer to Theo until our sides are pressed together, my warmth flowing into his. I squeeze his arm with mine, just to remind him that I'm here. He looks down at me, gratitude filling his eyes.

Thankfully, Theo doesn't stop for any photographs, much less to speak with any of the reporters yelling his name to get a statement. My stomach flips as I hear someone yell, "Mr. Carter, who is your guest this evening?"

I focus all my attention on putting one foot in front of the other. The last thing Theo needs is being tagged in a flurry of photographs with the idiot who managed to take a tumble in Converse.

We finally escape the lights into a dimmed room, decked out in expensive decorations and full of bodies sporting diamonds and Botox. It's all extremely *Gossip Girl.*

"So, uh, that was something."

"Yeah."

"The tiny little details of red carpets and paparazzi must have slipped your mind."

"I'm sorry I didn't tell you. I hate this side of my life."

I reach up and touch his face, not liking the tone his voice has taken one bit. "Let's get through tonight for the artists."

He grabs my hand. "Thank you. I couldn't get through this without you."

"You must find some way to reward me." I lift up to my toes, softly pressing my lips to his.

"How about some mini cheeseburgers?"

I mean, for once, my mind wasn't on food at all, but fuck if I can turn down some mini cheeseburgers. "Where?"

Theo smiles. "The one good thing about this event, the food rocks."

"I'll try not to embarrass you in front of the van der Woodsens and Waldorfs."

"The who?"

I wave him off. "Don't worry about it."

I'm halfway through my fifth mini cheeseburger when I hear a raspy voice, as if it's been permanently ruined from too much yelling, say, "Oh, aren't *you* a sweet thing?"

His words are like cough syrup, full of honey but still fucking gross, and have my beloved cheeseburgers rising up the back of my throat.

Theo stiffens beside me, face gone white, as if every bit of life has been sucked out of him at the sound of that voice, confirming who's just approached my other side. I can't imagine the kind of images it brings with it, ones of that voice greeting him in the middle of the night, with no effort spent on sounding civil before the wailing begins.

A callous look is easy to muster as I turn in his father's direction, giving him a once over. Aside from his height being roughly the same as Theo's, I don't see a *smidge* of him in this man. His father's skin is a worn, leathery texture, stained red from years of alcohol abuse. His features are too big for his face, as if even those are more domineering than anyone would want. Where Theo is handsome, sculpted and charming, this man is lined in a way where you can see his anger sitting a feather's brush away at all times. Something bubbles in my gut, begging for an outlet. Pure *rage*.

"Photoshop just gets better and better these days." I have never used this tone, but I can't stomach looking at this man who caused Theo so much pain. "I barely recognize you from the billboards."

I see Theo's head jerk in my direction, probably in shock.

Bill has the audacity to think I'm making a joke and laughs. "I like this one."

"Wish I could say the same." I reach over and grab Theo's hand, making myself his lifeline. Bill doesn't miss it.

"I'm sure poor little Theo here has told you all about his sad little life, where he's decided to write me in as a villain. He's always had such...imagination."

Bullies like to be heard. They like to be feared. I won't give him that. "Actually, I can't say that I've heard much about you at all."

He laughs again, and I decide that I'd rather listen to nails on a chalkboard. "I'm sure that's not true."

"Believe what you like, but I'm certain you spend more time thinking about you, than Theo does." I've spoken all of a few sentences with this man and I already feel like I need a shower. He's a disgusting slime ball, and I don't know how much more of this I can take before I physically scratch his eyes out.

Bill turns his focus on Theo. "Are you just going to let this *girl* do all the talking, son?" His tone drips with condescension. "I haven't seen you in a year, and you have nothing to say?"

"I hope you've been well," Theo manages. His voice is hollow, stiff. It twists my heart, and the burning in my stomach intensifies.

Bill breaks out into a counterfeit laugh. "Weak as ever, son." He turns his attention back toward me, letting his eyes glide down my body like I'm here for *him*.

"We were just going," I say as I wrap my arm through Theo's, giving us an out, before I end up needing a defense attorney of my own for assaulting this man in public.

Bill smiles again. "I'm sure you were."

Theo hasn't said another word. I can't take another minute of this, seeing the person who's brought so much brightness into my life being dimmed even a fraction. I need his witty banter. His ability to always say the right thing. Seeing him standing here like a ghost snaps something in me.

"Wish I could say it was a pleasure, Bob, but I'm sure you don't get that very often anyway."

"It's Bill."

"Isn't that what I said?" My voice cuts like a knife. I have no idea who this person is, but I'm so happy she came out to play tonight. I begin to turn us in the other direction to make our escape when Bill grabs my arm, pulling me to a stop.

His touch sends nausea roiling through me, which only increases when he leans in close, saying just loud enough for Theo to hear, too, "Let me know if you ever get sick of the child, and you want to know what a real man *feels* like."

Everything goes silent. This kind of hate is something I've never known. I want to *hurt* him. There is only burning rage, incinerating my insides, ready to burn this entire fucking place to the ground with him inside.

This disgusting excuse of a man, who made the person I love most consider something that would have taken him away from me forever, thinks he can not only make a pass at me, but take yet another piece of happiness away from Theo in the process.

I lean in even closer. He's got this smug look on his face as if he thinks he has an OUNCE of anything that could tempt me. My voice is a silenced gun when I finally speak.

"That CHILD is the most amazing person I have ever fucking met. Despite your BEST attempts at ruining anything good in him, he prevailed, making him stronger than you in *every* respect. You're just so fucking rotten on the inside, so far *gone* as a person, that you can do nothing but try to contaminate everything around you. Well, you FAILED. Theo is GOOD." Bill's mask falls, just in the slightest, and I keep going. "And it's a fucking *mercy* that your wife didn't have to stick around to see what you did to your son, what kind of monster you have become. It's a *mercy* that she doesn't know that you can still look yourself in the mirror every fucking day, despite being the *reason* someone had to SAVE YOUR SON'S LIFE. So, take your deadbeat, abusive, piece of shit drunk self and don't ever come within a fucking mile of us again."

I tear my arm out of his grasp, speaking loud enough for those around us to hear now. "And don't you *ever* make a pass at me again. I'm not into wrinkly, shriveled-up dicks."

I hear gasps all around us and don't bother to stick around to watch Bill struggle to ease the looks of horror on the eavesdropping faces.

"Now," I say pleasantly, like that didn't just happen, as I lead Theo to the dance floor. "Let's give these plastics something else to talk about."

I don't marvel at my bravery. Standing up to bullies is the bare goddamn minimum, and I should have started a long time ago.

As I come around to Theo's front, I have no idea why I brought us to the dance floor of all places. "I should have thought this through. I've got nothing to offer besides some below-average twerking."

Theo doesn't laugh at my joke the way I hoped, he just stares at me, silent. I find so much turmoil still left in his eyes, but they're no longer empty and dead. They are full of emotion, shock, maybe even a little regret. I'm busy sorting through it all when he reaches up, cupping my face.

"Ara?"

"Yeah?"

"That was the most badass thing I have ever seen, tied only with you decking that douchebag in the face." I wave him off, but he grabs my wrist. "*Nobody* stands up to my father. Even the judges, the politicians, they're all afraid of him."

I shrug like it's no big deal, like I haven't become an absolute *menace* to society this year.

"Ara, look at me."

I do, instantly recognizing the emotion in his eyes as the one I've always seen but never been able to place. The first time I saw it was the night we TP'd that asshole's house, and it's usually tucked away behind others, but right now it's front and center for me to see.

"I love you, Ara. I've loved you from the minute I saw your smile at the airport." His thumb brushes over my cheek. "I loved you then, and every day I love you more."

I should tell him how I feel. I should tell him that I feel the same way, that I love him so much it feels like my chest is caving in. But I just can't get the words out.

Instead, I grab his hand and drag him away.

# CHAPTER FORTY-ONE

## Present - Ara

Beyond words, I desperately search for somewhere private, away from the crowd bedecked in Cartier and Tiffany's.

A coat closet isn't an option, there being a literal coat check attendant whom I'm sure would not appreciate our presence. On second thought, maybe he would. *Nobody* is wearing a coat in Florida, so it would be the first activity of the night to come his way, but I'm not in the mood to share.

A supply closet isn't an option either, as those are tucked far away from this ballroom. God forbid one of these people would have to lay their eyes on such things.

All I know is I need to figure out something fast. That disgusting man needs to be purged from our thoughts forever. The spot on my arm where he grabbed me needs to be erased by Theo's touch. The shadows he cast over us need to be driven away by sparkling light.

*Finally.*

Up ahead on my left, I see a door which is seamlessly designed to not take away from the beauty of the wall. Made of the same texture and color as the walls, the only thing that gives it away are the tiny cracks and silver handle, which I almost missed.

I glance around, relieved to see that not a single person has noticed us, too busy climbing social ladders or staring at their reflections in the glasses of champagne. Grabbing the cold handle, I push the door open quietly so we can slip in before anyone spots us.

The room we enter is not some sort of service hallway to a kitchen, which I expect. The only thing I can think of to describe it is some sort of…gentlemen's club? It's the kind of room you see in movies where the mafia bosses come to smoke cigars.

There are beautiful mahogany leather chairs arranged around a low, wooden table in the middle, perfect for resting drinks while the men play cards. The carpet has beautiful, golden designs all throughout the burgundy color making it look even more expensive.

It's less modern than everything else I've seen throughout this hotel, making it seem frozen in time. Windows paned with gold run the entire length of the far side wall giving a stunning view of the other high rises. There are even desks, lined with decanters of amber liquid I can only imagine is the highest of quality.

The most beautiful part of the room is surely the wall to my left, lined by built-in bookshelves and leather-bound books. I drop his hand, moving to run my fingers across the gilded spines, awestruck.

I turn to Theo, who's been unusually quiet. Thankfully, he's no longer just the shell of the man I love, which I expect to see, quiet and caved. Instead, his expression is full of curiosity and trouble.

I smirk. "You've been quiet."

"I wanted to see where we ended up, though for someone who clearly had no idea where she was going, you picked well." He looks around, taking in the place. "I'm just wondering why we are here."

"I needed you alone." I lick my lips, my skin buzzing with anticipation.

"You want me?" Theo's eyes zero in, darkening, and he takes a step closer. "Right here? Right now?"

I nod, my chest heaves with my rough breathing.

Theo lifts a challenging brow as he takes a step closer. "Someone could walk in on us any moment."

"It would be their lucky day." The normal, not sex-crazed version of me would think about the ramifications of public nudity, but right now I'd risk anything, even solitary confinement in a maximum-security prison, if it got this man where I want him.

"There's a lot of windows." A devious smile spreads across his lips as he takes another step forward. "Anyone could be watching us."

I don't tell him that it makes me need him more, and thankfully, I don't need to.

Theo lunges for me, cradling my head as he backs me against the shelf. His mouth is on mine in an instant, his soft lips easing me open to explore. Body pressing into my skirts, he gets as close as he can manage, but there is still too much between us.

Theo's fingers sink into my hair, gripping it firmly, without making it fall to the other side of the knife toward pain. He trails kisses down my neck and across my collarbone, suckling along the way, making me want to scream.

His lips head south, brushing over the swell of my breast as Theo reaches for the laces on the back of my dress. I bat his hand away and shake my head. "That is *way* too much work."

I open my mouth to say something else, but stop in my tracks when he tugs down the cups of my dress, exposing my breast just long enough to take a long pull before righting it.

My knees almost give out as he slowly drops to his, keeping eye contact the entire time as he lifts my skirts and disappears beneath them. His fingers are unrushed as he moves my underwear aside, feeling how wet I am already.

The answer is plenty. Plenty. Fucking. Wet.

This isn't the place to take our time and I let him know, perhaps a bit too aggressively based on the chuckle I get in response. Surely one could die from the overwhelmingness of such sensation.

Grabbing the bookshelf behind me for support, I open my legs wider for him. My head tips back, resting against the leather spines, eyes closing as I relish in the work he does with his tongue.

So deep in bliss, I don't even hear the door open.

I let out a soft, almost inaudible moan, and then a throat clears, Theo's ministrations pausing with it. My eyes shoot open, landing on a young man in a catering suit holding a tray of glasses, looking mortified. I glance down, thankful that my skirts are big enough that Theo is completely concealed.

"Sorry, ma'am. I didn't know anyone was in here yet."

"I, um…" Theo's work picks up again and I'm breathless, having to grip the bookshelf to keep quiet. "…needed some air?"

"Of course." Indecision weighs on his face. I'm certain that I shouldn't be in here, but I don't get the idea he is brave enough to kick me out. For all he knows I'm the spawn of one of those horrible people out there waiting for an excuse to get him fired for shits and giggles. "Can I get you anything?"

"I'm okay." Just get the hell out of here, dude.

"Are you sure? Would you like some water? You look flushed."

Theo's tongue circles my center again, and I'm about ten seconds away from losing control entirely. This waiter needs to get the fuck out of here before I do it right in front of him.

"I'M. FINE." It comes out breathy, strangled, and perhaps a bit too emphatic for my liking, but he finally gets the point.

"Enjoy your night," he says with a bow as he backs out of the room closing the door behind him.

As I hear the soft click, I reach down for my skirt, uncovering Theo. "Up. Now."

"I'm not done." His voice vibrates against me, and I nearly finish right there, but I manage to hold out. We are doing this together, where I can see his soul and he can see mine.

"I need you. *All* of you," I say, but he continues. "*Please, Theo.*"

He gives me one last kiss and pulls away, coming back up for air.

I don't waste any time as I reach for his belt, quickly undoing it, followed by his pants. Theo watches my every move as I reach into his underwear, freeing his erection, and lean down to give him a little lick.

"This time, there is no hiding if someone comes in." Translation: hurry the hell up.

It's Theo's undoing. He reaches down, lifting me by my thighs to set me against one of the lower shelves before sinking inside. We both moan as he places his hands beneath my ass so he can work me, getting me exactly where we both need: as deep as our bodies will allow. The way he moves should be illegal, setting the perfect pace and moving in just the right way that I'm already on the edge.

"Theo." It's the only warning I can manage.

"I know, baby." He pumps inside me again, over and over and over. "Fuck. I'm not going to last much longer."

I groan, tipping my head back. Theo takes my weight into one arm as he reaches up, freeing both of my breasts this time. His gaze is locked on how my breasts move with every thrust, and watching him watch me is more than I can take.

I bite down as the pleasure shoots through me, unable to stop the sounds escaping from my lips. Theo reaches up, covering my mouth with his hand, and follows me into bliss.

The final wave crashes into us, leaving us breathless and speechless and spent. Theo places his forehead against mine, our eyes meeting. I find so much love and admiration staring back at me, my chest nearly caves in on itself. This man, who would follow me anywhere, would do anything for me. The man whom I can trust with my heart and offer my soul to.

"Theo?"

"Yeah?"

I've never used these words lightly, and I offer them to him now. "I love you."

He smiles, giving one of my strands a gentle tug before tucking it behind my ear. "I love you, too, Ara Scott."

• • •

*Buzz.*

*Buzz.*

*Buzz.*

The mosquito in my room is insane. Needing as little reminder of his father as possible, Theo wanted to stay at my place after the fundraiser, but he might regret it if he wakes up with fifteen mosquito bites.

*Buzz.*

*Buzz.*

*Buzz.*

I mean, mosquitoes are always obnoxious, but this is a whole new level.

*Buzz.*

*Buzz.*

*Buzz.*

It's been buzzing around for hours now.

*Buzz.*

*Buzz.*

*Buzz.*

Okay. Enough is enough. I'm going to slay this fucker.

*Buzz.*

I peel open my eyelids, squinting in the late morning sun pouring through the window.

*Buzz.*

Theo's arm is draped around my middle, where it rests every single night, and I slowly lift it so I can slide out from underneath.

*Buzz.*

I train my ears, listening for it, but soon realize it's not coming from a mosquito at all. It's my phone, which is buzzing nonstop. With Theo lying next to me, it could only be Lou.

Another day flashes through my mind and I reach for it, suddenly concerned that something has happened to her. The screen lights up with her contact, and my gut drops to the floor.

"Lou!?? Is everything okay!?"

"Ara!!! Where the hell have you been!?"

"Sleeping!! What's wrong?"

Lou laughs, hysterically. "What's wrong!!?!? Are you kidding!? It couldn't be better!!! Have you looked at your Instagram?"

"I just got out of bed, so no, I haven't looked at my Instagram." I rarely do as it is, but she knows that.

"Put me on speaker and look now. I want to hear your reaction."

I sigh, following her instructions. "Reaction to whaaa…" I trail off as I look at my app.

*Ten-thousand four-hundred and eleven.*

*Ten-thousand four-hundred and twelve.*

*Ten-thousand four-hundred and thirteen.*

*Ten-thousand four-hundred and fourteen.*

And *counting.*

My phone drops to the floor.

"Ara!? Ara!?" Lou squeals from the phone.

Theo finally raises his head, curious about what all the noise is about.

"We need to flee the country."

He gives me a sleepy chuckle. "Why?"

"I went viral."

"Ara!!!! They love it!!!!!!!!" Lou yells from the floor.

"What do you mean, they love it?" I lean down to pick up my phone.

"Your dress! Everyone is freaking out about it and asking how to get it. You could probably auction it for a million bucks!"

I would never, but I don't say that. Instead, I take a deep breath and touch the icon which opens my Instagram account. Thanks to a comment from Lou, letting everyone know who designed the dress, I've since been tagged in hundreds of posts about a mystery girl wearing a mystery label to Tampa's most prestigious charity event.

Follow after follow pops up, along with messages, comments, and even more likes. Nearly passing out as I see the amount of blue checks next to the names which now fill my inbox, I silently hand my phone to Theo (Lou still squawking), so he can have a look while I pace the length of my tiny room. Essentially, a lot of people now know that I exist, that I can make pretty stuff, and now they want something from me.

I remind myself that no one is laughing and take a minute to marvel at what is unfolding. Months ago had this happened, I would curl up in the corner of the room, unable to breathe while the monster under my skin reared its head, ready to destroy anything good which came my way.

But I've changed, haven't I?

"Wow," Theo says, taking it all in. "This is a lot."

"No kidding," I say dryly.

"Well, there is only one question."

I stop pacing and face him, heart pounding, adrenaline making me feel spinny.

"What do you want to do about it?"

Before I can come up with an answer, a knock sounds at my front door. I close my eyes, relieved at the sense of normalcy that I hope will be delivered on the other side of that door.

"Hold that thought," I say as I walk out of my bedroom and into my living room. Sure enough, Dave is smiling away on the other side of the door, light gray envelope in hand.

"Have you had a good month, Ara?"

I smile. "One of the best."

"That's good to hear, sweetheart." His eyes are full of warmth, and I can tell he is truly happy for me. "Tell Theo I said hello."

"Will do," I say as I shut my door.

"Another letter?" Theo asks from my doorway.

I nod, taking a seat on my couch, ready to find out what's inside.

*Dear Ara,*

*I've been watching a lot of TV recently, all kinds of shows really, but I've mostly been alternating between an old action series from the 80s and a funny one about a psychic detective. I've never been one to binge watch, but I've been enjoying it, having some really good laughs.*

*What I love about these shows is there is always another adventure, another risk they take without knowing what the outcome will be. It gets my heart pumping every time, wondering if this is the moment they get caught, or busted, or whatever.*

*I wish I had given you a life which had more adventure. I wasn't the most fun parent, having always been content to stay home and spend my time with you. Except, I should have encouraged you to get out more. To chase adventure and do things which get your heart beating out of your chest.*

*That said, I could never regret the time we spent together, even if it was mostly being plopped on your couch or mine watching movies. I would choose that over any other adventure in the world. But for you? I want you to see the very best that the world has to offer.*

*Which, of course, brings me to your task this month.*

*I want you to do something crazy, something that makes your heart beat out of your chest. I want you to know what it's like to have adrenaline coursing through your veins, not knowing what is going to happen next. I want it all for you, Ara.*

*And as always, I wish I was there to see it.*

*Since I know I won't, I'll imagine you came over to my house, barging in without a knock. You'd find me in the kitchen, preparing a new recipe I found online and printed out. I'd probably be frustrated about it not turning out right, but you'd come in and save my day by sharing a story of excitement.*

*You'd tell me all about it, or perhaps you wouldn't, depending on the content, you're a grown woman now, after all. But even if you chose not to tell me, I'd still see that look in your eye and know that my little girl was living.*

*I love you so much, Ara.*

*I miss you every day.*

*But you already know all of that.*

*So go get that heart beating.*

*Love,*

*Dad*

I look over to Theo, who's focusing all of his attention on making us coffee so as not to invade my privacy. It makes me smile, his thoughtfulness.

The memory of last night appears in my mind, the red carpet and paparazzi, verbally assaulting his father and everything that came after. I think about my phone and the thousands of people wanting to see more of my designs.

My heart doesn't stop, it continues beating faster and faster. It's a heavy, consistent rhythm, harder and harder, until I'm sure it's going to burst from my chest as I make my decision.

# CHAPTER FORTY-TWO

## Last Year - Theo

It took a few weeks, but we've finally finished throwing away everything William deemed to be "old crap." The house is squeaky clean and ready to be sold or rented or whatever will get done with the house.

William says he hasn't found it in himself to be able to write the letters to Ara. I know he tries to. I see him sitting at his desk in his home office day after day, staring at the blank paper. Sometimes, he has to toss the page on top when it becomes covered in tears.

That's where he is sitting now. I know he wants to finish them before things get too bad, but we don't talk about when that time will come as I can see that it's getting closer and closer.

I started staying with William two nights ago. I had to tell Connor that I was going to some author conference, and William told Ara he's been shipped off to some mandatory retreat. It won't be long before he's going to need care that I can't provide, and it's a hard truth to confront.

My phone buzzes and it's a message from Phil. I still feel the need to pinch myself when messages from the head of Puffin Press come in, after he decided to personally oversee the progress of my novel toward publication.

**Phil: Editor says it's looking good so far. Keep you updated.**

I type a quick message to thank him for the update and make my way to William's office. Even though the door is open, I lightly knock on the trim around the doorway, and he looks up.

"Come on in, Theo."

I walk over and take a seat. "Doing okay?"

He rubs his temples. "I've seen better days, that's for sure."

"Need anything?"

"No, I'm still working on that tea you made me earlier." He takes in a wet, wheezy breath that even as a usually non-aggressive person makes me want to throw something against the wall. If only my anger would be enough to drive that shit out of his lungs. "You know, nobody says how much impending doom gets the wheels turning in a head."

His dry humor, even at the worst of times, will never get old. I crack a grin despite myself. "What are the wheels turning around today?"

William smirks. He *SMIRKS.*

In the month that I've been following this man around, I've seen contemplation, kindness, amusement, regret, loss, and even despair but I have *never* seen Willaim smirk. "I was thinking about something I've never told anyone."

"Have you decided to finally share?"

"It was one of my proudest moments, so someone ought to bask in my glory, before it dies with me."

"I'm on the edge of my metaphorical seat already."

"Help me to the living room, that way you have an actual seat, and I can tell you."

I hate this part. Where the signs of his decline become so obvious. When he sits at his desk we can pretend. When we sit on the couch, laughing at something on the TV, we can pretend. We can pretend to be old pals in a bachelor pad enjoying a bromance-only version of the single life. But when it's time to move?

I give him my forearm for support as he heaves himself up, just as I duck down to wrap his arm around my shoulder and my arm around his waist.

"I better get over this drinking problem of mine pretty soon."

William likes to pretend that I'm getting him home drunk whenever we have to walk.

I give him a laugh, but we both know it's not a real one. We make it through the hall and I get him settled gently into his recliner. Taking a seat on the couch beside his chair, I watch him become more animated than I've ever seen.

"It's first period biology with Mr. Jenkins, who was a very loyal, very conservative, *proper* Christian man." He smiles a little, pleased with his description and set-up for the story. "You see, I knew that Tuesday afternoons he would stay behind and get the VHS for the next day's class set up on the TV. That way all he had to do was push play."

Before he can continue, he's taken over by a fit of coughs. I get up and run to the kitchen, coming back with a glass of lukewarm water. He takes it from me gingerly and sips it down to soothe his throat. "Thank you. Now where was I?"

"Mr. Jenkins was setting up the TV." I'm pleased when I manage to keep my voice level.

"Right." His smile has returned, and he launches back into his tale. "So after school I waited around long enough that most of the faculty would have gone home, including Mr. Jenkins. I snuck into the classroom and changed out the tape."

"What did you put on instead?"

He smiles victoriously as I ask the question he was *dying* for me to ask. "Porn."

I snort. "You fucking didn't."

"I. Fucking. Did." He smiles. "Right at the climax, too."

I laugh. A genuine, deep laugh.

"Mr. Jenkins jumped out of his skin. I'll never forget the look on his face as the moans rang out and the thrusting began. It's like he couldn't hit the power button no matter how hard he tried." I imagine poor Mr. Jenkins' hands trying to push a button, slipping around like everything was greased in oil.

We're both laughing now. I've got tears in my eyes and the melancholy feeling of wanting to sit here with this man forever. His laugh turns into coughs, his coughs turn into wheezes, and I'm reminded of the imminent reality instead.

With every day that passes, I understand his choice not to tell his daughter. Seeing him in pain is killing me. Changing me. I can't imagine having an entire lifetime to love this man and seeing it end this way.

"You know what's a weird thing, Theo?"

"What's that?"

"Time." William pauses. "In a moment it seems to crawl by, but before you know it, it's gone. Don't let time slip away from you, Theo, you have to promise me that you won't."

It's the easiest one I've ever made. "I promise."

I let myself absorb his warning about time, vowing that with every moment that passes, I will ensure that life grows from my time. One day, I'll mark a permanent reminder of it into my skin.

"Say, get an old man a beer?"

I give him a hesitant look, not sure what the right thing to do is.

"What? Is it bad for my health?"

Point taken.

We drink beer after beer until even the wallpaper is hilarious, making the most of our time, not letting even a moment slip away.

As every moment with him is doing.

OCTOBER
Dear Ara

# CHAPTER FORTY-THREE

*Present - Ara*

A knock on my door startles me, and I release the pedal of my machine as I yell for them to come in. There are only two possibilities for who it is, both male, and I know which one would knock and which one would barge in.

Theo pokes his head in, a smile on his face. "Hey, sorry to interrupt, but something arrived for you." He opens the door wider, and I notice that he's carrying a light gray envelope.

I've been so intent on completing this project, I'd totally overlooked the significance of today. I cover my mouth, not sure how to feel about the fact that I'd completely forgotten.

"Ara, he would want you to be doing exactly what you're doing." Theo's words settle over me, quelling the rising guilt and nausea with it. "You're healing."

My dad's message in every letter, over and over, is that he wants me to *live*. He wants me to experience everything that life has to offer. Pouring everything I have into something I love is exactly what he would want. In fact, the entire purpose of these letters was to ensure I did just that. I take the letter from Theo, thanking him as he ducks out the door to give me privacy.

Feeling my dad's presence, I hold the letter to my chest and tell him, "A lot has changed this month." One happy tear trickles down my face. With the increasing demand of my designs, and Theo asking me to move in with him, it's been a whirlwind. Of course, I'd accepted and submitted a formal change of address to the post office on the same day, also making sure Dave knew where I would be.

Theo and Connor gave me free choice of which room I wanted for my design room, Connor even offered to move out of his room if it had the best setup for what I needed. I responded to his sweet gesture by staying as far away from his room as possible, so as to never hear him with a girl.

That said, in the almost month I've officially lived here, and the countless nights before that, he's never *once* brought someone home with him. Theo says this is Connor's sacred space, and all the debauchery has to happen elsewhere so as to not desecrate it, but I've also gotten to know him better, learned what he's gone through, and it's forged a permanent bond between us. We understand each other in a way that's only possible when you've lost the person you care about most.

The requests for custom pieces haven't stopped flooding in either, since that day the starlight dress went viral. Ivy volunteered to help me make some content for my page, while showing me everything I can do with the platform, and it's resulted in so many requests that my time is completely booked up until March of next year.

Once I realized it wouldn't be stopping, I helped Jane find a new manager who can be there more time throughout the week. I still go in every weekend for the workshops, the budding artist community being my baby and all.

"You'll be happy to know I had to throw away my couch," I say with a chuckle. A moment later, I feel a warm presence surrounding me, and another tear escapes as I clutch the letter even closer. Maybe I'm imagining it, or maybe our connection is one that goes beyond the mere physical universe.

"And look, I've kept something alive." Oscar (like the grouch) sits in the corner, glaring at me. I've come to love the little cat with my entire heart, despite dirty looks being his love language. He may never be the cat that cuddles, but I'd jump in front of a bus for that cranky little thing. "I guess I'll open this now."

*Dear Ara,*

*There is something you should know, something I've been saving, wanting to make sure that I gave it to you at the right time. I needed you to be ready for it.*

*My lawyer should have contacted you long ago and arranged the inheritance be organized for you. I know I'm not a millionaire, but I've worked hard to make sure you would be set up, that amidst your grief and battle against life, you wouldn't have to worry about making ends meet.*

My stomach clenches, regret weighing on me. Not because I want his money, but because Dad worked hard for something to leave to me, and I brushed it off. The money never meant anything to me, but I didn't realize what it meant for him, the reassurance that I would be provided for.

*My lawyer was to keep this next part a secret until now, when you come to him with this note from me. There is another account, which is significantly more cushy. I put it together for when you'd be ready to (hopefully) use it as an investment into your future.*

*Whether that means you want to use it for real estate, to invest in something you believe in, or to fund your designs, there will be enough there to do it. My only request is that you use that clever mind of yours and use it well. There is enough there that I would recommend contacting one of my colleagues at the office to help you manage it.*

*It may be wishful thinking that you could use this money to take a chance on yourself, but part of me wonders whether it isn't. You could be ready by now. I can only hope these letters have helped to guide you, helped you to overcome your grief and helped you to grow.*

*Your task for this month is to visit my lawyer's office with this letter and gain access to the account. He will know what to do. What you decide to do with it afterward is in your hands.*

*Don't be afraid to believe in yourself, Ara.*

*The only limits you face are the ones you set for yourself.*

*And I hope you tell those limits to get fucked.*

*Love,*

*Dad*

My laugh is accompanied by the salty taste of tears, and I'm reminded of the moment that Dad fell in love with that phrase when he saw it on a bumper sticker. He rarely used it, but when he did, it became the highlight of my week.

I run my fingers through my hair, knowing I can't put it off any longer. Taking my phone off the *Making Magic* setting, I open the contact of my dad's attorney and press call.

It only rings a couple times before a disbelieving, "Sar- er, Ara? Ara Scott?"

I cringe at how many times this poor receptionist must have tried to contact me for her to remember my number and chosen name.

"Yep, this is Ara." I sigh. "I'd like to make an appointment with William Scott's lawyer for as soon as possible."

"Absolutely." Her mouse clicks a few times. "He actually had a cancelation for this afternoon, would you like to come in today?"

No. "Yes, that would be great. I can be there in an hour."

"We will see you soon, then, Miss Scott."

• • •

"Ara Scott."

"Yes, lovely to meet you, Ara." It took ten months to get me to step foot inside this office, it's not lovely to meet me. She definitely hates me, but she's paid not to say it. "Second door on your right, he is expecting you."

The office is one of those old-fashioned ones, and probably hasn't had a face lift since the 90s. Everything is in perfect condition and beautifully maintained, but not even remotely modern. The hallway is lined with wooden doors featuring glass windows and bamboo blinds.

*Warner Woods, Attorney At Law*

I snort. I'm sure he graduated law school long before *Legally Blonde* came out, but I can't imagine I'm the only client who thought that was funny. I make a little tapping sound before gingerly opening his door.

Mr. Woods stands up to shake my hand and motions me to a chair in front of his desk. "Please, have a seat, Miss Scott."

"You can call me Ara."

"Ara." He smiles. "We've had these documents ready for…a while…so you really only need to sign a few things and it will all be settled."

Good. The sooner I'm out of here, the better.

"I also have this." Thankfully, he only glances at the letter. I was afraid he would take it from me and keep it as evidence of some kind.

"Right. Let's start with these first, and I'll have Lois prepare the documents for that account as well." He makes a call, giving his secretary specific instructions before going into a very detailed description of my inheritance and the responsibilities which come with it.

The amount of work my dad put in to make sure I would be okay becomes quickly and obviously clear. It's not lost on me that due to my unwillingness to come in, Mr. Woods and his secretary have been managing everything for me until I was ready.

"Mr. Woods, I'm sorry about not coming in sooner, I just–"

He holds up his hands, pausing me. "Please, call me Warner."

"Warner."

"I've had no problem assisting, I can't imagine what you must be going through." He gives me a sad smile. "I knew you'd show up eventually and William was a friend. I was willing to help manage the affairs as long as necessary, until you were ready."

Warner hands me a small stack of papers, watching as my eyes physically bug out of my face when I take in the value of the assets and accounts I'm inheriting.

"Ara, while you're more than capable of handling things on your own, this is a lot to come into all at once. I would recommend getting the help of an accountant."

I nod. "I was planning to contact someone from the office where my dad worked."

"That sounds like a good idea to me."

We wrap it up quicker than expected, and I realize there is one more thing I need to do.

I text Theo an address and walk to my car, thanking Lois on the way out.

• • •

I had expected to find a year's worth of rotten food and layers of dust at least a few inches high, but I should have known better. Everything in my dad's house is perfect.

The kitchen pantry is empty, along with the refrigerator, which has been turned off and left open so as not to smell. White sheets have been draped over every piece of furniture, and the drawers and closets have already been emptied. The only things that remain are a box of sentimentals along with the furniture, someone having put in hours of work to get this place in such an organized, ready to be dealt with condition.

Theo drops to the couch next to me. Maybe it was the effect of walking into a home which is no longer a home to someone, but he had to take a few minutes to himself after coming in the door. He ran his hand over my dad's recliner and smiled at the closet near the kitchen.

"This seems like the place you can walk into, and five minutes later it feels like a home." Something about his words run deep. "What do you plan on doing with it?"

"I'm going to keep it." My dad was smart and paid off his mortgage as quickly as he could. It would be silly to sell an asset which will only increase in value over time. "Hopefully I can find a beautiful family to live here who will love it as much as he did."

Theo's arm wraps around my shoulder, bringing me in close. "And the rest of it?"

I know he's asking what I'll do with the inheritance. "Well, hopefully the accountants will have some input for whatever leftover there is, but I plan to use as much as it takes to create my own line."

Whether a woman is a size thirty or double zero, I want to create a brand that makes them feel nothing short of beautiful.

# CHAPTER FORTY-FOUR

## Last Year - Theo

William hasn't said anything to me in days. I've come to miss his smile and his laugh. It's as if the energy and light he pours into this world has slowly been slipping away. With every dose of painkillers and bout of pain, there is a little bit less of him left.

The past three days have proven to me that William has done right by his daughter. He's no longer the man I've come to cherish and love these past couple months. His decline came faster than I could have predicted, sweeping him away too fast. It feels like just yesterday that we were drinking beers, laughing at nothing, and yet somehow, it couldn't seem further away.

William can no longer stand, and I'd begun carrying his slight frame to and from the bathroom. When even that became too painful, I was forced to call in Hospice. He wanted to go before it came to that, but I guess some things aren't up to choice.

When the nurses arrived, he was still cognizant and he told them I was his son when they asked about my relation. It had sort of slipped out, shocking both of us, before he sheepishly looked to me for approval. Here I was, finally gaining the father I'd always wished for, just to watch him die.

I always imagined death to be tragic, but beautiful. It's not.

The movies make it seem like something which happens in a breath, a whisper. They don't add the days filled by screams of pain, the suffering that comes with the organs slowly shutting down. They don't show you the parts where you're forced to make decisions for your loved ones that you know they would never choose. There is absolutely nothing beautiful about death.

I'd previously thought I could write about it, do it justice with my imagination. Except after having seen it, I know that there are no words to accurately describe what it's like to watch the memories of them laughing, healthy and full of life, get replaced by memories of agony and helplessness as they suffer, while you can do nothing but hold their hand.

Their once comforting shoulder becomes skin and bone. Their smiles become a distant memory. You watch their dignity disappear with every simple task which is completed for them, and no matter how many reassuring words you offer, they go with the feeling of being a burden.

I have nothing more than a couple months of basking in this man's light, but his daughter? She has an entire lifetime of beautiful memories that stood to be tarnished by this merciless disease. A goodbye is an easy trade because I will be haunted by these moments for the rest of my life. Yet I willingly endure, knowing that William will not be alone.

My days and nights have become blurred, only his haggard breathing and the unsteady beeps of machines indicate that time is passing at all. The nurses believe he can still hear me, that he has taken the form of his astral self, so I put on The Eagles and tell him story after story, of faraway places and imaginary worlds.

I wish I could say there was a magical moment, with powerful last words that I could grasp onto forever, but that's another lie they feed you. This isn't a movie. This isn't a book.

With his last shuddered breath, gone is the humor and sound advice.

As his eyes glaze over, gone is the mischief and wisdom.

With his body's stiff, purpling limbs, gone is his once comforting embrace.

Gone is the life he once imbued into this world.

Gone is a friend.

Gone is a father.

Gone is the light.

NOVEMBER
Dear Ara

# CHAPTER FORTY-FIVE

## Present - Ara

"Kill shot." Connor laughs maniacally. "I'm coming for your mother next, asshole."

There's nothing classier than the stuff which leaves the mouth of a guy playing a high-stakes, combat video game.

Theo isn't any better. "Ha! Suck my dick, *laserpowder0604*."

Thankfully, the concierge called me instead of Theo this time to warn me of Dave's arrival. The elevator doors open a moment later, letting Dave into our apartment, letter in hand. Oscar sits next to me, giving Dave a little warning growl to let him know he's in charge of this turf now.

"Please, cover your ears, Dave," I say, cringing. "They're in ten-year-old-boy-who-just-discovered-trash-talking-and-cuss-words mode."

"We can hear you!" Connor whines before shouting, "What a pussy!"

"I best be on my way, then." Dave chuckles, handing me the letter before stepping back into the elevator. "Have a good month, Ara."

"You, too, Dave."

Their shouting follows me all the way to the hallway, where I make my way to my design room and close the door. I take a seat on the little couch that Theo surprised me with, where I usually sit and speak with my clients (it still feels weird to say that word) about what they're envisioning.

I take a deep breath and open the letter.

*Dear Ara,*

*It's November already, can you believe it?*

*The eleventh month. With that, it is officially the start of the holiday season.*

*It kills me to know that you had to be alone last year, but I couldn't stand the thought of the memories of me fighting a losing battle overtaking the good ones which came before.*

*Although you were alone last year, I imagine this year may be even harder. It's the first holiday where you know I won't be there for another, but hopefully (I'm looking at you, Universe) you won't be spending it alone.*

*This time of year is supposed to be a time of joy, food, and celebration. For you and many others it's also a time of sadness, missing those who you wish were there. It's sad for me, too. I can't accept that Thanksgiving will go by and I won't be able to cook for you, that Christmas will come and we won't be watching an array of bad movies just because it's tradition.*

*I would ask you not to be sad, but I know that's impossible, and I don't want you burying your feelings. So, instead I'm asking you to take a day. Take a day to listen to sad music and look at our pictures and cry if you need to. But once you're done, you have to promise me that you will do your best to smile again.*

*I want you to remember what you're grateful for, which leads me to one of your tasks for this month. Take a moment to appreciate the things you feel thankful for, whether it's a person, something you feel honored to have, or just a memory you treasure.*

*The second task is to find a really good meal (it doesn't have to go in that order). I'm not going to delude myself into thinking you're going to cook. Even if I forced you to learn, I know that you'd be miserable the entire time and never do it again. So, just find a good meal. McDonald's (or anything available through a drive-thru) strictly does not count.*

*I guess that's all I came here to say. I've been sitting here, staring at what I've written for almost an hour now, not knowing what else to write. These letters are difficult for me, but I've been wondering why this one has been the hardest of them all.*

*Then I remembered that this is the eleventh letter, meaning the next one is number twelve, and the last for…a while. I won't be able to put off writing it for much longer. Until then, I guess I should finish this letter by telling you what I'm thankful for.*

*I'm thankful for having found a career which allowed me to enjoy going to work every day. I'm thankful for being able to know love the way I knew it with your mother. I'm thankful for learning about loss so I could appreciate what I had. I'm thankful for the home I built for us and the life we lived within it.*

*And most of all, I'm thankful for everything which ever happened, that led to me becoming your dad. You have always been my greatest joy, my greatest love, and my greatest accomplishment.*

*Thank you for picking me.*

*Love,*

*Dad*

I gently set the letter to the side before the tears start to fall and splash over the page. With the rush of everything going on, I haven't stopped to *feel* in a while. Dad is right, I have so much to be thankful for, but I'm going to save that for later. Right now, I'm going to take the day.

My phone is heavy in my hand as I click play on the playlist I made, full of Classic Rock songs which were our favorites. I haven't listened to it since the last time we were together. After I found out he was gone, I didn't want to sink myself into a hole so deep I wouldn't climb out.

After months of healing and moving on, I need to feel it. I need to feel what it's going to be like to eat food that wasn't cooked by him on Thanksgiving. I need to process that I won't be drinking hot chocolate with him on Christmas Eve. I won't be opening presents with him on Christmas morning, or falling asleep on his couch before midnight on New Year's Eve. That when the day comes that I walk down the aisle, my dad won't be there to hand me off.

I let myself feel it all, song after song.

I *have* been healing. I've gone back out in the world, found love, friendship, joy, and even success, but that doesn't mean the wide gaping hole which he left will ever be filled.

I will *always* miss my dad.

There won't be a holiday or birthday or day of the week that passes where I won't wish he were there. It gets easier with time, but part of it is allowing yourself to feel the loss and the pain that comes with it.

I let myself cry and cry and cry and cry. Eventually the snot running down my face becomes too much. My eyes are swollen, and I need a tissue more than I need a liver right now.

Walking into the kitchen as quietly as possible, I pull a few out of the box before realizing I should just grab the entire thing. Suddenly, I feel eyes on me. Both guys have looked up from their video game, staring at me. I'm not sure who does it, but someone clicks exit immediately. My eyes widen, knowing that it was one of their online games, and exiting in the middle of a game is a huge no-no.

If that's not love, I'm not sure what is. The thought has my tears falling again.

Theo stands up first and walks over, taking me into a silent embrace and kissing the top of my head as the tears turn into sobs. Then, another set of limbs wrap around us, giving us another squeeze. My swollen eyes manage to open enough, despite being smushed against Theo's chest, to see Connor looking pretty emotional for someone who "doesn't do" feelings.

My crying slowly stops, replaced by a quiet comfort.

Then, from Connor, sniffling, "Who the fuck brought pollen into the house?"

Theo laughs against my hair. "It's fall, you idiot."

I smile.

With my family.

• • •

Lou's family home is beautiful. Nestled on what seems like a billion acres, the yellow-painted home with white trim brings a smile to my face as we drive up the last leg of the driveway lined by trees with orange and gold leaves.

When Theo found out about a massive author event that would be held on Thanksgiving weekend, I'd encouraged him to go. This is going to be Lou's first time seeing her family since she moved to Florida, and her mother has been begging for a chance to fix things with her daughter after everything that happened. Although I'd love to spend the holiday with Theo, she needed me. Plus, who could turn down a home-cooked southern meal for Thanksgiving?

We decided to drive, considering flight prices and airports are insane this time of year. Plus, Lou having the reassurance of being able to get the hell out of here if needed didn't hurt. She had pulled up this morning with her car *full* of road trip snacks, despite the fact we were driving to a Thanksgiving dinner, and I knew we would be eating our feelings today.

The car comes to a stop. Seven hours later and we've arrived right on time. After messaging Theo to let him know we arrived safely, I glance over and see that Lou's knuckles have turned white with her grip on the steering wheel. Reaching over, I pry them away, taking her hand in mine. "We got this."

She nods, clearly not convinced.

"Lou," I say, squeezing her hand. "You say the word and we'll drive away and go get drunk in a field instead."

Lou finally cracks, a bit of my friend shining through. "Let's do this shit."

I do the honor of knocking on the door, and a few minutes later, a middle-aged but insanely beautiful woman opens the door. With her tightly curled blonde hair, clear blue eyes and curves which are wrapped in an apron, I know immediately that this is Lou's mom.

For a moment they just look at each other, Lou unsure. Her mom's tears spill over, and she moves to wrap her daughter in the kind of hug only a parent who has missed their child greatly can give. "I've missed you so much, Louella."

I refrain from reacting to Lou's full name (something which she's failed to mention) to avoid killing the mood of this much-needed reunion. Lou visibly relaxes, wrapping her arms around her mom in return.

"I've missed you, too, Mama." Lou pulls away and introduces me. "This is Ara."

"It's lovely to meet you, Ara, we have heard so much about you," Lou's mom says as she pulls me in for a hug. "Please, call me Linda."

"It's lovely to meet you, too, Linda," I say, hugging her back. "You have a beautiful home."

"Well, thank you," she says, wiping her hands on her apron with shyness. "Now let's get inside, I don't trust your father to make sure nothing burns."

Lou snorts and leads me inside.

I wait until her mom has disappeared into the kitchen before I say, "Thanks for bringing me…*Louella*."

Lou turns on me with a glare, "If you tell anyone, you die."

"To my grave," I say as I cross my hands over my chest like a corpse.

"Good. I'll give you the grand tour."

Not even an hour later, after the tour and introduction after introduction to more cousins and relatives than I thought possible, we're seated at the large dining table lined with a feast.

"So, Lou," Linda begins, her husband offers her his hand in support, "How long have you and Ara been dating?"

Red wine spews from Lou's mouth, drenching her aunt sitting on the other side of the table who yells in surprise before standing from the table as wine drips from her face and down her front.

Lou lets out a hysterical laugh which sounds more like a strangled scream. "I'm sorry, *what*!?"

Looking around, gazes are pinned on Lou, then me, then Linda, then Lou and me again. I guess everyone is just going to pretend her aunt isn't running to the bathroom crying about her silk dress which is surely ruined.

"Isn't Ara your…*girlfriend*?" Linda laughs nervously.

"Mom," Lou says, covering her face in mortification.

"I'm sorry if that's the wrong word. I mean, I don't want to *assume*…"

"Mom."

"I just don't know how you like to be referred to, and oh gosh, this is so embarrassing. I'm already messing this up."

"Mom."

"I am *so* sorry." Linda looks at me now. "I'm still learning about these things."

"MOM!" Lou yells. "Ara is not my *girlfriend*. She is JUST a friend who also happens to be a female."

"Oh…" Linda says, processing. "*Oh.* So you're not…*together*?"

"No!! Ara has a *boyfriend*, and she's like my *sister*."

Pause. "Oh. Well, isn't this even more embarrassing now."

Everyone at the table looks like they're about to pass out. People are whispering in each other's ears. The aunt is wailing in the bathroom. Someone's grandmother starts to utter a prayer as she clutches her cross, and all I want to do is laugh. So, I do.

"It's okay, Linda. I'm not offended at all, and I think it's wonderful how accepting you were, thinking I was her girlfriend." I smile, sending an encouraging look to Lou. "We really are like sisters. My boyfriend had to go out of town, and Lou brought me along, not wanting to leave me alone during the holiday, especially since I can't cook."

"Well, of course, you're welcome regardless!!" Linda says sweetly. "Nobody goes hungry on Thanksgiving, and let's just pretend none of this happened, yes?"

Lou drags her hands down her face and laughs, "Mortifying family conversations? *Check.* Reminder that I'm the last single one of the family? *Check.* It's a real Thanksgiving now!"

We all laugh at that.

"Let's make a toast," I say, Dad's letter coming back to me. "I'll start. I'm thankful for having Lou as my very best friend, she has become my family, and I can't remember what life was like without her."

Taking turns, sharing what we are thankful for, we all laugh and drop our arms as they start to ache by the fifth person. Finally, we make it through the entire table and clink our glasses together.

I pause before taking a sip, thinking of everything else I'm thankful for. I think about Jane and the leap of faith she took on me, putting everything into motion after giving me my first dose of confidence in the workplace. I think about my designs, my beautiful machine and how happy I am to make a career out of something I love.

I think of Connor, my chosen brother.

I think of Theo, for walking into my life when I was shrouded in darkness and lighting a torch, for being the kind of person who makes me believe in this world again.

Then, I think of Dad. Most people never get to know what it's like to have a dad like him. A parent and a true guardian, but above all else, a friend. Even though my time with him was cut short, I would pick him every single time.

I am thankful for all of our laughs and our jokes and our moments. I'm thankful that even in death, he didn't abandon me, but instead held my hand. Perhaps the first few months I was so enveloped in my grief that I did not feel it. I was so focused on him being gone in the physical sense that I didn't realize that he's never left; that he will *always* be here.

Ever present. Ever existing. Ever alive.

• • •

"What are we doing here?" Suspicion creeps into Lou's voice as I pull into a parking lot in the heart of Tampa. The rest of Thanksgiving was beautiful, full of love and laughter, and I knew it was the perfect time to make a little stop on the way home. "Is this where you finally kill me after working so hard to gain my trust?"

I snort. "I would come up with something a lot more original than an abandoned warehouse."

"Fair." She looks around some more, peeking in through the little windows of the warehouse. Finally, she spots the little building, not much more than a shack that sits adjacent to the main building as she wanders over to check it out. "Oh, this is cute."

Lou takes in the baby blue painted wood and white trim which desperately needs a coat of paint. She runs her hand down the smooth, yellow door and touches the weeds which have taken over the little planters, her curiosity finally winning out. "So what are we doing here?"

"I wanted to show it to you because…I bought it."

"*What*!?" Lou spins on me, excitement and shock spreading across her face. "Are you fucking with me!?"

I laugh. "I'm not."

"You bought this whole thing!?" she exclaims, gesturing to the little shack, the warehouse which will become my design hub, and the parking lot.

I nod. "There is only one problem…"

"What?"

"I need a tenant for the additional space," I say motioning behind her. "And I won't be able to be here every day unless I have access to coffee at all times…"

"What are you saying?"

I smile. "Lou, will you be my tenant? Will you open your café here, next to my future design studio?"

Tears fill her eyes, and she starts rapidly blinking, trying to suck them back in.

"I know it won't be forever. People will go crazy for you, and you'll need to expand and get something bigger, but I just thought for starting out–" The breath is punched out of me as Lou crashes into me for a hug.

We both go down, hitting the ground, pain blocked out by our laughter. Gravel digs into my elbow and my hip, but I focus on my best friend, my sister, and the possibility that we can make our dreams come true together.

"Of course, I'll be your tenant!!"

A warm, happy breeze gently pulls through tendrils of my hair, and I know then that my joy rippled all the way to where my dad could feel it.

# CHAPTER FORTY-SIX

## Last Year - Theo

My fingers mindlessly trace over the folded-up piece of paper which has lived in my pocket for a week now. It's something that should be framed, never creased, but I need it too much. I need to keep it where it can be a lifeline. Where I can cherish his words. Where I can go for guidance.

When I stepped back into our home last week, the ruse was up. Connor knew something had happened, taking one look at my face and defeated posture and going straight for the top-shelf liquor. I'd gone to my room to drop my bag off and shower, something I hadn't done in days. I'd found the letter at the bottom of my bag, tucked below my things, where it had remained hidden for nearly a week.

It's why I'm here.

The airport is one of those places that doesn't change much. I haven't been here in nearly five years, yet the colored signs and curved roads are just as I remember, the lights of the airport becoming brighter as the sky dims to dusk.

After dropping my car off in the short-term parking, I make my way inside past the crowds and hurried travelers to the escalator which takes me up to the busiest terminal at Tampa International Airport.

I will admit, it's a great spot. Thousands of people rush by, offering a view of the entire spectrum of humanity from one little chair. There is even a little café across the way, offering respite from the exhaustion that comes with any journey.

Taking another good look around, I'm certain she isn't here yet. I've taken up a spot a ways away from where I'd assume she would sit, that way I can check on her while keeping my distance, leaving her none the wiser.

More and more people go by, and I lose myself in the potential. I am one person, sitting here with such a *heavy weight* of emotion. The loss of a mother before I knew her, of a father who was never really a father to me at all, and now the loss of a father figure who could have been. I sit here as one person, here only because I was saved by the love of a friend who's become a brother.

Love and loss are powerful things.

How much of it belongs to the thousands?

How much of it belongs to the millions? The billions?

When you walk into an airport or a crowded room, how much of that space is taken up by their trauma? How much of that space is taken up by their joy? How much of our planet is encased in grief, in apathy, or in anger? How could one tip the scales and fill our world with happiness?

Is it even possible? Is this world too broken? Are *we* too broken to try?

So wrapped up in the depth of it all I didn't notice when she walked up and took a seat closer to mine than I planned, just an aisle away facing me. My once steady heart becomes a cacophony. With just a turn of her head, she would notice me. She would look at me with those cognac eyes that I've seen in photos for weeks, finally knowing I exist.

Despite the shadows which follow her, she is beautiful in a way that even as a writer, I would have a hard time forming words for. Yes, her face is obviously stunning, and people would kill for her long, dark hair, but it's more than that. It's in the way that her freckles are scattered across the bridge of her nose, the way her lips sit naturally full, the way her eyelashes don't need mascara. She's been crying, probably for days, with her puffy eyes and rosy nose, yet it takes nothing away from her beauty.

I couldn't tell you how much time has passed as I sit here trying to figure out how I could ever do her justice with words. It's been long enough that the crowds have emptied out and most have boarded their flights by now. Long enough to lose my ability to form words, coherent thoughts, and for night to fall completely.

Then, like daybreak, she smiles, banishing the darkness around her for just a moment. Suddenly the grief, my heavy heart, and morbid thoughts about the trauma of a broken world take a back seat.

I need to know why she smiled.

And suddenly, the only thing which exists is making her smile again.

DECEMBER
Dear Ara

# CHAPTER FORTY-SEVEN

## Present - Ara

Ding.

The elevator alerts us of the arrival of another guest. The doors open revealing Ryder looking broody as ever, nothing Christmasy in sight, arms full of various bottles of hard liquor. I'd take a guess that at least half of that is just to get him through the night.

You'd think we asked him to be the test dummy for a new Taser or a grueling day of physical torture. Actually, now that I think about it, he would probably enjoy those two activities more than this ugly Christmas sweater party.

Both Lou and I have been curious about the boys' mission to bring him into our little crew. Whenever we ask, they share a silent look or two and tell us they feel bad for the guy. We don't buy it. There is definitely something else behind why they are trying, despite Ryder's best efforts to be left alone.

I haven't seen a trace of the sweet, even funny side of Ryder which I saw that night in the bar when I wandered in, lost in grief, looking for the way to get through my dad's birthday at the bottom of a bottle. It's almost as if once he realized the boys cared about him, he's done everything possible to keep them at arm's length. Connor and Theo had to threaten to turn up at his bar singing Christmas carols to get him to show up tonight.

"Aren't you supposed to do this shit on Christmas?"

"Merry Christmas to you, too," I say with an eye roll. "And actually, *most* people have their Christmas parties before Christmas anyway, but we share Christmas with Theo's birthday, and that's a lot to jam-pack into a day."

We had all decided to create new Christmas traditions together this year. I couldn't face doing my regular traditions without my dad. Lou had only ever gone to toxic Christmas parties in her community. Connor grew up in Australia where most of them celebrate by going to the beach, and with it being Theo's birthday (and therefore the anniversary of his mom's death), Christmas was never a time for celebrating for him or his father.

"Merry Christmas." Ryder hands me a bottle of vodka, tequila, and white rum, keeping one bottle tucked under his arm, which appears to be some sort of whiskey. "This one is mine."

I raise a brow. "Did you take this from your bar?"

Something dark passes over his face before he shrugs. "They owe me."

Ryder unscrews the bottle cap, taking a generous gulp that has me reaching for my own throat before walking toward the living room. Something is eating at him I realize, driving him further away from that bartender who helped me.

I follow him into the living room, finally figuring out why Connor has had a shit-eating grin plastered on his face this entire night.

"Seriously, Connor!?" His sweater seems as innocent as ugly Christmas sweaters go at first glance, but when you look closer, the red-and-white Christmas pattern is actually fucking reindeer. Not "fucking" as an exclamation, but as an activity. The reindeer are literally banging. "Where did you even find that?"

Connor smiles, proudly straightening it out so everyone can get a better look. "It's bloody great, isn't it?"

Lou cackles. "That's the best sweater I've ever seen."

Ryder pulls a stool into the corner of the room, taking another swig of his whiskey while I place the bottles of alcohol on the island with the rest of the "Christmas Potluck" items.

Doing the same thing each Christmas could get boring after twenty years, so I came up with the potluck idea. Instead of food, we each bring a different Christmas-themed gift or an activity for us to do.

This whole thing being my brainchild, it was my duty to bring the gingerbread house making kits, obviously. Theo brought an assorted pack of various Christmas hats, and we are *definitely* giving Ryder the grumpy elf one.

Lou brought her Polaroid camera, with a kit that has a slot for you to slide the Polaroids into a snow globe ornament (we've been told that we can only take ugly pictures). It's no surprise that Ryder brought alcohol, but we are all still in mystery as to what Connor's gift is.

Connor said he paid to get it wrapped up by one of those paid gift-wrapping stations at the mall because it's that good. He wouldn't let us open it until Ryder arrived, so now that he's here, I'm dying to know what's bad enough to make him so excited.

"Can I open it now?" Connor asks, rubbing his hands together.

"Um, definitely not." I grab the gift from him, tossing it to Theo.

Connor opens his mouth to argue, but Theo has already removed the bow and starts pulling back the paper.

"This better be good," Lou says with an eye roll.

It's not good.

It is so, so, *so* bad.

"Christmas-flavored… *condoms*?" Theo says, trying not to laugh (probably for my sake). "Candy cane…gingerbread…eggnog…and *cocoa*."

Smiling wide, Connor continues, "Isn't it great?"

We could make an entire orchestra performance out of the forehead slaps and aggravated sounds we make in Connor's presence.

"It's definitely something," Theo says with a chuckle, setting the box down next to him. "I guess I'll take it since I'm the only one with a date."

Connor reaches over and takes them back. "I don't need to have a date to get laid. In fact, I've figured out how to skip that step entirely."

Lou reaches over, ripping the box from Connor's shocked hands. Everyone turns to look at her for a moment. She snorts. "Just kidding, fuckheads, I definitely don't need these." Throwing the box at an unexpecting Ryder, he catches it with his face.

Connor laughs, standing up to go get the box. "I have higher odds of getting Lou to jump into bed with me right now than Ryder has of getting laid."

"What do you mean!? He has a different chick leaving a trail of drool after him every time I've seen him!" Lou exclaims.

"You can give a horse shit tons of water, buckets and buckets of water with great tits, but it doesn't mean they'll drink."

Lou snorts. "That's not even how the saying goes."

"I'm right here," Ryder says blandly, reminding them of his existence.

"Oh, come on, grumpy pants." Lou looks at him with her crystal blue eyes. "Don't you ever let yourself have some fun?"

Ryder looks at her a moment, eyes flat, and then almost as if it kills him, he says, "Is there any hot chocolate?"

"Duh! It's Christmas." Lou smiles. "I'll show you to it, bartender. You better whip us up something good."

As she leads Ryder to the kitchen island where the ingredients sit, Connor picks up the guitar that usually lays around the living room and starts playing around.

"So, boys," I begin. "We need to be out here by 6 AM on Christmas morning and be done with presents and breakfast by nine, that way we can make it to Theo's birthday surprise on time."

I've kept my plans for his birthday a secret from both of them, not wanting to risk it getting spoiled. Turning twenty-six is a big deal. I scored an early check-in to this incredible hotel a few hours away, and fast passes to the theme parks nearby.

The best part, though? The wife of Theo's favorite author reached out for a custom outfit recently, and I'd recognized her last name. As fate would have it, they will also be in Orlando for Christmas. She was happy to help arrange a lunch with her husband for Theo to pick his brain about all things author. Theo has no idea.

"We really don't need to do anything special, I don't want to take over Christmas and make it about me," Theo says humbly.

"Mate, enough of that. As if we're going to miss out on the chance to remind you that you're getting old and ugly."

"Speaking of being old…" A jolly, warm voice comes from the elevator.

Dave comes in, rosy as ever. The significance of how important of a role in my life he played this year tickles the back of my mind, and I can't help but jump up to give him a hug. He wraps his arms around me with a belly laugh, and takes a look around at my friends—my family—sitting around the living room.

We had prepared a Christmas gift for Dave, for his amazing service. I'd wrapped up a whole bunch of yummies, but wanted the chance to give it to him when he didn't have to dash off to his next location due to the busy Christmas deliveries. I'd invited him to bring the letter this evening, instead, so we could exchange them at the same time.

My attention snags on the light gray envelope, addressed in familiar handwriting.

The twelfth letter.

The twelfth task.

The last one for…a while.

"Thank you for coming tonight." I graciously take the letter from Dave. "I wanted to get the chance to say Merry Christmas and to tell you how grateful I am for making sure I got every single one."

"You're welcome, Ara. It was truly my pleasure. I don't know who wrote these letters, but I know they are important to you." He motions to my friends on the couch. "And whoever they are, they would be happy to see this, to know that this exists for you."

I smile, tears already threatening at the backs of my eyes.

"I remember meeting you that first month." An unprecedented, serious look takes over Dave's expression. "A beautiful girl, but so very unhappy. I'm glad I've gotten to see how much that has changed."

I give him another hug. "Thank you, Dave."

Connor yells something about being sappy and invites Dave to come take up a spot next to him on the large couch. Dave tries to be polite, saying he doesn't want to be the old man crashing the party, but Connor insists, giving me the gift of a moment to spend with my dad.

Before disappearing down the hallway completely, I look back, taking in the image before me. Connor strumming on his guitar, playing the acoustic version of a Christmas song. Lou is talking to Ryder, who actually just laughed a little, as begrudgingly it may be. Theo holds up the Polaroid camera, snapping a picture of Dave so he can make an ornament of his own, preserving this moment forever.

A family born not from blood, but from choice.

I take my letter to my design room, closing the door softly behind me and open it up.

*Dear Ara,*

*Merry (early) Christmas. I know it's still a couple weeks away, but I hope you find it in yourself to celebrate, to make your own traditions this year, and to find joy in whatever you decide to do.*

*Although this is the last letter for a while, I want to start off by saying that this is not goodbye. I've decided that I'll never say goodbye. I refuse to believe that this is where it ends for me.*

*The universe certainly wouldn't be cruel enough to design us in a way that after everything it puts us through, we disappear into nothing in the end. I think it gives us another shot to come back and try again. That said, I know this body doesn't have much longer, which means I've got to finish what I've started here.*

*With this being my last task, I will finally share my biggest regret, which is that I never gave myself more than one chance at love. I'd blamed it on the fact that if I'd found it again, it would mean that what I'd had with your mother wouldn't be as special. I'd blamed it on the fact that it would be unfair to you to bring someone into your life who wasn't your mother, because it should have been her who got to raise you.*

*Except I know now that your mother would have wanted me to love again, and I know you would have accepted it, had I found someone who brought me happiness. It was nobody but myself keeping it out of reach. It was my own fear of the unknown which prevented it.*

*I decided to leave this as your last task, because it probably won't happen overnight. In fact, I'd be worried if it did.*

*I want you to find love, Ara.*

*I want you to find real, true love. Someone who will love you at your worst and celebrate you at your best. Someone who gives you courage when you need it. Someone who doesn't walk away when the going gets tough. Someone you'd want by your side for every battle that life sends your way.*

*Don't be afraid to put your heart on the line.*

*Any hurt you experience along the way will be worth it.*

*Before I end this letter, I have one more request.*

*Please don't worry about me.*

*Unlike many others, I've been gifted the time to prepare and come to terms with the fact that my time has come. I can accept it now, knowing that I've gotten the chance to do what I could for you. To help you overcome your grief and find joy again. I can only hope that what I've done is enough.*

*I love you so much, Ara.*

*I am so proud of you.*

*And I miss you more than you can imagine.*

*Love,*

*Dad*

I take a piece of paper out of my notebook and a pen from my desk and do something I should have done a long time ago.

*Dear Dad,*

*I miss you, too.*

*I should have written this years ago. Not because I thought one day you wouldn't be around. In fact, it had never even occurred to me that something could happen to you, but because I'm not very good at saying the mushy stuff out loud. You know that, because I got it from you.*

*Our bond has always been stronger than mere words anyway, and I would have never been able to get through saying all this without crying my eyes out, the way I've been doing throughout the months leading up to this letter.*

*I want to tell you that I understand why you didn't tell me, and I'm not angry with you. The pain you must have gone through is unimaginable, and I can't even conceive how horrible it would have been to see you in that state, feeling helpless.*

*I would have done my best to put on a good face and be brave like you, but you would have seen through it. When I look back on our time together, all I see are the best times. I'd like to think that being there for you at the end wouldn't have changed that, but that pain changes people forever. It would have changed me forever.*

*You did everything right, and I know you fought every battle with bravery.*

*I'm not writing this letter to say goodbye, either. In fact, I can't physically bring myself to say those words because then it makes it real. Even now, I still have hope of seeing you again. Because if I didn't, well, then, I don't know, I just can't imagine my world without you in it.*

*So, I guess I'm writing this letter to say thank you. You lived an incredible life, so quiet about your kindness, your intelligence, and ability to make someone laugh. You saved the best bits of yourself for the ones who mattered most, and I will treasure that forever.*

*I want to thank you for the big moments and the little ones. The times you went swimming with me even if you were exhausted after work. The times you cooked me breakfast before school and listened to everything I had to say. For figuring out how to reach me after death, picking me up from rock bottom and putting me on the path that would save my life.*

*I will cherish every single moment we shared, but most of all I will cherish your character. The way you raised me and became my greatest friend along the way. The way you walked through life with courage, patience, and good will. I can only hope to do the same.*

*My fellow readers talk about fictional characters all the time, how much they wished that people like them would exist in real life. Well, I know firsthand that at least one has existed, and I was lucky enough to be the person whose life you lived in. Your character deserves to be written into a book, permanently etched into this world forever.*

*I hope one day, wherever you go next, you find the bits and pieces I left in this world for you. You'll know the ones.*

*No matter how many letters I write or what I manage to achieve, it will never be enough to express my love for you, or how honored I am to have had you as my dad, my best friend.*

*If I could go back in time, I wouldn't waste it on goodbyes. If I could see you one last time, I would hug you because I miss your hugs. I would rest my head on your shoulder because I miss the comfort and safety that came with it. I would walk out of my old bedroom to smell the breakfast you made and hear you say good morning. I'd never feared that there would come a morning where you wouldn't be there, and maybe it made me complacent.*

*I promise to never be complacent again. I will treasure every moment as it happens (even the tough ones). I will appreciate every single person I love, and I'm going to take a hell of a lot more pictures.*

*I want you to know that you succeeded. I am happy. Not in that shallow surface way either, but truly happy. I'll never stop wishing for you to be able to see it, but I promise to live every moment as well as you did.*

*The journey isn't over, I will have to wake up every day and put my mind to it, overcoming every barrier as it comes my way, but I know I will.*

*I am so proud of the life I am building, and I know the best is yet to come.*

*I love you so much, Dad.*

*I miss you every single day.*

*Thank you for leading me back to the light.*

*Love,*

*Ara*

*P.S. May we meet again.*

# EPILOGUE

## *Two Years Later - Ara*

Mindlessly toying with the ring on my left hand, I'd be lying if I said I wasn't nervous right now. Not because of who is waiting for me at the end of the aisle, I'll never be more sure of anything in life, but making it down the damn aisle, in this damn dress, without falling on my face? It will be a miracle if I can pull it off.

Lou (who is probably off somewhere screaming about something that needs to be perfected) and I went to three bridal appointments in search of *the one*. It was one depressing "Thank you so much for your time, but I think I have to keep looking" after another. After the third appointment, Lou physically smacked me upside the head and asked why on Earth I wouldn't be making my own dress. Weirdly, I hadn't thought of it.

Then the idea hit me. A simple satin bodice giving off the classic, timeless elegance with thick V-neck straps, while adding a plunging neckline and even lower back, leaving the skirt as the main event. Layered ivory tulle, beginning at my waist in true ballgown fashion, and continuing down into a train that runs the entire length of the staircase outside of my bridal suite. I'd thought I'd finished it, but I felt it was missing just a tiny bit of something, so I sprayed a thin layer of silver glitter on the tulle, creating a subtle shimmer when the light hits it just right.

Theo, thankfully, handled the suit for himself and his best man, Connor. For Lou, I'd thought of making her a Maid of Honor dress, but realized that I needed her for something much more important. She'd cried like a baby when

I asked her to be the one to walk me down the aisle and give me away. I let her decide what she wanted to wear, which was a formal corset jumpsuit that I'd made for her.

The wedding was supposed to be under ten people. *Total.*

Just our little family, which has gotten closer and grown in number, and a handful of others. Then I realized there were more people in my life who deserved to be invited. Dave, of course, was always going to come. Then there was Dan and Joel from the café, the latter greeting me with tears, and the former with a hug, when I showed up at the café that day to drop off their invites. They weren't surprised to hear about my success, which is wild, because sometimes I still don't believe it myself.

Then there was Jane, who played such a pivotal role in getting that cowed girl who walked into her material store that day to realize her true potential. Lou's family, whom I've grown even closer to over the past two years. Ivy who has become a friend and partner in taking over the fashion world. All of my models, all of my staff, and that's just the bride's side.

Case in point, that aisle is enemy number one.

The ceremony doesn't start for another hour, but I wanted to be ready early, which means I have sixty more minutes to imagine mopping the floor with my face in front of hundreds of witnesses.

Thankfully, a knock at the door interrupts my spiraling thoughts, probably some poor soul Lou sent here to check on me. I open the door to find Dave, jolly as ever, and I try not to let my heart jump with hope.

One thing I've learned over the past two years is that loss may become less poignant over time, but it doesn't necessarily get easier. Healing doesn't mean the sadness goes away entirely. There will always be the moments where I become crippled with grief, but they are less frequent and nestled between many more smiles.

I hadn't let myself get my hopes up. I haven't received a letter in over two years, and so many things could have prevented this letter from being delivered and so much mystery still remained on how my dad had managed to get them delivered so religiously in the first place.

"Is it a letter?"

Dave smiles, revealing a light gray envelope he had hidden behind his back. "You look beautiful, Ara, and I hope this brings you joy today." With that, he leaves me alone with the familiar handwriting I have missed so much.

A soft sob escapes, and I clasp my hand over my mouth. I've read his letters over and over, anytime I needed his advice, his comfort. Receiving this today, on a day where I'm missing him more than I could imagine, means everything.

I open the letter.

*Dear Ara,*

*Today is a pivotal day in your life. It's hard for me to accept that I won't get to meet the man you're marrying and threaten him with a shotgun a few times, just for good measure, but nonetheless, the day has come.*

*It's hard to believe that I won't be there to take you dress shopping, just for you to realize you could make something for yourself more unique and beautiful than anything you could find in one of those shops.*

*I can't accept the fact that I won't get to walk you down the aisle and do a bad job of guiding you around a very small portion of the dance floor while I cry and blame it on my allergies.*

*I can't imagine not getting to know the version of you who is ready to tie yourself with another for the rest of your life. It means you've changed. You've grown. You've opened your heart. You've trusted someone.*

*Please know that I'm there with you today, and I'll be by your side for every moment of it. I want you to know that I am happy for you. In my last letter, I said that I wanted you to find love and you have, provided this isn't one of those ridiculous fake marriages like you read about in your books.*

*After realizing what I did about love, I've since realized something about friends, too, and I can only hope that the person you love enough to marry is also your friend.*

*Friends are the true definition of unconditional. They don't have to be there unless they want to. Unless you're important to them. When you find a real one, there is nothing better out there. Supposedly it's called a ride or die.*

*There is something you should know. I've made a friend.*

*I know, shocking. It wasn't my doing. I only asked for a favor, and he sort of just noseyed his way into my life for the rest of it. But I gotta tell you, I'll be forever grateful he did. He is what every friend should be. He's been by my side through a lot already, and I trust that he will be here through the rest.*

*If I could change one thing, it would be that I remained your only friend. I think you got that from me, not wanting to branch out. I wish I'd given myself, and you, the opportunity to make more friends. I hope you've been granted that opportunity since I've been gone. You're going to need them by your side today.*

*In the beginning, I swore him to secrecy because he is the person I left responsible for getting you the letters. I didn't want to risk something petty happening and jeopardizing that. After getting to know him more, I'm wondering if that was the right call.*

*I've already given him the other letters, which you'll be getting every month. This is the last letter. I've been putting it off for quite a while and I'd planned to write more, but I've gotten to the stage where I don't think I'll have the time to write another.*

*I haven't known what to say, and I don't want to make you cry too much. So, I guess I'd like to be able to leave you something, or someone, rather. I don't know how many years have passed, but if you ever need a friend, you could find Theo. Theo Carter. He would be a good one to you, as he has been a good one to me.*

*A ride or die.*

*I met him outside my office building one afternoon, and if there was ever a time that I would believe in fate, it would be then.*

*Theo is sitting in the other room as I write this. His instructions were to keep this arrangement a secret no matter what, but I'm having second thoughts. That's because I want you to know that I haven't been alone. He's made sure of it. I also want you to know that if you ever needed anyone, I know Theo would be there for you.*

*When you meet him, or I guess I should say if you meet him, don't believe a single story he tells about me as a young man. None of it is true.*

*A small part of me wonders if you two will have found a way to be friends long before you get this letter. Your old man can only hope. But, if not, Phil from Puffin Press can tell you how to find Theo if you ever want to.*

*With that out of the way, I've somehow got to get through this next part before my allergies get too much, which I better stop joking about soon, otherwise Theo is going to come home with a box of Claritin one of these days.*

*So here goes.*

*If I could make a toast on this important day, I would say that my wish for you and your new husband is this:* Life goes by very, very fast, and I would just like to say that I hope you do your absolute best to make every day as much fun and great as it can possibly be.

*I wish I could be there today. I'm sorry that I'm not.*

*I wish I never had to write a damn one of these letters.*

*I wish I could say it all in person.*

*I am so proud of you.*

*I'm so happy that you're living, really living and that you've found love, just as I wished for in my last letter.*

*I love you so much, Ara, more than I could ever put into words.*

*May we meet again in another life.*

*Love,*

*Dad*

The tears begin falling in earnest.

They fall for my dad, and they fall for Theo.

Somehow, I always knew.

My legs begin moving before I make the conscious decision to do so. I gather my skirts, running for the door. I run through the hallway, down the steps, through another hallway before bursting through the door to the groom's suite.

Theo jumps, taking in my tear-streamed face and the letter in my hand. His tuxedo shirt is still mostly unbuttoned, tie dangling untied around his neck. His hair is styled to perfection, not a curl out of place. If I wasn't on the cusp of something so major, with his disheveled appearance and the Regency-styled room as his backdrop, my mind would be descending into some dirty *Bridgerton* places.

"What's wrong?" Worry touches Theo's face, whether for my well-being or for the contents of the letter I'm not sure.

Everything clicks. How Theo just happened to show up at that airport after my dad's funeral, how he found me at the diner the next day, and the emotions he fought to hide at the mention of him. "You knew my dad?"

Theo nods, somewhat reserved.

"You were his *friend*?" My voice cracks on the last word.

He nods again.

"And you were there with him?" A small sob escapes me at my next question. "At the end?"

Theo closes his eyes only to slowly open them again, as if to clear the images which just flashed in his mind. "I was there until his very last breath."

My hand clasps over my mouth, trying to quiet my sobs. Emotions and thoughts war with each other for my attention, raw with shock, but there are two words more important than all the rest. "Thank you."

The tears won't stop now, and for the first time Theo lets his tears for my dad fall, for me to see. One foot after another I bring myself closer to him, until I'm pressed against his warmth and in the comfort of his arms.

"You don't hate me? For keeping it a secret from you?" Theo's voice is broken, like he truly believes this could have changed the outcome of today. I realize then, when I entered his suite the way I did, he assumed the worst. That keeping this from me has been eating at him.

"Theo, it wasn't your secret to tell." I pull back, looking into his soul as more tears spill from our eyes. He reaches up with his thumbs, wiping mine away. "You were there for him when he needed someone the most… when I *couldn't* be."

"How much did he tell you?"

I hand Theo the letter, letting him see for himself. His eyes drift over the words, eager to consume every single one. The moment he reaches the part about friendship, he moves to the settee placing his face in his hand as he reads, trying to keep himself together.

When I read the letter, I knew that they had been close, my dad had never mentioned having a friend before. But seeing the way Theo feels about getting a little piece of my dad? I know that their friendship ran deep in the short time that they knew each other.

Losing hope of keeping even an ounce of my makeup intact, I squeeze in next to him, wedging myself under his arm so we can read it together.

*Again.*

*And again.*

"I wanted to tell you so many times, but he'd never given me any exceptions or conditions of when I could and I *couldn't* break my promise to him."

"You did the right thing, Theo. He trusted you and you never broke that trust. It meant something to him, and it means something to me." Theo pulls me closer and I go on. "Knowing that you knew him, that someone else misses him? It makes me feel less alone, because I'm not the only person who knows what it's like to lose him."

"You have *never* been alone in this. He loved you… more than anything." Theo shakes his head. "I'd never seen that kind of love before, and I don't think there is anything in this world which could have kept him from doing everything he could for you."

We're quiet for a moment.

"There is something else you should see."

Theo pulls a worn, but cared for, piece of stationery from his pocket and I recognize it immediately. "He wrote you a letter?"

Theo nods, passing it over. "I found it in my bag after he passed."

*Dear Theo,*

*You've probably gathered by now that I'm not very good with my words or expressing how I truly feel to someone I care about and well, I care about you.*

*In the beginning, I thought you were put on my path to help me make sure Ara would be okay. You were the way I could get the letters to her, and I could trust that you would do it.*

*Though, after the last few months together, I'm starting to think that you were put on my path to teach this old man a little more about life before mine was over.*

*Just over fifty years, and I'd never learned the meaning of true friendship. I'd known the love of a woman and the love of a daughter, but you taught me about the love of a friend.*

*I learned what path I needed to guide Ara to follow because you showed it to me.*

*I've done what I could with Phil to ensure your brilliance and care becomes known throughout the world. If I'm right about you, your stories will inspire the masses. It will inspire them to make meaningful connections and seek the beauty in life which can remain hidden at first glance. I can only hope that Ara can have a friend like you one day. Please watch over her for me. If you decide to get close, though, know you'll be risking your hand, potentially other limbs.*

*You've been putting on a brave face for me, but nobody should have to watch this slow torture that is this disease. Thank you for being here so I do not have to burden Ara with this pain, too.*

*You're a good man, Theo.*

*Since we don't have much longer, I wish we could have met earlier. I only wished for two things for my soul. I wanted to be happy and find peace.*

*Thank you for bringing me happiness.*

*Thank you for bringing me peace.*

*Love,*

*William*

The last bit of mascara smears down my face, and I hold the man next to me as we mourn the man who brought us together.

After a while, Theo breaks the silence. "There's something I've always wanted to know."

"What?"

"Why did you smile at the airport that day? You were so sad and then suddenly this smile overtook your sadness, and I just knew there was no way I was walking away from you."

I snort. "I was thinking about where my dad had gone after he died, and I started wondering whether the dead have a one-way looking glass into our lives whenever they want and what if…what if he popped in to check on me just to find me having sex."

A shocked, choking laugh escapes Theo. "Oh God, that is one hell of an image. I can only imagine William's face…"

We're both laughing as Lou barges in, tornadoes in her eyes, a force ready to destroy everything in her path. "What the fuck…" She trails off, taking in our tears, the letters, and snot running down my face.

"Oh dear God." She turns around. "No mascara is waterproof enough for me to keep looking at your love and the letters in your laps. Should I tell everyone to leave and we can have all the cake to ourselves and cry the rest of the day?"

I chuckle to her back and look at Theo. The man who stayed by my dad's side when he needed him the most. The man who never broke the trust of someone he cares about. The man who my dad believed will inspire the world.

There is nothing I would rather do than hitch myself to him for life.

I take Theo's hand, his thumbs coated in the remains of my eye makeup. "Let's do this thing."

He smiles, leaning in to kiss me on the lips. "Let's do this thing."

We both feel the warm, peaceful presence as I walk down the aisle, as I kiss Theo for the first time as my husband, as Lou and Connor make their toasts which have champagne shooting from our noses, as Theo guides me around the dance floor to a song for us and a song to honor my dad.

We feel his comforting presence, offering guidance and comfort when we need it the most, for the rest of our lives and into eternity.

Until we meet again.

**LOOK OUT FOR BOOK TWO:**
***LAST STAND FOR GENEVIEVE***

**How Does It Feel To Be The One Who Survived?**
**When Substance Abuse Becomes A Crutch,**
**Your Life Is No Longer Yours.**

Connor decided a long time ago that life is a lot simpler when emotions are kept out of it. As far as he's concerned, there is only room in life for two things:

1. The family he chose
2. Music

But after meeting the secretive and enigmatic Brooke, Connor finds himself questioning everything. Greeted by nothing but her icy exterior, he becomes determined to discover if anything warm lies beneath.

What turned Brooke, the beautiful, some would even say perfect 4.0 GPA girl-next-door into a ghost who's been off the radar for over three years?

Will Brooke find it in herself to finally share her secrets?

Will the truth set her free?

If you love getting your heart shredded and put back together, then this book is for you.

*Last Stand for Genevieve* is a dual point-of-view romance novel with alternating timelines that will have you laughing, crying, and possibly cursing the author.

With its own happily ever after, it can be read as a standalone novel or as *Book Two* in *The Last Series*, following *Last Letters to Ara*.

Visit My Website To Subscribe and Receive Bonus Chapters
(PLUS, a sneak peek of Book Two!!)

www.kaymiewuerfel.com

Follow Me On Socials For More Updates
Instagram: @kayywuerf
TikTok: @kayywuerf

# ACKNOWLEDGMENTS

This is in no order of thanks because that would be totally impossible. Instead, I'm going to start my thank you's at the beginning of what brought this story to fruition and write something linearly for once in my life.

I want to thank my dad, for being the kind of person whose character deserves to be permanently etched into this word. Our bond and friendship are everything that inspired this book, and there are absolutely no words in the English language (or any other), to describe my gratitude for all you brought to my life.

Thank you for making a teenage girl feel seen and heard, whether it was watching *Gossip Girl* or listening to me talk about trivial drama which happened at school that day. Thank you for teaching me about hard work, persistence, and courage. Thank you for showing me how important it is to find adventure, for encouraging me to find what I love, and showing me the ingredients of success. Wherever you are, I hope there is home-made popcorn with lots of butter, and brownies with the perfect ratio of vanilla ice cream. I miss you every single day, and I can't wait for the day that we meet again. I'm busy making sure we have a hell of a lot to celebrate.

I want to thank my mom. For teaching me to read, for taking me to the library every single month, and helping me haul thirty books to and from the car so I could read a book a day. Thank you for encouraging me to write my first book, which was about giving a horse a carrot (I know, guys, riveting stuff).

You helped me publish it by stapling it together and teaching me how to draw a horse so I could design the cover. You are the person who has taken every dream of mine, every creative urge or wild side and coaxed it to life. Most parents look at their child's imagination as something to fix and try to bring them back down to reality. You gave mine life. We've got the dreamer's disease.

I want to thank the rest of my amazing family for being the best people on the planet. I love you guys so much.

I want to thank my brother for letting me add his song to the playlist. He wrote and played "Try" as we sat with our dad, and I typed the ending to Ara's story. Every time I listen to it, I feel the song in my soul. Thank you for bringing something so beautiful into such a hard time, and for recording it so I could share it with the world.

I want to thank my friend, Stephanie, for sharing my love for books and encouraging the stories that I wrote for us in high school. Thank you for finding my old notebook last year and sending me the contents, reminding me that I used to love telling stories as much as I loved reading them. Thank you for convincing me that I could try again, for finding time between being a boss bitch, caring for your babies, and being an absolute god on the daily, to listen to me spitball ideas until this one stuck. Thank you for reading my first draft, for finding it in yourself to tell me it was good. I know you were lying, it was dog shit and we both know it, but I'm all the more grateful. This story would have never existed without you. Thank you for being the catalyst of my dreams.

I want to thank my husband for being the kind of person who doesn't think I'm insane when I wake up one day and say "I'm going to write a book," the kind of person who when I say "You know what would be cool?" responds with "Your book becoming a bestseller and you becoming a full-time author?" (I was thinking about a new way to make nachos, but that answer was way cooler.) You believed in me before you'd read a single word that I'd written, and I will be forever thankful. Dreaming with you is the best part of life. You are my best friend, my soul mate, and I love you so much.

My cat gets half a thank you for being the terror who forced me to wake up at the ass crack of dawn, every single day. (It's only half a thank you because who actually likes waking up that early?) If there are any typos, I blame him for walking all over my keyboard.

I want to thank my friend Rachel, for making Alpha Reader into a new identity. Thank you for listening to all of my ideas, for reviewing every microscopic change I ever made, and convincing me that all 119,000 words shouldn't be permanently deleted. This one's for you.

I want to thank my friend Sydney, for being the person I'd call if I needed to bury a body. For breathing and just existing on Earth at the same time as me. For meeting me at fourteen and deciding to keep me. I love you more than words.

I want to thank my friend, Britt C, for being an alpha reader and convincing me that I could do this for real. Your feedback was everything to me and I am forever grateful. Thank you for being my twin flame.

I want to thank my friend, Britt B, for being my writing buddy and so much more. You inspire me, encourage me, and make me feel like I can fly. Thank you for having me in your life.

You guys were my first readers and my biggest fans. Your friendships are EVERYTHING to me. I couldn't do life without you, nor would I want to.

Thank you to my editor, Elaine, for taking a chance on a first-time, self-published author and not refunding my money when you got a glance at my manuscript. I appreciate your kind words and helping hand, resulting in this dream of mine coming to fruition.

Thank you to my cover designer, Jules, for taking something I love so much and giving it life. You are my hero. (If you need someone for a cover, I HIGHLY recommend her. Her communication and service is unmatched. You can find her at coversbyjules.crd.co)

Thank you to all of my future readers, even if there is only one of you. I hope you enjoyed this novel which came straight from my heart and tear ducts. I'd love it if you stuck around for the next one.

And to Madison, my friend and fellow author, because I saved the best for last. Honestly, fuck you. Nobody else will understand that, but you know it's a compliment of the highest magnitude. We fell in love as friends over our love for books, started on this journey together, and you've been by my side through every wobbling step.

Thank you for being everything I needed to take this story to the next level, for convincing me to write outside the lines I'd drawn for myself. Thank you for talking me off the ledge as I tried to purge more than half this story, on more than one occasion. This book (but especially chapters fourteen through seventeen) exist *because* of you. The flashbacks exist *because* of you. We know what Ara's apartment looks like *because* of you. Books two and three in this series exist *because* of you.

If it weren't for you, I would have given up. Between losing 60k words of my work and the constant battle against imposter syndrome, thank you for always reminding me that this story was worth it all. So here I stand, at the threshold of my dreams, because you held my hand.

Love, Kaymie

# ABOUT THE AUTHOR

Originally from the United States, Kaymie Wuerfel now lives in Sydney, Australia, with her husband and two fur-babies.

She's a verified TikTok creator known for her comedic skits, and has successfully pursued a career in fashion, owning her own business which sells exquisite dresses worldwide.

During the few hours she finds between her eleven-hour days and seven-day work weeks, she can be found reading a book, writing her own, or laughing with her friends.

Kaymie's dream is to live on a mountain with her friends and family, all while visiting far away worlds through the written word.

Made in United States
North Haven, CT
13 September 2023

41491133R00215